MATTHEW

The JADED GENTLEMEN series

GRACE BURROWES

Published by Grace Burrowes Publishing, 21 Summit Avenue, Hagerstown, MD
21740.

ISBN for *Matthew—The Jaded Gentlemen Book II*: 978-1941419182
Cover by Wax Creative, Inc.

To unwed mothers

CHAPTER ONE

In Matthew Belmont's world, a damsel in distress took precedence over an early morning inspection of the pear orchard, particularly when the damsel weighed close to a ton and had a foal at her side.

"I wouldn't ask it of you this early in the day," Beckman Haddonfield said, as one of Matthew's stable lads took Beck's sweaty gelding to be walked out. "But if we lose the dam, we could well lose the foal, and neither Jamie nor I can figure out what ails the mare."

"Best saddle Minerva," Matthew called to the groom. "You, Beckman, will wait a few moments before joining me at Linden. Your horse needs to catch his wind, as do you."

A father of three learned to speak in imperatives, though unlike Matthew's sons, Beckman would probably heed the proffered direction.

Minerva heeded Matthew's direction—most of the time. She was a game grey mare, approaching twenty, but spry and flighty. On a brisk autumn morning, she made short work of the trip to Linden, negotiating cross-country terrain like the seasoned campaigner she was, though she over-jumped a rivulet for form's sake.

Matthew was soon handing her reins over to old Jamie, the Linden head stable lad. "Who is our patient?"

"It's Penny," Jamie replied, loosening Minerva's girth. "The autumn grass must be too rich, or maybe the filly's upsetting her. Damned wee beast is at her mama all the time."

The proper office of children was to upset their parents, something Jamie couldn't know.

"The nights are getting cold, Jamie. The filly's bound to nurse a lot."

Jamie hobbled beside Matthew into the barn, Minerva clip-clopping along behind them.

"I know racehorses," Jamie said, "and I manage with the hunters, hacks, and carriage horses, but a colicky brood mare flummoxes me."

Females of any species flummoxed Matthew, and he thanked the Almighty regularly that his children were all boys.

"I'm none too fond of colic myself," Matthew said. "Is Penny in the foaling stall?"

"She is, and the filly is in the next stall over. Miss Theresa Jennings is keeping an eye on 'em both."

Miss Jennings would be a sister to Linden's owner, Thomas Jennings, Baron Sutcliffe. In the excitement of the baron's recent wedding, Matthew had not troubled his host for an introduction to Miss Jennings. Sutcliffe and his bride were off on their wedding journey, and thus nobody was on hand in the stables to make the introductions.

Needs must when valuable livestock was imperiled. Matthew moved down the barn aisle to the foaling stalls, where a tall brunette stood outside a half door.

"Miss Jennings, Matthew Belmont, at your service."

She brushed a glance over him, her blue eyes full of anxiety. "Mr. Belmont, my thanks for coming. I know little of doctoring horses, but Penny is special to my brother, and Jamie said—"

The mare switched her tail, as if to say the idle chat could wait until later.

"Jamie was right," Matthew replied. "Sutcliffe would happily look in on a mare at Belmont House in my absence. I'm pleased to do the same for my neighbors." Often at a less convenient hour than this, and to a less pulchritudinous reception.

Miss Jennings was long out of the schoolroom and into the years when a woman's true beauty shone forth.

The massive copper-colored equine known as Penny had pricked her ears at the sound of Matthew's voice, while the "little" filly—easily three hundred pounds of baby horse—in the next stall over danced in circles.

"Are you comfortable with horses, Miss Jennings?"

"Reasonably. I know which end does what."

The same starting point from which Matthew had embarked on his parental challenges.

"I'd like to bring the filly into her mama's stall, though somebody should hold her while I look Penny over. I can wait for Jamie to finish with Minerva if you'd rather."

"That won't be necessary. I've held horses on many occasions."

"The little one's name is Treasure," Matthew said, opening the door to the smaller stall. "The Linden stable master halter-trained the filly before he left for London."

Matthew slipped the headstall over the filly's ears, scratching at her fuzzy neck as he did. He kept up a patter of nonsense talk, telling the foal how fetching she looked in her halter, and how cozy she'd be in her woolly winter coat.

Matthew passed Miss Jennings the lead rope and preceded her from the stall.

"And now," he said in the same conversational tones, "we'll step over to Mama's stall, so we might—"

The instant Matthew slid the half door back, the filly shot forward, yanking Miss Jennings with her. The lady wisely dropped the lead rope as she stumbled, and Matthew found himself smack up against a lithe, warm human female, one whose lemony scent blended with the earthier aromas of horse and hay.

In the next instant, Matthew tramped on Treasure's lead rope, though the filly had slipped through the narrow opening to her mama's stall and was nuzzling the mare with obvious relief.

The instant after that became both awkward and... interesting. As Miss Jennings struggled to find her balance, and Matthew struggled to know where to put his hands. "I beg your pardon, Miss Jennings." Matthew's grip closed on the lady's upper arms. "Are you all right?"

Stupid question, when the lady was gasping for breath. She'd been flung at Matthew with enough force to knock the wind out of her.

"Relax, madam." Matthew probably ought not to have *ordered* her to relax. "You'll get your breath back if you give yourself a moment. The fault was entirely mine. I should have known the filly would be frantic. I should have kept hold of that lead rope, and I do apologize—"

Miss Jennings held up a hand, then gestured at the mare and filly. "If the mother's ill, should the filly be doing *that*?"

The foal was nursing, her little tail whisking gleefully about her quarters.

Matthew removed his hands from Miss Jennings's person. "I expect she's hungry. I tend to forget my manners when I'm peckish. Then too, a determined female of any species should be not underestimated."

For the foal, who'd never been separated from her mama to speak of, nursing would be both physical and emotional sustenance. Matthew did not share that indelicate observation as he approached the mare. He talked nonsense again, a patter of flattery and small talk intended to let the mare know exactly where he was at all times.

"Now sweetheart," Matthew crooned, "you won't give me trouble if I merely want to admire your smile, will you?" He gently pried up the big mare's lips and pressed on her gums. "There's a love, now let's have a listen, shall we?"

He ran a hand down the horse's shoulder and pressed an ear to her side, all the while letting the filly nurse.

"You must tell me, Penny, if something is amiss." He switched sides and listened again to her gut, though that required maneuvering the filly about. "I expect you miss your Wee Nick, don't you, hmm? You have the look of a female pining for her favorite."

Miss Jennings flicked a wisp of hay from her sleeve. "Penny seems calmer with you in her stall. When Jamie tried to get close to her, she pawed and circled in the straw."

"Making the proverbial mare's nest." Matthew moved to the horse's shoulder. "Let me have a look at your legs, my girl." He ran his hands up and down each sturdy front limb, Penny having been bred to the plough. "No heat, no swelling, no bumps, no sore joints… You're being coy, Penny, my love."

The mare turned a limpid eye on him, as if to confirm his accusation.

"Is she eating?" he asked as he started on the back legs.

"Like the proverbial horse. The stable master wrote out the rations for each horse, and Penny gets as much as any other two horses put together."

A parent's lot was arduous, regardless of the species, particularly a lactating parent.

"Have you those written instructions on hand?" Matthew asked as he pressed on the mare's spine, vertebra by vertebra. "She's may have a bit of indigestion, but it isn't colic. Her limbs are sound. Eyes, ears, teeth, and mouth are all in fine shape. She's producing milk, she's not noticeably dehydrated, and mastitis doesn't seem to be the issue."

"Mastitis?"

"Inflammation of the…" *Well, hell.* Matthew waved a hand in the general direction of his chest. "Of the… udder. If the mare is sore, she won't let the filly nurse, so she gets impacted in addition to the underlying inflammation— it's quite painful for the horse. Happens more often in cows," he went on, wishing his idiot country squire mouth would shut itself.

"Cows, Mr. Belmont?"

Had the lady taken a step back?

"I beg your pardon." Matthew avoided the consternation in Miss Jennings's gaze by scratching Penny's hairy withers. "A rustic life familiarizes one with animal husbandry."

Rural surrounds did not, however, require that one bleat on in the presence of a lady as if one were a sheep stuck halfway over a style.

"I'll find the stable master's instructions." Miss Jennings passed Matthew the foal's lead rope and nearly ran down the barn aisle.

Matthew leaned his forehead against the horse's neck.

"God help me." At thirty-five years of age, he was turning into that pathetic caricature, a bumpkin who cared for naught but his hounds and horses, a man without conversation or sophistication of any sort. An embarrassment.

At least he was an embarrassment who took the care of his land and livestock seriously. Matthew toed through the straw, and his boot came in contact with the inevitable horse droppings.

Miss Jennings reappeared at the door to the stall, a piece of foolscap in her hand. "I have Nick's list."

"What proclamations did Wee Nick make for his Penny?" Matthew crossed the stall to peer down at the paper. "This is quite detailed. I would need my spectacles to decipher the handwriting. Would you mind reading it for me?"

The damned dim light was the trouble, and too many late nights attempting to make sense of legal tomes or his sons' handwriting.

"That's no bother at all, Mr. Belmont."

Miss Jennings stood right next to Matthew and scanned the written instructions. This gave him his first opportunity to focus on Miss Jennings, to inventory her features and assess her attire.

Matthew enjoyed most of his job as magistrate because the post involved solving the little mysteries that passed for criminal mischief in the wilds of Sussex. Who let Mrs. Golightly's heifer out, and who might have stolen three of Mr. Dimwitty's handkerchiefs from Mrs. Dimwitty's clothesline?

Theresa Jennings struck Matthew as a puzzle with missing pieces. Something about the woman was *off*, like a column of even numbers adding to an odd total. She was tall, brunette, blue-eyed, and wearing a dress nondescript enough to be appropriate in the stable, but still something....

"The stable master is a man given to detail, isn't he?" she concluded after rattling off a list portions and a schedule of activities.

"Nicholas loves this mare," Matthew replied. "Risked his life for her when the old stable burned, and suffered injury himself while rescuing her." But then, Nicholas Haddonfield was partial to females on general principles. "Does he write anything more?"

Matthew told himself to move, to leave the mare and foal in peace, but here he was, lounging shamelessly against the stall door, appearing to read over Miss Jennings's shoulder when in fact he was imbibing the lemony scent of her hair and admiring the swell of her bosom against her modest brown walking dress.

Matthew's yearning for closeness with Miss Jennings wasn't even sexual—not *very* sexual, anyway—which was vaguely alarming. He simply longed for the softness and sweetness of a woman.

"Nicholas says Penny isn't keen on ice in her bucket, particularly when the first hard frosts come through." Miss Jennings squinted at the paper, which gratified Matthew exceedingly. "She prefers carrots to apples."

"Fussy old thing." Matthew stepped over to the horse and scratched her great ears before the temptation to smooth his palm over Miss Jennings's shoulder overcame his manners.

"That's probably what's troubling you, isn't it?" Matthew asked the horse. "You don't have your personal body servant on hand to see to your every whim and pleasure, and your morning tea isn't brewed exactly to your liking."

The horse reciprocated Matthew's sympathy by wiggling her lips against his hair, a gesture he tolerated from one fussy old thing to another. He and Minerva had the same sort of relationship, and it was not eccentric.

Despite what his sons might think.

"I'll have a word with Jamie and with Beckman," Matthew said as he closed the stall door. "The mare needs the chill taken off her water in the morning. She'll drink more, and her belly will ease as a result."

"Of course."

Miss Jennings eyed Matthew assessingly, looking something like her brother. She and the baron shared a particular curve of the lips, a quirk of the mouth when thinking. While Matthew tried again to figure out what about Miss Jennings didn't quite sit right, she ran her fingers over his hair.

"The mare destroyed your coiffure, and I don't suppose a cowlick"—she repeated the gesture several times—"would comport with your manly dignity. There."

Matthew's own wife had never... his own children... if he'd permitted a valet to dress him, he wouldn't have allowed... He blinked down at Miss Jennings, resisting mightily the urge to investigate the state of his hair with his fingers.

"I'm sorry." She took a step back. "I didn't mean to presume, but Thomas has always been particular about his turn-out, and men can take their appearance quite..."

Matthew offered Miss Jennings the smile his sons referred to as *the harmless old squire smile*, which served nicely for inspiring confessions from miscreants under the age of ten.

"No matter, Miss Jennings. I haven't been properly fussed over by anybody in a very long time. You're... sweet to trouble over me."

Odd—exceedingly odd—but sweet. Matthew left Miss Jennings by the brood mare's stall and went off to find Jamie, intent on lecturing the head groom about the proper preparation of her ladyship's morning tea.

* * *

Squire Belmont sauntered away, moving like a man at ease in a stable, at ease in his life. The look in the big mare's eye when she'd spied him had been nothing short of adoring.

If a horse could have said, "Thank God you've come," the mare would have been that horse. She'd wiggled her big lips across Mr. Belmont's blond hair as if he were her favorite fellow of any species.

And the squire hadn't taken the least umbrage.

He'd easily sorted out Penny's problem, suggesting he was a man of discernment, but what man of discernment would have called Theresa Jennings *sweet?*

Jamie came bustling out of the saddle room. "You'll feed the lad, won't ye?"

"Feed whom?"

Jamie jerked his chin in Mr. Belmont's direction. "Yon squire. He's notorious good at appreciating his victuals, and his cook done took off for Brighton again. Least you can do, being neighbors and all. So what's ailing our Penny?"

Thomas had the most impertinent help—a divine irony, considering how prickly Thomas could be—though every person at Linden worked hard.

"I believe Mr. Belmont is searching you out to discuss what ails the mare," Theresa said. "He suggested she was missing the stable master."

"Never thought of that. Might could be. Mares are particular. Squire!"

Jamie trotted off, amazingly spry when he wanted to be, and flagged down Mr. Belmont, who stood in the stable yard conferring with Beckman.

When Theresa joined them a few moments later, she had the sense she was interrupting a religious service.

Jamie pushed something Theresa did not examine too closely about in the dirt with the toe of a dusty boot.

"You say she's not drinking enough, Squire?"

"Exactly, which means she isn't producing a lot at one time for Treasure," Mr. Belmont went on, "so the filly is at her, and the mare is cranky and out of sorts, and probably getting a tad corked up as a result."

Theresa was not an equestrienne, but she knew enough not to ask what corked—what *that* term—meant.

Beckman cleared his throat and cast a desperate glance at the squire.

"Beg pardon, Miss Jennings." Mr. Belmont nodded at her, though Theresa had the sense the squire barely noticed her. "So what the mare needs is a little more attention to the temperature of her morning water bucket, and she should come right in a day or two." He swung his attention to Beckman. "Some extra coddling from you wouldn't go amiss either, because you most closely resemble Wee Nick."

"In miniature," Jamie chortled.

"The stable master is that grand a fellow?" Theresa interjected. Beckman was every bit as tall as the squire and as muscular as regular stable work could make a man. Beckman's hair was a lighter blond, his eyes a lighter blue. He was, in short, a less weathered, less honed version of the squire.

Beckman's smile held a touch of pride. "My older brother is that grand in many respects."

"Pride goeth," the squire muttered, though he smiled. "You'll keep me informed?"

Jamie winked. "Bet on it."

Mr. Belmont pulled gloves from his pocket. "Then my contribution here is complete. A word with you, Miss Jennings?"

He offered his arm, a quaint gesture under the circumstances. Thomas offered Theresa his arm, and she tolerated it because he was her brother. Brothers could be old-fashioned where sisters were concerned—even sisters who had fallen so very far from grace.

Maybe, especially those sisters.

"You are preoccupied," the squire observed as he walked with her across the drive to a bench under a spreading oak.

"Thinking of my brother."

"Baron Sutcliffe is a capital fellow, and he has found a lovely bride, one well worth his notice."

Mr. Belmont could not know how talk of happy nuptials still had the power to wound Theresa. The dart of pain came as a small surprise to her too.

"You know Miss—her ladyship, Mr. Belmont?"

"I've known Loris for almost ten years. Shall we sit?"

"Of course." Theresa had forgotten the strictures of ladies and gentlemen in company with each other. She hadn't considered herself a lady for years, nor had she enjoyed the company of a true gentleman since well before that.

Mr. Belmont was a gentleman, even if he did air his veterinary vocabulary with astonishing capability.

Theresa's escort seemed in no hurry to resume the conversation, and she was content to sit beside him. Matthew Belmont was at ease in proximity to her, and simply being close to him was soothing.

That shouldn't be—he was an *adult male*—but there it was.

"I proposed to Loris at one point," Mr. Belmont said, smoothing out the wrinkled fingers of his riding gloves against his thigh. "She turned me down, for which I suppose I should be grateful."

A breeze stirred the remaining oak leaves, a dry, sad sound. "Grateful to be rejected, Mr. Belmont?"

"I wasn't asking for the right reasons, and my proposal flattered neither of us."

A failed proposal could not possibly be what Mr. Belmont had wanted to discuss, and any woman with sense would have changed the subject.

Theresa had not visited with a neighbor for years, though, much less a male neighbor. "What are the right reasons?"

"There are many right reasons." Mr. Belmont sat back, stretched an arm over the back of the bench, and crossed long legs at the ankle.

The topic was not unnerving him. Maybe nothing unnerved him.

"What's most important," he went on, "is to be honest about what one's reasons are. I married out of familial obligation, duty, and, for want of a better term, youthful eagerness—my late wife was very pretty. She married me out of social necessity and gratitude. We understood one other's reasons, and the union functioned adequately as a result."

What did this have to do with an ailing mare? And yet, Theresa was curious, for Mr. Belmont's adequate union sounded... lonely.

"Were you happy?"

"We grew to be content," he replied, as if reciting a catechism. "We were happy raising our children."

"Content. A consummation devoutly to be wished."

Mr. Belmont brightened, like a hound who hears a rustling in a nearby thicket. "You enjoy Shakespeare, Miss Jennings? My oldest went on a Shakespeare spree two summers ago. He nigh drove his brothers to swear eternal illiteracy."

Safer ground, this—much safer. "I like to read, Shakespeare among others. And you?"

"Living in the country, one acquires an aptitude for either reading or drinking. I have the Bard's complete works in my library, if you're due for an infusion."

He'd regret that offer, though Theresa wouldn't presume on his books in any case.

"You give me leave to raid your library, while I invite you to join me in a figurative raid on the larder. Penny would insist I offer you a meal for your trouble." As would Thomas, oddly enough.

Mr. Belmont rose and drew Theresa to her feet, then placed her hand on his arm.

"I'm utterly harmless, Miss Jennings, in all settings save one. Put me before a hearty meal, and my focus narrows as if I were Wellington advancing across the Peninsula. No larder is safe when I'm in the neighborhood."

He gave her the same smile he'd offered her in the barn. Charming, friendly, and as deceptive as Priscilla when reporting last night's bedtime.

Theresa walked with him through the Sutcliffe gardens, which were fading as gardens did when autumn had supplanted summer. The chrysanthemums were putting on a good show, and heartsease was enjoying the cooler weather, but winter was edging closer, and the flowers knew it.

Mr. Belmont made small talk, and yet, Theresa was not fooled.

Any man who could diagnose something as obscure as a mare's persnickety preferences regarding her water bucket, any man who inspired even the mute beasts to watch him walk away, any man who called Theresa Jennings sweet and made her wish it was so, was not a harmless man.

* * *

Breakfast passed pleasantly, much to Theresa's surprise. The squire had the gift of conversation, and he was acquainted with every soul for twenty miles in any direction, as well as their dogs, horses, ailments, and legal complaints.

And yet, as he recounted anecdotes or judicial contretemps, he never named names, or sermonized about his neighbors' foibles. If anything, he viewed life from a tolerant perspective Theresa hadn't encountered for too long.

"When you are both neighbor and magistrate," he said, "people will tell you of any and every mishap, spat, or peculiar circumstance, most of which has no bearing on anything, save a need to talk."

Despite his ability to converse amiably, he also paid assiduous homage to the offerings on the sideboard.

"How did you become magistrate?" Such a fate typically befell an older fellow.

"My late neighbor, Squire Pettigrew, was prepared to bear the dubious honor for at least another twenty years, but he was the victim of food poisoning, and I was the next likely choice because my father had held the post prior to Pettigrew's tenure. The job has been interesting, if occasionally inconvenient."

For Matthew Belmont "occasionally inconvenient" was doubtless the equivalent of protracted cursing from another man.

"To sit in judgment of one's neighbors," Theresa replied, "without becoming arrogant would be a challenge." For Thomas, that challenge would have been considerable, at least the Thomas whom Theresa had known ten years ago.

"Arrogant?" Mr. Belmont peered at his plate, from which every morsel of eggs, toast, ham, bacon, and stewed apples had been consumed. "Holding parlor sessions is often a humbling business, because one can so easily be in error."

"But who is to know that? People usually come to their own conclusions, and the truth has little to do with it." Theresa kept the bitterness from her words, barely, but the squire wasn't deceived.

She liked him a little less for his perceptivity, and respected him more.

"You have been tried, judged, and executed in the court of public opinion, I'd guess. Not a pleasant experience." Mr. Belmont shared his evidentiary conclusion gently.

Worse yet, his blue eyes were kind.

Theresa pushed her eggs about on her plate. "You however, have likely never endured such an experience." Nobody should have to endure public censure, however silent or subtle it might be.

Mr. Belmont moved the teapot closer to her wrist—the good porcelain, suggesting the kitchen was on its best behavior.

"There, madam, you would be wrong, and I notice you do not gainsay my conclusion. Do you intend to eat those eggs?"

He'd put away a prodigious amount of food, but for all his leanness, he was a good-sized fellow.

"You're welcome to them, if that's what you're asking."

He reached for her plate. "I realize I am risking quite the bad impression, but my cook has run off to Brighton—she's always running off somewhere now that my sons reside in Oxfordshire. Your cook, on the other hand, has a fine hand with the omelet, and an empty stomach has no pride."

Theresa sat, nonplussed and charmed, as her guest scraped her untouched food onto his plate.

"I haven't seen a man demolish a meal like this since Thomas lived at Sutcliffe," she said. "He grew so quickly and was always active. Food disappeared whenever he was around, just plain disappeared."

Thomas had had no pride then. He'd been all appetite—for food, for knowledge, for books, languages, and life.

"I share the same ability," Mr. Belmont said between bites, "to make food disappear. While my sons' handling of a plate of food defies description. Gustatory legerdemain is the closest I can come. Food vanishes. Fortunately, your cook is aware of my tendencies and provides portions in abundance when I'm on the property."

"So when were you pilloried by the local gossips?" Theresa asked.

He frowned at the eggs on his fork. "Any man serving as magistrate comes in for a deal of criticism. He charges those whom public opinion would forgive, he does not charge someone who is unpopular. Evidence matters naught when the yeomen gather around their pints, and in some cases, I am not free to disclose the entire basis upon which I make my decisions."

The eggs, which had to be cold by now, met their fate, while Theresa remained quiet in hopes Mr. Belmont would continue his recitation.

"It's a d— deuced thankless job," he went on, "and that's before we consider what the judges at the assizes have to say about one's work, or the vicar judging from his pulpit each Sunday while he exhorts the rest of us to judge not. Then too, Mr. Burton Louis fancies himself the local equivalent of Dr. Johnson because he manages to print a broadsheet of purest blather each—"

Mr. Belmont put his fork down. "I am whining. Forgive me."

The charming smile was nowhere in sight, and yet, Theresa liked this version of Squire Belmont—a little testy, running low on neighborly good cheer, not too proud to eat cold eggs.

What a shame they'd never have a chance to further their acquaintance. She ignored her heart's plea for just a few more minutes of friendly, adult company with Mr. Belmont, and instead let the truth loose between them.

"You may assume, Mr. Belmont, that the mother of an articulate eight-year-old has overlooked whining far more protracted than your little lapse."

Mr. Belmont stilled, as if he'd heard a sword drawn from its scabbard in the next room. His eyes were the predictable blue of the Englishman descended from Saxon ancestors, and Theresa braced herself to see his gaze grow chilly, or worse—speculating.

The corners of those eyes crinkled, and his expression became, if anything, commiserating.

"You'll miss that whining someday, I assure you. You'll miss the mud on your carpets, the slamming of doors above stairs, the inability of the child to recall where—in the space of two minutes—gloves, boots, books, or common sense has got off to. Would you like more tea, Miss Jennings? I'm after the last of the toast and want to wash it down properly."

What Theresa wanted, was to ask if Mr. Belmont had heard her. *Miss* Theresa Jennings had an eight-year-old daughter. A man who prided himself on his animal husbandry needn't any clearer clue to his hostess's unsavory past.

Mr. Belmont's hand was on the teapot, his expression hinting at both humor and regret. The service was decorated with a shepherd boy and a goose girl casting coy glances among twining flowers and gilt vines.

Mr. Belmont's index finger bore a scar, a slash of white across an otherwise elegant, if unfashionably tan hand.

The sight of that scar—small, old, unremarkable, but suggestive of a story—provoked a peculiar insight: Theresa and the magistrate had in common the joys and frustrations of parenting.

The same reality that had ruined Theresa's good name once and for all, gave her common ground with the king's man. The sense of connection was so unexpected and rare, she might have turned up sentimental over it, if she hadn't sworn off that useless proclivity years ago.

"You really do take your nutrition seriously," she said, or maybe Mr. Belmont really did know how to change the subject. "If you're still hungry, we have apple tart on the sideboard. Shall we enjoy it on the terrace with a fresh pot of tea? The southern side of the house is protected from the breezes and lovely at this time of the morning."

"A wonderful suggestion." Mr. Belmont rose and assisted Theresa to her feet, another quaint, disconcerting display. "Will I ever meet this whining prodigy who calls you mother?"

He missed his children badly. Thomas had said something about them visiting cousins or going up to university.

Theresa pondered the conversational options all the way to the terrace, where she decided on the only course she'd ever been able to tolerate where Priscilla was concerned: honesty.

"I am not in the habit of socializing with neighbors, Mr. Belmont. My life at Sutcliffe Keep was nigh monastic, and I preferred it that way."

Mr. Belmont plucked a sprig of lavender from the border edging the flagstones, despite the blooms being well past their best season.

"Sutcliffe Keep is along the sea, isn't it?" he asked, twirling the lavender beneath his nose. "The seacoast has always struck me as lonely."

Matthew Belmont was not a stupid man, and yet, Theresa needed to be very clear with him regarding her situation.

"The sea wasn't what isolated us, Mr. Belmont."

Her comment was an invitation for her guest to recall a pressing engagement, bow politely, and take away his full stomach, kind eyes, and feeble attempt at whining by the simple expedient of striding off through the gardens.

"You have me at a loss, Miss Jennings." His gaze was steady, his expression giving away nothing—not dread of another prickly subject, not avaricious anticipation of juicy gossip. He spun the lavender idly between his fingers, not a hint of tension in even that small gesture.

He was not outstandingly handsome, but he was attractive. This realization evoked sorrow—Theresa had not found a man attractive in years—and justified a ruthless display of common sense.

"My daughter is a bastard," Theresa said. "I would not want to cause you or her embarrassment should the facts of her birth be revealed to you in her hearing."

Mr. Belmont stood at Theresa's side, while a pair of sparrows flitted among the nearby oaks, and a frisky breeze fluttered leaves donning their autumn glory. He didn't clear his throat, didn't narrow his eyes, didn't quirk an eyebrow in invitation as other supposed gentlemen had many times before him.

"For your daughter," he said, tucking the lavender into his jacket pocket, "I am sorry. Some will treat her unfairly on the basis of her circumstances, and for you…"

"For me?" Theresa prompted, ready to snatch up her skirts and whirl back to the safety of the house.

"I am sorry as well. Your trust was quite obviously betrayed. Fortunately, I conclude you treasure your daughter and she, you, and that is what matters most. Somebody did mention apple tart, if I recall. Shall we?"

He offered Theresa his arm again.

Shall we?

Two unremarkable, cordial words that swept aside judgment—and worse—dispensed with the prurient interest that often followed disclosure of Priscilla's bastardy. *Shall we?*

Theresa laid her hand on his arm. His bare fingers closed over hers with a little pat, and he escorted her down the steps to the lower terrace.

CHAPTER TWO

Mr. Belmont did the male version of prattling on as they walked, about tutors, about nannies, about how his two oldest sons had taken to their studies at university, about being unable to part with any of the ponies his sons had outgrown—ponies whose acquaintance Miss Priscilla might like to make.

His neighborly baritone filled a quiet morning, and filled an emptiness inside Theresa too. As a much younger woman, she'd had glimpses of what Matthew Belmont represented: decent society. He was kindness itself, civility, fair play, and all the classical virtues in a winsome package.

She should have met such a man ten years ago, though even ten years ago would have been too late, and even Matthew Belmont's quiet gentlemanliness wouldn't have affected the decisions she'd made then.

For Theresa, Mr. Belmont would have been—as he still was—too little and much, much too late.

They ate large servings of apple tart, and Mr. Belmont accepted a second helping without even a pretense of polite demurral.

A woman could enjoy feeding such a man, planning menus to delight him and to appease that prodigious appetite. She would look forward to sharing meals with him, and to simply being in his company.

"I'm off to finish my correspondence and balance ledgers that have been glaring at me for the past week," Mr. Belmont said. "I enjoy the physical labor of harvest, but it generates a great deal of paperwork as well, and that, I confess, I find tedious."

"I love the ledgers and balance sheets and figuring," Theresa said, accepting his proffered arm with an ease that she would ponder when she had the solitude to do so. "At Sutcliffe, I did not trust the stewards and land agents to operate in

Thomas's best interests, so I supervised their every transaction."

"They were not honest?"

"They were far from honest." Weasels had more honor than that pack of vermin. "I pensioned off as many as I could before our grandfather died, and did the bookwork myself thereafter."

"And where was our Thomas while you were busily defending the family seat?" Mr. Belmont asked. "He doesn't strike me as a man who would allow his dependents to be taken advantage of."

Theresa would also be honest with Mr. Belmont about this, in part because he'd whined a little and in part because nobody—not one person in Theresa's hearing—had ever wondered why the wealthy Thomas Jennings, now Baron Sutcliffe, kept his sister moldering away at the family seat.

"Thomas and I had a significant falling-out before Priscilla was born. Despite every probability to the contrary, he did not expect to come into the title—didn't want it, didn't aspire to it, didn't even acknowledge it at first—so the business of the estate was of no moment to him until about two years ago."

The words were truthful, the way the visible portion of an iceberg could not be called a misrepresentation.

"I understood his succession was recent. Your family, like all families, apparently has its share of challenges."

Challenges, yes, and Theresa was perishing sick of them.

"I looked after Sutcliffe, because from a young age, I understood that Thomas would likely become its owner someday. Shall I send some food home with you, Mr. Belmont? I cannot abide the thought of you going hungry while we have such abundance here."

"I would not starve, but I might be tempted to accept an invitation from one of the marriage-minded mamas in the district. A man shold consider a bread-and-water diet before yielding to such folly."

Thank goodness he was leaving. The longer Theresa was in Mr. Belmont's company, the more she liked him.

"You will not remarry?"

"If I remarry, it won't be to some girl half my age who thinks only to satisfy the dictates of her parents."

His blue eyes were positively glacial as he voiced that sentiment, the sternness of his expression making him impressive in a different, intriguing way. He was the king's man, prosecutor and judge when the situation called for it.

Though he was also a lonely papa.

"Mr. Belmont, I do believe that is the closest sentiment to irritation I have heard in your voice since meeting you." The closest emotion to *anger*.

He'd been leading Theresa around the house, so they now stood at the bottom of the front steps, Theresa's hand on his arm, his hand over hers.

"The ambushes started at Matilda's very wake, if you must know. Neighbors typically provide meals for the aggrieved, and I swear I met more single young women over ham casseroles than I knew lived in all of Sussex. At the time, I was too upset to notice, and thank goodness my brother Axel shielded me from the worst of it, but the campaign didn't stop there and hasn't really stopped since."

He seemed to realize he'd trapped Theresa's hand on his sleeve and unlaced their arms with a sort of bow, then fished his riding gloves out of his coat pocket.

His tirade—for Mr. Belmont that surely qualified as a tirade?—merited a response.

"One wonders if widows endure the same sort of pursuit." The pursuit Theresa had endured had been so much less genteel.

"The wealthy ones do, and they expect me to commiserate and even provide—"

Theresa could imagine what the local widows wanted from the tall, cordial squire. Their pigs probably went missing regularly—or their earbobs or their wits—as a result of what they sought from Matthew Belmont.

He fell silent while trying to button his second glove.

Theresa took his hand, glove and all, between her two and did up the button with the dispatch of a mother experienced at buttoning moving targets.

Though Mr. Belmont held absolutely still. "Thank you," he said when Theresa turned loose of him.

"I have fussed at you twice in one day."

"And I still find it sweet—wonderfully sweet—but what was that look about?"

He wanted more honesty from her, and what was the harm in one more little truth between them?

"I never grasped that men might feel as pestered as women do by unwanted attentions. Women can flounce off in high dudgeon, be insulted, plead a headache, or set the fellow down, but a gentleman…"

"Does so at his peril," Mr. Belmont finished. "One doesn't want to hurt the feelings of the sweet young things, but their mamas are quite another matter. For a time, I dreaded the churchyard after services and even procrastinated opening my mail."

"Let's go around to the kitchen, sir. I cannot bear the thought of what enduring more ham casseroles might drive you to."

* * *

By the time they reached the kitchen, Matthew had figured out what bothered him about Theresa Jennings. The insight had come to him when the lady had buttoned up his right glove. She'd stepped closer, scenting the moment with lemon verbena and taking his hand in both of hers with a confident grasp.

For a succession of instants, he'd stared at the nape of her neck, at the curve of her jaw, at the way the morning breeze tried to wreak havoc with her dark hair—and failed. In profile, her features revealed the sort of classic proportions that gave her face a quality of repose and agelessness.

She was a beautiful woman and determined to hide it.

She did nothing—not one thing—to call attention to her feminine attributes. Her attire was not noticeably plain, it was *un*-noticeably plain. Her hair was swept back in a pretty, utterly unremarkable bun. She wore no jewelry. Her rare smiles bore no hint of flirtation, her gestures were contained.

Theresa Jennings hid in plain sight, and as Matthew studied the flawless, downy skin of her nape, he wondered if she hid even from herself. She was a spinster masquerading as a fallen woman, and the combination bothered him.

He wondered when a man had last pressed his grateful, hungry lips to that skin and made her sigh with passion?

Then he wondered if he—the sober, mature widower, the fellow hostesses prevailed upon to make up the numbers at the last minute—had misplaced his wits.

"The kitchen is always quiet this time of day," Miss Jennings said, taking a wicker container down from a high shelf.

Matthew was too busy cadging a peek at her ankles to assist her. She bustled about, putting together a hamper of provisions in no time. A fresh loaf of bread, a mold of butter, some hard cheese, shiny red apples, cold sliced beef, grapes, and a half a loaf of spice cake all disappeared into the hamper.

"I cannot imagine this will hold you even until sundown, Mr. Belmont."

"I will survive. The vicar's oldest daughters do temporary duty for the evening meal, and we make do otherwise. You are most generous." Also more competent in the big kitchen than a baron's sister should be.

Her gaze inventoried the shelves like a general reviewing her troops. "You watched me cut that cake as if you were a starving raptor. What are you doing for dinner tomorrow night?"

A cold tray in the library, ledgers, a ham casserole of boredom, solitude, and duty.

"Imposing on you?"

Miss Jennings's smile became one hint worth of wicked. "If you can bear Priscilla's company, you are cordially invited to join us. It's time to work on her company manners, and you've raised children. I feel certain you're up to the challenge."

A child at table was a splendid idea. Such company would preserve Matthew from lunatic speculations about napes and sighs and the taste of lemons.

"I didn't simply raise children, Miss Jennings, I raised *boys*, that species of primate who finds rude noises produced with the body to be a form of entertainment, particularly before guests."

She passed him a surprisingly heavy hamper. "My brother and my cousins weren't like that. Even Grandpapa had his limits."

"I'd forgotten Thomas had cousins." Much less that Thomas had been raised with them by a titled grandfather. "He hasn't mentioned them."

"They are… deceased," she said, opening the back door. "I shall walk you down to the stable."

"I would enjoy that." Matthew also enjoyed offering her his arm, and enjoyed even more when she took it—and then refrained from leaning, pressing, stumbling, or otherwise drawing his notice to her attributes.

Lovely though those attributes were.

"You are such a gentleman, Mr. Belmont." Alas, this did not sound like a compliment. "I hardly know what to do with you."

"Are you complaining?"

"I'm lamenting," she replied softly, as they passed blown roses and withered salvia.

While Matthew, with a full hamper in hand and an invitation to dinner tucked beside the spice cake, grappled instead with an odd sense of rejoicing.

* * *

"Mama looked very nice," Priscilla said as Miss Alice tied a perfect pink bow to the end of Priscilla's right braid. Governesses could do that—tie bows that matched exactly—but Mama had the knack of leaving a bit of ribbon trailing on each side, which looked more grown-up.

"We will all present quite nicely," Miss Alice said, finishing the second bow. "Do you have any questions, Priscilla? We didn't have much company at Sutcliffe Keep."

They hadn't had *any* company, and not because Priscilla had been too young to leave the nursery. Even though she'd eaten nearly every supper with Miss Alice and Mama, she was still too young for company, according to Miss Alice.

That meant tonight's meal with Squire Belmont was a Very Special Occasion.

"We practiced at breakfast and luncheon," Priscilla said. "I'm not to speak unless a grown-up asks me a question, and I'm not to kick my chair. I am to be a pattern card of good manners and charm."

Uncle Thomas had charm, and he could be silly, greeting Priscilla in a different language each time he saw her.

"I might have overstated the objective a trifle." Miss Alice leaned closer to the folding mirror on the vanity and used her little finger to smooth the hair at her temple.

Miss Alice was pretty. She had dark hair, a nice voice, and she was smart. She was also Mama's only friend.

"You look fetching, Miss Alice."

Miss Alice would say that was forward of Priscilla, but Miss Alice was always going on about honesty being the first requirement of virtue—virtue had *a lot* of requirements—and Miss Alice had never, ever told Priscilla a lie.

"Thank you, Priscilla. We will give your mother and Mr. Belmont a few more minutes, then join them in the parlor. Are you nervous?"

Priscilla was supposed to say yes, but Miss Alice was the one who was nervous.

"Maybe a little. Mama said Mr. Belmont is a papa and that he's nice. I won't kick my chair even once, Miss Alice."

Not quite a lie. Priscilla had learned to weave truth carefully, because sometimes, a girl needed to choose in which direction to be honest.

Priscilla wasn't nervous, she was *excited*, for Mama's brown dress was the same one she'd worn to Uncle Thomas and Aunt Loris's wedding, the very best dress Mama owned.

Miss Alice checked the watch pinned to her bodice. "Five more minutes. I intend to be very proud of you by bedtime, Priscilla."

Priscilla was proud of Mama. Yesterday, from a vantage point in the hay mow, Priscilla had watched as Mama had stood guard over Penny and Treasure, and then had helped Mr. Belmont figure out what ailed Penny.

Mama had been *normal* with Mr. Belmont. She had stood right next to him to read about Penny's hay and feed, and she'd barely fussed when Treasure had knocked her right against Mr. Belmont.

Mama was a prodigious good fusser, sometimes.

Mr. Belmont had been *normal* with Mama too. He hadn't sniffed and scowled and acted like Mama had embarrassed him by burping at the table or using bad language on Sunday.

Then, according to Cook, Mr. Belmont and Mama had *had breakfast together*. Mama never had company for breakfast, not even Mr. Finbottom, the curate who came around twice a year to collect for the Widows and Orphans Fund.

Mr. Belmont was ever so much nicer than Mr. Finbottom, and Mr. Belmont had come cantering up the drive on a *white horse*.

"What are you thinking about, Priscilla?" Miss Alice asked, giving her chignon a final pat.

"I'm thinking about my storybooks. If I am very good, may I read a whole story tonight?"

Miss Alice checked her watch again. She wore no other jewelry, ever, but her dresses were as fine as Mama's, and her boots were newer.

"Company dinners can take longer," Miss Alice said. "If we're not too late in the dining room, then you may read one entire story of not more than twenty pages."

Priscilla mentally inventoried her stories and came up with half a dozen short enough to qualify.

"I will be better than I've ever been before. Is it five minutes yet?"

Miss Alice's mouth twitched, which meant she was trying not to smile. "Approximately five minutes," she said, holding out a hand to Priscilla.

Priscilla let herself be led to the steps at a pace so ladylike, her ninth birthday would probably arrive before they got down to dinner, but she was determined to be very, very good, so she didn't complain.

"I'm nervous," Miss Alice said at the top of the steps. "I suspect your mama is too, Priscilla. We mustn't muck this up."

"We'll be pattern cards of good manners and charm, Miss Alice. Don't worry."

A girl learned to manage on her own when she had nearly a whole castle to herself. Mr. Belmont was nice—Penny wouldn't like him if he was a rotter—and thus nobody should be worried.

Priscilla would, however, be as well-mannered as she knew how to be, for in every one of her stories, one fact remained reliable: The fellow who rode the white horse was the one to rescue the princess. Mr. Belmont rode a lovely white mare, had the golden hair required of all self-respecting princes, and he had got himself invited to dinner with Mama and Miss Alice.

All that was needed was a magic spell or two, and nobody would have to go back to that miserable, cold, damp castle by the sea ever again.

* * *

"Mr. Matthew Belmont," Harry, the senior footman announced, stepping back to admit Matthew to the Linden library. "Shall I tell the kitchen our guest has arrived, ma'am?"

"Thank you, yes, Harry." Miss Jennings rose, and in evening dress her efforts at camouflage were significantly less successful. Her gown, while several years out-of-date, was a chocolate-brown velvet that flattered her hair, her eyes, and her figure—most especially her figure.

"Miss Jennings." Matthew bowed over her hand. "How lovely you look. I would not have thought to attire you in that shade, but it is most becoming."

She appeared pleased by his compliment, also flustered, like a lady who'd left the schoolroom not many years past, rather than the mother of a precocious eight-year-old.

"I am always relieved when the cooler weather appears and I can get out my velvets. You are a splendid sight yourself, sir."

Splendid? *Well.* Matthew was abruptly glad he'd bothered with a sapphire stick pin, gold watch fob, and matching sleeve buttons, though finding the entire set had taken him nearly half an hour.

"I have little call for proper evening attire anymore, but the clothing still fits, and the company is well worth the effort." *Laying it on a bit thick, old boy.*

"May I offer you a drink, Mr. Belmont?"

God, yes. Yesterday, the idea of an evening meal in Miss Jennings's company had seemed like a fine notion, particularly in the opinion of that vast cavern known as Matthew's belly. Tonight, he had stared at himself in his dressing mirror and realized he was... nervous, to be sharing a meal with a woman whose company he enjoyed.

"A tot of brandy wouldn't go amiss."

"Brandy it will be." Miss Jennings poured a hospitable portion from the decanter on the sideboard.

"I know some ladies are reluctant to take strong spirits," Matthew said, "but we're likely to get frost tonight. Shall you have a nip to keep the chill off?"

Matilda had sworn by regular medicinal nips. Miss Jennings looked far less taken with the notion.

"Perhaps a drop," she said, pouring not much more than that into a glass. "Shall we be seated? We have a few minutes before Priscilla shatters the king's peace in the name of showing off her manners."

Matthew took a seat on the sofa and tried to ignore the sense that he'd misstepped somehow regarding the spirits. Miss Jennings hadn't struck him as a high stickler, but perhaps he ought to have asked for a glass of wine?

She settled herself in a rocking chair at right angles to the fire, her drink untouched in her hand.

"Were you raised here in Sussex, Mr. Belmont?"

Onward to the small talk, then. "We were, my brother and I." He and Axel had endured childhoods in Sussex, at any rate. "I grew up at Belmont House, and my parents are buried there. I suppose I will be too."

"One hopes not for quite some time."

Matthew took a cautious sip of his drink. "Sometimes I feel as if I've already been interred." His admission was uncharacteristically morose, and personal—honest, too—but Miss Jennings continued to rock serenely.

"I feel the same way about Sutcliffe Keep. I should love it, because I'm raising my daughter there, where my father was raised. But for so many years, I've looked at Sutcliffe as a resource I had to protect for my brother, as an obligation. Priscilla says the castle doesn't look like a place where people live. It looks like a place where armies fight with spears and boiling oil. She's right."

"From the mouths of babes." Though thank God that Matthew's sons didn't feel that way about Belmont House. "If you dislike Sutcliffe Keep, why not leave?"

The rhythm Miss Jennings set up, rocking languidly before the fire, soothed as the brandy did not, excellent potation though it was.

"Why don't you leave Belmont House? We set down roots, and there we are, whether the place we planted ourselves ten years ago is where we wish to be planted today or not."

In other words, Miss Jennings had wanted to leave the ancestral pile by the sea, just as Matthew had often wanted to turn his back on Belmont House.

"I do leave," Matthew said. "I go up to Town when my schedule allows. I visit my brother. I went to Oxford to fetch Christopher home between terms last year."

Matthew had felt like a truant first former on every one of those excursions, vaguely anxious about livestock and servants who likely hadn't spared him a thought.

Miss Jennings held her glass up to the firelight, as if she might read portents in the flames' reflections.

"This trip to Linden is the first I've left Sutcliffe since Priscilla was born."

Eight years in a place meant for spears and boiling oil? "You were rusticating with a vengeance."

She set the drink down, again without taking a taste. "It's only rusticating, Mr. Belmont, if one has another option. I was simply living my life."

Miss Jennings did not bumble. She advanced through a conversation with the confidence of a French cavalry unit charging an English infantry square. Fearsome, unstoppable, all business at a steady, ground-eating trot that boded ill for Albion, and could break into an all-out gallop at any moment.

So Matthew met her charge with a volley of curiosity. "Would your brother have assisted you to find a more hospitable domicile if you asked him to?"

"My brother is a good man," Miss Jennings replied, addressing the fire in the hearth more than her guest. "Thomas is also as stubborn as a lame mule, and when he left Sutcliffe after university, he was not in charity with me. We had enjoyed a lively correspondence, but after that, my letters were returned unopened until he came here to Linden."

Baron Sutcliffe *was* stubborn, stubborn in the way of a man whose determination had saved his soul. Alas, the trait was apparently common to both siblings.

"To what do you attribute your brother's change of heart?"

"The title, to some extent. Thomas has ever been responsible and as head of the family, he was responsible for me. Then too, his best friend—Viscount Fairly—married, and happily so. But it wasn't only that...."

Harmless old squires heard many confessions, most of them not remotely criminal. Matthew *wanted* to hear this one, for Miss Jennings carried mystery about with her like a favorite shawl. He took a dilatory sip of a dangerously pleasant brew rather than interrupt her.

"Thomas didn't know about Priscilla. She has helped tip the balance."

Matthew and his hostess had passed from small talk to philosophy to confidences. Watching Miss Jennings rock quietly in her chair, her brandy untouched, her outdated gown flattering a figure Matthew could not quite ignore, he had the sense these exchanges were the least of the shadows Theresa Jennings carried in her heart.

Generally, Matthew kept the confidences imposed on him as a matter of responsibility—as a neighbor, as an exemplar of the king's peace, as a gentleman.

Hetty Longacre's youngest bore a strong resemblance not to the blue-eyed Mr. Longacre, but to Tobias Shirley, right down to the Shirley brown eyes. Even

Matthew's sons had remarked the likeness, which had given him many a bad moment.

The upright Frampton Jones, brewer of the finest ales in Sussex, went to London for mercury treatments.

The list of woes and secrets Matthew was privy to was endless, and like the horse hair that accumulated on his wardrobe by the end of some days, he ignored the lot. With Theresa Jennings, ignoring the shadows in her eyes would be unkind in the first place, and impossible in the second.

A woman who had the courage to reveal her heartaches on her own initiative, rather than as a matter of official investigation or neighborly inquisition, would not expect endless sunshine and small talk from those around her.

"I should not be telling you this, Mr. Belmont, and you likely hear enough useless chatter without my adding to your store."

Of useless chatter, Matthew had a king's ransom. His shelves were nearly bare of honest conversation, though.

"You should be telling someone, madam. How did Priscilla tip the balance between you and your brother?"

Matthew already had an inkling, because the children had tipped the balance between him and Matilda, for a time anyway.

"A child…" Miss Jennings looked away, out the mullioned windows to where nightfall wasn't yet relieved by a rising moon. "A child reminds one of one's own youth, and in Priscilla, Thomas was able to see parts of me that as a younger, angrier man, he could not acknowledge. I am his elder, but that doesn't mean I was always an adult."

Except in some sense, she had been an adult since birth. Matthew recognized the breed, for he saw it in the mirror and in his brother Axel. Christopher had an element of the same quality.

"Thomas loved his sister, when she wasn't an adult," Matthew said, "when she was a little girl with a big imagination and no friends. Isn't it wondrous how children allow us to love?"

Miss Jennings rose and stood with her back to him. "Unfair, Mr. Belmont." The rocker went on moving, slowing gradually.

"My apologies." Matthew rose as well, and not because manners required it, and not entirely because he wanted to stand behind Miss Jennings breathing lemon verbena and studying the intricate braiding she'd woven in her hair.

"Forgive my presumption, madam, and allow me to point out, whatever the cause, you and your brother are reconciled, and into the bargain, Priscilla now has her Uncle Thomas, who I am sure will make up for the time lost as best he can."

Miss Jennings nodded, but still didn't turn, and Matthew resisted the urge to take her by the shoulders and make her face him, so that he might see her extraordinary blue eyes and the emotions they held. His gaze fell again on the nape of her neck, graceful, tender, and abruptly, quite… kissable.

If he wanted his face slapped.

"More brandy?" he asked, stepping over to the decanter, though the ploy was absurd. Miss Jennings hadn't touched her drink.

She turned, her expression composed, her eyes painfully bright. "No thank you, though you must help yourself to as much as you like."

"You were generous,"—he held up his unfinished drink—"and I am trying to demonstrate restraint by savoring such fine libation."

A soft tap on the door heralded Harry's reappearance.

"Dinner, Miss Jennings, and Miss Alice and Miss Priscilla are on their way down."

"Priscilla's governess usually joins us for the evening meal, unless Priscilla has been boisterous and Alice wants a break," Miss Jennings said. "Ours was a very humble household."

Household? At least Matthew's prison had been commodious.

He offered his arm. "With three ladies to grace the table, I will be the most envied of men."

"Reserve judgment on that. Your companions will be a child, a confirmed bluestocking, and me."

Not a one of whom would be trying to inveigle Matthew into taking liberties or offering marriage.

"And *your* companion will be Squire Belmont, or as my boys christened me, Squire Bottomless. We shall make a delightful company, and your cook will be in alt."

CHAPTER THREE

Despite Mr. Belmont's regalia and the unsettling conversation, dinner with *Squire Bottomless* would be informal, with both Alice and Priscilla on hand to ensure nothing untoward was said.

Nothing *more* untoward. Theresa had nearly come undone at what Mr. Belmont had deduced about her upbringing at Sutcliffe.

A little girl with a big imagination and no friends. What a recipe for misery that had become. As she allowed Mr. Belmont seat her, then watched him display the same courtesy to Alice and even Priscilla, Theresa reminded herself that her guest was dangerous.

He was attractive, with height, blond hair, blue, blue eyes, and a sense of contained, competent energy—a fine specimen, like a well-bred horse or a fit hound. If anything about him was bottomless, though, it was his calm spirit.

Matthew Belmont viewed life with a tolerance as startling as it was alluring. Others might take that broad-mindedness for granted, but Theresa wanted to probe its edges and origins.

Thank the kindly powers, Alice and Priscilla would prevent such folly.

Mr. Belmont turned to the child as the last course was served, and the topic of the Belmont pony herd had been discussed at length.

"What have you found most interesting here at Linden, Miss Priscilla?"

Priscilla's brow puckered, which made her look more like her uncle. "Linden Hall is *easy*. If you want to go from your bedroom to the kitchen, you needn't travel up two flights and down one, then cross the bailey to get there. Linden likes the light, it doesn't huddle up in its stones like it's always happier in the dark. Uncle Thomas has a stable, not just a few stalls under the gatehouse, and Aunt Loris has flowers and flowers and flowers."

"Have you helped her make scents?" Mr. Belmont inquired.

He had excellent instincts with children. Alice acknowledged as much in the look she sent Theresa across the table.

Priscilla beamed at their guest. "I do help, and Aunt made a scent for me. Here." She stuck out her arm and waved her wrist under Mr. Belmont's nose.

He sniffed delicately at her wrist. "Lovely. Sunny, like daffodils, and you."

"That's what I asked for," Priscilla replied. "Uncle Thomas likes it when Aunt Loris smells like biscuits, but we haven't found scents yet for Mama and Miss Alice."

"More complicated ladies need more complicated scents," Mr. Belmont said—and with a straight face too. "Are you missing your Uncle Thomas?"

Theresa sat back and watched as an adult male held a conversation with her daughter. The experience was appallingly novel. Thomas teased the child and indulged in linguistic antics Priscilla found delightful. Viscount Fairly had joked and tickled and similarly entertained Priscilla, but neither man had engaged the girl's mind.

"I miss Uncle lots," Priscilla said. "I think that's because I only just met him here at Linden. If he lived with us, I would probably miss him less. I want Mama to let us live here, but she keeps telling me not to pester her."

Mr. Belmont's expression remained respectfully attentive. "Pestering is hardly ever a good tactic with one's mama. Surely you must find fault with some aspects of Linden?"

Alice stepped into the breach, for Priscilla could be an eloquent critic. "Perhaps you might consider your answer at your leisure, Priscilla?"

"I'll think about it," Priscilla said. "May I come see your ponies, Mr. Belmont?"

Mr. Belmont pretended to ponder the question. "That might come close to pestering, child."

"Was I pestering, Mama?"

"More wheedling than pestering," Theresa temporized. "You have done an excellent job with your studies since Uncle Thomas and Aunt Loris left for Sutcliffe Keep, and you've completed all your stories. If the squire is willing, we can schedule a visit."

To see the ponies, which spared Theresa admitting she'd like to call upon the squire himself.

"Do you enjoy horses, Miss Portman?" Mr. Belmont inquired of Alice.

"From a safe distance. Upwind, if it can be arranged."

"A town lady, then? One comfortable going all year without hearing the cows low or the roosters crow?"

"You have me." When she smiled, Alice was quite pretty. Theresa had known the woman for nearly five years and was astonished to note this. "Unfortunately for Miss Priscilla, I am very good at devising ways of entertaining and educating that do not call for excursions beyond the house."

"But Mama rescues me," Priscilla interjected, "so I can go outside, and Miss Alice can have a break from me, because I am a handful."

Grandpapa had called Theresa so much worse than that.

"And because you need to stretch your legs," Theresa said, "as do I, from time to time. We would be pleased, Mr. Belmont, to come see your ponies. Now then, who would like some chocolate cake?"

Theresa had gone to trouble with this cake, making it herself that very afternoon. Life at Sutcliffe had been isolated, with the nearest market town seven hilly miles distant. If Theresa had wanted confections and fancy dishes, she'd learned—partly out of sheer boredom—to make them herself, and this sweet was among her favorites. The cake itself was rich, moist chocolate, the filling raspberry, and the lot was served with whipped cream.

The staff might have disapproved of her presuming on the kitchen, but they'd never declined a serving of cake.

The squire's eyebrows rose as dessert was brought to the table. "My compliments to the cook, again. Appearance alone suggests this will be as delicious as all the preceding courses."

They tucked into their cake, Mr. Belmont going silent, perhaps in the pursuit of alimentary bliss. When his portion had been consumed, he sat back. His smile was bashful, likely the reaction to the three pairs of female eyes watching him with amusement.

"I enjoyed the entire meal, Miss Jennings, but the company and your cake have to win top honors for the evening."

Alice rose. "Some of the company must depart for their beds, and that includes you, Priscilla."

Priscilla scrambled out of her seat and scampered over to Theresa, dark braids bouncing.

"Good night, Mama." She wrapped her arms around Theresa's neck and squeezed. "Will you tuck me in and hear my prayers?"

"Later, Priscilla." Theresa kissed her daughter's forehead. "You should be very proud of yourself. Your manners were lovely and your conversation gracious."

"Am I growing up?" Priscilla asked, nose in the air.

All too quickly. "You are. You are becoming quite the young lady."

Alice extended a hand. "Come along Priscilla, before you say something outrageous and your mother will have to revise her opinion."

"Good night Mr. Belmont." Priscilla trotted over to him and held out her arms.

Mr. Belmont, who had risen when Alice had stood, scooped the child up as naturally as if it were part of his evening ritual.

"Pleasant dreams, Princess." He smiled through her fierce hug and bumped her cheek gently with his nose. "Don't be in too big a hurry to grow up, and don't forget that you promised me a story with a happy ending."

"You shall have it soon," Priscilla said as he deposited her on her feet.

"Genius cannot be hurried," Mr. Belmont murmured, as the child led her governess from the room. "What an utter delight she is. Boys are such busy creatures and charming in their own way. A fellow can *do* things with his sons, show them how to go on, teach them all sorts of useful and arcane lore, but a little girl is such a lovable creature."

"That one is." Mr. Belmont's observation invited Theresa to look beyond Priscilla's table manners, penmanship, and diction, to the miracle of the growing child herself. "I am no end of relieved that Thomas has acknowledged her as his niece. She is much like him, busy, studious, imaginative, and she can mimic anyone so closely you'd think she'd trod the boards."

Mr. Belmont resumed his seat and peered down the neck of a wine bottle still more than half full.

"You persisted in mending the breach with Thomas because of Priscilla and her right to know and be loved by her family."

A hypothesis, for Matthew Belmont had that sort of mind. Curious, analytical, interested in others. Theresa had once been burdened with a lively curiosity too.

"Some of my persistence was on Priscilla's behalf. Shall I ring for tea, or would you perhaps like another brandy to finish your meal?"

"What I would like is a turn in the garden with a congenial lady on my arm. The meal was by far the best I've had in months, but my digestion would benefit from some movement."

"Fresh air appeals." As did avoiding any more discussion of Theresa's differences with Thomas. She and her brother were talking, true, but difficult words still needed to be said—eventually. She rose, as Mr. Belmont drew her chair back for her.

"I bet I can find you a sprig of lavender on the south terrace," he said, "and we'll be out of the evening breeze as well."

"Priscilla is right about the flowers here," Theresa replied, grateful for the change in topic. "The place is just short of overrun with them, particularly the steward's cottage."

"Loris likes her flowers and loves making scents," Mr. Belmont said as they made their way through the library to the terrace beyond. "If Sutcliffe were so inclined, he could turn the flowers into a successful commercial venture."

"Have you mentioned that to him?" Theresa asked, stepping out onto the flagstone terrace and leaving Mr. Belmont's side to test the dampness of the soil in the pot of pansies on the table.

The pansies were thirsty, which Theresa would mention to Harry. She'd neglected to have the torches lit, though a full harvest moon was clearing the horizon to the east. Were she a different woman with a different past, she'd take a moment to consider the propriety of a moonlit stroll with an unmarried gentleman.

She'd lost the right to that hesitation long ago. Instead, she'd considered the bother to the servants of having to light a garden full of torches for a short constitutional on a chilly evening.

"I've mentioned my ideas regarding the flowers to Loris," Mr. Belmont said. "The recipes and labor are largely hers. Tell me, Miss Jennings, have I given offense?"

Theresa stood on her side of the terrace, feeling awkward, because she'd no handkerchief with which to wipe her hand clean. "I beg your pardon, Mr. Belmont?"

"You disdain to take my arm," he said, flourishing white linen in the darkness, "though I recall you allowing me the privilege of providing escort on previous occasions."

He was smiling, *teasing* her, the handkerchief dangling from his hand like a slack flag of truce.

"I beg your pardon." Theresa made use of the handkerchief, passed it back to him, and wrapped her hand around his elbow. "Now we might stumble around in the dark as one."

"You are so wonderfully tart, madam. Like a bracing lemonade punch on a hot, dull day."

"Food is very important to you, isn't it? And yet I can't liken you to any one single dish or drink."

"Perhaps I am like that marvelous cake you served. Tall, sweet, and elegant."

More teasing—Theresa had nearly forgot that adults could tease each other. "How can I trifle with your arrogance without insulting my dessert? Are you also perhaps sinfully rich, wickedly decadent?"

As soon as the words were out of her mouth, Theresa regretted them. They were the mindless banter of a sophisticate, a tease, a woman who might be trolling for custom, and who might not.

"Are you flirting with me?" He sounded hopeful. They had wound their way around the south side of the house to the gardens bordering the back lawns.

"I don't mean to." Theresa's days of purposefully courting perdition were long past. "I do beg your pardon."

She dropped his arm and walked off a few paces to settle on a worn wooden love seat. She realized the error of that decision when Mr. Belmont simply sat himself down beside her, and let a silence bloom between them.

"Here." He shrugged out of his coat and wrapped it around her shoulders with a gentle brush of his hands down her arms. "The air is cooler than I had anticipated."

"Mr. Belmont, you ought not," Theresa began tiredly, but the warmth and spicy scent of him were seeping into her from his coat. To be the object of such consideration felt wretchedly lovely.

Also absolutely, shamefully wrong.

* * *

Matthew lounged back and crossed his ankles, prepared for Miss Jennings to finish a wonderful evening on a sour note.

"I believe you are working up to more of that tartness that I find so intriguing," he said. "If you're trying to offer a set-down, you'd best adopt another tactic."

"I am out of practice," she said. "You can tease and flirt and make pleasant conversation by the hour, and yet for me…. I'd forgotten what an effort it is."

"You needn't make an effort with me, Miss Jennings," Matthew said when it became obvious she would say no more. "I am a simple man who appreciates his friends and the many blessings of his bucolic existence. I mean no offense with my remarks."

"None taken."

In that terse phrase, Matthew heard a world of resignation, loneliness, and weariness, emotions with which he had become all too familiar. On impulse, he took Miss Jennings's hand in his, surprised at how cold her fingers were, and equally surprised that she let him. Emboldened by her acquiescence, he laid a careful arm around her shoulders, saying nothing, merely holding her against the heat of his body.

For a brief eternity, she was still, tacitly resisting, but then, on a soft sigh, she let her head rest on his shoulder and relaxed against him.

The moon rose higher, clearing the horizon and bathing the world in benevolent, silvery light.

This was what Matthew longed for. Not to tease, flirt, or banter, not to toss inane compliments at Miss Jennings, or match wits with her prickly nature and lively mind. He wanted simply to hold her, and watch the moon rise silently over the lovely autumn landscape.

* * *

By the time Theresa reached the sanctuary of the nursery, Priscilla was fast asleep.

"She's exhausted from her great adventure," Alice said, taking one of the rocking chairs by the hearth in the playroom. "She did very well at dinner, though Mr. Belmont is a treasure. Any girl would be on her best behavior around him."

Theresa took the other rocker, for Alice's interrogation would start any moment. "Not you too, Alice." Alice was a treasure. Theresa had no idea how she'd managed before the shy, bookish Alice Portman had become Priscilla's governess.

"Your brother is to be complimented on his friends," Alice replied. "I liked the viscount, but he had too much dash for me. Mr. Belmont is salt of the earth in a very handsome package."

Handsome hardly mattered compared to the knowledge in Matthew Belmont's eyes, the quiet sense of—

Oh, dear. "Alice Portman, are you *smitten?*"

"Most assuredly not, but neither am I dead yet, and you would be a fool, Theresa Jennings, not to admit that man could be interested in you."

Theresa had been the crown princess of fools until Priscilla had come along. "What if he is interested? I know what comes of gentlemen who are *interested,* Alice, as well as you do. A lot of clammy-handed groping, foul breath, and misery."

From most men. Theresa had met a few of the other kind. Priscilla's father had had more to recommend him than that. Somewhat more. He'd at least asked if she'd known how to prevent conception.

"You call your only child misery, Theresa?"

Friends were a blessing, even if they failed utterly to provide sympathy and commiseration when a woman badly needed both.

"My daughter is a bastard." Theresa never used the word in Priscilla's hearing, and never entirely forgot it either. "She will know a great deal of misery because I let some handsome young fellow be *interested* in me." A handsome, kind-hearted, well-placed fellow, whom Theresa had carefully chosen, which only made the memory worse.

"You let the wrong fellow be interested in you. Mr. Belmont is honorable."

"You can tell this, how?" They kept their voices down from long habit, but Theresa had nearly wailed the question. "By the elegant fit of his evening attire? By his genial repartee? By the way his sapphire cravat pin complements his marvelous blue eyes? By his appetite for chocolate cake?"

Alice peered over at Theresa, her governess-inquisition eyebrow cocked. "Did Mr. Belmont make untoward advances?"

"He did not." Whatever Mr. Belmont had been about on that moonlit bench, it hadn't been *advances.* His arm around Theresa's shoulders had been comforting, also awkward.

She'd waited for his hands to wander, his mouth to smother hers, his conversation to turn beseeching and vulgar.

A star had fallen, the merest sigh of light against the soft, night sky. Theresa would not have seen that small miracle had Matthew Belmont not asked for a stroll in the garden. To share that fleeting wonder with him had been...

Theresa had no words for what that moment had been, no frame of reference for it at all.

Alice, however, was just full of words.

"Mr. Belmont is honorable," Alice reiterated, nodding in agreement with herself. "He was beyond charming to Priscilla, who is not the most scintillating conversationalist for a man grown."

"He was charming, and Priscilla would be in transports over attention from any grown man who treated her decently. That worries me."

Theresa was *relieved* to have an articulable worry.

Alice closed her eyes, a woman weary of dealing with her charges. "Priscilla is a little girl. Why shouldn't she have some attention from the man sharing an informal evening meal at her mother's table?"

Old bewilderment threatened Theresa's composure. *You are a pest and an embarrassment, Theresa Jennings. Be gone from my sight.* How many times had Grandpapa said those very words, then smiled at the twins, whose every stupid wager or mean prank was indulged as "boyish high spirits"?

"Priscilla hugged Mr. Belmont," Theresa said miserably. "She hugged me good night then romped over and hugged the squire."

"What was he supposed to do?" Alice snapped. "Lecture her on proper manners with dinner guests? Priscilla is eight years old. She hugs her aunt and uncle, she hugs you, she hugs me. She hugs the horses and the dogs and, when she can catch them, the cats. Mr. Belmont was a neighbor at a family meal in a country household, nothing more. You want her to behave as if she were eighteen on the verge of making her bow."

What Theresa wanted was to cry, to abandon her composure, and succumb to the bewilderment and anxiety that so frequently characterized her maternal burden. Her upset was somehow Mr. Belmont's fault, though she had the sense she could have raised even this topic with him and earned a fair, compassionate hearing.

She also wanted to be back out in the garden with him, listening to slow, doomed crickets and watching stars fall.

Theresa stood, intent on seeking her bed, because fatigue had never improved a mother's disposition.

"If one doesn't understand how to go on with men at age eight, then when does one comprehend, Alice? Age ten, age thirteen, age fifteen? I certainly didn't, to my everlasting shame and peril."

Alice remained seated, though Theresa could feel the frustration quivering through her. Alice often limped, a result of a bad fall from a horse. When she was tired, her hip pained her, and standing became a trial.

"You had no mama worth the name," Alice said. "No papa since you were in leading strings, and no one to take any interest in you at all, save your little brother. Of course you made mistakes and lacked sound judgment, but Priscilla has you, me, and now her uncle and aunt to help her go on."

This was the voice of reason, the voice of true friendship, and yet, Theresa was not reassured.

"God help me, but some part of me wishes we were back at Sutcliffe Keep, preparing for another siege of cold, sleet, and darkness. At least there, I knew everybody on the property and exactly what to expect from each encounter."

"You were dying at Sutcliffe," Alice rejoined. "Emotionally, intellectually, socially, you were at the end of your tether. One ancient estate on the coast is not enough for you, Theresa Jennings, no matter how large, prosperous or well managed you made it."

"I wasn't dying." Theresa had laid some particulars to rest long ago—hope, innocence, *foolishness*—though she'd been pathetically grateful to accept the olive branch Thomas had extended. "Where is it written that we are due unrelenting happiness in this life? Sutcliffe Keep is a more than adequate abode."

"Coward." Alice smiled, and for the first time, Theresa wondered what Alice was hiding from. "Sutcliffe Keep holds few happy memories for you, save for those you've created with Priscilla. You are safe under your brother's roof, and so is your daughter."

Safe. Was a woman ever safe? Safe from her memories, safe from her past?

"I am also tired. You are a dear to listen to me go on, Alice, and I am sorry to be so trying."

Theresa made her way to her bedroom, part of a pleasant, spacious suite in a back corner of the house. The fire had been banked, the wash water left on the hearth, and the covers turned down to warm the sheets—all amenities that would have been unusual at Sutcliffe Keep. There, the house staff was getting older, and since Thomas had acquired the title, Theresa hadn't presumed to replace any of the servants.

They tended to get up late, move slowly, and turn in early, leaving the details of domestic service untended to.

Alice was right, Theresa reasoned as she took her hair down and brushed out the chaos resulting from an evening in myriad small, tight braids. She and Priscilla were safe under Thomas's roof, and Mr. Belmont was merely a pleasant neighbor....

Who had held Theresa so tenderly, as if she were precious, sharing his warmth and the uncomplicated pleasure of his bodily presence. That was all they'd done—a simple, protracted embrace, his arm around her, his hand in hers, as the moon spread its cool light on the autumn gardens.

The feel of those warm, strong fingers sliding across Theresa's palm and closing around her cold hand had been enough to steal her wits. Sitting with Matthew Belmont, Theresa had known she would suffer doubts and recriminations for her behavior later, but while she'd been with him, peace had flowed through her.

Matthew Belmont was warm, physically, but also warm-hearted. He would doubtless ascribe the state of his heart to the children he'd raised, and she envied him that. Parenting Priscilla had not left Theresa warm-hearted; it left her tired, worried, and very, very careful.

And for Priscilla's sake, if not for her own, Theresa would indulge in no more such embraces with Mr. Belmont. He had not presumed, exactly, but he had exceeded the nearer limit of propriety—or rather, Theresa and he had. Both of them.

Theresa fell asleep, lecturing herself sternly about lapses of judgment and wondering why, if Mr. Belmont had been intent on exceeding the bounds of propriety, he hadn't at least tried to steal a kiss from her.

CHAPTER FOUR

Matthew made his way home on Hermes, content to let the horse amble along the lane in the moonlight. He had a hamper tied behind the saddle again, this one full of sautéed vegetables in a crock, perfectly cured and cooked ham, another loaf of fresh bread, and—glory of glories—a fat slice of chocolate cake.

When Miss Jennings had risen from the garden bench, Matthew had expected a stinging rebuke for presuming on her person, or at the least, a chilly comment that indicated she would ignore his forwardness.

Women were like that. A fellow might hold a lady's hand for twenty minutes, let the fragrance of her lemony perfume entrance him for the duration, wrap her up as closely against his side as he dared, and still, she might hare off without a backward glance, never to acknowledge that poor fellow again.

Miss Jennings had merely stood, smiled an odd, wistful smile, and offered a polite comment.

"My thanks for your company," was all she'd had to say. Then, "Shall we raid the larder before sending you home?"

He'd walked beside her the length of the house, followed her in through a back door that led to the kitchen, and let her fill up the hamper.

Matthew had known better than to kiss her. Fifteen years ago, even ten, he might have tried to steal that march as well, in the gardens, in the kitchen, or in the darkness of the front terrace as she'd waited with him for the horse.

But Theresa Jennings was not a woman to be trifled with or underestimated. She inspired both Matthew's highest virtues and his base urges, and simply taking her in his arms had attained the summit of some lofty, majestic peak.

When the moment of parting had come, Matthew had bowed over his hostess's hand, thanked her for a lovely evening, and established that he would retrieve her and Priscilla the next day after luncheon for a visit to the ponies.

Well done of him, he thought as his gelding came to a halt in the Belmont stable yard. Maybe next time, if the lady seemed willing, he might find a moment to steal a kiss.

* * *

"Do you have lots and lots of ponies, Mr. Belmont?" Priscilla asked before they were out of the Linden stable yard. "And do they like treats? Can I ride them, please?"

"May I," Theresa corrected from Evan's sturdy and comfortable back. "Priscilla, remember what we talked about?" Theresa fired a silent maternal admonition at her daughter, who was perched before Mr. Belmont on his gelding, an elegant grey named Hermes.

"But Mama, I am not pestering. I am only *asking*."

"I think your mama is suggesting that we neglected the pleasantries, Miss Priscilla. The oversight is entirely my fault, so I'll begin: Such a pleasure to see you, and might I inquire as to how you fare this lovely day?"

"I'm fine, thank you," Priscilla replied, drawing her fingers through the gelding's mane. "And how are *you*, Mr. Belmont?"

"Never better." He lowered his voice to a conspiratorial whisper. "Is this the part where we talk about the weather?"

"It is." Priscilla's nod almost clipped him on the nose with the back of her head.

"We have a glorious day for our little jaunt," Mr. Belmont went on. "Perhaps you could tell me which of the autumn flowers you find most attractive?"

Priscilla turned to her mother. "What am I supposed to say? Do I ask if Mr. Belmont has a favorite flower?"

Theresa rummaged around in the bottom drawers of her memory, where her governess's futile lectures about deportment lay collecting dust.

"You could, or you could ask if Mr. Belmont spends much time in the out of doors when the weather is so fine. You could ask him about his ponies, or how his sons are getting along at university."

But not if he slept well the previous evening. Never that.

Priscilla peered up at Mr. Belmont, her gaze so eager and innocent Theresa had to look away.

"*Do* you have a favorite pony?"

"My heavenly stars!" The squire appeared utterly flummoxed. "How could I choose among my ponies?" He launched into a detailed description of each little equine's personality, appearance, and skills, and added several anecdotes regarding his sons' mounted exploits.

As they walked their horses down the sunny farm lanes, a sentiment grew in Theresa's heart. She was out in the fresh air, honestly enjoying herself with her daughter. Priscilla was in transports, chattering and pointing, then squirming around to visually reassure herself of her mother's presence nearby.

Theresa regarded Priscilla and Mr. Belmont, chatting happily about nothing, and tried to locate some guilt, some worry, anything familiar, and found only a sense of… freedom.

"Belmont House's drive will come up on our left," Mr. Belmont informed his guests some ten minutes later. "The house sits on a considerable rise, hence the name, *belle monte.* Somewhere back several generations, my ancestors included a ration of rabid Francophiles."

"What is a Francophile?" Priscilla asked.

"Somebody who adores all things Frankish, or French. I am a chocolate cake-o-phile."

"I am a horse-o-phile," Priscilla said, grinning. "Mama?"

"I am a peace-and-quiet-o-phile." Though Matthew Belmont's embrace in a moonlit garden was also quite lovely.

Mr. Belmont sent her a curious look over the child's head. "That is a contradiction in terms. How can one be passionate about peace and quiet?"

"Live with Priscilla, and you'll acquire the knack."

Priscilla sat straighter in the saddle. "I am not that noisy. Certainly Mr. Belmont's sons were far noisier than I?"

"They were," Mr. Belmont said, "and now I miss their noise. Let's turn in here, shall we? Would you like to canter up the drive, Miss Priscilla?"

"That would be lovely!"

"Grab some mane." He took both sets of reins in one hand and wrapped an arm snugly about the child. "Ready, Miss Jennings?"

Theresa nodded, but was still taken by surprise when Hermes sprang forward and Evan followed suit, albeit at a more sedate pace. She was even more taken aback to see Mr. Belmont turn his big gray toward an old horse trough that had been planted with pansies and chrysanthemums. Heart in her throat, she watched as he guided the horse to a foot-perfect approach, take-off, and landing, Priscilla laughing uproariously as they came back down to the walk.

"Mr. Belmont! Can we do that again? Please may we?"

"If your mother has no objection, though based on the expression on your mama's face, I should have asked permission first."

He hadn't asked permission in the garden last night either. Was he alluding to that presumption?

"Mama?"

"Of course you may," Theresa replied, forcing a smile. The dratted man had likely seen her, gloved hand smacked over her own mouth so she wouldn't scream and upset the horses. "But you must not pester, Priscilla. Twice will have to be enough for now."

"Thank you!"

Mr. Belmont obligingly wheeled the horse into a rocking canter, and put him to the jump again.

"That was the best!" Priscilla announced, patting Hermes's neck in solid thumps. "That was top of the trees. All the heroines in my stories will jump enormous banks of flowers."

"Hermes is a talented and experienced jumper," Mr. Belmont said, "but you must promise me that you will never, ever, attempt to take a horse over an obstacle without supervision. I've seen more horses than I care to count maimed and mortally injured when carelessly put to a fence."

Mr. Belmont had been clever to add that last, about the *horses* being injured. Priscilla's soft heart would never jeopardize a beast, though she'd defy her mother's commands when tired or provoked.

"I promise, Mr. Belmont. May we see the ponies now?"

"We'll let Evan and Hermes blow while we walk out to the pony paddock." He swung down, then lifted Priscilla to the ground as a stable lad appeared to take the horses.

"Good day, Squire." The man's smile suggested friendly respect toward his employer. This fellow was only an inch or so taller than Jamie, though dark-complected and much younger. "I saw you and himself showing off for the ladies."

"Good day, Spiker," the squire replied, looking just a touch… *smug.* "You can hardly call hopping a bed of flowers showing off." He passed over the grey's reins, then walked over to Evan's side.

Theresa didn't grasp Mr. Belmont's intentions until his hands were at her waist.

"Watch the whip," he cautioned as she unhooked her knee from the horn. Surely Mr. Belmont was simply being his typical courteous self when he didn't simply swing her down from the horse. He settled Theresa on the ground, his strength guiding her descent along his frame until her feet were under her and she had her balance.

For a moment, she stood where she'd landed, like some drunken bee in the vicinity of its preferred blossom. Her imagination suggested Mr. Belmont's hands lingered at her waist, while her common sense declared her daft.

"My sons are doing famously with my brother in Oxfordshire," Mr. Belmont said. "Two of them even managed to write their old papa this week, and I love to be out of doors in weather like this, particularly in such wonderful company." He stepped back. "I have no favorite autumn flower, but I rather admire the pansy."

He'd recalled Theresa's questions.

"You admire pansies? Heartsease is considered nondescript by the serious gardener." While blessed with vivid coloring, the little flower could not tolerate heat and had little fragrance.

"They are the furthest thing from nondescript." Mr. Belmont let Priscilla take one of his hands, even as the child grabbed for her mother's hand on the other side. "Pansies are not afraid to be bold, to put purple right next to yellow, or white in the middle of a soft blue. They brave cold and wind and even a light snow and keep blooming, heedless of impending doom. And yet they are the softest-looking flower, as velvety as that habit you wear, Miss Jennings, and even softer to the touch."

"You should write a poem," Priscilla interjected, "about the noble pansy."

"I will leave that to you, as the literary talent in the neighborhood. How is my story coming?"

Mr. Belmont was talking to Priscilla again, holding a true conversation with the child and drawing her out in subtle, easy degrees. Priscilla regaled him with myriad details of the draft she'd penned for him—a draft that had yet to reach its mandatory happy ending.

"What of your mama's story?" Mr. Belmont asked as Priscilla wound down. "Are you planning an epic tale for her?"

He appeared happy to dawdle along at a pace comfortable for Priscilla, which allowed Theresa to take in the surroundings. Belmont House sat on its hill, a serene testament to the last century's passion for landscaping. Oaks and maples were turning golden about the house, shedding a carpet of luminous leaves on lush green grass.

Chrysanthemums provided dashes of russet, white, and yellow, and a simple circular fountain added the soft splash of water to a pretty day. Nothing about Belmont House suggested boiling oil or pitched battle. Mr. Belmont's estate was a lovely haven, a well-cared-for home.

Though rather a lot of home for one man.

"Mama's story will be hard to write," Priscilla said. "She is my mama, after all, and I am not sure a mama can have exciting adventures."

Mr. Belmont smiled at Theresa over the child's head, his expression managing that blend of naughty and bland known only to parents in the company of small children.

"When you solve that puzzle, you will be able to buy your own castle on the proceeds of your writing, child."

"You are my exciting adventure, Priscilla," Theresa said, because that was in every way the truth. "If you wrote the story for me and my brave and clever daughter, you might find the task easier."

"Shall I do that? I could, you know. I could call it, 'Princess Priscilla to the Rescue.' Oh Mama!" She dropped the hands of both adults and raced up to the nearest fence. "Look at the lovely, lovely ponies!"

She was trying to clamber up the fence rails when Mr. Belmont swung her up to the top board and kept a hand on her waist.

"I have seven in all," he said. "The oldest is over there, by the gate, and her name is Dandelion, or Dandy…" He described each pony, including the origin of the animal's name, its breeding, and its current state of health.

Priscilla listened, rapt, through the entire recitation. "Can I pet them?"

May I? Though what mattered grammar when a child was falling in love?

"They would be offended if you didn't." Mr. Belmont lied well, in the parental sense, though his equine piglets had barely looked up from their single-minded attempts to ingest every blade of grass in the paddock.

He vaulted over the fence in a single athletic maneuver his sons had likely been trying to emulate for years, grabbed Priscilla off the top rail, affixed her to his hip, and approached old Dandy.

"Dandy doesn't see well," Mr. Belmont said. "I am careful to always speak fairly loudly—Miss Jennings, my humble apologies, I should have at least opened the gate for you."

He sounded genuinely distressed as Theresa climbed over the fence, a complicated undertaking in a riding habit.

"One doesn't interrupt a man holding forth about one of his passions," she said, shaking out her skirts.

"May I get down, please?"

For him, Priscilla recalled her grammar.

"Of course." He set her on her feet, produced several hunks of carrot from his pocket, and let Priscilla make what friends she might—or her carrots might.

"To see these old rascals is shamefully gratifying." Mr. Belmont said. "I never get a chance to prose on about their adventures with the boys, to see the magic that the mere sight of an equine can light in a small child's eyes."

He watched Priscilla with such wistfulness, Theresa wondered what, in truth, he was seeing.

"When was the last time you paid a call on them?"

"With company? Not since Remington and Christopher walked here with me the evening before the boys' departure this summer."

Which suggested without company, he came here often—perhaps in search of company?

"So who is this?" Theresa asked.

"That is Gowain," Mr. Belmont replied, petting a portly little piebald. "Because he belonged to Richard, my youngest, his name was transmogrified into 'Go Away' by the older two. He and Richard had their revenge, though. Gowain is faster than lightning and will jump anything you put him to, rather like Richard."

"May I ride Gowain?" Priscilla asked, obviously taken with the idea of being fast as lightning and able to jump anything.

"If you ladies will accompany me back to the house, we can talk about that while we enjoy a glass of lemonade or cider."

Priscilla looked over the little herd, clearly torn between the desire to stay with the ponies and the chance to discuss how she might ride them.

"Lemonade would be lovely," Theresa replied, lest winter arrive before Priscilla made up her mind.

"One of my favorites," the squire rejoined gravely, winking.

Oh, the scamp.... Theresa wanted to be stern with him, to discourage such blatant teasing, but he was so friendly with it, and the day was proving to be so otherwise enjoyable that she simply couldn't locate her usually endless supply of sternness.

It was only a wink, after all.

Her first wink in years.

Mr. Belmont led them to the nearby gate, and when he'd seen both ladies through, Priscilla tore off along the hedgerow, bent on picking purple asters closer to the house.

"My apologies for jumping with her earlier," Mr. Belmont said as soon as Pricilla was out of earshot. "I used to tear all over the countryside with the boys, and they loved it."

"Did their mother love it?"

His smile dimmed as Priscilla ran riot along the hedgerow. "Matilda was something of a hoyden. If I had one child up with me, she'd have the other two on a lead line. She taught them to row, went fishing with us, and hiked over every inch of the property with us. The way she threw herself into bucolic pursuits with her sons was one of her endearing qualities, and the boys loved her for it as well."

"She sounds like a wonderful woman." What would it have been like to have such a mother? "Not a lady cowed by the dictates of proper society."

Mr. Belmont's smile disappeared altogether, leaving a serious, even bleak countenance in its wake.

"Far better for her, if she had been more respectful of those dictates, and for those who cared about her as well."

For once, Theresa wished she had taken her escort's arm. Mr. Belmont walked along beside her, his long legs adjusting their stride to hers, his hands linked behind his back. He gave off an odd tension, one Theresa might have better been able to interpret were they arm in arm.

"I hardly think that hiking and fishing on one's own property should earn a mother approbation, Mr. Belmont."

He stopped, his gaze going past Theresa's shoulder, back in the direction they'd come.

"If you are in this area for any length of time, Miss Jennings, you will soon be informed, for the kindest possible reasons of course, that my oldest made his appearance a scant six months after Matilda and I said our vows. The boy already stands over six feet and is hardy as a goat. The notion of a premature birth in his case is preposterous."

"You anticipated your vows." Would that Theresa's own transgressions had been half so mundane. "It happens, and you and your bride were quite young."

"I did not anticipate my vows." Mr. Belmont's tone wasn't mean, but it was… angry. "I was seventeen, Matilda eighteen, and while your conjecture is the locally accepted version of the tale, she came to me bearing another man's child."

The meaning of his words took a moment to sort itself out in Theresa's mind. The day was too pretty, the man too proud of his sons. He had a *herd* of pensioner ponies, for pity's sake, and he missed his sons so badly she could feel the ache of it.

Theresa did not want to hear this confidence, and yet, Mr. Belmont's marital history explained some of his extraordinarily tolerant attitude.

Also the hint of disquiet Theresa detected behind his smiles and cordial manners.

"I might as well tell you the whole of it, for you're too much a lady to inquire," he said. The ponies went on munching grass and swishing their tails, while Theresa wanted to slap her hand over Mr. Belmont's mouth.

She was not a lady in any sense, but Mr. Belmont needed to tell her this sad tale. For once, her past created privilege rather than burden, so she plucked a sprig of aster and bit back words of sympathy.

"When Matilda's circumstances became known to her parents and her older sister," Mr. Belmont went on, "the women in the family put their heads together and came up with yours truly—a second cousin once removed, at least—as a convenient groom. I was not coerced, precisely, but Matilda came with a dowry, was honest about her situation, and I was seventeen."

"What has your age to do with it, other than to connote a general lack of worldly experience?" Though at seventeen, Theresa had been woefully familiar with vice for a baron's granddaughter.

Mr. Belmont plucked the asters from her hand and tucked them into the lapel of her riding jacket.

His presumption had the brisk competence of a man who'd taken small boys to Sunday services, and yet… Theresa was pleased by the gesture.

He surveyed his work and went back to studying the ponies. "I had enough worldly experience to comprehend that a wife could afford a randy young fellow certain comforts, and because Matilda was quite pretty, and no virgin, my judgment was not objective."

He'd been *seventeen*. Theresa had known—though not quite in the biblical sense—young fellows down from university. They were a plague on society whose lustful inclinations were dampened only by liberal applications of strong drink or stupid wagers.

Priscilla had rambled halfway back to the house, a veritable sheaf of wildflowers in her arms. She could turn around any moment, and then this exchange would be over.

"In certain matters, Mr. Belmont, few of us have objective judgment, at any age, much less before our majority."

A beat of fraught silence went by, while Theresa wished she could offer Mr. Belmont words of greater comfort. Though why should he accept her absolution when she couldn't forgive herself for the same lack of judgment?

He touched the little wild flowers gracing Theresa's lapel. "Did you love him?" he asked softly.

CHAPTER FIVE

"I hate to see you so worrit, young Beckman."

Beckman continued raking the barn aisle, his rhythm never faltering, because Jamie Hannigan lived to disrupt those intent on completing a task.

"You can tell I'm worried from how I rake a barn aisle, old man?"

Jamie *was* apparently worried, and when Jamie fretted, he muttered and stomped until somebody investigated or the horses grew restless.

"It's the sound, ye see, my boy."

Beckman saw only a paisley pattern in the dirt, like successive waves approaching the shore. Horses and people would obliterate that pattern within fifteen minutes, though creating the design twice a day still gave Beckman satisfaction.

A tidy barn was a safe barn.

"The sounds and speed of the rake," Jamie clarified, hoisting himself onto a trunk. "You have one rhythm for thinking, another for fuming, and another for gnawing on a problem."

"Maybe I'm worried the stalls won't get mucked, because you sit about on your skinny arse listening to rakes when you ought to be working."

Nobody loved a good row more than Jamie, and the horses had learned to ignore him most of the time.

"You young people work until you drop, then boast of your exhaustion. When you're my age, you'll know better. Your brother will be fine."

Well, damn.

"Nick knows London like you know the back of a horse. Of course, he'll be fine." Nick would not be happy in the refined company in London though, and that was a shame for a man doomed to inherit an earldom.

"You will manage without him too," Jamie said, taking a pipe from his pocket. He dug in the bowl of the pipe using a nail secreted in some other pocket, and dumped the leavings on Beck's tidy aisle. "We'll miss him though. The horses miss him. Squire was right about that."

Beckman raked over the small mess Jamie had created. "You've been tossed on your head a few too many times. Nick and I have been separated on many previous occasions, often for months." With oceans between them, if Beck had been able to arrange it. "Nick is probably relieved to be away from the stink of horses."

The smell of the stable had become a comfort to Beckman, oddly enough, and the company of the horses soothing.

"I've been tossed on every part of me a man can land on, young sir, and I came up ready to ride another race every time. If you're not worrit about your brother, then what's troublin' ye?"

"Muck me a stall, Jamie Hannigan, or you'll be the one with something to worry about."

A stall set fair by James Michael Patrick Hannigan was tidier than a parson's parlor, a work of art in Beck's eyes, and in the horses'.

"You need the practice, lad, though I'll grant you, you've improved. Some." Jamie lifted his boots so Beck could rake beneath them, but the older man wouldn't leave his perch until Beck confessed a credible worry.

"Maybe I'm uneasy about the baron's sister, going off without a groom in Matthew Belmont's company."

Jamie clamped the cold pipe between his teeth. "Our Mr. Belmont is a gentleman, and they had the child with them. Won't be any mischief with a child underfoot."

Beck reached the end of the aisle and leaned on his rake. "How many brothers and sisters do you have, Jamie?"

"Thirteen, that I know of. Some of the publican's boys looked an awful lot like my younger brothers, when they had hair."

"And you were raised in a three-room cottage. Children underfoot are no guarantee of propriety, though I agree, Matthew Belmont is a gentleman. It's the baron's temperament that troubles me."

Until the words left his mouth, Beckman would not have given a thought to Thomas Jennings's opinion of Miss Theresa's outing with Matthew Belmont. In the past two years, though, Beckman had learned to observe the people around him and to take their concerns to heart.

Miss Theresa Jennings had strayed from the straight and narrow, and Beckman knew firsthand how long and hard the journey back to respectability could be. Her titled brother might well judge her first for this foray among Polite Society and make apologies later—if at all.

Jamie hopped off his trunk, leaving two boot prints amid Beckman's careful work.

"The baron has acquired a baroness. If that don't turn him up sweet, nothing will. You're worrying for nothing, and your brother likely is too."

Beck hung the rake on the wall, where no horse could trip over it. "Why would Nick be worried? He's heir to a title, the world soon to be at his feet. His days as stable master are over."

Jamie cuffed Beck on the arm. "He'll worry about you, ye dimwit. Must I explain everything to you?"

"You do, whether I ask you to or not."

"Young people are enough to make an old man long for the company of the angels. I'll settle for the company at the Cock and Bull, if you'll join me."

The stable was tidy, the horses content. "One pint," Beckman said. "We'll have one pint, and then, by God, you'll get after your half of the stalls."

Which Jamie would have neater than a pin in half the time it took Beckman to do half the job.

"One pint then, ye miser. Have I ever told you, you can't hold your liquor?"

"Have I ever told you, you need to learn to hold your tongue?"

They squabbled good-naturedly halfway to the village, though as they passed the Belmont lane, Beckman admitted that he truly was just the smallest bit uneasy that Theresa Jennings had gone calling on one of the most eligible bachelors in the shire without a chaperone or a groom.

* * *

Did you love him?

Mr. Belmont had let the question stand, no apology, no dodging about to preserve Theresa's dignity, and that in itself was a form of respect. They would do each other the courtesy of being honest, here along the hedgerow dying back to yellow and scarlet.

"I did not love him. I tried to talk myself into the notion that I did, and I have often wished that I did, for Priscilla's sake, but no. I was fond of the man, I respected him, and I liked him, but I knew better than to love Priscilla's father."

Even before she'd reached her legal majority, Theresa had claimed that wisdom, which was beyond pathetic.

Priscilla rambled along the path, the ponies swished flies and munched grass, while Mr. Belmont stood immobile, as the gentry of England had stood solid and steady through centuries, wars, and revolutions.

"I am sad for you," he said, gaze on the lush pasture. "You gave up much, and your sacrifice has not been rewarded with the results it merited." Despite the placid surrounds, Mr. Belmont sounded... quietly enraged. "Does this great fool, this blunderer who could not inspire you to love him, does he take any interest in his daughter at all?"

The moment took on a strange quality, as if Theresa had stepped into one of Priscilla's fantastical realms, where dragons danced and princesses flew over enchanted forests.

Mr. Belmont was not calling *Theresa* a fool or a blunderer. He wasn't even implying it, wasn't hinting it.

"Priscilla's father was killed on the Peninsula before Priscilla was out of leading strings. His death was sad, but I am ashamed to say that for me, his passing was not the tragedy those closest to him must have endured."

Theresa was not nearly as ashamed of that admission as she would have been in other company. Mr. Belmont solved crimes in his capacity as magistrate, and he sorted the guilty from the innocent. He did not, apparently, feel a need to sit in judgment, even as he adjudicated.

"You never told him. He died without knowing the child existed."

And Mr. Belmont occasionally erred. "I wrote to him, but who knows where letters end up in times of war, or whether knowing about Priscilla would have been a blessing or a curse as he lay dying. He made me promise that I would inform him if our acquaintance bore consequences. I kept my promise, and then he died."

Theresa had cried for the fallen soldier, though. Cried for another daughter who would never know her father too.

"I am so sorry." Mr. Belmont took Theresa's hand and linked his fingers through hers, a slow slide of warm, masculine strength that surprised even as it comforted. "I am even sorry for the blunderer."

Theresa's own brother hadn't thought to comfort her. Hadn't done anything but blame her for nine long years.

"Shall we join Miss Priscilla?" Mr. Belmont asked. "She will denude the estate of flowers if somebody doesn't distract her."

Theresa walked with him in silence, her hand in his, her prodigious talent for recrimination stirring to life. She should never have blurted out the unfortunate facts of Priscilla's parentage, never invited such confidences from Mr. Belmont. Now they'd have nothing but awkwardness between them.

She should drop his hand, immediately, lest the awkwardness grow any worse.

Except Theresa didn't *feel* awkward.

She felt lighter, as if those four little words, "*I am so sorry,*" had turned a key in her emotions. The squire didn't express pity, he offered compassion.

Then he'd taken Theresa's hand.

"You have gone quiet," Mr. Belmont said some moments later. "Are you shocked that the prosy old squire would disclose family secrets?"

If he lived to be ninety-four, he would never be a prosy old squire.

"Surprised, more at myself than at the squire—who is the opposite of prosy. I can hardly be shocked by another woman's indiscretion when I was indiscreet myself. I still don't comprehend why you would marry into such a situation. Were you in love with her?"

"Thank God, I was not. After various wrong turnings and flailing about, I came to love Matilda, but neither she nor I wanted me *in* love with her. Her affections had been elsewhere engaged, and no man, no matter how young, randy, or well motivated, wants to compete with another for his wife's regard."

That was not the conclusion of the seventeen-year-old, regardless of how eager he'd been.

"You began your marriage on difficult and lonely footing." Much as Theresa had embarked on motherhood.

"The situation grew easier," he said, after they'd walked the bridle path hand in hand, back to the edge of the garden. "When the boys came along, we found a rhythm. We had uncomfortable years of muddling along first, uncomfortable for both of us. For about two straight years, I woke up angry every single day. I suspect Matilda cried herself to sleep for those same years."

Theresa nearly stopped walking with the impact of the next insight. "You told me of your marriage so my situation with Priscilla would not seem so unusual. I appreciate that." Interrogating criminal defendants, Mr. Belmont would be very clever, indeed. "Does Christopher know?"

"He does." Mr. Belmont kicked at the ground, sending yellow and red leaves flying. "Mostly because his dear Uncle Emmanuel could not resist one sly comment after another, about six months' babes, the passions of youth, and so forth. Explaining that I wasn't Christopher's true father was an uncomfortable interview all around."

Probably as uncomfortable as some of the discussions Theresa had had with Priscilla, and would have with her.

"What about his real father? Those feelings have to be complicated too." And not a little of the complication would be from anger, though Matthew Belmont had married with his eyes open—if any seventeen-year-old could be said to have his eyes open.

"We don't know who that blunderer might be," Mr. Belmont said, as Priscilla trotted backward a few steps, waved at her mother, then returned to her explorations. "Matilda never said, and I didn't feel it my place to press. She told me only that he wasn't in a position to claim her or his offspring, and she had known that when she took the risks with him that she did."

"Poor Matilda," Theresa murmured. "Poor Matthew. Poor Christopher." Though she had no pity for the blunderer. None.

"Poor Theresa," Mr. Belmont added, "and poor Priscilla. But today is beautiful and the company wonderful." He lifted Theresa's hand and kissed her knuckles. "There is more to life than our misguided pasts, and on such a lovely day, that is worth remembering."

On that philosophical note, Mr. Belmont escorted them into his home, taking the flowers from Priscilla and leading his guests not to a parlor, but to his library. He went off to order them a tray, while Theresa arranged the flowers in four different vases, and Priscilla alternately gawped at the wealth of books and petted a brindle hound dozing on the hearth rug.

Theresa tried not to gawp. She'd envisioned Belmont House as a cozy country manor, a home weighed down with fresh thatch and at least two centuries of history and human wear. The sort of home where everybody knew where everybody else was at all times, simply as a function of proximity.

Though Belmont House's dimension weren't apparent from its façade, the manor house was easily twice the size of Linden, beautifully appointed, and intimidatingly spotless.

Mr. Belmont returned, bearing a tray with two glasses, a pitcher, and a mug. The tray was silver, the glasses crystal, while Mr. Belmont's boots were comfortably worn.

"Priscilla," Theresa called up to the reading loft, "come sit while you drink your lemonade. Shall I pour?"

"Would you please?" Mr. Belmont waited until Theresa had settled herself on one end of the sofa, then took an armchair to her right. The hound propped her chin on the toe of his boot, as naturally as if that were the intended purpose of any handy riding boot.

Priscilla paused long enough to pet the old dog, whose state of wakefulness was manifest only by an occasional thump of its tail.

"I want a room like this, Mama, with huge windows, and a balcony, and a twisted staircase in midair."

"We have spiral staircases at Sutcliffe, though granted, they are made of stone." Theresa poured two glasses and one mug of lemonade. Either Mr. Belmont had his own ice house, or Thomas kept his neighbor supplied. Sprigs of mint sat on the tray in one porcelain bowl and sprigs of lavender in another.

"I'll take a touch of lavender in mine," Mr. Belmont said, lifting a sprig of silvery green. "My sons call me eccentric, but the occasional hint of lavender, particularly in a beverage such as lemonade or even hot tea, appeals to me. I also like it on my pudding."

"You eat flowers?" Priscilla asked, wide-eyed.

"Not eat them exactly. Here, try it." He extended his glass to Priscilla, who took a tentative sip, her expression of skepticism comical.

"It tastes like it smells. Try it, Mama."

Mr. Belmont next held out his glass to Theresa, raising it to her lips rather than surrendering it to her grasp. He left her no choice but to wrap her bare fingers around his and guide his hand to her mouth.

"I like it," she said. "It's refreshing and unexpected, though I can't imagine lavender in a cup of hot tea."

"When next you ladies are at Belmont House," their host said, finally taking a sip of his own lemonade. "We'll try lavender in our tea."

When next you ladies are at Belmont House.... How casual he was, as if neighborly invitations came Theresa's way once a week instead of once a decade. He drank from the same spot Theresa had, more casual familiarity, nothing the least bit flirtatious about it.

Merely a sip of lemonade. Only a wink, simply a clasp of hands…. And Matthew Belmont was only her brother's neighbor. That's all he was, that's all he would ever be.

They finished their drinks with Priscilla hinting broadly that now might be a good time to discuss riding the squire's lonely, neglected, sorry old ponies.

"The loan of a pony would be no imposition," Mr. Belmont said, rearranging the sprig of lavender in his half-empty glass. "The ground isn't frozen enough to allow me my hunting yet, and the crops are in. I have the time to impart some horsemanship basics, if you can spare Priscilla for a few mornings a week, and Tut would enjoy the exercise."

"Tut?" Theresa asked. "As in tut-tut?" Odd name for a pony.

"Tutankhamen," Mr. Belmont said. "The boys were going through a study of ancient history, hence Tut and Cleo. He's the perfect little gentleman to start riding lessons on, if you're inclined to permit them."

Priscilla, to her credit, held her peace, but the longing and anxiety in her eyes made the decision a foregone conclusion.

"If it won't be any bother," Theresa said, "but Priscilla, you will be at Mr. Belmont's beck and call, and at the first sign that you can't keep up with your studies, the riding lessons will be cut back."

"Oh Mama!" Priscilla flung her arms around Theresa's neck. "Thank you, thank you!" She raced over to Mr. Belmont and treated him to the same exuberant display, barely giving him time to set his glass down first. "May I go pick some more flowers now? Please?"

"Priscilla Jennings," Mr. Belmont said, sounding very much like a man who'd raised three rambunctious boys, "you may pick one more small bouquet, but I warn you now, no flowers grow inside the pony paddock. I can tell if you've been in that pasture simply by studying the grass, and you are not to hop that fence unless your mother or I are with you."

"I won't." Priscilla fairly bounced from foot to foot with anticipation. "I promise."

"See that you don't," Theresa said, though Mr. Belmont's warning probably could not have impressed Pricilla more if it had been rendered on a stone tablet.

Priscilla bolted, the library door nearly slamming behind her in her headlong rush to inform Tut of his impending honor.

"That sound." Mr. Belmont leaned back against his chair, a slight smile bowing his lips. "I haven't heard it for months."

He missed that sound terribly and wasn't ashamed of his sentiments.

Ye gods and little fishes. Theresa rose, for she was alone behind a closed door with a man about whom she could all too easily get disastrous ideas.

"You have a lovely library, Mr. Belmont."

"A consolation," he said, rising as well. A gentleman did when a lady stood. "Might I lend you a volume or two?" If he found Theresa's abrupt change of subject unusual, he was too well-mannered to remark on it. "The collection is eclectic, and you might see something Priscilla would like as well. Here,"—he led Theresa to the far wall—"I kept a number of the lighter novels the boys enjoyed."

Mr. Belmont stood directly behind Theresa, an attentive host whose cedar and spice scent wafted into her senses along with a damnable awareness of his body heat.

"This one." He reached over Theresa's head and plucked a volume off the shelf above her. "This tale is about a fellow who was shipwrecked on a tropical island. All three boys devoured it several times, and I enjoyed it too."

For that instant, when Mr. Belmont had reached up, and his body had been only inches from Theresa's, she'd felt *covered*, as a mare is covered by a stallion. He'd loomed so large, and so near, and so… present, she'd resisted the impulse to duck under his arm and retreat to a safe distance.

Instead, she merely stood, her back to him, ignoring the book he expected her to turn and take from his hand.

"Miss Jennings?"

She heard Mr. Belmont put the book aside. Her peripheral vision told her he hadn't stepped back. He was immediately behind her, tall, muscular, and as still as she.

A whisper of sensation on the back of her neck kicked Theresa's heart into a pounding trot.

"Theresa?" His voice was at her ear, and she knew he was inhaling the fragrance of her hair, breathing her in much as she'd attended the sensation of his hands on her waist in the stable yard.

Theresa faced him, and he was, indeed, standing very close. He peered down at her, his expression unreadable.

"Did you kiss me, Mr. Belmont? Did you *kiss* the back of my neck?"

His expression cooled, with indignation or—possibly—amusement.

"I did not. I brushed my fingertip along the collar of your habit, where you had a strand of hair snagged on your dress hook. You would have snarled your hair, when you disrobed."

Theresa was relieved, pathetically so—also disappointed. "You did not kiss me?"

"I did not, but if you've no objection, now I shall."

CHAPTER SIX

Matthew settled his lips over Miss Jennings's and waited for her to wrench away—or slap him—but when she merely went still, he cradled her jaw with his palm and slid his other hand around her waist in a snug embrace.

Her contours were exquisite, all womanly grace, warmth, and pleasure. Matthew wanted to savor each morsel of her—to wallow in the sheer, male joy of appreciating a woman lip to lip. For too long, he'd stayed busy, he'd ignored a gnawing restlessness, he'd denied a yearning for a woman with whom to share more than simple desire.

His entire adulthood had been spent either married to a spouse who hadn't loved him, or dodging women who'd marry him based on greed and desperation. Thirty-five more years of avoiding the marital hounds would drive him mad.

While kissing Theresa Jennings soothed and aroused, both.

Matthew called upon his patience, lazily coaxing her to open for him. She tasted of lemonade, with faint overtones of lavender and reluctance, though on a sigh, she allowed him to deepen the kiss.

That sigh had suggested she shouldn't be doing this, she really, really should not, and Matthew's heart sank.

Then her hands slid up his chest and linked at his nape, her fingers toying with hair in need of a trim.

"Better," Matthew murmured, resting his forehead against hers.

"What's better?"

"You touch me too." Theresa Jennings had all the signs of a woman who'd want to talk about a first kiss. Matthew would happily oblige her, *later*.

He touched his mouth to hers again, and this time, he used the arm around her waist to urge her more fully against him. When she acquiesced, he yielded to instinct, put some rhythm into the movements of his tongue, and widened his stance.

He and Miss Jennings were healthy, unattached adults, and surely life was not intended to be an endless progression of parlor sessions and Sunday services?

After an agreeable, and by no means sufficient, amount of kissing, she tucked her face into the crook of his neck.

"What you must think of me, Mr. Belmont."

He thought her delicious, intriguing, and lonely. If he told her that, she'd likely disappear down the drive at a dead gallop and never return.

"Let me hold you for a minute, hmm?" Matthew angled himself so he could lean against the library's shelving and hold her close. "Lean on me," he whispered, kissing a spot below her ear.

She shivered at his kiss, then settled, and gave Matthew a moment to analyze his motivations. Sooner than most young men, he'd learned to manage lust. The circumstances of his marriage had required that much.

He had not learned to manage a growing sense of pointlessness. His children were all but grown, his estate thriving, his place in the community secure, if not always appreciated. His life might not be even half over, and yet, the challenge and joy of living were increasingly difficult to find.

Matilda's portrait on the opposite wall stared blankly across the library, a room she'd never had much use for—much as she'd had little use for Matthew, at least in the early years of their marriage. Matthew had come to honestly pity her—after he'd spent a few years pitying himself.

The lady in his arms stirred, and Matthew loosened his embrace without letting her go. He liked holding Theresa Jennings, liked the bodily reminder of his maleness. He liked the puzzle and prettiness of her, and he liked kissing her.

"I don't bite," Matthew said, when she braced slightly away from him. "You needn't poker up merely because I'm prone to normal male responses."

He'd pokered up, or started to.

"We should not have done this," Miss Jennings muttered, even while she burrowed against him. "We most assuredly should not have done this."

Matthew would have preferred to *do* a bit more, though only a bit. A child was loose on the premises, after all.

"Where is the harm?" A legal question that came in handy in many walks of life. "I enjoyed kissing you, and I very much enjoy holding you."

"One can enjoy jumping off a cliff," she countered, twiddling the hair at Matthew's nape. "But then one lands."

Or two landed. "Hopefully, in a nice deep pool of water. When was the last time you jumped, Miss Jennings?"

"Nine years ago, and the landing is an ongoing disaster."

As much as Matthew hurt for her—why hadn't her family found *her* a convenient fellow to rescue her good name?—he was also aware that disasters had a way of becoming life sentences, unless one took steps to leave them behind.

"Perhaps you jumped from the wrong cliff." Or perhaps she'd been pushed, which thought gave him pause.

When she stepped back, Matthew let her go.

"A cliff is a cliff is a cliff," she said, swishing across the library to stand before a tall window.

Maida bestirred herself to rise and poke her nose against the lady's hand.

How lovely Theresa Jennings looked, absently petting the old hound as she regarded the Belmont gardens, back straight, coiffure beginning to unravel at her nape. Matthew took the place immediately behind her, though that tempted him to again touch her.

"May we talk about this, madam?" Matthew was the one who wanted to have a discussion now—also more kisses, provided those kisses were welcome.

She rubbed her fingers across her forehead. "Conversation won't change anything, Mr. Belmont."

And yet, converse with her, Matthew would. He turned her by the shoulders and led her to the sofa, gesturing for Maida to resume her nap on the carpet. When Miss Jennings was seated, Matthew took the armchair on the other side of the low table, the better to gauge the lady's reactions.

The better to keep his hands to himself.

"Have my instincts gone totally around the bend," Matthew began, "or were you enjoying that kiss too?"

"My body was enjoying it." Miss Jennings crossed her arms like a vexed governess. "Some."

Which meant other parts of her had not been enjoying Matthew's attentions.

"You did not protest." She still wasn't *exactly* protesting.

"Your kisses are pleasant." Her aggrieved posture faded, leaving a thoughtful expression, as if she contemplated not a high, dangerous cliff, but perhaps a small, leap-able stream bank.

"I have grown accustomed to being invisible," she said. "With the exception of Priscilla, nobody touches me. It's as if…"

Invisible? As a harmless old squire was invisible, save to matchmakers and other miscreants?

"Go on."

"It's as if I have no physical person anymore."

She swallowed, and Matthew could feel a damnable ache in his own throat, for she was confiding in him, sharing pain too vast and bewildering for tears.

"It's as if," she went on, "having used for unworthy ends the one body the Lord gave me, I am now neither male nor female, pretty nor ugly, old nor young. I am not ever acknowledged as any of those things by the touch of another— or certainly not the caring touch of another."

"You are young, female, and *lovely*. Pretty is for debutantes, landscapes, and flowers, and you are more than simply a pleasing appearance."

Matthew would like *her* touch, to remind him that he was a man not yet old, with something to offer a woman besides small talk, civilities, or a few minutes of fumbling oblivion stolen from the boredom of a house party.

Miss Jennings picked up a pillow—two white doves embroidered on a maroon velvet background, a curving green bow over their heads. She traced the bow—an olive branch?—with the fourth finger of her left hand.

"I've found a kind peace in being nobody, nobody but Priscilla's mother. The other.…. I never really learned how to go on, when I was young, pretty and female. I rather botched it."

"Because you conceived a child?" For more than a simple misstep lay behind the lack of a ring on that elegant finger.

"That too." She put the pillow aside, dove-side down. "One doesn't conceive a child by sipping lemonade."

"Conception is supposed to be a far more enjoyable process than sipping lemonade."

Oh, he ought not to have said that. Miss Jennings's chin came up. "Supposed to be, for the man."

Matthew abruptly reconsidered his strategy. A woman might be indifferent to him physically, and no disrespect to either party lay in admitting as much. His own palate had become increasingly diffident with respect to potential intimate partners, and he would not abide being merely tolerated in a woman's bed.

He had learned years ago that he *could not* abide it, in fact.

In addition to the possibility of bodily intimacy, Matthew was asking Theresa Jennings, whose confidence had been betrayed in the past, for her trust.

And that… changed what he must offer in return.

Miss Jennings was attracted to him, but she'd got nothing whatsoever in exchange for the risks she'd taken when Priscilla had been conceived. Not pleasure, not affection, not a fleeting infatuation, nothing.

Not a promise of marriage, should a child be conceived, suggesting Priscilla's father had been a rogue in addition to a blunderer.

Matthew fell back on a barrister's oldest tool for exposing buried truth—the hypothetical question.

"If there were no threat of another child or no threat of public censure, then would you kiss me again?"

Miss Jennings's smile was rueful and adult. "Kissing is not what gets us into such trouble."

"That does not answer my question."

"I would kiss you again," she said, humor flickering out and leaving testiness in its wake. "Or allow you to take me in your arms."

Allow him? Well, yes, as it should be. Matthew savored the victory in that—

the victory of Miss Jennings's self-respect over her loneliness, and his.

"Then let me give you those simple gestures of regard for now," Matthew said, rising. "We can leave the rest of this discussion for another day." Or another evening in a chilly garden, or a ride through the autumn woods on a crisp, sunny morning, or a picnic without benefit of Priscilla's chaperonage.

Matthew repositioned the armchair by the hearth, then came down beside Miss Jennings on the sofa.

She sat rigidly, as if the town drunk had taken the pew beside her at church.

Matthew was tipsy, at least, on hope, on possibilities, on puzzles.

He traced a finger along her jaw—so resolute, so smooth.

"Let me hold you. This will cost you nothing, not one damned thing. Not a glance from your brother, not a question from Miss Portman, nothing. You can get up, call for your horse, and leave whenever you wish. My discretion is utterly trustworthy. I promise you this."

For one instant, Miss Jennings's gaze was so tormented Matthew nearly withdrew his request. Had the blundering rogue promised her discretion, only to ruin her good name? Had Thomas Jennings any idea of the depth of his sister's suffering? Had anybody taken a moment to see the *person* enduring years of self-censure in that lonely castle by the sea?

Matthew was on the point of declaring himself a presuming fool when a feminine hand slid across his belly. Theresa rested her head on his shoulder, carefully, tentatively.

An olive branch.

He angled his body toward hers, brought his arms around her, and tucked his cheek against her hair. When she seemed comfortable with that much, and only then, he assayed a slow caress to her back. She tensed at first, but slowly, slowly eased under his hand.

Matthew wanted to kiss her until he could loosen their clothing, slide her beneath him, and pleasure them both to a mindless stupor. The realization was heartening, for he hadn't wanted to kiss much of anybody—excepting perhaps his horses—for some time. But he merely held her, and not only because a child was loose on the property.

He'd thought Theresa Jennings an attractive, experienced, possibly available woman, and that characterization was likely true, though far from a complete truth.

Any relations they undertook would be complicated, but also substantial— real and meaningful. *Meaningful* intrigued Matthew, like a faint game trail twisting through lush undergrowth.

Of course she'd been dishonored—she had the child to prove it—but something in her manner, in her sad blue eyes, suggested the story wasn't so simple, and the solution to her sadness wasn't a carefree romp in the hay with an affable neighbor.

How to bring the smile back into Theresa Jennings's eyes was a mystery. The even greater puzzle was why Matthew, who finally had life much on his own terms, would want to unravel that mystery.

For unravel it, he would.

* * *

Theresa curled next to Matthew Belmont in his pretty, light-filled library, her mind racing in all directions.

She should not allow herself the comfort of his affections.

Where was Priscilla?

Matthew Belmont smelled good, of green pastures, autumn sunshine, horse, cedar, and spices.

Hold me, please. Hold me.

Did the Belmont staff know the squire was sequestered with an unchaperoned female of marriageable age and tarnished reputation?

Into this flapping, fluttering flock of thoughts, another intruded: Matthew Belmont was different. Desire formed a part of Theresa's reaction to him, but so did affection, respect, discretion, and—Theresa pounced on this insight as if it were her last sovereign—*intimacy.*

Not a mindless relinquishing of physical dignity in exchange for favors or pleasure, but an intentional vulnerability far more dangerous and lasting.

To her relief, Mr. Belmont made no further attempts to kiss her, nor she him. His hand on her back soothed her nearly to slumber, but when the clock on the mantel struck the hour, he lifted his arm from Theresa's shoulders and shot his cuffs.

"I could do with another serving of lemonade. Shall I pour you some as well?" he asked.

"Please." For Theresa needed something to do with her hands, something to do with her mind.

"You needn't be nervous of me," he said, garnishing Theresa's drink with a sprig of mint. "I will not presume, though you are invited to take whatever liberties with my person you please."

He passed Theresa the cool glass, no brushing of fingers, no lowered lids, no lascivious smile. Had his flirtations been that gauche, Theresa would have known how to react—ignore them, take a brisk leave of her host, and never again be alone with him.

She sipped her lemonade as Mr. Belmont took his to the shelves along the wall. Even that—the courtesy of some physical distance—might have been a purposeful kindness from him.

"Will Priscilla enjoy a tale of adventure?" he asked. "Shall I find her an illustrated herbal or a book about birds of darkest Africa?"

"All three," Theresa replied, while she would have appreciated a manual for how to navigate the bewildering waters of mutual adult attraction. She'd banked her oars years ago and was entirely at sea in the Belmont library.

A door slammed, and Theresa nearly spilled her lemonade. Mr. Belmont pulled three volumes—two slim, one stout—from the shelves, and came back to the sofa with his lemonade.

"The watch approaches," he said, tipping his glass to his lips. "Let's make our return to the stable by way of the grape arbor."

Priscilla burst through the library door a moment later, her pinafore streaked with green, a leaf caught in one of her braids, a few stems of aster in her hand.

"I gave my flowers to the maid," she announced. "I found some white ones to go with the purple. I didn't go into the pasture, but I greeted the ponies because that's polite when you make a call."

Priscilla's chatter continued as Mr. Belmont led them out the French doors and through his gardens, until they approached a long arbor laden with fat clusters of purple grapes. He passed Theresa a handful and gave Priscilla a smaller bunch before selecting a few for himself.

"Watch out for bees, Priscilla," Theresa warned. "The later the season, the worse their sting."

Mr. Belmont hadn't taken Theresa's hand, hadn't done more than remark on the changing leaves as he'd plucked ripe fruit from the vines.

"And here,"—he found another cluster—"you can take these to Spiker, Priscilla, and let him know we'll need the horses in a few moments."

Priscilla bounded off, leaving her mother alone with Matthew Belmont in the privacy of the grape arbor.

"I would like to kiss you again, you know," Mr. Belmont said, as bees droned nearby and a gentle breeze set green and yellow leaves twittering.

He'd planned this route, planned for the shelter of the thick vines.

"Are you warning me, or seeking my permission?" Theresa wanted to kiss him again too, intentionally, with forethought and focus. Part of her hoped his first kiss had been a fluke, that what had felt like patience, confidence, and respect had been caution and novelty, no more.

"I am asking your permission and warning you, both. Also stating a fact." He slipped a hand around Theresa's waist and lowered his lips to hers.

He doesn't rush. Thank all the naughty saints, he doesn't rush, and he doesn't dawdle. He didn't haul her roughly up against him and mash his face to hers, didn't try to gag her with his tongue, didn't manhandle her breasts as if they were so much under-ripe fruit.

Didn't thump his hips against her as if she had no awareness of where a man's arousal centered.

Matthew Belmont prowled his way through a kiss, building desire by deliberate degrees, and giving Theresa time to adjust to each minute maneuver. As his tongue parted her lips and tangled plush, fruity sensations with anxiety about Priscilla's whereabouts, Theresa admitted she was in the arms not of a boy or a prancing lordling, but an adult in his prime.

Matthew Belmont was all muscle and man, no waste, no false moves, no excess about him.

Theresa was both disappointed and relieved when he eased his mouth from hers and merely held her for a long moment. His cheek rested against hers, his breath gently fanned her neck.

Merciful devils, she *liked* this. Liked how Matthew Belmont's kisses had a beginning, a middle, and an end. Only a confident rider took his time and let the approach, the jump, and the landing all have their moments.

"My dear,"—he nuzzled at her neck—"we should be going, or Priscilla will come patrolling for you. Have another grape and say something. You're too quiet."

He moved away to find the requisite grape, then slid his palm down Theresa's arm to capture her hand in his. They stood thus, munching on grapes, in a moment prosaic, disconcerting, and precious.

"Would you like me to tell you if your tongue is purple?" Theresa asked.

He set her hand on his arm. "You might tell me if my tongue tastes purple."

"Your..." Theresa shaded her eyes, as if the stable lay not beyond the garden wall, but across a brilliantly sunny lake. "You taste like pure sin."

"Wonderful," he replied, patting her knuckles. "I can hardly wait to learn what every part of you tastes like."

Theresa hadn't any reply for him, didn't know how to meet such frankness without turning the discussion naughty, and that she did not want when Priscilla might dart from behind any hedge.

A few minutes later, Theresa was peering down at her host from Evan's saddle, for Mr. Belmont remained standing at the horse's side after boosting Theresa aboard. Was he about to announce another intention to kiss her? Surely not in front of Priscilla?

"I've appropriated the use of your Christian name on at least two occasions," Mr. Belmont said. "You might do me the same honor."

Honor? To assume familiar address?

He petted the horse's shoulder rather than meet Theresa's gaze, and insight illuminated the moment, like the autumn sunshine turning the crown of Mr. Belmont's head golden.

He was *asking* Theresa to use his name, not telling her, not assuming such informality was his due. Behind the skill in his kisses lay a man who'd feel rejection keenly, but endure it with good grace.

Theresa twitched her habit so the skirt lay more neatly over her boot and took up the reins.

"Priscilla, put that kitten down. It's time we were on our way. My thanks for a pleasant afternoon, *Matthew*."

* * *

"Priscilla's handwriting resembles yours," Loris observed, draping herself over Thomas's shoulder. "At her age, I was barely making legible letters."

Thomas set his niece's letter aside—he had it nearly memorized—took off his spectacles, and drew his new wife into his lap. He'd left Loris sleeping in Sutcliffe Keep's baronial bed in the next room and wandered to the sitting room, goaded by a need to think.

"You are a bad influence on a man's ability to concentrate, Baroness." A fragrant, lithe, beautiful bad influence who was wearing nothing but one of her husband's shirts despite supper being hours away.

"This is our wedding journey," Loris replied, settling in. "I'm dedicated to being a bad influence until we must return to Linden. Priscilla's letter doesn't make you smile, though she's an excellent correspondent."

Priscilla's *existence* didn't make Thomas smile, for all the child was endlessly dear. Because Thomas and Theresa had been estranged, and he'd refused to open letters from his sister, he hadn't even known about the girl until recently.

"Her mother has a way with a pen too," Thomas said. "Theresa wrote plays and tragedies by the hour when she was a girl."

A young girl. As she'd approached adolescence, Theresa had become high-strung and difficult. She'd switched to poetry and then satire, by the time Thomas had left for university.

"Does Theresa have your gift for languages?" Loris asked, scooting around as bad influences were inclined to do.

"I don't know. Grandpapa provided governesses for her, but they had little more than parlor French and an abiding affection for Godfrey's Cordial."

While Thomas had been able to learn French, German, Italian, Latin, Greek, Spanish, and—as Fairly's man of business—smatterings of everything from Yiddish to Hindu to Arabic.

As a young man, Thomas had accepted that boys and girls faced different lots in life. Grandpapa had said an educated female got into mischief. Theresa had been denied much of an education, and mischief had become her stock in trade.

"Write back," Loris said, kissing Thomas's nose. "You're Priscilla's only uncle, and she will treasure your every word."

Thomas scooped up his wife and carried her to the bed. They occupied the master suite, an apartment that had known no occupant since Grandpapa's death. The delicate gilt furnishings were decades out of date, the wallpaper faded to a pale blue, and the woodwork in need of polishing.

Like Thomas's anger, the entire suite had a faded quality.

"I want to be furious," Thomas said, climbing onto the bed beside his wife. "I came here hoping to find that my sister had idled away her years at Sutcliffe in undeserved luxury."

Loris sat up and pulled the nightshirt over her head, then straddled Thomas.

"Theresa disappointed you bitterly all those years ago. Of course you're angry."

Thomas drew Loris down to him, the very feel of her in his arms a comfort. He could think when he held her, he could admit to feelings as awkward as they were surprising.

"Theresa worked like a dog turning a spit to keep this decrepit pile of stones from going to ruin," he said. "She kept nothing for herself, or for... the girl. Every penny was either ploughed back into the estate or set aside in the estate accounts. I can only assume the solicitors then kept the twins from frittering away every groat."

How had Theresa, a selfish, impulsive, inebriate on the road to certain destruction, learned to manage thousands of acres, a dozen tenant farms, and an entire castle staff? Grandpapa had died shortly after sending Thomas away, and Thomas had never made inquiries regarding the state of his cousins' holdings. Theresa had apparently been keeping the estate functional, despite the neglect of Thomas's predecessors.

"You have an aptitude for business," Loris said. "That's why Viscount Fairly relied on you. Your mercantile instincts are impeccable. Perhaps Theresa has a similar gift."

Thomas did not want to even glance at some of the tasks he'd undertaken for Fairly, not now, not here, not ever.

"His lordship sends felicitations, by the way," Thomas said, drawing a quilt over Loris's shoulders. "Her ladyship is in good health and invites us to visit in Town or at their estate in Kent whenever we please."

Loris left off nibbling his earlobe. "Thomas, you are the bravest man I know, and running off to see friends you recently entertained at our wedding is not worthy of you. You've invited Theresa to Linden, and now all that remains is to become reacquainted with her. Priscilla adores you, and Theresa isn't the licentious bawd you feared she'd become. She's your only living family besides Priscilla. Give this some time, and all will be well."

Thomas had put nearly ten years of *time* between himself and his older sister, and still, he was unable to trust that all would ever be well.

"Theresa was licentious enough, else I'd not have a bastard niece."

Loris climbed off of him and ranged herself beside him on the bed. "Priscilla is a delight, and many a good family has representatives from distaff branches. What is this about, my love?"

Thomas did not know how to answer her. He'd already come to value Loris's ability to sort through problems, so he blundered on.

"The staff here is ancient, and they do not speak of Theresa with respect. They sniff with censure about her parenting of Priscilla, her lack of attendance at services, her assumption of the authority that was Grandpapa's."

Whom they referred to as "the baron" in Thomas's hearing. Not "the late baron," or "your grandpapa, the baron," but *the* baron. As if Thomas were still an untitled adolescent without expectations to speak of, rather than immensely wealthy, well-traveled, and the present titleholder.

"We skipped services this week," Loris said. "You said the vicar was an awful old Presbyterian who ranted for hours when you were a boy."

Because no parish with any sense would welcome the Rev. Hesikiah Saunders, he'd apparently rant on in the village of Pendlegast for another twenty years.

"The staff don't bestir themselves to go to services," Thomas said. "Theresa made the coach available to them, and still they don't go." Theresa had probably paid any fines resulting from their hypocrisy too.

Despite enjoying the privileges of a man on his honeymoon, Thomas had not slept well the previous night. Being at Sutcliffe Keep brought back memories and raised questions that had no simple answers.

"I had almost arranged the past in such a way that I could excuse my sister's wild behavior," Thomas said. "She had no mother, no guidance. My cousins were a wicked pair, and Grandpapa paid Theresa no mind, ever. She was bored, she wanted attention... I can concoct all manner of excuses for her now, and yet, I cannot comprehend what she's become."

"A mother?" Loris asked, smacking a pillow. "If you turn up Puritan on me now, Thomas, I can promise you a very lonely honeymoon. No woman gets herself pregnant."

"I am aware of the mechanics of procreation, madam."

Loris hit him with a pillow, then curled up, her head on his shoulder. "You excel at the mechanics of procreation. Married life will surely leave me exhausted by Yuletide."

At the very least, Loris would sport a different shape by Yuletide. Thomas knew the look of a breeding woman, even in the early days of gestation.

"Theresa endured ten years of hard work here in virtual isolation," Thomas said, "but for lazy servants and judgmental neighbors. She could have gone elsewhere, presented herself somewhere up north as a war widow, sent Priscilla to a vicarage in the Midlands. Neither I, nor my cousins before me took any interest in Sutcliffe. The funds here were more than sufficient to allow Theresa to leave and let the castle fall into the sea."

Loris kissed Thomas and remained poised on her side. She brushed his hair back from his brow in a soothing caress, while her gray eyes held only compassion.

"You are ashamed," she said, and though Thomas himself hadn't been able to label his emotions, when Loris said those words, he could not deny their truth.

"I'm something. I've been furious with Theresa for a decade or more, and she's spent most of that time protecting my birthright. Maybe she did it for Priscilla's sake, maybe she did it out of guilt, but the benefit of her efforts goes to me."

"She wrote to you," Loris said. "She didn't give up on you, which suggests your stubbornness is a family trait as well."

Stubbornness or determination? Theresa had written over and over, probably relying on the family solicitors to search out Thomas's direction. He hadn't been hiding from her, precisely.

"I don't even know Theresa anymore," Thomas said. "I don't want to like her, but I must respect what she's done here. The estate would have fallen to ruins without her efforts, and after a millennium in the care of our family, for Sutcliffe Keep to falter would have been... regrettable."

Would have been a disgrace, as Theresa had become a disgrace in earliest adulthood.

Dozens of families relied on Sutcliffe for sustenance, and times had been hard. Thomas had visited enough tenants in recent days to know Theresa had not only held Sutcliffe together, she'd made a good job of it, despite Thomas's prolonged silence.

Despite an aging, disdainful staff, despite two previous owners whose passings none had mourned.

"Close your eyes," Loris said. "When you go back to Linden, I'll be with you. Take an interest in Priscilla, and her mother will appreciate you for it. That's a place to start."

Thomas drew his wife into his arms, but left desire for another time. A question plagued him: He respected what his sister had done with the estate, if not with her life, and yet, he was also still that furious young man whose only sibling had sided against him all those years ago.

Theresa had agreed with Grandpapa's plan to send Thomas away from Sutcliffe after university, away from all he'd ever known and loved. She'd told Thomas to stop clinging to her skirts and go make something of himself.

The words had hurt, the betrayal had hurt worse yet, and leaving Sutcliffe had nigh torn Thomas's heart from his chest.

So why should it matter now that, just perhaps, Thomas ought to have defied his sister and his grandfather both, and stayed by her side at Sutcliffe?

CHAPTER SEVEN

Priscilla's first lesson on Tut consisted of an extended game of follow-the-squire in a closed arena. Matthew stood immediately before the pony, then backed up ten paces, and explained to Priscilla how to make the little beast close the distance.

To Matthew's relief, she was instinctively respectful of her mount and grasped the essentials quickly. Within the hour, she was turning Tut, stopping him, and even backing him a few steps.

Beckman and Theresa watched from the rail, eventually joined by Jamie and Nicholas, the Linden stable master.

"Is that man a giant?" Priscilla whispered when she'd successfully steered Tut over that most daunting of initial obstacles, a pole on the ground.

"The fellow standing next to your mother is called Wee Nick," Matthew said. "He's your uncle's stable master, though I suspect he'll soon leave his post. Nick was visiting friends in Surrey after spending time in London. He's a nice man and particularly fond of children."

What fellow with seven younger siblings wouldn't love children?

Priscilla sent Nick another dubious look. "Will he be nice to Tut?"

Matthew's sons operated under a handicap, having been raised in recent years without a mother. He'd seen the same puzzled uncertainty on their faces, when they discussed the challenges of standing up at an assembly for the first time, or walking a young lady to services.

Women, on some level, did not make sense to his sons, because their mama hadn't been on hand to help unravel the mystery, and Matthew's limited understanding had been a poor substitute.

Perhaps men didn't make sense to Priscilla.

"Nick will spoil Tut rotten," Matthew said. "I'm surprised you haven't heard how Nick risked his life to save Penny and Treasure this summer. Beckman is very proud of his brother."

Priscilla fiddled the reins, which she held in her bare hands. "That man is Beckman's *brother*?"

Beckman had four brothers that Matthew knew of, but in this too, Priscilla's world had been limited by her mother's circumstances.

"I have a brother too," Matthew said, taking the pony's reins and leading him toward the gate. "And a brother-in-law, sister-in-law, and nephews, just as you have an uncle, and your mother has a brother. Let's call it a day, shall we? You've done quite well, but Tut might be tired."

Tut was barely awake, and not as a result of overexertion.

"You were a good boy, Tut. Thank you ever so much," Priscilla said, thumping the pony on the shoulder. Dust rose along with the fragrance of equine.

"Maybe Nick will show you how to give Tut a bath," Matthew said, for which mischief he would likely pay. "Ponies love to be clean."

Tut nearly stepped on Matthew's boot.

"Mama! Did you see us?" Priscilla called. "We rode all around the arena and even went over the pole!"

"I saw you," Theresa said. "Not a foot wrong, and you even backed your pony. An excellent start, Priscilla. You should be very proud of yourself."

"You should," Matthew said, passing the reins back to Priscilla as Nick opened the gate. "Not every child has the patience for riding, but you and Tut will get on famously."

Until the first time Tut dumped Priscilla. The course of true love between child and pony could come to an abrupt end.

"King Tut is smitten," Nick said, fastening the latch when Priscilla had steered her mount through the gate. "I know horses, and that pony has found his match."

"You're Nick," Priscilla said.

"Nicholas Haddonfield, at your service," he said, sweeping a bow. "That was good riding, Miss Priscilla. Shall I show you how to put Tut up?"

Yes, please. If Nick took over instructing the child, Matthew might embark on another interesting discussion with her mother, who had figured prominently in his dreams the previous night.

"I'll help," Beckman said. "Then we can show Priscilla the proper way to clean a bridle."

"And scrub a water bucket," Nick added. "Very important skill, scrubbing water buckets. Fortunately, we have at least a dozen Miss Priscilla can practice on."

"Don't forget that raking a barn aisle is also an art," Beck replied, as Tut's eyelids drooped over big brown eyes. "Nobody learns to do that in a day."

"Too bad Miss Priscilla's not strong enough to push a muck cart," Nick lamented.

"A real shame," Beck said. "Takes years to develop muck-cart muscles, though."

Tut woke up enough to toddle along between the Haddonfields as they sauntered off in the direction of the stable, with Priscilla chattering about being quite strong for her size

"She'll be fine," Matthew said, when Theresa's gaze remained on the plodding pony and the blathering Haddonfields. "They won't let her near a muck cart, and they'll keep her safe."

"You know them that well?" she asked as Tut's dusty little backside disappeared behind a hedge.

"I do. Walk with me?" Matthew didn't offer Theresa his arm, didn't gesture in the direction of the trail that led from the arena, along the stream, and into the Linden home wood. Matthew well knew a parent's struggle not to hover. His brother-in-law, Emmanuel Capshaw, loved nothing so much as to tease him about overprotectiveness.

"I'd rather not go far," Theresa said. "Priscilla might have need of me. Horses seldom mean to hurt us, but they're enormous animals, and Priscilla's not that familiar with them."

"Let's admire your brother's gardens, then," Matthew suggested, though the gardens were far less private than the woods. "I have a lilac bush that has decided to offer a few blooms, probably because we had some warm nights immediately before the harvest."

"They get confused," Theresa said, falling in step beside him. "I'm confused."

Matthew mentally braced himself to get tossed out of the saddle, though he and Theresa Jennings had barely left the figurative starting line.

"I dreamed of you," he said, idly tracking Nick's sizeable boot prints on the path back to the stable. "Dreamed of you in my library, reading Byron, of all things. I don't care for his sarcasm, but I suspect he's at heart a bitterly bewildered man."

"Bewildered," Theresa said, nodding. "Matthew, I have a daughter."

Hardly news, but at least she'd called him Matthew.

"A lovely girl, who is at this moment having a lovely time, getting her boots dirty and giving two grown men an excuse to avoid their less appealing chores. I'd like to kiss you again."

He ought not to have said that. Theresa waved a hand, as if batting aside a pesky bee inebriating itself on ripe grapes.

"Priscilla is fascinated with her uncle," Theresa said. "To his credit, Thomas has been very good with her. Very patient."

The season was changing, the undergrowth in the hedgerow dying back to yellows and browns, the leaves drifting from branches overhead. The time of year was sweet, though the direction the conversation was taking wasn't sweet at all.

"Thomas ought to be horsewhipped," Matthew said, "not venerated."

Theresa rounded on him as they reached the knot garden farthest from the Linden manor house.

"I beg your pardon, Mr. Belmont."

Matthew took a half step closer to her, so they were nose to nose. "No, you're begging your brother's pardon, and probably have been for years. Have you cousins or uncles, Theresa?"

"None," she said, "and I cannot afford to alienate Thomas now, when after years of ignoring my every letter and overture, he's finally turning up civil."

Arguing with a woman was a slippery, dangerous undertaking. A man had to defend his honor, uphold the truth, and respect the lady's sensibilities, while she fought him at every turn and foiled his own pretenses to reasonableness.

"You are about to tell me," Matthew said, "that I must not show you any favor, because your brother is entitled to punish you yet further for the mistakes of your past. The self-same brother who could not be bothered to open your letters, learn of Priscilla's existence, or make any provision for you or her. *He* is judge, jury, and executioner of your free will?"

Theresa patted Matthew's lapel. "You are magnificent in a temper, despite all your gentlemanly manners and affable conversation. Woe unto the criminal who seeks to disturb the king's peace in your shire."

Nobody had called Matthew magnificent, ever. Theresa stood close enough that the scent of the stable upwind blended with lemons, and the point Matthew needed to make nearly went wafting away on the autumn breeze.

"Shall we sit, madam?"

"Let's take the bench across the lane from the stable. Priscilla will find me there."

And Matthew would be precluded from taking liberties. How badly Theresa's trust had been abused, that she must protect herself from even respectful kisses—which Matthew would never have pressed on an unwilling lady, in any location.

As he escorted Theresa along a paddock and across the lane, his mind arranged facts as if he were analyzing a crime scene. Theresa, at a young age, had been taken advantage of. Her grandfather had died, then her cousins, leaving her—and Priscilla—only Thomas's dubious generosity to rely upon.

One casualty of the crime had been Theresa's good name, another the option of a good match at an early age.

The greater loss had been her ability to trust, particularly to trust men, and in a greater sense, to trust life.

"My wife was not faithful to me," Matthew said as Jamie emerged from the stable and tossed half a bucket of dirty water onto a bed of heartsease.

"You told me Matilda came to the marriage carrying another man's child. You married her anyway."

"Of course, I married her," Matthew snapped. "She was not of age to marry without her father's permission, she was gently bred, she was in difficulties not entirely of her own making. What does it mean to be a gentleman, if not to offer protection to those unable to protect themselves?"

Theresa took a seat on the wooden bench, Matthew came down beside her uninvited.

"I'm not sure what it means to be a gentleman," Theresa said. "Priscilla's father was a commissioned officer, the son of a lord, and by no means a bad fellow. I liked him. He was kind to me, in his way, and his friends were even kinder."

This dubious kindness puzzled her. Matthew was abruptly glad that Thomas Jennings was off on his wedding journey, lest Matthew search him out and thrash him.

"Had you met Nicholas Haddonfield before today?" Matthew asked.

"He and Beckman were at the wedding. You were too, I think, as was Lord Fairly. I don't know as I've ever seen so many well-dressed, handsome blond men."

Magnificent, and now handsome too. Matthew fortified his patience with those observations.

"Nicholas is the son of the Earl of Bellefonte," Matthew said, "as is Beckman. Did Nick let you know that?"

Jamie came out with another bucket of dirty water, Priscilla beside him. He passed her the bucket, and she dribbled it over various pots of salvia situated around the stable yard.

"Younger sons are expected to make their own way," Theresa said.

"Nick is the heir, Beckman the spare," Matthew said. "Younger sons of earls don't typically make their way in rural stable yards, but there they are. If you want to surprise Nick, refer to him as Viscount Reston."

Priscilla and Jamie disappeared back into the stable.

"Nicholas Haddonfield has a *courtesy title?*"

"He was visiting among others, the former owner of this estate, Lord Greymoor."

A leaf came down and landed on Matthew's shoulder. Theresa brushed it away. "I don't know this Greymoor fellow. Loris might have mentioned him."

"Greymoor is an earl, his brother a marquess. I was on excellent terms with Greymoor, and had no reason to doubt him when he reported that the marquess quite ruined his marchioness before he married her. Has Loris mentioned Greymoor's cousin, Miss Guinevere Hollister? Miss Hollister visited Linden last autumn with Lord Amery."

Matthew had Theresa's attention now, and he did not intend to relinquish it until he'd made his point.

"I don't know any of these people," Theresa said, almost as if she knew what came next.

"Miss Hollister and Lord Amery are married now, and their son and heir made his appearance less than nine months after the wedding. *Her* daughter, a child of perhaps five, was supposedly the by-blow of a ducal spare, one of Moreland's sons."

"One of the Duke of *Moreland's* sons?"

"The present Baron Berwick married his mistress only several years past, and she a confirmed member of the demimonde. My point, Theresa, is that your tale is not so very wicked, or even unusual. We're not angels, none of us, and if Thomas expects you to live like a nun for the rest of your life, then he's being ridiculous and hypocritical. Whether or not you ever permit me to kiss you again, I'll tell him as much if you give me leave, and perhaps even if you don't."

* * *

Matthew Belmont was deceptive. He appeared to be an affable country gentleman, on good terms with all and sundry, but he was also... more than that.

He was shrewd, fierce, and very much his own man. Unfortunately, Theresa was not her own woman, and never would be again. She was like this season, between summer and winter. Not without joy, but helpless to prevent whatever frost and storms inevitably arrived.

"Thomas is stubborn," she said, "and he's in a position to do Priscilla a great deal of good, or to remove her from my care and ensure I never see her again."

Matthew shifted to rest his arm along the back of the bench. Somebody was burning leaves or brush nearby, and the scent, while pleasant, was a melancholy harbinger of bitter weather.

"Allow me to point out that if the child is illegitimate, then you are her sole guardian, madam. Legally, Thomas can do nothing."

"Thomas can petition to become her guardian, and a part of me wishes he would. As Baron Sutcliffe's niece, the stigma Priscilla faces—"

"For God's sake, if the Duke of Devonshire can live in an open liaison with his duchess and his mistress for decades, then marry the mistress upon the duchess's death, what matters the irregular birth of a baron's niece? I can assure you Thomas and Loris anticipated their vows, and prior to purchasing Linden, your self-same puritanical brother worked for Lord Fairly. That worthy, whom I happen to like quite well, married the madam maintaining his very profitable common nuisance. Ask Thomas about that, why don't you?"

Matthew spoke quietly, but the words were clipped to razor-sharp enunciation.

He wasn't angry, he was furious, *and on Theresa's behalf.*

"I know what a common nuisance is." Theresa's grandfather had accused her of being one, though the term was more commonly applied to houses of ill-repute. Then the import of Matthew's words sank in. "Lord Fairly owned a… a place like that? And he married—they were at the wedding, and Thomas was quite…"

A memory came to mind, of Thomas leaning close to Lord Fairly's quiet, dark-haired viscountess, kissing her cheek and murmuring something in her ear that had made her smile. The moment had hurt, because Thomas's attitude toward the viscountess was both affectionate and respectful.

When Thomas had seen Theresa for the first time in ten years, he'd bowed. Slightly. Stiffly.

"I apologize for raising such a topic in the presence of a lady," Matthew said, "and I consider your brother a friend. I do not consider him the moral arbiter of the shire, and neither should you."

Thomas had invited a former madam and her brothel-owning husband to this wedding, but had refused to touch his own sister.

Theresa put a hand to her middle, which was abruptly disquieted. Perhaps the scent of smoke had done it, or perhaps last night's poor sleep was catching up with her.

"Thomas could not have condoned the viscount's business activities," she said. "My brother was always a proper little fellow, the one our cousins were sure was headed for the church. They ridiculed him."

Theresa had too, in the end. She'd ridiculed Thomas right out of her life.

"Are you well, madam? Have I upset you? I apologize, but your situation matters to me."

Theresa mattered to him, and that was unsettling too. "I'm fine, but you've given me much to think about. Thomas has changed, if he'd work for a man who owned an establishment of women like me." Perhaps Thomas had become more tolerant, and surely that was for the good?

"Is that all you see of yourself? You surrendered your virtue years ago to some scurrilous bounder, and all the years since, all your love for your daughter, your years of sober and responsible living, of accepting quiet obscurity, mean nothing?"

Matthew's blue eyes were so sad.

"I cannot forgive myself," Theresa said, the words making her throat ache. "Maybe I haven't forgiven myself because the greater transgression was against my younger brother. He looked up to me, and I disappointed him." To say nothing of the transgression against the child.

Matthew leaned closer, and Theresa closed her eyes in anticipation of a kiss, right there on a bench across from the stable yard.

Lips brushed gently across her forehead.

"And thus," Matthew said, "you've spent ten years castigating yourself for being human, and in those ten years, your dear, perfect, wealthy, worldly brother disported as he pleased. I fail to see how this qualifies him to sit in judgment of you or of anybody."

Disported as he pleased. That's what men did, most men—disported as they pleased.

"Will you and Priscilla come to services with me on Sunday?" Matthew asked.

Good God. "You excel at the art of ambush, Matthew Belmont. I haven't been to services since before Priscilla's birth."

"Then you're overdue for some poorly sung hymns, churchyard gossip, and mild flirtation from the proverbial lonely curate. Say you'll come."

Theresa knew all about lonely curates, and yet, she was tempted. "Priscilla will fidget."

"You'll fidget. You'll peer up at the rafters and hope the roof doesn't cave in on your sinful self. Matilda went to services any number of times, and I can assure you, the church roof endured her presence. She even managed to look fetching in her Sunday bonnet most of the time too."

Matthew was so casual about the concepts that had defined Theresa's life for years. Fallenness, worthiness, acceptance.

"I took all three of my boys to services with me for years," he went on, rising. "Priscilla cannot possibly fidget as much as three active boys did."

"Perhaps not, but I can."

Matthew extended a bare hand down to her. He had beautiful hands, elegant, sun-browned, competent, and strong. He'd have an equestrian's calluses and a loving father's patience in those hands.

As a lover…

Theresa gave him her hand and rose. "I'll attend with you, but be prepared for awkwardness."

"Excellent," he said. "A little awkwardness livens up the service wonderfully. I warn you now, I can't carry a tune in a bucket, so don't smirk at me if I only move my lips during the hymns."

"I sing rather well," Theresa said, starting off for the stable, from which her daughter hadn't emerged for some minutes. "Or I did as a girl. I suppose we'll find out if I still can."

Matthew tucked her hand into the crook of his arm and led her across the lane. He had asked much of her in this simple Sunday outing. Asked that she risk censure and gossip, as well as Thomas's wrath when he returned home and found she'd fraternized with the neighbors.

Matthew Belmont had made a telling point, however. If Thomas counted a brothel owner and a madam among his friends—Theresa knew far more wanton names for such an establishment than that—then Thomas's outlook on life had shifted considerably.

Thomas and Loris had anticipated their vows too, though many couples did.

"I'll come by for you after breakfast," Matthew said. "Do not think of pleading a headache, madam."

"I'll be ready."

Theresa would never be ready to face the gauntlet of a local congregation, but because Matthew had asked it of her, she'd try. She would rise to a challenge she'd dodged for years for one reason.

Matthew Belmont would be by her side for the duration, regardless of the reception she received.

CHAPTER EIGHT

Theresa Jennings did not fidget, and she had a lovely soprano voice. She did hide, though, in the plainest brown carriage dress Matthew had seen in years—and a rural squire saw many a nondescript dress. Rather than sing the melody, she discreetly harmonized among the contraltos and tenors.

"The pews get harder each year," Matthew murmured, when the service had concluded. The organist plodded through a postlude as the congregation rustled and shuffled to its feet, while Theresa gathered up her reticule.

"Let's use the side door," she said. "Less congested."

By no means was she a coward, but she was afraid, and Matthew wanted to thrash her brother all over again. He wanted to thrash all the men who attended the services of a God of forgiveness and honor, while they worshipped at the altar of judgment and hypocrisy.

"I did not quibble when you told me Priscilla had developed a slight cough," Matthew said, tapping his hat onto his head. "One falsehood per Sunday morning ought to suffice."

Theresa sent him a look that emphasized the resemblance between mother and daughter.

"You are awful, and you lied too," she said. "You sing quite well."

Awful surely qualified as an endearment of some sort. "I love to sing, as do my boys. Christopher lives for glee club, and Remington's voice is solo quality. They get that from their mother."

Theresa pretended to busy herself with her bonnet ribbons. To complement her sober brown dress, she'd donned a simple, wide-brimmed straw hat. Her strategy had failed, though she couldn't know that. Instead of creating a nondescript, unremarkable appearance, she'd chosen a color that flattered her dark hair and blue eyes, and a simplicity of attire that called attention to her beauty.

For she was lovely, did she but know it. Her movements, her voice, her way of holding herself, were attractive.

"I suppose we'd best get this over with," she said, clutching her beaded bag in gloved hands. "If I recall, the sermon was on.... I can't recall."

Matthew cast back over the last hour, most of which had been spent staring at the Book of Common Prayer while trying to limit his awareness of the woman beside him.

The Rev. Thaddeus Herndon had only so many sermons, and in the autumn...

"Those who come late to work the harvest," Matthew said. "An apt topic, one of his better and braver homilies. Stop dawdling, my dear."

They were getting looks. Matthew always got looks, and the looks were usually followed up by smiles and invitations. Would the squire like to join this or that family for the Sunday meal?

"That woman by the baptismal font seems angry," Theresa muttered before leaving the pew.

"She has three unmarried daughters over the age of twenty," Matthew whispered back. "Mrs. Birkman has plans for my bachelorhood with which I have long taken issue, despite their cook's genius with a joint of beef. I suspect her daughters are waiting for my sons to come of age, which is part of the reason I've sent the boys off to safety with my brother Axel in Oxfordshire."

The crowd shuffled forward, while Rev. Herndon stood at the back door, beaming good cheer in all directions.

Herndon must have heard the siren call of his own Sunday meal, because he merely bowed over Theresa's hand, thanked her for attending, and asked her to extend his felicitations to the baron and his lady upon their return from their wedding journey.

Theresa was cordially invited to call on Mrs. Herndon, provided her hearing was up to the rigors of ten children living cheek by jowl in a humble vicarage.

"The sky did not fall," Matthew said, as he assisted Theresa into his gig. "Admit it. The church rafters will hold up for another century at least, the goodwives of the parish did not pelt you with mud—at least not as a result of your past."

Matthew had smiled, nodded, and otherwise slipped through the lines of neighbors who would have kept him and Theresa in the churchyard all afternoon. The goodwives had wanted to pelt Theresa with questions, that much had been obvious.

"They weren't exactly friendly," Theresa said, as Matthew took the place beside her and gave the horse leave to trot on.

"Loris Tanner, whom most of them merely tolerated, ensnared the handsome, wealthy baron in holy matrimony," Matthew said. "They wonder about the baron's sister, and her plans for the confirmed bachelor, Mr. Belmont. I'm sure they would have gladly extended their supper invitations to you, had we tarried long enough to draw that fire."

The day was beautiful, warm in the sun, cool in the shade, as the best autumn days could be. The harvest had gone well, the orchards offered handsome yields, and Matthew had taken a woman to services whom he esteemed and was attracted to.

As the gig rattled out of the village, more gratitude filled his heart than he could ever have experienced sitting on a hard pew among his curious neighbors.

"You love this," Theresa said. "You love being out in the fresh air, the ribbons in your hands. You trained this gelding, didn't you?"

"Foaled him out, trained him in harness, and taught him to go under saddle," Matthew said. "Leo is a smart fellow and enjoyed having a succession of new challenges. He can do some tricks too."

"You enjoyed the challenges," Theresa said, turning her face to the breeze and closing her eyes.

Matthew enjoyed *her*. "Would you like to drive?"

"No, thank you. You deserve the pleasure. Some people don't have to over-imbibe, over-wager, or indulge in opium, hashish, or other vices. They have the great gift of intoxicating themselves on legitimate diversions."

As if thunder had rumbled to the south, Matthew's joy in the morning's accomplishment dimmed.

"Now you will tell me that your youthful excesses included those intoxicants you listed, and then you'll regale me with a description of your scandalous wardrobe when you embarked on this dissipation," he said. "I did go up to university, you know."

He'd had a year and a half to sample the vices of the wider world before holy matrimony had cut short his education.

"Matthew, I wasn't wearing nearly enough on some of the occasions when I abused those intoxicants."

The notion that she'd been twenty years old, a gently reared lady of the baronial manor, and so fallen into wickedness sickened him. She'd had a grandfather, a brother, two cousins, and none of them had intervened as she'd courted disgrace.

For a young lady did not pitch her good name that far into the weeds on a single toss.

"Tell me the rest of it." Matthew had heard confessions of murder that troubled him less than the truths she wanted to inflict on him. "Tell me whatever horrors and sins you think will give me a disgust of you, for that's your aim."

She'd fail, of course. If Matthew admired one virtue above all others, it was honesty. His own wife had never been honest with him, while Theresa Jennings had never dissembled.

"You think I was some delicate creature, taken advantage of by a charming scoundrel," she said. "I was... awful, Matthew. I had my reasons, at first, but then I had no reason, or so it seems in hindsight. My cousins were a pair of ne'er-do-well wastrels, my grandfather a tired old man. I was lost and I ran wild."

Matthew passed Theresa the reins, which she accepted. She wasn't wearing the right gloves for driving, but Leonardo had a delicate mouth, and the distance to Linden was short.

"You were lost, you ran wild, for years," Matthew said, slipping an arm around the lady's waist. "Your cousins were a pair of bad influences, your brother left in a peevish tantrum, your grandfather washed his hands of his grandchildren, and of life."

"Thomas didn't—"

Matthew kissed her cheek. "I'm not finished. You were sunk in disgrace, headed for a bad end, the despair of the house of Sutcliffe, and then you conceived a child, the inevitable wages of your folly."

She gently checked Leo, who'd sped up, probably at the ire in Matthew's voice. "My situation was worse than that, but you've grasped the main points."

What could be worse than the road to perdition? "And then, rather than throw yourself into the sea," Matthew went on, "or blame the authors of your ruin, or drown yourself in years of self-pity, you righted your ship, found calm waters, and got on with the business of a raising a daughter."

"I was the author of my own ruin, mostly," Theresa said as they tooled past the drive to Matthew's estate. "I became the author of my own ruin."

"And you became the sole author of your own salvation, and your daughter's," Matthew said. "I admire that about you. Rather a lot. Would you like to join me for supper at my in-laws'? Agatha is a dreadful bore, Emmanuel a bit too jovial, and the roast often undercooked, but they're family. You know how it is with family."

* * *

The trip to church had broken Theresa's heart all over again, when she'd thought that traitorous organ too far gone to fracture anew.

Matthew's grand scheme to return her to propriety in the space of a Sunday morning had been ridiculous and dear. She'd indulged him, hoping a few glaring biddies, or a snub from the pastor would make her point eloquently enough. The congregation hadn't obliged, and so she'd loaded her cannon with greater, sadder truths.

"I tell you I was as debauched as a decently reared woman can be, and you threaten me with undercooked roast?" she asked.

"You're pulling a bit to the right, probably because I'm distracting you."

Matthew was nearly sitting in Theresa's lap, his arm around her waist, his warmth a pleasure on a crisp autumn morning. Courting couples occupied the bench of a buggy like this, and in no regard could Theresa consider that she and Matthew...

She scooted a few inches away and corrected her contact with the gelding's mouth.

Matthew withdrew his arm. "Agatha and Emmanuel mean well. Agatha is Matilda's older sister, and they have me to dinner one Sunday per month, weather permitting. The weather today, alas, permits."

Theresa hadn't told Matthew the whole of her descent into vice and oblivion, but she'd told him as much as she dared and even exaggerated a bit for the sake of emphasis.

"You are determined to minimize my unfitness. Why, Matthew?"

"Why are you determined to see yourself only as you were years ago?" he countered. "Years ago, I was a miserable, angry, widower; an irritable father; a negligent brother; and a poor choice as magistrate."

He propped a boot on the fender, the casual gesture of a man bracing himself for verbal fisticuffs, when Theresa truly hadn't an answer for him.

So she asked a question. "You were angry?"

"Furious," he said, gaze going to the scythed hayfield beside the lane. "I'd always thought that someday, Matilda and I might come to a sort of peace. She could explain to me why, for the duration of our marriage, she had given her heart to a man who treated her dishonorably. I could explain to her how much I loved the children, and wanted to love her as their mother, despite all the other mess and complication in our lives. When she fell ill, I tried—"

The shrewd, relentless Mr. Belmont hadn't intended these words. He liked Theresa for her honesty, but wasn't so keen on sharing his own truths.

"You tried?"

"Matilda was not interested in any great, dramatic rapprochement with her husband of convenience. As she lay dying, she grieved not the life she might have had with me and the boys, but the life she'd never have with her old love. I was enraged, with her, with him, with the marriage that was dying even as she too faded."

Theresa blinked at a lane gone blurry. "I'm sorry, Matthew. For you, for her. Were you ever tempted to call her old love out?"

"Before she wed me, I assured her I'd never ask her for his name. I was young, and yet, I think that promise was wise."

Kind, in any case. Kind to the young couple married amid so much sadness and necessity.

"The turn to Linden is coming up," Matthew said. "Shall I take the ribbons?"

Theresa passed them over. She'd intended to set Matthew straight, to save him from his own good intentions and tolerant nature, and she'd failed.

Which was a relief, albeit bewildering. Matthew was not a rural innocent, caught in the grip of an honorable excess of tolerance for a neighbor's tarnished sister. He was a man wrestling with his own bitterness and unhappy past.

And Theresa—may heaven help her—hoped he'd ask her to drive with him to church again next week.

* * *

"Squire, have a seat. It's only sporting to let you finish your ale before I thrash you." Nick slid over on the bench that ran the length of the tavern's snug, taking his own ale with him.

"We have rules here in England, Haddonfield," Matthew said, settling in on the opposite bench. "You can't arrest, try, and convict a man without letting him know how he's transgressed. Why is it, the pews in the church always feel so much harder than the benches of the local tavern, when both are made of simple wood?"

Why was it, having enjoyed Agatha's Sunday fare, Matthew was still hungry, for both company and food?

Nick pushed a tray of bread and butter at Matthew. "The Papists generally start off with 'Bless me father, for I have sinned.' I dispense with the popery and generously administer a restorative beating to those clearly in need. You took Theresa Jennings to services this morning."

Matthew had taken the lady somewhat to task too. He saluted with his tankard. "Your powers of observation appear to be quite in order, Nicholas."

Nick cut off a slice of bread, dabbed butter on it, and set it on a wooden dish. "Do you fancy strawberry jam?"

Strawberry was Rem's favorite. "No, thank you, Nicholas. If this is the condemned squire's last meal, will you at least finish reading the charges against me before I go nobly to my fate? The last time I checked, taking a lady to services was hardly a threat to the king's peace."

Nick fixed himself a serving of bread and butter, and topped his slice with a dab of preserves. He was the largest man Matthew knew, his present position one of mostly manual labor, and yet, his table manners were exquisite, his hands always clean.

"Thomas, Baron Sutcliffe, should have been the one to take Miss Jennings to services," Nick said. "He declined that honor, for the present, and we must conclude he did so for reasons."

Matthew took a sip of ambrosial ale. Soon the publican would switch to the winter brews, which were too dark and bitter for Matthew's palate.

"Did Thomas decline the honor of escorting his sister to services, overlook the obligation in the uproar of the wedding, or did he neglect the privilege?"

Nick sat back, his bread and butter in his hand. Not a crumb dared fall before he popped the sustenance into his mouth.

"Did you imbibe too much wine with your Sunday viands, Squire?"

"Too much of my in-laws' company. At some point, Agatha and Emmanuel came to expect that one-quarter of my Sunday afternoons belonged to them. I complied with this assumption because the boys needed to know their aunt and uncle, but the time has come to reclaim my Sabbath. What is wrong with me, Nicholas, that I am increasingly vexed with my late wife's only relations?"

What was wrong with Matthew, that he'd stop off at the local watering hole of a late Sunday afternoon rather than go directly home to his own hearth? A toddy or three, a cozy fire, a riveting pamphlet on the benefits of running sheep over fallow turnip patches… These appealed more strongly than another serving of Agatha's pear compote, and another hour of Emmanuel's jovial insinuations about debauches on the banks of the River Isis.

"I don't much care for in-laws on general principles," Nick said. "The presence of in-laws implies the presence of a wife."

"Bless me, Father, for an earl's heir must marry, Nicholas?"

"My father's health is not good," Nick said, dusting his hands over the bread board. "But he can wield a pen with the accuracy of a coachman's lash, stinging my filial devotion down to the bone. I can't ask Beckman to marry again, George is hopeless, and Adolphus will likely take up academics rather than holy matrimony."

Such was life as a magistrate often saw it.

Mr. Dweedle complained about Mrs. Puckett's dog barking at all hours, though Dweedle himself still missed the hound he'd buried last summer. Mrs. Puckett relished her imbroglios with old Dweedle, mostly because she'd been sweet on him half a century ago, and he'd offered instead for Maude Peckley, gone ten years past.

If Dweedle had had the sense to marry Dorie Puckett upon Maude's death, then Dorie would not have bought the dog for company, and nobody would lose sleep over endless barking.

Nicholas needed a wife, while Matthew needed another ale.

"I have in-laws but no wife," Matthew said. "You adore the ladies, love children, have a duty to marry, and yet want neither in-laws nor a wife. Perhaps we should switch to brandy."

"He who mixes the grape and grain is sure to have a very sore brain," Nick muttered. "How are the Capshaws, and why are you still enduring their company when you've long been a widower?"

Matthew had dragged Nick along to the Sunday feasts a time or two. Nick was a good friend, but undercooked roast, along with Agatha's sniffy manners, was penance such as even friendship ought not to endure. When Agatha was on her mettle, she could come up with a grace as long as Matthew's arm.

On the ride back from Trieshock, Matthew had pondered Nick's question, in a different light: Why endure the Capshaw's company with such frequency?

What was it about Matilda's older sister and brother-in-law that made Matthew increasingly want to upend the entire table and stomp off in a tantrum worthy of his youngest son?

"They insist on treating me as if I'm still that seventeen-year-old boy," Matthew said. "The youth who quaked at the altar, certain only that a gentleman would never leave a lady in the circumstances Matilda faced. She was distant kin, and I was very young, but determined to uphold the family honor."

"You were randy," Nick said charitably. "Maybe you're still randy."

Back to this. "I am lonely, Nicholas, and I see in Thomas's sister another person whose youth and uncertainty led her to make unfortunate choices. Thomas has hardly been a saint."

Nick cut another slice of bread. The knife could have been sharper, so the undertaking required patience and a light hand.

"I'm the last to judge anybody for youthful folly, but Theresa Jennings is a troubled woman," Nick said, applying butter and jam to the bread.

Matthew swiped the food from Nick's hand before Nick could take a bite.

"Emmanuel Capshaw made the same point, and without having so much as laid eyes on Miss Jennings." Bread, butter, and jam were good for the soul. Pear compote was… too sweet and a waste of good spirits.

"In-laws are like that," Nick said, slicing off yet more bread. "They have powers of divination. If you marry Theresa Jennings, Thomas will become your brother-in-law. Ponder that."

"If I marry Theresa Jennings, Loris would also become an in-law," Matthew said, taking a sip of mellow ale.

Marry Theresa Jennings.

"Half the congregation was buzzing about your choice of companion this morning," Nick said. "The other half, as usual, was asleep."

Beckman came sauntering into the common, winked at the barmaid sitting on a stool and polishing glasses, then took the place beside Matthew.

"Jamie's knees are acting up," Beckman said, taking a sip of Matthew's ale. "Rain before morning."

Nick slathered butter on his bread and added more than a dab of jam. "Or maybe, Jamie took a look at the sky and saw clouds gathering to the southeast. Nothing but trouble comes from the direction of France."

Nick lifted the bread and even had his mouth open when Beckman neatly appropriated it, took a bite, and passed it back.

"I come here for the bread and butter," Beck said. "Not for the weather predictions. How was Sunday penance, Squire?"

Beckman too, had once been dragooned into joining Matthew at the Capshaws' table.

"My Sabbath meal was undercooked and preachy," Matthew said. "I accompanied Miss Jennings to services. I have accompanied any number of ladies to services. When Clarissa Springdorf broke her ankle, I spent an entire summer playing coachman. Dorie Puckett prevailed on my good offices not a month past when her gig needed a new wheel."

The barmaid delivered Beckman's ale, along with more butter and a wedge of cheese.

"Linden aged cheese is the finest," Nick said, cutting the wedge into three parts. "And you accompany only widows, spinsters, and dowagers to services, Matthew. Miss Jennings is none of the above."

Matthew ate his portion of cheese for two reasons. First, Agatha's meal had left him hungry. She arrayed her table beautifully. Her porcelain matched, her silver gleamed, her serving dishes were coordinated and placed just so.

Of food, however, there was far less than Matthew required. Matilda had once said her sister excelled at the art of extravagant miserliness.

The second reason he munched his cheese in thoughtful silence was that Nick had asked a question.

Theresa Jennings was not a widow, a spinster, or a dowager—so what was she?

"Miss Jennings is brave," Beckman said, dipping his cheese in his ale before taking a bite. "I like her."

"Are you warning me of something, Beckman?" Matthew asked. Emmanuel had been full of warnings. "I took the lady straight home, in an open gig, mind you, and then I took myself home. I did not set one handsome, booted foot inside the Linden manor house. Once under my own roof, I made myself a few sandwiches of ham and cheddar, three to be exact. Then I sat in my library for more than an hour procrastinating the afternoon's call upon the Capshaws while writing to my offspring."

Matthew had muttered a few complaints in Maida's sympathetic direction too, and in an egregious breach of library etiquette, fed her the crusts of his final sandwich.

"By the time I arrived on the Capshaw doorstep," Matthew went on, "Emmanuel already knew with whom I'd attended services and something of her circumstances."

Nick and Beck were both apparently fascinated with their drinks, or trying to hide matching smirks.

Nick spoke first. "Are you warning us of something, Belmont?"

"I'm warning you to mind your own business," Matthew said. "Emmanuel blathered to me about my own sons being at impressionable ages, about Matilda's memory deserving respect, about foolishness being a single man's lot at *my age*. I nearly backhanded him for his presumption. He hasn't even met Theresa, and he's decided she's Jezebel's more wicked sister."

"What have *you* decided?" Beckman asked, tearing off a piece of bread and taking a bite.

"A man in love doesn't decide anything," Nick said, passing his brother the butter. "Such a pathetic creature has no rational processes to his name. He aches, he yearns, he speaks nonsense, which is nonetheless the most honest discourse of his entire life. He is a creature both pathetic and noble, ecstatic and miserable. His honor reaches to celestial heights at the same time he plots endlessly to take liberties with his beloved. We pity him aloud, while we envy him in our hearts."

The barmaid left off polishing glasses. "Mr. Haddonfield, will you marry me?"

Nick blew her a kiss. "I'm unworthy of your regard, Daisy my love, but bring us another round, and my resolve might weaken. Put the drinks on Belmont's tab, and it will weaken yet further."

Beckman dipped another piece of bread. "You got a letter from Papa, I take it?"

"One from Papa, one from Nita." Nick fished inside his jacket and passed two epistles to his brother. "Our sister sends greetings. Papa is not doing well, but he's in good spirits."

"Same as last month and the month before," Beckman said. "While the squire's situation appears to be changing."

Yes, by God, Matthew's situation was changing. He'd lectured his sons about change being inevitable and desirable, and then he'd gone right back to reading pamphlets on the proper use of horse lineament and the wonders of manuring vegetables with chicken shit.

"I miss my boys," Matthew said. "I will always miss them, but at some point in the last eighteen years, I also lost track of myself. I don't even like pears."

"That's the honest discourse part," Beck said.

"Or the nonsense," Nick said. "Hard to tell the difference when a man is truly smitten."

Matthew sipped his ale and let them have their fun—they were envying him in their hearts, after all, or they soon would be.

CHAPTER NINE

Agatha was growing plump, a testament to what three rounds of tea cakes per day—mid-morning, late afternoon, and late evening—could do to the figure of a woman whose "elegant" table servings bordered on stingy. She was coloring her hair too, according to the maid of all work, and kept a lurid novel in her lap desk.

Emmanuel would never begrudge his wife her vanities or pleasures, even if she spent money on them that was better invested in stocking the larders.

"I do believe Matthew was in a hurry to leave us," Emmanuel remarked, as he pushed coals to the back of the fireplace. They were in the family parlor, the one Agatha called comfortable, the one Emmanuel called dowdy, and small enough to heat easily.

"Perhaps Matthew was anxious to avoid the rain," Agatha said. "I'm certain we'll have a proper downpour by morning. Are you retiring already, Emmanuel?"

He'd go up to bed. He would not retire. "Soon, my dear. Matthew's situation worries me."

Agatha's needle paused between one stitch and the next. She embroidered beautifully, though how she could tolerate sitting hour after hour baffled him.

"Matthew has been without female companionship for years," Agatha said, "but he's stood up with this lady, driven that one to church, turned pages for another, and none of it has ever amounted to anything. The Jennings woman's circumstances are pathetic, if gossip is to be believed. A gentleman would pity such a creature."

Though Agatha heard gossip in quantity—witness, her immediate knowledge of Matthew's outing earlier that day—she repeated none of it outside her own home.

Emmanuel had had the great misfortune to marry a genuine lady. Agatha was not warm, and God knew she wasn't affectionate, but she took her station to heart, maintaining a virtuous dignity in all situations.

She did not, however, take her husband to bed, thank the heavenly powers.

"I'm not judging the Jennings creature," Emmanuel said. "Our own dear Tilly, may she rest in peace, nearly found herself in pathetic circumstances."

"We would have taken her in," Agatha said, jabbing at the fabric. "I told her, we would have provided a home for her. Compassion for those who've erred is preferable to casting stones."

Emmanuel set the poker on the hearth stand. The fire was an extravagance, but now was not the time to harangue Agatha again on the need for economies.

"You are without doubt the most loving older sister ever to grace this shire, madam. I'm sure Tilly had her reasons for choosing Belmont's charms over our humble household."

Emmanuel was, in fact, quite sure that marriage to Belmont had been a less disagreeable existence for Matilda than years of enduring Agatha's charity would have been. He'd shared his conviction in this regard with Agatha's sister too, and she—canny young lady—had heeded his guidance.

"Would you be very vexed if I pleaded a head cold next month, Emmanuel?" Agatha asked. "One doesn't like to dissemble, but I get the sense Matthew regards our monthly meals as a duty, rather than a pleasure. Matilda has been gone for years, after all."

Eight years and three months, in fact, but Emmanuel was not about to cut the thread that reliably bound them to Matthew Belmont. If Agatha could see beyond her embroidery hoop, she'd realize she didn't to cut those ties either.

"We have a duty to Matthew, my dear. He's family, and the boys need to know we're not neglecting him. They're good boys, and they worry about their old papa. I was once a university scholar, and I know how their minds work. The more diversions they have, the more guilty they feel about leaving their father back in the shires, there to grow old and content."

For a moment, Agatha looked unconvinced—she was not stupid, but she was the product of a strict upbringing. Tilly had rebelled against that upbringing, while Agatha, as the older sister, had upheld her parents' expectations at every turn.

"I suppose you're right," she said. "Matthew has ever been his own man. He occasionally begs off, after all. Our table is hardly impressive though, and his appetite remains appallingly robust."

Ah, so Agatha was ashamed rather than miserly. She excelled at being ashamed, which would have surprised most who knew her. She was ashamed of her younger sister's memory, ashamed of her own inability to produce children, and probably ashamed of her inability to make her pin money stretch as far as it needed to.

Emmanuel brushed aside the possibility that she might be ashamed of her husband.

Or that he should be ashamed of himself. A man, God's least perfect creature, did what he could with the resources available to him.

Emmanuel patted Agatha's shoulder. "Matthew can afford to feed himself exceedingly well, my dear. The point of our Sunday meals is to gather as a family, not to impress a wealthy relation with pointless extravagance. My concern is that a woman of loose morals will stop at nothing to get her hands on Matthew's wealth. The more often we can remind him of that, the better for the boys. She'd squander their inheritance without a thought."

Agatha yawned, covering her mouth with the back of one plump hand. "You're good to be concerned for the boys, Manny. They still have a quite a bit of growing up to do."

Emmanuel did not love his wife, but her management of the household made his life easier. By virtue of Agatha's sheer, unrelenting respectability, Emmanuel's reputation remained spotless by association. His meals were hot, his linens clean, his house tidy. He esteemed Agatha, which she probably preferred to the messier emotions sometimes associated with marriage.

He kissed her brow and wished her pleasant dreams, as he had for years.

"Sleep well, Emmanuel."

She went back to her embroidery, though Emmanuel knew from long experience that within ten minutes, she'd go up to her bedroom. He'd listen for her step in the corridor, and ten minutes after that, let himself out the kitchen door. While Agatha said her prayers, and dreamed of embroidery, Emmanuel would have a few brandies at the local posting inn, and then offer to escort one of the friendlier barmaids back to her lodgings.

* * *

"Are you hiding, or trying not to be obvious about avoiding Mr. Belmont?" Alice tossed that question into the library's quiet, then came limping in after it.

"Did the damp weather earlier in the week grieve your hip?" Theresa had appropriated the estate desk, the place from which Thomas ran his many properties and investments.

And yet, it was also just a comfortable chair at a big, old desk. A good place to hide.

"I haven't decided if the change in the weather bothers my hip, or if the problem is simply that I sit for too long. Rainy days are the best for reading or catching up on correspondence."

Halfway through Alice's second winter on the Sussex coast, Theresa had asked to whom Alice wrote so faithfully. Alice had a sister in the north, a full brother, and a half brother. She never mentioned them by name, but Theresa had seen the addresses on the letters.

Alice's letters had been regularly answered, unlike Theresa's to Thomas, and some of the letters were franked.

Boots thumped in the corridor, the confident stride of a sizeable man.

For an instant, Theresa was certain Thomas had cut his wedding journey short and returned home to castigate her for attending services the previous Sunday with Matthew. While part of her accepted that Thomas had a right to be upset—she was his disgraced sister, and this was his home parish—another part of her had begun preparing for a long overdue row.

"Ladies, may I join you?" Matthew Belmont asked, marching into the library. "Miss Priscilla has once again acquitted herself magnificently with her gallant steed. She's cantering up to the nursery to change and will then render a full report, I'm sure. Her braids are somewhat the worse for her outing, though her spirits are excellent."

"She'll want to write a story," Theresa said, rising. "Tut must be immortalized as the first flying unicorn ever to grace Linden's pastures, and—"

"I'll tend to the child," Alice said. "She and I are due to take tea in German today, and that slows Priscilla's chatter considerably. Squire, good day."

And thus Theresa was cast unchaperoned into the company of the man she'd avoided for the past three days—except in her dreams. Years from now, she might still encounter Matthew Belmont in her dreams, if she were lucky.

"Priscilla does well with old Tut," Matthew said, closing the library door. The wet weather had been followed by cooler days, so a fire blazed in the library's fireplace.

Fire blazed in Theresa's memory too. The fire of Matthew's kisses, the fire in his eyes when he'd raged against Thomas's stubbornness.

"I loved to ride when I was a girl," Theresa said, resuming her seat at Thomas's desk. "I had two older cousins, twin boys, and Thomas was a demon in the saddle from a young age. Keeping up with the cousins while trying to look after Thomas meant I learned to love horses early and well."

Matthew was in riding attire, tall boots, sober colors, the fingers of worn riding gloves poking out of one jacket pocket. His hair was windblown, and a faint odor of leather and horse clung to his person.

To see him, to catch that scent, to feel the sense of energy he brought to the library's quiet pleased Theresa.

Pleased her terribly, and that would not do.

"My brother Axel and I practically lived on our ponies," Matthew said. "Do you mind if I have a nip?"

"Of course not."

He poured himself a tot of brandy, but didn't taste it. Instead, he cradled his glass in his palm, the perfect accessory to a country gentleman at his most delectable.

He gestured with the drink. "Care for a sip?"

"No, thank you." Theresa was sufficiently inebriated on Matthew's mere presence, which was very bad of her. Men had lost the ability to make her silly more than a decade ago.

"Are you abstemious as a form of self-punishment, madam, or out of caution?"

He wandered to the family Bible, which Theresa had brought with her from Sutcliffe Keep. That book should dwell where the head of the family dwelled, and the sea air wasn't kind to books, particularly not to old, precious books.

"I simply lost the habit of consuming spirits," Theresa said, though that answer didn't satisfy even her. "Before I grasped that I was with child, the taste of spirits had begun disagreeing with me. I never recovered it."

Matthew opened the Bible. "Matilda was much the same. Her tastes grew eccentric when she was expecting, which is how I knew Remington and Richard were on the way. She loved the juice of Spanish oranges, unless she was *enceinte*. I do believe this Bible goes back to when Bibles were first printed."

"The Sutcliffe barony is ancient." While Theresa felt like a girl again, reckless, uncertain, and stupid with longing for Matthew's attention. Maybe this was normal, or more normal than the indifference or revulsion she'd felt toward most men from a young age.

"I am not ancient, and neither are you." Matthew gently closed the Bible. "How are you, Theresa?"

He remained halfway across the carpet, but Theresa felt the impact of his focus. The small talk was over, and now she'd learn why he'd sought her out in her brother's library.

"I am well. You?"

He passed his brandy glass under his nose. "I am lonely. I had suspected as much when I surrendered my sons into my brother's keeping, and then spent the next month staring at ledgers any junior clerk could have brought up to date. When I study on the matter, which I've recently had occasion to do, I conclude I have been lonely for most of my adult life."

This loneliness had not made him weak and foolish, though, it had made him honest.

"Loneliness is not mortal illness, Mr. Belmont."

He set the drink down, though he'd yet to taste it. "Do you know how many years I bludgeoned myself with that very platitude? The corollary makes an equally stout cudgel: Hard work never killed a man."

Nor a woman. Theresa had assured herself of this while staying up late to balance Thomas's books, then waking early to start the bread, because the Sutcliffe kitchens could not be relied upon to keep the supply fresh.

"We endure what we must," she said, scrabbling mentally for a change of subject. Instinct warned her Matthew was about to deliver some mortal blow to her carefully constructed peace, and this time, it wouldn't be with a kiss.

He gave the globe a spin. "We endure what we must, assuredly. Do you endure my kisses?"

"Matthew, what are you about?"

"I'm focused on the motive here, Theresa. The crime is not difficult to identify. Two grown people, free of other encumbrances, are attracted to each other, and yet, I sense nothing will be done to explore this precious, happy development. I'm attracted to women occasionally, but my transgression in your case is apparently that I *like* you. I *admire* your devotion to your daughter. I *respect* the effort you've made to reclaim a life free of vice. My high regard for you somehow renders my attentions undesirable. Why?"

He was hurt, though he would not have put that word on his feelings. Men claimed to be unclear, confused, or possibly bewildered, and their heartaches thus were never directly acknowledged.

Matthew Belmont was not most men. He flung his pain at Theresa's feet, a verbal gauntlet. Theresa was hurting too, but she could locate just enough determination to repel Matthew's charge.

"You and your brother nearly lived on your ponies," Theresa said, abandoning the Linden mercantile throne. "He was your great friend and playfellow, and you've entrusted your very children to his good offices now. Growing up, you had parents, a home, a place in life. You have friends now, you are respected. I had nobody and nothing but a succession of tipsy governesses expected to discreetly entertain my grandfather late at night."

"How could you—?"

"I'm not stupid, Matthew. I could not afford to be stupid, not once I understood that my grandfather wished I'd never been born. He told me when I was eight years old that girls are nothing but a drain on a family's finances, and the pretty ones the worst of the lot.

"The only person whose regard ever mattered to me," she went on, "is Thomas. I tolerated my cousins' snide company and their equally unpleasant charity solely because I owed that to my brother if I was to preserve the Sutcliffe legacy for him. Thomas was the last hope the family had of ever coming right, and I cannot afford to sacrifice his regard again."

The old recklessness threatened, the despair that ripped good sense and civility from Theresa's grasp. The young woman who had surrendered to despair had owned a handy set of verbal bludgeons too: *Might as well be hung for a sheep as a lamb. In for a penny, in for a pound. Needs must when the devil drives. You're already ruined, might as well make a thorough job of it.*

Matthew took two steps closer, close enough that Theresa could see the dust creased into the folds of his cravat.

"Your objection is not to my person, then?" he asked.

"I am out of the habit of allowing objectionable men to kiss me."

He almost asked the question Theresa would never answer. *Why would you ever have allowed objectionable men to kiss you?*

She saw the hesitation in his eyes, the compassion, and lost a piece of her heart to him for his reluctance to hurt her.

Why must falling in love with a good man be so painful and pointless?

"I cannot change the past, Matthew, but I will not sacrifice my future and Priscilla's for a passing dalliance. I return to Sutcliffe after the holidays, sooner if Thomas tires of my company. I'm half-hoping he'll offer to keep Priscilla here, and shower her with tutors and ponies. I will ask Thomas for this very boon, in fact, when the moment is right. My duty as a mother requires this of me."

The lump in Theresa's throat prevented further babbling.

Matthew regarded her for a long moment, while Theresa's heart beat a steady ostinato of *"please go/ don't leave me."* She craved his company, but knew well where unbridled craving could leave her.

A clean white handkerchief appeared before her eyes, one devoid of even a monogram.

She clutched at it and barely resisted the temptation to bunch it under her nose.

"You labor under a misapprehension, madam, for which I must take responsibility. A dalliance will not answer." Matthew probably pronounced sentence in those same grave tones.

"I'm glad you agree." Glad and devastated.

"A dalliance will not answer when I seek to pay you my addresses, Theresa Jennings. My most respectful, affectionate addresses."

The idea of leaving Priscilla at Linden, of merely visiting as the child grew into a well-educated, well-dowered, well-received young woman, had cut Theresa to her soul.

And yet, that prospect was also her last prayer each night and first wish every morning. She would manage to part from Priscilla with an encouraging wave, a smile, and a good, stout hug—not a tear to be seen.

Matthew Belmont's sincere, respectful declaration, however, left Theresa crying like a motherless child.

* * *

"The child has returned to the house," Nick said. "You can use whatever foul language you've been holding back."

Beckman kept swatting at the aisle's dirt floor with his rake. "Nicholas, who is responsible for our farm equipment?"

"Archibald Everly manages the home farm, if that's what you're asking."

Beckman was in a lather about something and had been since returning from his errands in the village. He'd also been broody throughout Priscilla's riding lesson—if the girl's ceaseless raptures could be considered a lesson—and now he was raking as if his credit had been permanently cut off at the posting inn.

"Somebody needs to tell Everly not to leave his harrows out in the rain,"

Beck said, backing up to start a new row. He worked methodically, rhythmically, a far healthier and happier man than when he'd come to Linden two years ago.

Beckman wasn't happy now.

"Everly wouldn't leave a harrow out in the rain," Nick said. "The baroness would never permit such poor husbandry. We have sheds for the field equipment, and this time of year, the harrows should all be in them."

Harrows were for working the soil after the ploughs had turned the sod. Their sturdy iron teeth broke up the earth so planting could take place with little additional effort.

"Well, somebody left a harrow out," Beckman said, "right against the stone wall that divides our south pasture from Belmont's woods."

"You took the shortcut."

Beck paused to scratch Tut's chin. "Everybody takes the shortcut."

Not *everybody* took that shortcut. "The people who take the shortcut all have horses fit enough to jump the stone wall." The gentry, in other words, not the yeomanry. "The baron should have a stile built there."

Beckman resumed raking. "Not if some fool leaves a harrow right against the wall where the path comes out of the woods. If the footing hadn't been a tad sloppy, if I hadn't been carrying a bag of nails, if I'd been in a hurry… I'd be shooting my horse, Nick, or you'd be saying last rites for me."

Unease stirred through Nick like a serving of bad ale. "You would have jumped that wall and landed on the harrow?"

"Unless my horse badly over-jumped a familiar obstacle, he would have landed right amidst those iron teeth," Beck said. "From the woods side, you couldn't tell there's anything but the same old pasture on the other side. I wouldn't have noticed, except I used the gate farther along the tree line and still nearly trotted through the tall grass right into the harrow. Where are you going?"

"To goddamn move that harrow. Matthew Belmont uses that path more often than he uses the lanes. Spiker could ride that path in pitch darkness. I use it, the baroness, the baron, the dowager flight of the hunt field, half the damned children on their damned—"

"I moved it," Beck said, starting another row. "I stood it up against the wall, so anybody can see it from either side. A harrow is damned heavy, but I was furious."

Beckman was also damned strong. Two years of mucking, raking, pitching hay, rebuilding pasture walls, riding, hauling water buckets, and generally working his backside off had made him so.

"I'll have a word with Everly before the baron comes home," Nick said. "Harrows don't just appear where they're not supposed to be."

"They don't, but the rain obliterated any tracks that might have told us where the harrow came from."

Beck had looked for tracks, in other words, and found none. Matthew Belmont was the best tracker Nick knew, but even he couldn't read fresh mud.

"You think somebody deliberately left a piece of farm equipment where it would cause injury or death?"

Beck's raking had tidied up the barn aisle, while Nick's emotions were in riot. Linden had been through a stable fire that very summer, seen gates left open at random, and endured a plague of small boys bound for big mischief, but those troubles had come to their apparent conclusion.

Or had they?

"I don't know what to think," Beckman said, leaning on his rake. "People are stupid all the time. I've certainly been stupid, thoughtless, distracted… but between Monday and now, somebody took a piece of farm equipment that won't be missed until spring, used at least a two-horse team to position it where it was bound to cause harm, and left that harrow sitting out in the rain. What do you think, Nick?"

What Nick thought was too foul to share with even his brother.

* * *

As Matthew resisted, barely, the compulsion to take Theresa Jennings in his arms, the analogy of a crime scene again came to mind.

The clues weren't adding up. Theresa Jennings had had motive of a sort to seek her own ruin—boredom, adolescent rebellion, a need for acknowledgement from a resentful patriarch—and with her cousins leading the way, she'd also had plenty of opportunity to become debauched.

Matthew brought her his brandy—Sutcliffe stocked a lovely vintage—and led her by the wrist to the sofa before the fire. That she had allowed him such a presumption gave him heart.

"You will indulge in a medicinal tot, if not to steady your nerves, then to humor my need to feel useful," he said, bracing himself against the mantel rather than take the place beside her.

He badly needed to hold her, but she needed even more to recover her dignity.

The discussion Matthew intended to embark upon had to yield the results of an effective interrogation without making the lady feel like a prisoner in the dock. She'd shackled her happiness in some dungeon or other, and Matthew's aim was to free that captive.

She took a ladylike sip of the brandy and set the glass aside.

"Someday, Theresa Jennings, I hope to see you tipsy."

She touched Matthew's handkerchief to the corner of each eye. "Why?"

Brilliant. The seasoned interrogator was now answering the questions, but at least Theresa's tears had slowed.

"Because you are a woman grown, in full possession of your faculties, and occasional silliness over a dusty bottle of elderberry cordial is your right. I'm not proposing the fall of Rome, mind you, merely some genteel latitude among friends."

"You're proposing marriage," she said, running a finger around the rim of her glass. An elegant finger it was too and, like the rest of her, completely without adornment.

"I'm asking permission to court you. Not the same thing at all."

The very same thing, if a man's intentions were sincere, and Matthew's were.

"You're not supposed to ask *me* for that permission, you should ask Thomas. I can't allow that."

"Who loves you, Theresa Jennings?"

The glass tipped over. Its shape—wide at the bottom, narrower at the lip—was designed to contain the remaining brandy without spilling.

When Theresa righted the glass, her hand trembled minutely. "What a question. Priscilla loves me. Alice is a dear friend."

"Then I will ask Priscilla for permission to pay you my addresses, should you give me leave. I will ask Alice. I will ask the very walls of Sutcliffe Keep, for they at least sheltered you when you were in harm's way. I'll be damned if I'll ask your negligent brother for the time of day where you're concerned."

Matthew hadn't lost his temper since he'd deduced that Matilda was carrying Remington. Even then, he'd been unable to raise his voice to a woman. He was losing his temper now, and he half-hoped Theresa might lose hers as well.

When passion charged to the fore, honesty was sure to follow.

"You are a fraud, Matthew Belmont," she said, taking another tiny sip of the brandy. "You trot about the shire, mild-mannered gentleman at large, but you are fierce and far too noticing. What will it take for you to stop noticing me?"

"You have gone unnoticed for too long, and so have I. If my attentions are distasteful to you, then I will quit the premises and limit our future dealings to civilities. I am a gentleman, and you are a lady, despite all protestations to the contrary."

He was a gentleman having trouble looking anywhere besides Theresa Jennings's mouth, God help him. He stayed by the mantel though, for she must come to him this time.

The choice belonged to the lady, and always would.

"I am a poor relation at best," Theresa said. "I have no funds. Not a competence, not an unspent dowry. I am a charity case, Matthew. The only reason my cousins didn't cast me and Priscilla on the parish was because they feared Thomas would get wind of their behavior."

Well, damn Thomas Jennings all over again. No mature woman with a dependent child should live without means when her family was able to remedy that lack.

"I am angry on your behalf in so many different ways, I can hardly number them," Matthew said. "There you were, likely still a child in many ways, no mother to guide you, no maiden aunt to protect your good name, and off you went on some spree of youthful indignation, determined to gain the notice showered on your cousins and brother. You might have been sent to a finishing school, or to a widow of your grandfather's contemporaries. Your cousins might have been kept away from you. Any number of—"

He'd raised his voice, not to shouting, but certainly above a conversational level. Theresa regarded him as if he'd burst forth into one of Mozart's more extravagant tenor arias.

"Go on," she said, taking another sip of the brandy. "You weren't finished."

Matthew had barely begun to argue his case. "You were doomed," he said, as gently as he could. "Unless you'd developed a religious obsession at the age of eleven, you were doomed."

Theresa patted the place beside her on the sofa. "Were you doomed, Matthew?"

An invitation was as good as an overture. Matthew strolled—he did not run—to the sofa, and eased himself down beside her.

"What can you be alluding to?"

"You married at seventeen. I went wild at about the same age. Were you doomed?"

Back to this, back to answering questions instead of asking them.

"Perhaps I was a bit doomed," Matthew said. "Mama was fading, and Axel buried himself in his botany studies and his music. Papa was drinking rather more than he should have, and I…"

Theresa passed him the glass, which held a final swallow of comfort. "You grew up overnight, except one can't. Marrying Matilda was the act of a boy trying to become an honorable man, and a youth who needed to find a purpose in life while dwelling in a house of grief."

Her insight burned its way into Matthew's belly like the brandy, only far less sweet.

"Christopher turned seventeen earlier this year," Matthew said, setting the empty glass aside rather than hurl it into the fire. "The weather was fine at the time, so the boys and I made it a day for shooting at targets. An Oxford education doesn't include the proper use of weapons, and anything as dangerous as a gun in the hands of a creature as dangerous as a high-spirited young man…"

He trailed off as Theresa scooted closer. "At seventeen, I wanted to feel dangerous too, Matthew. I hadn't realized that."

"I missed every damned thing I aimed at," Matthew said. "The boys accused me of missing on purpose, but there was Christopher, more boy than man, and I kept thinking, *I was seventeen*. Why had my father given his blessing? What was I thinking? I was only seventeen years old…"

The conversation had gone all wrong, for Matthew had failed to secure the lady's leave to embark on a courtship. And yet, Theresa remained right beside him.

When she leaned over to kiss Matthew, her aim was impressively accurate.

CHAPTER TEN

Theresa could not have said why she was kissing Matthew Belmont, could not have formed a coherent sentence, in fact. She needed to kiss him, to be close to the beating heart of a man as decent as he was intelligent as he was desirable.

You were doomed.

Theresa had never dared characterize her situation thus, not in years of introspection and regretting. She was still doomed, but kissing Matthew Belmont savored of salvation, albeit temporary salvation.

He was kissing her back too, with a fervor that gratified as it intrigued.

She drew away an entire half an inch. "This doesn't change anything."

"Damn right it doesn't," he muttered, hoisting Theresa up to straddle his lap as if she weighed no more than a cat. "You make the very point I was—"

Theresa got hold of the hair at his nape and shook him gently. "No more making points. That's for later."

She excelled at holding on to regrets, and this occasion would likely join the heaping pile she towed with her everywhere. Unlike those regrets, however, this one would come with an aura of joy.

Matthew Belmont was still intent on making his almighty points, with his hands as they roamed Theresa's back, with his mouth as his kisses became diabolically gentle, with his—he arched up, his arousal evident.

He desired her.

In Theresa's heart, mind, and body, her sole reaction to his overture was feminine jubilation. Too often, she'd endured a man's attentions, her greatest challenge to hide her boredom. Matthew Belmont desired *her*. He didn't seek a mere stolen moment with a baron's wicked granddaughter.

He wanted *her*, not bragging rights, not oblivion, not fleeting, selfish—

His hand, warm and confident, slid beneath Theresa's skirts. She knew that sensation, of soft fabric sliding over her calves and thighs, warm flesh against her knee, knew the susurration that portended further intimacy.

And for the first time, she delighted in it. "Stop teasing me, Matthew. Kiss me like you mean it."

Theresa had been slobbered over, mauled, and groped, until she'd learned to limit her indiscretions to men who brought some skill and consideration to the matter.

Matthew's kisses tasted of exquisite passion straining at the leash of gentlemanly respect, and Theresa was famished for them.

"Matthew, I want you." The words were out, inelegant and honest. He wanted her too, else Theresa might have had a prayer of maintaining some dignity.

Thomas would come home any day, and then even stolen moments would be beyond her grasp.

"You shall have me," he said, sitting back and letting Theresa's skirts fall. "Though I warn you, madam—"

Theresa went to work on his falls, which required a frustrating amount of concentration. She wanted not one spare moment for common sense to find her, not an extra instant for Matthew's gentlemanly scruples to overcome his passion.

How novel, to want a man for himself, to want only him, and to fear not that he'd dawdle and make maudlin declarations, but that he'd take himself off, relieved to have pulled his horse up before a bad fence.

And yet, this was Thomas's house, where Theresa was a guest. "Matthew, the door is unlocked."

"I locked it," he said, starting on the second side of his falls. "A man seeking permission to pay his addresses cannot risk interruption by stray unicorns."

A man who'd raised three boys would know of such interruptions first hand. All over again, Matthew Belmont stole Theresa's heart.

And her breath. His clothing was undone, and the sight of him, attire in disarray, hair tousled, and arousal clearly evident shocked her in a way drunken viscounts and strutting ducal heirs never could.

Want uncurled low in Theresa's belly, hot and urgent. Ten years fell away, and she was once again a young woman capable of reckless determination. She took him in her hand and knelt up, cursing her stays, his waistcoat, and every other article of clothing in the library, but grateful for them too. At some point, she'd regained the modesty she'd discarded long ago. A surprise that, and a comfort.

"Slowly," Matthew said, wrapping his hand around hers. "I will savor this experience, and please God, you will savor me."

Theresa wanted to sink down over him, to fill herself with him, and let passion obliterate the last of her reasoning powers.

Matthew kissed her, sweetly, tenderly, and between one moment and the next, all of the anxiety went out of her, leaving only the urgency of healthy desire.

She was with *Matthew*, who respected her and admired her. She'd be foolish to hurry through what might be her only experience of making love with a man she respected and admired too.

* * *

A sharp double rap on Christopher Belmont's door meant he could give up trying to stare polite words onto the blank page before him.

"Come in, Uncle."

The door opened, and Uncle Axel sauntered into the room. He and Papa had very different walks, but they both arrived exactly where they intended to be, exactly when they intended to be there.

"You have foregone the weekly billiards debacle in favor of your correspondence," Uncle said, taking the reading chair angled near the fire. "Should I worry about you, Nephew? You're a university scholar and idle dissipation is your due."

Latin, Greek, and self-gratification were the subjects Christopher spent the most time on.

"Richard beat me in the first round," Christopher said, "and if I expect Papa to correspond regularly, then I had best set him a good example."

Uncle whipped out a handkerchief—wrinkled but spotless—and pulled off his spectacles, which made him look more like Papa. They were both tall, lean, blond, and blue-eyed, but Papa cultivated an approachable quality Uncle didn't bother with.

"Your father told you to set him that example," Uncle said. "Just before he hugged you for the last time, swung up on his charger, and rode back up the Belmont House lane, there to ensure the safety of clean laundry and barking dogs throughout his corner of the realm."

Well, yes, Papa had. Fortunately, he hadn't looked back, or he would have seen his oldest son blinking madly at his father's retreating back, again.

"I miss him too," Uncle said, holding a sparkling pair of spectacles up to the firelight. "I see your correspondence has yet to gain your whole attention."

Like Papa, Uncle took his turn serving as magistrate. That ability to ask a question by casual observation was probably a parental talent, though.

"I've written to Papa," Christopher said, passing a single folded and sealed page to his uncle. "I'm trying to write to the Capshaws. It's their week."

Uncle settled back, and the chair creaked. "You've told them your studies progress well, but Virgil is something of a challenge?"

Virgil was a joy. "I used that one last time."

"You've inquired after your aunt's health?"

"One does."

"You've expressed your longing for your aunt's cooking?"

Aunt ran a very indifferent kitchen. Her cook tippled, according to Papa, though this was possibly a euphemism for Aunt's own habits. Christopher had never been quite sure what to make of his aunt.

"One of the reasons I rejoice to leave Sussex is to escape her desserts. They are invariably drowned in some indifferent cordial better used to attract bees."

Uncle folded his handkerchief—though what was the point of folding a wrinkled handkerchief?—and tucked it away, then set his spectacles on the corner of Christopher's desk.

"You don't care for your Aunt and Uncle Capshaw." A conclusion, not a question.

"They aren't so bad." Except, in Axel Belmont's usual fashion, he'd seized upon the inconvenient truth. Papa was more of a diplomat, while Uncle Axel leaned in the direction of the scholar. Blunt, practical, and willing to sacrifice decorum to necessity sooner than Papa would have.

"Agatha Capshaw is a trial," Uncle said, "so bored she has nothing better to do than keep track of her neighbors' peccadilloes when she can rise above her various megrims and chest colds. Emmanuel ignores her, exacerbating the problem, and does little to look after his own interests when he can instead flirt, drink, and strut about, as should be the right of every third son of a baronet."

"Not politics, Uncle, please."

Uncle crossed his legs at the ankle, exactly as Papa did—right ankle over left. "I always wind up in the same place: Reform is preferable to revolution. I don't much care for the Capshaws, and if you asked your papa in a private moment, he'd admit as much, though he'd be oblique about it."

Becoming an adult wasn't the unbridled joy Christopher had envisioned as a child. He stayed up until all hours, true, and drank to excess on occasion, and was making new friends at university, but the southerly end of adulthood also meant an unrelenting preoccupation with females, which frequently destroyed a fellow's dignity.

"I think Papa has met a lady," Christopher said.

Uncle yawned, closed his eyes, and folded his hands on his flat belly. "Do tell."

"He sent along his usual report this week, about dreading his ledgers, Cook decamping to Brighton, the hounds being in fine form for the approaching season, and Maida seldom leaving her post by the library hearth."

"We'll ride in the local meets," Uncle said, twirling a wrist. "Tell me about the lady."

"Papa took the fence at an angle, of course," Christopher said, as Christopher was doing with his own recitation. "He mentioned that his neighbor's niece was visiting at Linden, and the child's equestrian education has been neglected."

Uncle opened his eyes, his gaze on the fire. "Matthew started both of your cousins in the saddle, and like you lot, they both have a fine seat."

The Belmont family was small, but close, and very loyal. Christopher unfolded his father's report and read verbatim.

"With the permission of the girl's mother, which lady accepted my escort to services this week, I will prevail on old Tut's good offices to teach little Priscilla a few basics."

Uncle uncrossed his ankles and recrossed them, left on top, which was Richard's and Rem's preferred arrangement. Christopher didn't cross his legs much of late, because it drew his awareness to parts of his anatomy all too likely to wreck his concentration.

Though sometimes, he'd cross an ankle over a knee.

"You conclude if the girl had a papa," Uncle said, "then Matthew would gain the father's permission for these riding lessons rather than the mother's. The mother is of an age with your father, having a child who can be described as little, but who must be old enough to sit Tut, who is not the smallest of the pensioners. What else do you conclude?"

Experiments and investigations ordered Uncle's botanical world. Christopher suspected they played a part in managing Uncle's loneliness too.

"Papa took the lady to services, though if this woman is Lord Sutcliffe's sister, and biding at Linden, she had no need of Papa's escort. She could have had John Coachman, Nick, Beck, or even Jamie drive her."

"Ergo," Uncle said, "your papa enjoys the woman's company. Does this bother you?"

"A fellow has no privacy with you, Uncle."

"I knocked before coming in here," Uncle said, getting up to poke at the fire. He threw another clump of peat on the flames—Uncle was comparing the effectiveness of various fuels—and took up a lean on the edge of the desk. "Your father has been widowed for some years. That wears on a man."

Uncle had been widowed even longer.

"I don't begrudge Papa the company of a woman whom he esteems."

"You begrudge somebody something, young man." Uncle stood, the desk creaked, and Christopher realized why the letter to the Capshaws was distasteful—why all the letters to them were a chore.

"Last summer, Papa and I went to Trieshock to pick up my new boots. He wanted me to break them in before I came back to school."

"New boots can lame a fellow," Uncle said, nudging the fire screen flush against the bricks with his toe.

Christopher was learning to enjoy the scent of peat, which few people burned in the south. Now, its toasty aroma reminded him of these jaunts out to Candlewood, where for a few days, Oxford scholarship could be forgotten, and a fellow could get a decent meal and sleep in a warm bed.

"My boots fitted me perfectly. There's a boarding house in Trieshock, or that's what I'm supposed to think it is."

Christopher studied his boots, which now fit him better than perfectly. He wasn't blushing yet, but it was a near thing.

"Mrs. Henderson's," Uncle said, stuffing his spectacles in his breast pocket. "A genteel version of a bordello. The gentlemen callers all seem to enter the premises from the rear, mostly after dark, though few stay more than half an hour. The residents socialize only with each other, albeit nothing about their dress or demeanor renders them overtly suspect... but a fellow wonders, how do tenants without visible occupations pay their landlady?"

Christopher was nearly halfway through his three years at Oxford. He knew of young widows who had reputations among the scholars for friendliness. The Oxford taverns boasted barmaids who supplemented their wages with a casual tup, though Papa had cautioned Christopher about the health risks of sampling their wares.

"Uncle has visited that establishment," Christopher said. "I don't know if Papa saw him going in the back door. We were cutting through an alley, and plain as day, I saw Uncle letting himself in Mrs. Henderson's back door."

"One mustn't judge, Christopher. Every marriage is different."

"He had a key," Christopher said, wondering what Uncle Axel's marriage had been like. "In the middle of the afternoon, he let himself into that place with a key. Whenever Emmanuel Capshaw sees me, he asks me—in front of Rem and Richard—if I've come across any *tasty morsels* on the curriculum here. He tells me seasoned game can be the most succulent, but a fresh pullet is always a pleasure. Rem is subject to the same nonsense."

Uncle Axel resumed his seat. He and Papa moved silently, as if quiet could hide the fact that they were both big, fit fellows who could give a good account of themselves in a dark alley.

"Emmanuel is a gentleman by economic privilege," Uncle said, "not in the truest sense of the word. He is, unfortunately, unexceptional in this regard, but he's family, so you wonder where to place him in your social taxonomy."

"I don't like him, I don't respect him, and I'd like to place him in darkest Peru along with Aunt's desserts."

What did Axel Belmont know about his brother's family? Christopher understood the genesis of the marriage between Matthew and Matilda Belmont more clearly than he wanted to, and Uncle Axel was a shrewd fellow.

"And thus you see how difficult the lot of a true gentleman is," Uncle said, every bit the professor coming to the point of the lecture. "If Emmanuel is a disgrace, he's a petty disgrace whose private challenges we cannot assess. He means nobody any harm, provided his privileges and funds accrue to him without any effort on his part. My approach to such a fellow is to extend him courtesy at all times and tolerance for his minor transgressions."

"Do you respect him?"

Uncle stood to bring a branch of candles from the mantel to the desk, which nearly doubled the light falling on Christopher's blank page.

"I respect snakes, my boy, and poisons, and matchmaking mamas, and thorny roses. I don't think you're confused about who is worthy of your respect."

"Good point. You don't trust him, then."

"I don't enjoy his company, but I trust him to ever be himself. He's asked me the same questions he's asked you, about pullets and morsels. Emmanuel spent all of one year at university, he made no Grand Tour, and like your father, he married young, though in his case economic expedience led the way to the altar. It's as if, having been denied a few years to drink, carouse, and spout Latin, he can't escape a fascination with those pursuits in others."

Christopher took up his white quill pen and brushed it over the end of his nose. "If my brothers have sons, I won't be that sort of uncle." Christopher would be the sort of uncle Axel Belmont was, a cross between a papa, brother, mentor, conscience, stern tutor, and guardian angel.

"What shall you write?" Uncle asked, refolding the extra blanket at the foot of the bed.

"Dear Aunt and Uncle Capshaw, I have come upon the most riveting translation of Caesar's Gallic letters. The author has a grasp of the realities of the campaign, and a sensitivity to the perspective of the native Gaul that leaves all other translations begging...."

Uncle scrubbed his knuckles over Christopher's crown. "A paragraph or two of that should suffice handily and allow you to join the next round of billiards. I don't intend that we allow your papa to spend his holidays alone, you know."

Christopher hadn't figured out how to raise this topic. "He's alone in that big house, with nothing to do but teach some little girl how to stay awake on old Tut."

Uncle leveled a look at Christopher that blended amusement with warning. "He's likely up to more than that, my boy, and we will not judge him for it."

"No, we won't," Christopher said, which left the dilemma of what, exactly, to pass along to Rem and Richard. "But we'll jaunt down to Sussex and make the acquaintance of this little Priscilla person, and her mother."

"Perhaps we'll do just that."

Uncle was out the door before Christopher had even uncapped the ink.

* * *

Complications loomed, not the least of which was Theresa Jennings's mulishness concerning her brother's regard for her. Matthew would get to the bottom of that familial felony later, when he could once again think.

For the present moment, he was too busy rejoicing.

Theresa wore no drawers, and thus when she gave up her grasp of Matthew's breeding organs, eager flesh met happy flesh, and confirmed that the lady was interested in the proceedings.

She had kissed *him* this time, after all, and she was kissing him again. Her hands drifted over his features, her touch both curious and delicate. His jaw, his brow, his eyebrows, his hair… she explored Matthew with a thoroughness that brought him awareness of his own dimensions and features.

Since Matilda's death, he'd not been celibate. A discreet liaison at the occasional house party, an evening with a friendly widow when passing through London… forgettable and vaguely sad, all of them.

Matthew would never forget the sense of homecoming he felt when Theresa eased her weight onto him, and brushed her thumbs over his lips.

"Madam, what are you about?"

"I'm untying your cravat." She *had* untied it, in fact, and piled it next to the empty brandy glass. "Now I'm unbuttoning your shirt. Soon, I'll be moaning in your ear."

"And I in yours. Very soon." Not quite yet, though. Matthew had found the woman in whom protectiveness, respect, desire, liking—all the fine, lovely emotions he could feel for a woman—came home.

"You have the most complicated, masculine, attractive scent," Theresa said, nuzzling his neck. "Have you ever considered wearing a gold ring in one ear?"

"For you, I'd consider wearing a gold dressing ring, and aught else. Damn your blasted corset, madam."

Her sigh breezed across his throat, her sex glossed over his cock. "I like that you're swearing. I'll regret this entire—"

Matthew kissed her to silence, and then simply kissed her for the pleasure of feeling her tongue move in the same languorous rhythm as her hips.

"No regrets, Theresa. I like that I needn't dissemble with you," he said. "I needn't pretend I'm some callow swain unacquainted with honest desire. Make your demands of me, and I will meet them."

Thank God, she wasn't a blushing virgin who'd take years to develop the confidence to state her intimate preferences.

She pressed her forehead to his and her hands fell away. "You like that I'm not chaste?"

"You are not *ignorant*. You are wise, lovely, and for the present moment, mine, as I am yours."

Theresa did the honors, as Matthew had hoped she would. She took him in her hand and showed him where she needed him to be.

"Move," Matthew whispered, flexing his hips slowly. "Please, love. Move."

The sensations were lush and delightful. Heat, desire, the greatest possible physical closeness. A slow, lovely, blissful joining, gilded with yearning and anticipation of greater pleasure.

As Matthew wrapped Theresa close and found a rhythm with her, he buried his lips against her throat, lest he burden her with other intimacies she would not welcome.

He was staring at the male equivalent of spinsterhood, his children had all left home, and his dreams—few though they were—had apparently left with them. Life had stretched before him, an endless manicured landscape of boring meals with boring in-laws, stolen laundry, and interminable assemblies.

With the prospect of Theresa Jennings at his side, the entire vista changed into beautiful, untamed wilderness. He'd been married, raised children, and had his pick of the local beauties should he wish to remarry, but his heart had remained innocent of love shared with a woman who was wholly his to love in return.

Theresa's breathing changed and her movements became more focused. She shifted the angle of their joining, and Matthew's self-control suffered a bad moment. His rhythm faltered, and she went still.

"Matthew? Should we stop?" Her question held all manner of worries and topics they ought to have discussed.

He brushed her hair back from her brow. "I will not spend, Theresa. Next time, I'll use a sheath."

"There can't be a next—"

Matthew parried that thrust with a slow, hard, roll of his hips. "Take your pleasure of me, Theresa. I give you my word, we'll have as many rousing arguments as you please, *later*."

The intermission steadied him, which was fortunate, for Theresa Jennings was magnificent in her passion. She went about satisfaction with a silent vigor that ended in only one soft, sighing exhalation after she'd beaten Matthew's self-restraint to flinders, and done wonders for his self-esteem.

Next time, and all the times after that, they'd use a sheath, unless and until they were married, and Theresa was comfortable with the idea of having another child.

When she was drowsing on his shoulder, two reprises of bliss later, Matthew reached for the handkerchief crumpled next to the empty brandy glass.

"Stay with me," he murmured as he gently unjoined them. "Stay right where you are."

Theresa did better than that. She kissed him witless as he brought himself off, then snuggled in close when he'd tossed the handkerchief in the direction of the table. Not nearly the same as having consummated the act as a couple, but intimacy upon intimacy nonetheless.

The fire popped and crackled, Theresa dozed in Matthew's arms, and as pleasure ebbed to mellow satisfaction, regret stole up on Matthew from within.

He and Matilda had attempted marital intimacies, but they'd been young, their situation burdened by her past, and that path had led nowhere happy. He'd been doomed, as Theresa had suggested. He grieved for that young man in a way he hadn't allowed himself to previously—wholly and passionately.

He wasn't doomed now, though. For the first time in his life, Matthew Belmont was in love. He raised Theresa's hand to his lips and kissed her knuckles.

Against his shoulder, she stirred, then kissed the back of his hand. She raised beautiful, sleepy eyes to his, and Matthew braced himself to hear that his addresses would be welcome.

They'd gone about the courting business a bit backward, but the critical elements would all be addressed eventually.

"Shall we have one of those rousing arguments now?" she asked, smoothing her free hand over Matthew's hair. "Thomas will be home any day, and I'm sorry, Matthew. I did not mean for this to happen. You must not think I've given you leave to pay me your addresses."

She was to lead him on the hunt of his life, then. Fortunately, he was a mature fellow, fit, determined, and highly skilled at pursuing an elusive quarry.

"Tell yourself that if you must, my love, but without uttering a word, you've given me all the permission I need. Prepare to be courted."

CHAPTER ELEVEN

"He has no scruples," Theresa wailed, a mischaracterization worthy of Priscilla's fictional excesses. "Alice, what am I do to with a man who has no scruples?"

Alice put her cards face down on the table. "You're accusing Matthew Belmont, the king's man, of having no scruples? The fellow who's patiently teaching Priscilla to keep her heels down as she bounces around the riding arena again and again? The man who has escorted you to services twice and introduced you to half the gentry in the shire? That unscrupulous Matthew Belmont?"

Alice didn't list Matthew's worst transgression, which was to treat Theresa with unfailing courtesy, genial warmth, and occasional dashes of affection. Since their encounter in the library the previous week, he'd comported himself like a proper and entirely self-restrained suitor.

Damn him for that most of all. Theresa's hand of cards was full of sixes and sevens, appropriately.

"He's resorted to puppies, Alice. What man of honor involves puppies in a flirtation?" Not a courtship, never that, despite Matthew's determination.

"A shrewd man of honor." Alice tugged Theresa's cards from her hand. "Shall I go with you? I know how to sit a horse, though it has been a long, long time."

The offer was brave. Alice never even went to the stable if she could avoid it. She claimed horses made her sneeze, though Theresa suspected they brought to mind her riding accident.

"I can withstand a few wiggling puppies," Theresa said, hoping it was true. "Priscilla wheedling for a dog of her own will be another matter altogether."

Withstanding Matthew's mannerly company was beyond her. When Thomas came home, Theresa might be sent packing back to Sutcliffe Keep, but until then, she'd take what time with Matthew she could have.

Alice shuffled the deck, the sound stropping against Theresa's nerves.

"If we're to return to Sutcliffe after the holidays, Theresa, then a puppy might be a good idea. Puppies grow into nice, big dogs with nice, big teeth. I'm rather fond of dogs, myself."

Alice was fond of a life free of any and all risk. When had Theresa adopted the same outlook?

"Matthew has offered to teach me to shoot. Thomas probably won't approve." The list of items Thomas would not approve was growing long—longer, rather.

"I'm very sure the baroness is skilled with firearms," Alice said, cutting the deck and shuffling again. "To hear the Linden housekeeper tell it, her ladyship all but ran this estate. Rabid animals, foundered horses, feral dogs who plague henhouses—they all require that somebody be handy with a gun."

Theresa rose from the card table. She ought to change into her habit, for Matthew was soon to escort her and Priscilla to visit with the latest batch of puppies to grace his kennel.

Puppies, for God's sake. She cracked a window, because the library was nearly stuffy, and all too soon she'd be shut up at Sutcliffe for months breathing coal fumes and reading, reading, embroidering, and reading...

And missing Matthew.

"Thomas seems to love his new wife very much," Theresa observed. Out in the garden, the chrysanthemums alone were still in good form. Everything else had surrendered to the march of cold nights and crisp days. Today, however, a Martinmas summer was upon them.

Theresa knew better than to trust warm weather this late in the season. They'd wake up to sleet, or worse.

"Does your brother's affection for his wife bother you?" Alice asked.

Matthew Belmont bothered Theresa, and yet, she longed to see him trotting up the drive on his handsome grey mare.

"I love Loris, or I love what I know of her. She welcomed me as if I were family and she's very patient with Priscilla."

"For mercy's sake, you *are* family." Alice rose and put the cards on the same shelf that held the chess set, the dueling pistols, and the cribbage board. "Go change. I'll entertain your favorite scoundrel should he arrive ten minutes early."

As it happened, Matthew was on time to the minute, according to the library clock. Priscilla was on her best behavior, the prospect of visiting puppies too delightful to risk jeopardizing the outing with the slightest infraction against good manners.

The puppies were puppies—silky soft, wiggly, warm, lovely little balls of canine curiosity.

Matthew Belmont with the puppies… Theresa had known her defenses would crumble, but her well-constructed battlements had fallen straight into a sea of tender sentiments.

"The mama's name is Orbit," Matthew said, passing Priscilla a puppy. "She likes to circle the pack in her quest to find the scent, and she's often the first to sniff old Reynard out."

"You could name the puppies after the planets," Priscilla suggested. "This one could be Mercury."

Mercury commenced licking Priscilla's chin, which caused a prodigious outburst of giggling.

"He likes you," Matthew said, stroking a gloved hand over the pup's head. The little hound, predictably, became fascinated with Matthew's glove, while the mama dog looked on, tail thumping gently against the whelping box.

Orbit's tail had been doing that since she'd caught sight of Matthew.

The kennel was unlike the few Theresa had visited previously, in that the air was fresh and the light abundant. Every pen connected to a lengthy run, and a common area joined several runs apiece beyond that.

"Would you like to help my shepherd school one of the young collies?" Matthew asked.

"Can Mercury come with me?" Priscilla asked.

"Mercury is a little too young to leave his family," Matthew said. "Perhaps another time. Mr. Riley is working with a promising youngster today by the name of Mortimer. He's almost as friendly as Mercury."

Priscilla set Mercury down next to his mama. "Is Mr. Riley friendly? You said Tut likes it best when I ask nicely, and dogs like us to be on our manners too, don't you think?"

Matthew and Priscilla left the kennel, while Theresa lingered for a moment, kneeling beside the whelping box to pat Orbit.

"Look after your little ones," she told the hound. "They are very dear and only yours for a short time. Then you'll be back among your pack, chasing after some feckless fox."

The hound spared Theresa a limpid gaze, then went back to nuzzling the puppy, who was squirming his way in the direction of sustenance.

"I'd rather stay with you," Theresa went on, "than subject myself to more of Matthew and Priscilla's good cheer. Matthew talks to Priscilla, he doesn't lecture her or tease her. I doubt I'll be back."

Tears threatened for no discernible reason. "I hate to cry. I thought I'd lost the knack, then I come to Linden, and I'm a watering pot."

"You are entitled to your tears," Matthew said, "though you are also entitled to the comfort of my embrace when you weep."

"You shouldn't sneak up on a pair of mothers having a nice chat," Theresa said, rising. "Though I can hardly imagine how Orbit will part with six children at once. Perhaps exhaustion will aid with the separation."

Matthew slipped his arms around Theresa's waist. She didn't return his embrace, but simply stood in the circle of his embrace, her forehead resting against his shoulder.

"Pride helps you let them go," he said. "Not the arrogant sort that refuses to acknowledge pain, but the pride you take in your offspring, to see them going forth, taking their places in a greater world. You've prepared them as best you can, you're there to catch them if they fall, and they'll make their way to destinations you could not have foreseen, all with their own style."

Theresa eased away. "A fine theory, Mr. Belmont."

He picked up another puppy who'd been about to spill out of the box and placed it next to Mercury.

"When will you stop punishing yourself for running amok in your youth?"

"I've been thinking about that." Theresa had also been thinking about Matthew Belmont, and about Priscilla. "One doesn't wake up one morning and decide the past no longer matters."

Matthew looked away, to the puppies snuggling so contentedly beside their mother. She was a handsome, sizeable hound, and apparently a conscientious parent.

"One doesn't," he said. "Though one can learn from the past and move on from it. Am I given any credit for not offering Priscilla a puppy?"

An attempt to change the subject. Theresa was not inclined to let him off that easily.

"I asked my grandfather for a puppy. I would have been younger than Priscilla is now, and Thomas would have adored having something of his own. I knew the twins would inherit all of Sutcliffe one day, and I wanted Thomas to have something none of his elders could claim. The Sutcliffe kennels were extensive, and surely, I thought, Grandpapa could spare a single small hound?"

Had Matthew tried to put his arms around her then, she might have smacked him.

"Your grandfather denied your request."

"He regularly had the runts drowned, said he was sparing them a worse end among the pack. He wouldn't even spare me a runt to give to my brother."

Orbit rose, circled, and re-established herself among her offspring, but she spared a moment to lick Matthew's glove first.

Matthew patted the hound. "So now you're steeling yourself to offer that same brother your only begotten daughter. Why would you cast your daughter into the hands of a man who neither knows her nor loves her, when an upbringing under similar circumstances still has the power to hurt you?"

No wonder he was the magistrate, with insight like that. The battle-readiness coursing through Theresa confirmed that Matthew's questions deserved answers.

"Might I suggest," Matthew went on, "that if we're to have a rousing disagreement, which I am more than willing to have, that we do so outside the hearing of the hounds?"

He offered Orbit a final caress to her ears, then gestured toward the open door to the kennel.

Wise of him, not to expect Theresa to take his arm.

"You sent your boys to your brother," Theresa said. His nearly grown boys, all together or nearly so.

"Remington went up to university this year, Christopher began his studies last year. My brother's estate is close to Oxford, and his two boys have excellent tutors, among whom their father numbers. Richard and I were often cross with each other, and just because I—he was better off among his brothers and cousins. Your brother can offer Priscilla advantages. I do take your point."

Matthew had, in fact, taken Theresa's heart.

"Do you know why I'm attracted to you?" she asked as they emerged into the pleasant sunshine.

"Allow me a moment, madam, to rejoice in the admission itself. You are *attracted* to me. I'm most comfortable among my hounds and horses, my latest accomplishment was identifying which small boy stole Mrs. Magillacuddy's only lace-trimmed petticoat to use as a sail on his raft, and I can eat more than even Nicholas Haddonfield and still have room for dessert. For some reason, you are attracted to me. I own I am pleased to hear it."

He was shy too, but Theresa kept that item off the present list.

"You are honest," she said instead, "with yourself, with others, with me, and yet, you are also kind. I have never met a man so lacking in insecurities. I don't know what to do with you, and when you say things to me that Alice has hinted at for years, I can hear them. I don't want to hear them, but I listen to you because you listen to me. I am so thoroughly vexed with you and utterly besotted—"

He stepped closer, though out in the pasture, Priscilla and a tall young man were working with a black and white collie, and over in the stable yard, Spiker was mending harness.

"Vexed and besotted," Matthew said. "An apt description of my own state, though I'm mostly vexed on your behalf. I cannot abide injustice, and your situation provokes me to cursing."

Spiker gathered up his harness and took it into the stable.

"I love it when you curse," Theresa said. "I love that we can have a difference of opinion and yet remain in charity with each other."

She loved Matthew Belmont, which was both glorious and sad. Thomas would never bless such a union, and Matthew's reputation would suffer if they married, and yet, to love, to trust, to give her heart into another's keeping…

Had these gifts befallen her as a younger woman, then much misery could have been averted.

"I am not in charity with you," Matthew said, standing nose to nose with Theresa. "I am in love with you. How love and a renewed propensity for foul language relate, I cannot say. If you don't decamp for the pasture this instant, I will soon be kissing you, though I cannot explain how that will aid matters either."

He was magnificent when he was in a temper—or in love.

Theresa slid a hand around Matthew's lean waist. "Enough saying and explaining. Allow me a moment to savor your declaration, and to kiss you for it."

She was just about to press her lips to his, intent on expressing all the warm, wild, wonderful feelings that defied words, when the report of a gun exploded at close range.

*　*　*

"Uncle says we're to return to Belmont House for the Christmas holidays," Christopher said. "Be good to see home again."

"Be good to have some of Mrs. Dellingham's plum pudding," Remington replied. Because Uncle Axel had influence at the college, Christopher and Rem shared a room. Richard was at Candlewick, studying like a fiend so he could start university earlier than most, and all five cousins could matriculate together for one year.

"Mrs. D is still in Brighton," Christopher said, setting aside old Virgil. "I worry that Papa is starving."

Rem had inherited Papa's gift for sketching, or at least learned it from him. He was sketching a still life now, a boot, a riding crop, an old-fashioned hunting horn, and a long whip, such as the whippers-in used to keep an unruly pack together.

"Papa was starving before we came up here. Tell me about Priscilla's mama. Papa always writes the good stuff to you, and you never share it because you're an idiot."

Christopher kicked Rem's feet off the corner of the table that doubled as a desk, chair, clothes press, dining table, and work bench.

"Have some respect for your elders, Rem. Papa wasn't starving."

Rem blew on his sketching paper and brushed graceful fingers over the image taking shape.

"Who is Papa's best friend?" Rem asked, pencil resuming its steady scratching. "Nick Haddonfield is quitting his post at Linden if he hasn't already. Beckman barely speaks unless it's to argue with his brother. The baron is new to the neighborhood and enthralled with his new baroness. The vicar has ten children and doesn't ride to hounds to speak of. Uncle Emmanuel rides to hounds and tells the same tiresome jokes on every outing. Papa was starving."

"Everybody loves Papa," Christopher said, though Rem, as usual, had a valid point. Richard was all storms and brilliant sunshine. His laughter was contagious, his bleak moods—much in evidence of late—could suffocate the entire shire. His emotions fluctuated more rapidly than Scottish weather in spring. Richard took after Mama, of that Christopher was certain.

Rem was more like Papa. A quiet, steady fellow who missed nothing and was not to be underestimated.

"Everybody loves Papa," Rem said, "but Papa loves only his family, and we're here and he's there. Nick writes that Papa has taken Miss Jennings to church twice now, and that Miss Priscilla and Tut are getting on famously."

"You rode Tut, before Richard stole him," Christopher said. Rem had stolen Tut from Christopher first, of course, stealing being more dashing than simply outgrowing one's pony. "Nick is spying for you?"

"Spying for us, and I didn't even have to ask it of him. Richard doesn't want to go home for Christmas. He's afraid Papa won't let him come back to Oxfordshire with us."

"Richard is an ass. Papa wouldn't do that, not if he's intent on courting Miss Jennings."

Richard had been a merry boy, but at his present age, he was no recommendation for the Belmont menfolk generally. Of the three brothers, he alone seemed to share Papa's knack for pondering a conundrum until a solution emerged. Lately, Richard had been a puzzle, with his endless dark moods and ferocious determination to arrive at university knowing more than the professors.

"*Is* Papa courting the lady?" Rem asked, holding his sketch at arm's length. "You have noticed the irregularity of her situation, haven't you?"

"You've drawn Belmont House all the while you've stared at that pile of nonsense," Christopher observed. "You want to go home for Christmas."

So did Christopher, and in fact, he wanted to become his father's steward. Belmont House wasn't entailed, and while Richard had a head for figures, Christopher longed to once again ride Belmont's metes and bounds with Papa and count lambs as an excuse for a morning hack.

All three of them were Papa's son in some regard, a comfort and an irony.

Rem flipped over a new sheet and once again propped his feet on a corner of the table. Big feet, and sporting a pair of Christopher's clean stockings.

"Now I know why men have their every handkerchief and cravat monogrammed," Christopher said. "It's so their thieving younger brothers can't steal them permanently."

"You stole mine first," Rem said. "Miss Jennings isn't married, and she has a daughter. Do you suppose Papa's intentions are honorable, or will he follow Uncle Emmanuel's dubious example?"

The question was not as casual as Rem wanted Christopher to think it was.

"Papa could never be like Uncle Emmanuel, not in that sense. Richard would kill him for one thing. Baby Brother is at that serious age, when honor is another term for having a poker up one's arse. Richard reads too much and doesn't sing enough."

"Maybe the lady isn't interested in marriage. Thank the gracious Deity, such women exist."

And all of them, from the friendlier tavern maids, to the laundresses, to the mamas who came to visit their sons at school, were drawn to Rem's dark-eyed good looks. Richard had been appalled when he'd seen Rem's appeal to the ladies, while Christopher was envious. All three brothers were brown-haired and brown-eyed, for pity's sake, but Rem had *something*, a diffident charm, and the ladies adored him.

"Every woman is supposed to be interested in marriage," Christopher said. "I can't say it made Mama very happy, though."

As the oldest, he'd known their mother the best, though he suspected his brothers missed her more. Mama had occasionally been difficult, something Richard refused to recall, and Rem never mentioned.

"Mama and Papa both muddled on as best they could," Rem said, "which suggests Miss Jennings might not be in contention for step-mama honors. Richard will not be best pleased to find Papa preoccupied with the lady at Yuletide. Between Papa's new love affair, Aunt Agatha's tippling, and Uncle Emmanuel's dirty jokes, we should have interesting holidays."

Christopher had no wise, elder-brother rejoinder to make to that lowering observation, so he grabbed the nearest pillow and brought it down on Rem's handsome head.

* * *

The gunshot didn't bother Matthew half so much as Spiker's cursing. At Matthew's order, guns were fired regularly in the vicinity of the stable and the kennels, so neither horses nor hounds would be afraid of gunfire.

But Spiker's language, hurling invective in both English and a language Matthew couldn't name, wasn't appropriate for the ears of a lady or a child.

"Go to Priscilla," Matthew said, stealing a quick kiss on the lips from Theresa. "Spiker's apparently had a mishap."

Theresa kissed him back and strode off. Her idea of a difference of opinion was, without doubt, the most agreeable form of argument Matthew had encountered. He appreciated her retreating form for the space of a breath, then jogged around to the back of the stable, from whence came Spiker's diatribe.

"What happened?" Matthew asked, though the evidence was plain enough. The fingers of Spiker's right hand were a bloody mess, and Matthew's hunting pistol lay in the dirt, the mechanism mangled and covered in black powder.

"Rubbishing, bedamned worthless piece of shite misfired on me," Spiker said, shaking his hand. "By the Virgin's balls, I just cleaned it last week too."

"Let your hand bleed for a moment," Matthew said, taking Spiker by the wrist and examining the injury. Thank God, it was more mess than anything else. "You still have all your fingers, though why would you have the gun out now when you know my guests include a child?"

Spiker snatched his hand back and shook his bloody fingers, scattering drops of blood about the stable yard. He was a former jockey, short and wiry, with large hands.

"As long as I can hold a pint or a pair of reins, I'll manage, Squire. I saw that vixen who's dug the covert by the stream. Saucy little thing was peeking out at me from the bushes past the gate. I meant to warn her off, just in case she was thinking of snacking on a stray puppy. She'll spend half the winter laughing at me, doubtless."

Spiker's hand had to hurt like blazes. "She has a litter of kits, and I don't blame her for scouting the possibilities. I can't see that you need any stitches, but the wound should be cleaned and bound."

In Matthew's household, Cook tended to minor injuries, but Spiker's hand was still bleeding, and the injury was more than minor. Then too, Cook was in Brighton, where one of her countless nieces, cousins, nieces-in-law, passing friends, or possibly even a nephew, was having yet another baby.

"Come along, and I'll tend to you," Matthew said, picking up the gun by the barrel. "Don't touch the wound and come up to the—Miss Jennings, greetings. No cause for alarm, merely a mishap."

Some people fainted at the sight of blood. Theresa was apparently not among them.

"I can help," she said. "At Sutcliffe, we're seven miles from the nearest market town or surgeon, and one learns to make do. Where are your medicinals, Mr. Belmont? We'll need clean linen too, for in no case should Mr. Spiker's fingers be wrapped together. As the flesh heals—"

"I'll thank you kindly for your assistance, missus," Spiker said, swiping off his cap with his uninjured hand. "Squire, if you'd lead the way, my hand is paining me something awful."

Theresa merely looked amused, bless her.

"Stop trying to flirt with Miss Jennings, or loss of your position will pain you more." Matthew offered Theresa his arm and led the way to the Belmont House herbal.

While he lounged in the doorway, and Spiker trotted out his best Sunday manners, Theresa made a thorough and skilled job of cleaning the wound.

"Do not be pigheaded about this," she said, tying the last of the linen strips around Spiker's palm. "The wound must be kept clean to heal properly, or you could lose your hand, your arm, or your life. Use the sling, have the binding changed every day, and be patient. It's a nasty injury, and you'll want some laudanum to help you sleep for the next night or two. If you suspect infection, send for me immediately."

"Now you'll have him shooting at his own toes," Matthew said. "Spiker, you're not to lift a hand for the next three days, except at the tavern before your favorite pint. Obey Miss Jennings's instructions or answer to me."

"I like it better when she scolds me, Squire," Spiker said, snatching his cap off the table and strutting away.

"Spiker, a moment please," Matthew said.

His stable master paused, cap in hand, doubtless prepared to memorize every word Matthew exchanged with Theresa.

"Miss Jennings," Matthew said, "I'll have the horses saddled and see you and Priscilla home now, if you like." Matthew did not *like*. Visions of a lazy afternoon flirting with Theresa and sipping lemonade while Priscilla visited ponies had exploded along with Matthew's pistol.

"I'll be down to the stable in a moment," Theresa said. "Let me tidy up here."

"Then I'll see to collecting Priscilla and let her name a few more puppies."

Theresa had kissed him in the stable yard, or kissed him back, and if she wanted to kiss him now, right in front of Spiker, Matthew would bear up under the indignity with excellent good cheer.

"You'll not offer her a puppy, Matthew, promise me."

"No puppies. They really are too young to leave their mother." Priscilla was too.

"Be off with you, then."

Spiker smirked at his cap, while Matthew dutifully accompanied him across the back terrace.

"The first formal meet is next week," Matthew said, "and I always carry that pistol with me in the hunt field."

"If you'd asked me, I would have said that was a trusty little gun and a handsome piece too. All guns get old, though, no matter how carefully you clean and store them."

Matthew's steps slowed, though Spiker kept up easily. "That gun was less than five years old, Spiker, and you are conscientious about the maintenance of the sporting pieces. I'm the only person who uses it, typically."

Spiker scrubbed his chin with his bandaged hand, then winced. "You might well have used it next week, checking the sight, doing some target shooting, or signaling the start of the hunt breakfast. I don't like this, Squire."

"I don't like that you nearly got your hand blown off." Even more than Matthew didn't like giving up his afternoon with Theresa.

"The hand will heal," Spiker said, "slowly, I hope. For that gun to misfire isn't right, though. Has a stink about it, like somebody leaving a damned harrow smack in the middle of your bridle path."

Matthew stopped in the garden, beside a bed of roses already trimmed down to stubby canes of thorns.

"What damned harrow left smack in the middle of which bridle path, Spiker?"

By the time the stable master's explanation was complete, Matthew was cursing too, in English, French, and, because his sons were not on the property, Latin as well.

CHAPTER TWELVE

"Might I say, Miss Jennings, that you make a very fetching addition to the gathering? Very fetching, indeed. That shade of blue becomes your charms most agreeably."

The weather was too crisp for flies to be a bother, but Emmanuel Capshaw annoyed Theresa more than any winged pest could have. She'd let Matthew talk her into joining the hunt party, and for the first two runs, she'd enjoyed herself tremendously. Then Mr. Capshaw had appeared at her side, and the day had deteriorated apace.

"Thank you, Mr. Capshaw, but I've borrowed this ensemble from the baroness. I'll pass along your compliments to her."

Would that Loris was on hand to deflect Mr. Capshaw's attention.

He offered Theresa an exaggerated wink and a wiggle of his eyebrows. "I daresay, she would not do the habit half as much credit."

Matthew was serving as master of fox hounds and had thus remained ahead of the first flight, managing the pack and directing the hunt staff. Theresa had enjoyed the company of the other ladies and the older squires in the second flight, where socializing often took precedence over sport.

"Miss Jennings, may I ride in with you and Mr. Capshaw?" Beckman Haddonfield asked from the back of a lovely bay gelding.

"Of course," Theresa said, and thank the angels, Beckman's presence put a stop to Mr. Capshaw's most effusive overtures.

Emmanuel Capshaw was at that point in life where he'd not accepted that his youthful good looks—along with a quantity of his graying brown hair—had departed. The flesh beneath his eyes tended to pouches. The last button of his hunt coat strained against a slight belly, his equestrian skills were somewhat wanting, and despite having undergone no significant exertion in the last fifteen minutes, his complexion was ruddy.

Perhaps the frequency with which he drank from his hunting flask had something to do with his heightened color.

"Haddonfield, good day," Mr. Capshaw said. "A pity the sport wasn't more exciting this morning, wouldn't you agree?"

"If you rode with us more often," Beckman replied, "you'd find not a member of this hunt is truly interested in ending Reynard's existence, Mr. Capshaw. We've gone multiple seasons without a kill, and yet, half the shire shows up to the meets when the weather's fair. A good gallop after a pack in full cry, a good gossip over the hunt breakfast, and we're happy."

"Damned odd, if you ask me," Capshaw retorted. "If I were master here, the chickens would be much safer, I can tell you that."

"We build sturdy coops," Beckman said, "and stout fences. That seems to work quite well. Miss Jennings, did you enjoy yourself?"

"Very much." At least until Mr. Capshaw had attached himself to her side. "I'd forgotten what tearing across the fields and leaping the ditches can do for one's spirits, particularly with a solid fellow like Evan under saddle."

The gelding enjoyed hunting, as some horses did. On the lanes, he plodded. Aim him across an open field or show him an obstacle, and he became a different fellow altogether.

"Mr. Belmont is a first-rate master," Beckman said. "He knows the terrain in every corner of the fixture, and can read signs like you read your Bible. I never enjoyed riding to hounds until I rode with him."

This panegyric was offered with a straight face, and from Beckman, who never seemed to speak unless words were necessary.

Oh dear. Matthew's courtship campaign had acquired foot soldiers.

"Hardly worth getting in the saddle," Capshaw countered, gesturing with his flask, "if you're not riding for blood sport. What's the point? I was in on my first kill practically before I was breeched. Wore the blood proudly for the rest of the day too."

The party turned up the lane to Belmont House on that unappetizing note, and not a moment too soon for Theresa's patience. No wonder Matthew dreaded Sunday dinners at the Capshaws'.

"Miss Jennings, may I assist you to dismount?" Mr. Capshaw asked, heaving himself off his horse.

"No need, thank you. I'm quite capable of reaching the ground on my own."

Beckman hovered, though Theresa knew he was expected to help deal with the guest horses lent from the Belmont stable.

She unhooked her knee from the horn, gathered her skirts, and slipped off the horse before Capshaw could interfere. Nonetheless, for the next half hour, he persisted in trailing her about the buffet, then to the punchbowl, and then to a bench a few yards from the larger tables.

Best get it over with. "Mr. Capshaw, won't you join me?"

"My pleasure, Miss Jennings." Predictably, he sat too close for propriety. "Your quarry will soon learn of your past," he murmured, breathing fumes in her ear. He'd yet to eat anything, and Theresa was fairly certain he'd started on a second flask.

She took a nibble of a succulent pear. "I beg your pardon?"

Capshaw's gaze swept over her in a manner not remotely gentlemanly.

"I refer to Matthew. He buries himself here in the provinces, so the reputation of the Sutcliffe Strumpet wouldn't be known to him. I, on the other hand, have circulated in the wider world and recall well the tales I heard even ten years ago. You'd best leave the field before your past catches up with you."

The pear was perfect—juicy, sweet, crisp, and flavored with a hint of spice. All around Theresa, people were laughing and talking, just another social gathering among the good, decent folk of a good, decent parish on a beautiful autumn day.

She'd been part of the gathering too, albeit a quiet, somewhat self-conscious part.

And that had felt... like one of the most precious gifts Matthew could have given her. Not simply a pleasant outing among friendly people, but the hope that someday she might fit in with such a group.

Emmanuel Capshaw was trying to tear that hope to bits, much as the pack descended on the fox after chasing it to exhaustion by virtue of forty-to-one odds, predator against prey.

Theresa wasn't stealing any chickens that she deserved such treatment. "Mr. Capshaw, if all you have to offer by way of conversation is ten-year-old gossip, then I will ask you to inflict your company on somebody else."

He leaned closer, his breath reeking of gin. "You needn't put on airs, missy. I'll happily compensate you for lost custom if you'll simply take yourself off. My nephews should be protected from influences such as yours, and the boys will be home in a few weeks. If your animal spirits are in want of a good, hard swiving, I daresay I'm more than—"

Theresa rose and brushed out her skirts. Capshaw had ambushed her. She'd mistaken him for a garden-variety lecher, when he was instead a noxious, thorny vine, the kind that stank when it bloomed.

Matthew was several yards away, so Theresa kept her voice down.

"I *daresay*, Mr. Capshaw, that if I inquired into your youthful indiscretions, I'd find enough tattle to mortify both you and your lady wife, who is entirely undeserving of such embarrassment. Keep your money, keep your filthy overtures, and keep your mouth shut. Relevant particulars of my past will be shared with Mr. Belmont as I see fit."

She wanted to stomp away, but Matthew was watching her over his cup of punch. He was surrounded by neighbors, whom hunt protocol required to wish him good night before they departed. With his windblown hair and mud-spattered boots, he was entirely in his element and painfully attractive.

"You'd best not be hasty," Mr. Capshaw said, remaining seated and picking up Theresa's plate. "I mean you no harm, Miss Jennings. I'm trying to prevent trouble, not cause it. Matthew is family, and you'll not get your hooks into him while I have breath in my body."

Theresa might have resumed her place beside Capshaw and explained to him that she fully expected to return to Sutcliffe after the holidays. She might have bowed her head and let his damned innuendos and propositions slide past her unacknowledged, as she had on many similar occasions with similar obnoxious men.

Now, as then, she was angry, which did not for a moment disguise the fact that she was also embarrassed. Capshaw was her worst fear, the upstanding citizen who could pillory her with a word, and thus pillory Priscilla's future as well.

Matthew smiled at her and lifted his silver stirrup cup in her direction. The gesture was noticed by the group around him, who shot Theresa indulgent looks.

Theresa picked up the pear before Capshaw could touch it. "You will excuse me, sir. Rather than endure old tattle about the distant past, I will find company less judgmental, more tolerant, and more to my taste. Half-pickled men who mention their base impulses at a polite gathering are tedious in the extreme."

She did not flounce off, she wandered away, nibbling on her pear, and wondering at her treatment of Mr. Capshaw. All the years at Sutcliffe Keep had been spent in hiding, doing penance for choices that had in truth been the best decisions Theresa could have made at the time. The world would never see her past thus, Thomas would never see the situation thus, and that was sad and unfair.

Matthew, however, had revealed to Theresa a healthier perspective on a young woman who'd been given no real chance to preserve her good name. Standing in the sunshine, neighborly socializing all around her, Theresa's heart eased.

As angry as she was, as much as she regretted her past, for the first time, she was not ashamed of what she'd done. She was not ashamed *of herself.*

She caught Matthew's eye, waved with her pear, and as all the world looked on, smiled at the man she loved.

* * *

"Cease your mooning," Beckman said quietly, though Matthew heard him. "People have already noticed you noticing her."

"I intend to do a great deal more than notice Theresa Jennings." Bathed in late autumn sunshine, cheeks rosy, wearing a habit that flattered in both color and cut, Theresa Jennings was pretty. When she smiled at Matthew over a half-eaten pear, she became *stunning*.

Lovely, mischievous, alluring, sweet... lowly adjectives failed. Entire rapturous paragraphs threatened.

"You'll marry her?" Beckman asked.

"If she'll have me. If her clod-pated baron of a brother doesn't convince her to go dodging back to Sutcliffe Keep, my heart firmly in her grasp."

Beckman took a sip of his ale. Matthew had never known him to imbibe strong spirits to excess.

"You should speak with Nicholas," Beckman said. "Miss Jennings's past might not comport entirely with your perceptions of—"

Beckman was a friend, and a friend wearing what was possibly his only decent hunt coat, thus Matthew did not knock him on his arse in public.

"Shut your mouth, Beckman."

Beckman also had four brothers, two older, two younger, and was thus not easily put off, rather like Remington.

"I like her, Squire. I like her a lot, but having acquired something of a bad reputation myself in the not-distant-enough past, I can tell you people have long, nasty memories for every foot I've ever put wrong. If you were some knight ruralizing in the Outer Hebrides, I might hold my tongue, but if you marry her, you're taking scandal to wife right on her brother's very property line. Thomas Jennings is not a man to trifle with."

He wasn't now. Ten years ago he'd been an arrogant sprout, apparently. "I *am* a man to trifle with, Beckman? Perhaps you'd like a turn serving as magistrate."

"Think of *her*, Belmont. She'll be cut every Sunday at services by her only sibling. Think of Priscilla, who won't understand why Uncle Thomas never comes to call. He's a reasonable man and not one to judge, but you must approach him properly before you steal the sister he barely speaks to."

"Matthew, excuse me."

How long had Agatha Capshaw been standing there, and what had she overheard?

"Agatha, good day. You know Mr. Haddonfield, I believe."

"Mr. Haddonfield." She bobbed a curtsey. "Matthew, Emmanuel and I will take our leave of you, but you should know the punchbowl is nearly empty, as are the tart trays."

More helpfulness that nearly motivated Matthew to violence. "Thank you, Agatha, for keeping a sharp eye on the buffet. I'll alert the kitchen."

Matthew had given the vicar's two oldest daughters strict orders regarding the quantities of punch and tarts to be prepared, because his dear neighbors would not leave until the stores were all consumed.

He'd been ready for every one of them to go to blazes an hour ago.

Agatha was darting glances at Theresa, who held the vicar's youngest, a scapegrace little fellow known as Wee Ralph. If anything could have enhanced Theresa's beauty yet further, it was the sight of a small child cuddled in her arms.

"Mr. Haddonfield," Agatha said, "might you excuse us?"

"I'll see that your horses are ready, Mrs. Capshaw," Beckman said, bowing. "Then I'll be on my way home as well. Good night, master."

"Good night, Beckman." Though for deserting Matthew to Agatha's dubious company, Beck deserved to be knocked into the mud, hunt coat and all.

"She's very pretty," Agatha said, when Beckman was out of earshot.

Matilda had been pretty. "If you refer to Miss Jennings, I can assure you she's also sensible, kind, tolerant, and honest. Shall I introduce you?"

"Yes, please. I'm not a hypocrite, Matthew. My own sister would have found little welcome at such a gathering, but for your timely gallantry."

Agatha had not ridden with the hunt that morning, not even at the back of the second flight, though in years past, she had. Today, she'd remained behind to supervise the preparation of the hunt breakfast, though the vicar's daughters had had all in hand when Matthew had left the house.

Matthew offered Agatha his arm, for as she'd circulated among the guests and made several trips through the buffet, her gait had been uneven.

"Does the cold weather not agree with you, Agatha?"

"A sore hip, nothing more. Do you fancy Miss Jennings?"

Was this how Reynard felt, with the pack baying his doom? "I do fancy her, and hope to offer for her, though she might not look favorably on my suit."

"You're a fool if you're concerned she'll reject you," Agatha said. "Miss Jennings would be lucky to have an offer from you, Matthew—any offer."

Not only was Agatha's gait uneven, but she'd also lost some height. She'd been many years Matilda's senior, as much a mother as a sister.

"Agatha, are you well?"

Agatha's gaze strayed to Emmanuel, who would be lucky to sit a horse all the way home.

"I am content." She was resigned, in other words, not the same thing at all.

"Is there anything I can do, Agatha?" For a woman whom Matthew really didn't know all that well.

"Be happy while you can," she said. "And take good care of my nephews."

* * *

Except for Emmanuel Capshaw's tipsy meddling, Theresa's day had been lovely. When Matthew had plucked Wee Ralph from her arms, though, and informed her the time had come to return to Linden, she'd been glad to go.

"Agatha Capshaw wasn't what I expected," she said as they turned their horses up the lane to Linden. "She strikes me as a sad woman, but a good woman. One who's made a practical peace with life's challenges."

"Not another soul would characterize Agatha Capshaw as sad, but I think you have the right of it. You would make a fine magistrate, my dear."

"I've known my share of sadness. Then I think of the women who lose their children as infants. They would dearly love to trade their sadness for mine."

"You lost your only sibling, more or less," Matthew said. "You also lost both parents, a grandmother, a grandfather."

Thomas had endured the same losses, but he'd chosen to divest himself of his only sister. Why? What would an occasional letter have cost him?

"That doesn't excuse what I became," Theresa said, because she needed for Matthew to understand this. "I had my reasons. Grief wasn't among them."

The horses, having enjoyed the morning's hunting, were content to walk along, and the sun's rays were gathering strength as the day progressed. Theresa enjoyed a sense of normalness, of a morning devoted to an enjoyable pastime too long denied her, and an afternoon full of lovely possibilities.

If she'd never fallen from grace, she'd have accumulated a store of such days, as Thomas doubtless had. More and more, she was prone to comparing what Thomas's banishment from Sutcliffe had earned him, versus what her tenure at the Keep had cost her.

The reckoning was overdue, and… disquieting.

"What did you think of Emmanuel?" Matthew asked. "I apologize for not seeing to the introductions."

"He is a trial, which is odd. I had anticipated that his wife would be the harder company to endure. Mr. Capshaw suffered a fascination with my bosom." And with Theresa's past.

Matthew drew his mare up. "Shall I call him out?" He was abruptly no longer the genial, handsome squire, he was a man who'd hunted down felons and brought them to justice.

"You can't call him out—you're the king's man. Dueling solves nothing and spreads scandal, but thank you for the gesture."

"As to that, Baron Sutcliffe should consider taking his turn serving as local magistrate."

"Thomas lacks…" He lacked the tolerance that added so much to Matthew's appeal. Theresa had the cheering thought that Matthew's tolerance was a product of years spent wrestling with a younger man's penchant for anger. "Thomas is newly married, and inflicting parlor sessions on him would be unkind."

Matthew's mare toddled forward, and Evan fell in beside her.

"You nearly criticized your darling baby brother. There's hope for you. I'll have a word with Emmanuel, one he won't soon forget."

Some of the day's joy wafted away on the brisk breeze, like so many leaves twirling to earth.

"Matthew, please say nothing to your brother. Other people will recall that I was known as the Sutcliffe Strumpet." The sobriquet hurt, for Theresa's own cousins had inflicted it on her.

"Because you were the disgrace of southern England, the shame of four shires, the bad example of the modern age, et cetera, et cetera. My neighbors don't agree with you, Theresa. More to the point, I don't agree with you. When I kiss you, do you feel like a strumpet?"

She did not dare lie to him, did not want to. The day had lifted a weight from her heart and replaced it with a luminous dawning of hope above the limitless seascape of her regrets.

"When you kiss me, I feel... lovely."

Matthew remained silent the rest of the way up the drive, which meant he was considering strategy. Theresa did not need to consider strategy, because with Matthew, only unrelenting honesty would do.

He assisted her off her horse. "This morning, I rode hard for more than two hours, I greeted every neighbor who owns a decent mount. I prevented several grown men from falling face first into the punchbowl, and I kept the hounds occupied and the fox entertained without anybody coming to grief. The entire time—"

Theresa kissed him, because she could, because that's what he'd been about to ask of her. A fine, enthusiastic kiss on a lovely, happy day. The holidays would come, Emmanuel Capshaw would make his ugly threats, but Matthew would not be deterred. Thomas, of course, would present a problem, but for a few moments, Theresa allowed that sliver of hope to widen, to become the beginning of a sunrise on new dreams.

The passion of the kiss was sumptuous, like the day. Fresh, clear, with an edge that delighted even as it hinted of the more dramatic winter weather in the offing.

"We shouldn't—" she managed a breathless moment later.

"All morning, I was a perfect gentleman, an agreeable neighbor, while I starved for the feel of you in my arms," Matthew whispered, his embrace wonderfully snug. "If I can't soon—"

"*Theresa Jennings.*" Thomas's voice cracked across the stable yard like lightning forking through a storm. "You will get your filthy, shameless hands off the king's man this instant or be escorted to the foot of the drive like the baggage you are."

* * *

Matthew had once found himself face-to-face with a fugitive from the law who'd been charged with arson, a hanging felony. The man had been armed, with nothing to lose, and had had the advantage of surprise. Matthew had been distracted, reading the quarry's trail while mentally sorting through the latest row with Richard.

And then, he'd been facing a loaded pistol held in a shaking hand, and all the many rows with Richard had dwindled to so much noise.

Matthew had gambled his life on the moral distance between arson and murder. He'd not allowed himself to think of his boys, who'd be orphaned by their father's death. He hadn't contemplated his own demise, hadn't allowed a flicker of regret to pass through his mind for dreams and hopes that would never see the light of day.

Axel would take care of the boys, Emmanuel would manage the Belmont estate until Christopher could fill that role, and every man should die with a few dreams unfulfilled.

Matthew had instead put himself in the shoes of his quarry and talked of justice, of a chance to clear a name unfairly tainted by accusation, of the king's mercy and his regard for the yeomen who kept Britain fed and defended.

The fire had been ruled accidental, and two lives—Matthew's and the accused's—had been saved by nothing more than faith and hope.

Now, facing an irate baron, Matthew thought of his brother Axel, the man who'd kept him sane when Matilda had been dying, the brother with whom he'd fought, laughed, argued, and grown up.

All of Theresa's timidity where her brother was concerned made sense as Matthew studied the disgust in Thomas Jennings's eyes. For Theresa, the great risk she took when she showed Matthew her favor wasn't material—she was a resourceful woman, she'd manage to procure the necessities even if her brother cast her out.

What she risked was the *hope* that her only sibling might someday once again respect her—a precious hope, indeed. Too precious for Matthew to jeopardize. Tact suggested he ought to withdraw and allow Theresa and Thomas to sort out their differences without an audience.

Tact be damned. Matthew kept his arm around Theresa's shoulders and turned a calm countenance on the seething baron.

"Sutcliffe, welcome home. A pleasure to see you, though your greeting to your sister suggests your eyesight is failing."

Theresa gave a half-hearted squirm. "Matthew, Thomas has every right—"

The hell he did. Matthew kissed her again, a little hush-now of a kiss. "A grown woman guilty of nothing more than kissing in the stable yard ought to be able to rely on her only sibling, and the head of her family, for civility at least."

"My eyesight is fine, Belmont," Sutcliffe spat. "My sister's morals, however, remain in want of—"

Loris, Baroness Sutcliffe, emerged from the stable. "Matthew, Theresa, hello."

"Baroness, welcome home," Matthew said, keeping his arm about Theresa's shoulders. "Your husband interrupted Miss Jennings and myself in the midst of enthusiasms best expressed in private. My apologies. They were mutual enthusiasms, Sutcliffe, or has your wedding journey left you too fatigued to see straight?"

The baroness linked her arm with her husband's. "We're very glad to be home. I think."

"We're disgusted," Sutcliffe countered. "The first time I open my home to a sister whom I feared lost to all discretion years ago, and I find not only has she completely ignored the bounds of propriety, she's turned her sights on a neighbor and a man I would have thought too worldly to fall for her schemes."

Oh, for God's sake. Matthew gave Theresa the space of two heartbeats to scold her dunderheaded brother for his presumption, much less his hypocrisy, but Theresa remained pale, tense, and silent.

Sutcliffe had mucked things up nearly beyond repair.

"Ladies, will you excuse us?" Matthew asked, with his best, harmless smile. "Miss Jennings, my thanks for joining us this morning at the hunt meet, and I do hope you'll ride with us again. Baroness, perhaps you'll take Miss Jennings to the house and see that she gets some sustenance. Hunting is a hungry business."

The baron snorted at that observation, and the last of Matthew's considerable patience scurried away amid the undergrowth.

"We'll just be going," Loris said, taking Theresa's hand.

Theresa allowed herself to be led away, her expression suggesting she couldn't recognize when a man was about to wage battle on her behalf—a long overdue battle, in which Priscilla's and Matthew's own happiness had no little stake.

Alas, one could not simply spank fifteen stone of tantruming baron in that baron's very own stable yard.

Matthew tucked his riding gloves into his coat pocket, made sure Sutcliffe had left off glowering at the retreating ladies, and clipped his lordship with a satisfying left cross to the baronial jaw.

* * *

"We start for home in less than two weeks," Remington said, letting himself into Richard's room without knocking. Rem was still growing, and worse, he was growing faster than Richard. Older brothers were God's plague on the undeserving, and bigger older brothers were penance personified.

"I'm not going home," Richard said, pretending to be fascinated with his Greek. Why a lot of buggering catamites in dressing gowns deserved study two thousand years after warring their civilization into oblivion, Richard did not know.

"You're coming home with us," Rem replied, lounging on Richard's bed, boots and all. "Papa will be heartbroken if you don't come home, and Uncle Axel won't let you stay here anyway."

Here was Candlewick, Axel Belmont's estate in Oxfordshire and the salvation of Richard's sanity. He and his cousin Phillip were in a neck and neck competition to master the most material by next autumn, so all five cousins could spend a year together at Oxford. Dayton, Phillip's older brother, had proposed this scheme, and Richard had leapt at the challenge.

"I'll be too sick to travel." Richard could do a convincing megrim, because he'd been getting them with increasing frequency before leaving Sussex. Bloody awful they were, too.

"For an entire month, you'll be too sick?" Rem asked, folding his hands behind his head. "Christopher and I won't go home without you, so you'd better tell me what this is about, Dirty Dickie."

The nickname had been an occasion for fisticuffs when Richard had been younger. He'd spent enough time visiting at the colleges to grasp that everybody had a nickname. Dirty Dickie for a fellow who prided himself on his spotless attire wasn't half bad.

"This is about me," Richard said, "trying to learn a few things before I start school next year. Wasting the holidays visiting the ponies for old times' sake won't aid in that cause."

"You're lying," Rem said, yawning and cracking his jaw. "Bluster all you like, have your tantrums—Mama certainly had hers—and pretend to enjoy that stinking Greek, but you're lying to your own brother."

Mama had had tantrums. Richard could recall that much about her, in addition to occasional laughter and a winsome smile. Her husband, by contrast, had never raised his voice indoors, and had always seemed to Richard to be busy with somebody's ailing bullock or missing goose.

"You're jealous because I enjoy Greek," Richard said, turning a page he had not read. "Go away, now that you've tended to the obligatory disruption of my studies."

Rem sat up in one quick movement. "Stop being an ass. *I am your brother*. If you got some tavern maid in trouble, then tell me. Christopher and I will do all in our power to help you, and no, we won't go running to Papa telling tales."

Richard hadn't had the *opportunity* to get a tavern maid in trouble, though he well understood that tavern maids figured prominently on every young man's list of amatory challenges. The prospect was daunting and alluring at once.

"Would you tell me if you'd got a woman in trouble, Remington?"

"Of course," Rem said, rising. "You'd become an uncle. Not something I'd want to keep from you. If something happened to me, you and Chris would have to care for the child, wouldn't you?" He smoothed the wrinkles from the coverlet, his gesture reminiscent of Matthew Belmont, another inherently tidy person.

"Please don't get any tavern maids in trouble, Rem. I'm not ready to be an uncle yet." Did Rem ever wonder if he'd inherited his tidiness from his father?

"Neither am I," Rem said, spearing Richard with a look. "So I haven't risked the near occasion, so to speak."

Richard turned another page. "You're at university. Why comport yourself like a monk?" *Why pretend to bury yourself in your studies when you'd rather bury yourself in a willing female?*

"Not like a monk, like a gentleman. Papa raised us to be gentlemen."

And there was the rub, as the Bard might have said. Matthew Belmont, by example and exhortation, had raised Richard, Christopher, and Rem to be gentlemen. If Richard went home for Christmas, all he could promise the man who'd provided him every necessity and more than a few luxuries was a lot of bad manners and silence.

"Oxford is full of gentlemen," Richard said, closing his book and resting his chin on his stacked fists. "The streets are full of their bastards too."

"When did you become such a cheery little soul?"

Richard knew when, to the day, but Rem, mercifully, was wandering toward the door.

"I get my excellent disposition from my older brothers," Richard said. "I really do not want to go home to Sussex." Not ever, and that hurt too badly to think about. Lots of fellows spent holidays with a schoolmate or a relative. Lots of fellows who didn't have a lovely home in Sussex and Matthew Belmont writing to them conscientiously every week.

"I want nearly every tavern maid who bats her eyes at me, and a few who don't," Rem said. "Wanting means little. Whatever bee has got in your bonnet, Richard, get rid of it. Soon enough, we'll leave home to seek our fortunes in the wider world, and then you'll rue the day you disdained a family gathering at your birthplace."

Richard thought of old Tut, who was stealing treats from some little girl these days.

The notion nearly had him in tears. "Be gone, Remington. I'll never get to my Latin if you insist on blathering at me the livelong day."

Rem crossed his arms and leaned ever so casually against the door. Christopher was handsome, but Rem was attractive, while Richard was neither. Not yet. A headache threatened behind his eyes. He set his Greek across the table, beyond throwing range.

"I don't trifle with the ladies," Rem said, "because I am yet dependent upon my father's generosity. Should I get some woman with child, my allowance would be all I could offer for the infant's care and the mother's well-being. Many make do on less, but I didn't. Respect and affection for my own children require that I give them the same advantages I had, at least."

Respect and affection for one's own children. Now there was a concept to wreck a fellow's remaining self-discipline. Richard grabbed a handy boot awaiting a proper polishing and pitched it in the direction of his older brother.

"Take yourself off. Your sermonizing is wasted on a dedicated scholar."

Rem studied Richard for an uncomfortable moment, gently tossed the boot back to him, and slipped out the door.

CHAPTER THIRTEEN

Betrayal, nauseating and familiar, washed through Thomas as he watched his sister swish off hand in hand with his baroness. Panic threatened, a boy's panic at being closed out, shoved aside, ignored by his elders, and by his only sibling.

If Theresa stole Loris's loyalty from him—

Belmont's fist caught Thomas on the chin before that thought could fully form. The pain was welcome, too compelling to dismiss even in the face of Theresa's latest betrayal.

"Now that I have your attention," Belmont said, "you will cease fuming and admit that you and the fair Loris did more than kiss in the stable yard when you were courting."

Belmont was so calm, so bloody composed. Thomas's smarting chin was the only evidence a punch had been thrown—a very competent punch.

"Belmont, have you taken leave of your senses?"

"Answer the question, Sutcliffe. Of all women, all women of mature years and sound judgment, is Theresa Jennings alone to be judged by puritanical standards? You nearly venerate your lady wife for having granted you privileges far in excess of the liberties your sister was just now granting me."

"My wife *is* a lady," Thomas said, spoiling to return fire, though Loris would not approve.

Belmont took out his gloves and pulled them on, his movements casual. "Must I take you in hand, Sutcliffe? Unless I miss my guess, Loris will become the mother of your firstborn something less than nine months after taking her marital vows. This is the same woman who dwelled here at Linden for two years without a chaperone, working as the estate's steward in all but name. "

When Loris had found herself living alone at Linden and shouldering her father's responsibilities, Matthew Belmont had proposed to her. She'd gently rebuffed him, and Thomas suspected the squire had been relieved.

This tirade was not a criticism of Loris, which fact alone allowed Thomas to keep his fists to himself.

Barely. "Loris cannot help that she was abandoned by the very man responsible for safeguarding her welfare."

Belmont remained silent while Jamie led the horses into the stable. Even when privacy was once again assured, Belmont studied the few yellow leaves remaining on the oak across the lane. He studied the sky, a lovely blue and white canvas despite the nip in the air.

Thomas's own words hung in the air… *abandoned by the very man responsible for safeguarding her welfare.*

All over again, Thomas wanted to hit somebody. "Did Theresa tell you I abandoned her?"

Belmont swung a pitying regard on him. "You must cease insulting your sister, else I shall have to thrash you properly, Sutcliffe, in which case the ladies would be wroth with both of us. Theresa defends you at every turn. I cannot hint that your actions in any regard have been remiss, but most especially she defends your behavior toward her."

Bewilderment and weariness edged aside temper. "She defends me, then plasters herself to the nearest wealthy bachelor where anybody might see. She's a conscientious parent, her daughter is a pure delight, and yet, at the first opportunity, she sets her sights on you, who ought to know better."

Theresa should have known better. "I want her gone, Matthew. I've extended the obligatory olive branch to appease my wife, who has no siblings, but at the soonest opportunity, I want Theresa gone, back to Sutcliffe at least, if not consigned to the Yorkshire dales."

"We have a dilemma then, Sutcliffe. Walk with me?"

For the first time in his adult life, Thomas had looked forward to coming home, to the home he shared with his new wife. After university, he'd had lodgings, even owned property, but he'd never replaced Sutcliffe Keep in his heart as *home*. Linden was home now, because Loris loved this place, and Thomas loved Loris.

"I'd like to look in on Dove Cottage," Thomas said. For two years, Loris had resided in the small dwelling at the edge of the home wood. The place stood empty now, unless Thomas was of a mind to idle a day away there with his baroness.

Belmont obliged by ambling off in the direction of the lane that led to the cottage.

"Do you hate your sister, Sutcliffe?"

"I do not hate—" Thomas walked along, wishing Loris were beside him, not this patient, implacable inquisitor. "I've loathed what she became."

"The opposite of love is not hate, but indifference. My son Richard could tell me which philosopher said that. The boy has taken me into dislike at present, which assures me he still cares for his old papa in some regard."

"You're not old," Thomas said as they reached the edge of the wood. Thomas felt old, and he felt nineteen, powerless, and revolted by his only sibling. His cousins had been rotten as far back as he could recall, but that Theresa had cast her lot with them—

"I am not old," Belmont said, "and you, my friend, are no longer a boy."

In some sense, Thomas had never been a boy. He'd lost his parents early, and his grandfather had been curmudgeonly on a good day. His cousins had been wastrels who'd delighted in shocking Thomas from a young age with their vices and venery.

"I'm not proud of how I feel," Thomas said, "but she was a good girl, Matthew. Long, long ago, Theresa Jennings was a good girl."

Kind, bookish, patient, willing to take the blame to spare her brother. Thomas had thought all sisters were like that, until he'd gone up to university and heard some of his schoolmates disparaging their siblings.

"She was a good girl, and now, she is a good woman," Belmont said. "You've admitted that her regard for her daughter is beyond reproach. Sutcliffe Keep has prospered because of her attention to it. You will not insult her again in my hearing without suffering the consequences."

Belmont was as relentless as the wind on the moor, eroding Thomas's carefully constructed righteousness without striking another direct blow. Gratitude to the squire, for assuming the role of champion, warred with guilt.

Thomas had once been his sister's friend and confidant, if not quite her champion. He'd been something worthy, to a sister who'd been worthy.

"Until two years ago, my cousin held the barony," Thomas said, though the former baron had been a Town man. Thomas had carefully ensured their paths never crossed, which had taken a fair amount of travel and avoiding Polite Society.

"Your cousin was a wenching, drinking disgrace who came with an identical twin. Were these wastrels destined to live long lives, siring many children?"

Wenching wastrels were often unable to sire *any* children, thanks to the virulent strain of syphilis that had mobilized with the Corsican's armies. Thomas had managed a brothel, and such knowledge had been unavoidable.

"You're saying Theresa managed Sutcliffe because she knew I'd inherit it?"

Belmont made no reply. In the wood, the air was quieter, though the carpet of fallen leaves crunched underfoot. The season had changed at Linden in Thomas's absence, gone from mellow autumn to early winter.

Loris had hinted at the same conclusion Belmont was suggesting—that Theresa had preserved Thomas's birthright, all the while Thomas had been refusing to open his sister's letters. The notion was preposterous.

Almost. "Had Theresa allowed Sutcliffe to fall into ruin, she and Priscilla would have had no place to bide, Belmont. Looking after her home was in her own interests."

Thomas had told himself that lie any number of times. He'd married a woman who knew how to look after a property though, and Loris had effusively admired Sutcliffe's apiary, the spotless dairy, the tidy wood, the neat stone walls. The family seat was in excellent repair as an estate, though as a household, the Keep itself was... fraying.

"I cannot have Theresa living here, Belmont," Thomas said, kicking at the leaves as the gray cottage came into view. Without Loris's flowers rioting about its porch and yard, the little dwelling looked forlorn.

As Thomas felt forlorn.

"Theresa hasn't asked you if she can bide at Linden, has she?" Belmont kept walking, around to the back of the cottage.

"Not yet, but she's biding her time, waiting for a moment when Loris won't let me refuse her. You don't know what Theresa became, Belmont. She was hell-bent on having her own way, and nothing, not pleading, promises, or threats, could stop her."

Ugly, was the best word Thomas could put on what his sister had become. She'd sneered at him to run along back to Town, to stop clinging to her skirts, and leave her in peace.

She'd been ugly, but Thomas had been pathetic.

"You managed a brothel," Belmont said, climbing the porch steps and taking a place on the swing where Thomas had fallen in love with Loris.

"For a time, and under protest."

Belmont gave the swing a push, and the chains creaked. "That's all right, then."

Creak... creak... creak.

"Somebody had to keep the peace among the patrons, sort out squabbles, and—hell." Thomas had hated every moment of it, hated being cast in the role of both protector and exploiter.

"You ensured that women were intimately available to any man who came along, ensured a profit resulted from what these women did, and assured yourself you *had no alternative* but to include these tasks in your duties. So helpless, for such a strapping, intelligent fellow. Were these women born wicked, I wonder? When they were Priscilla's age, did they long to become debauched?"

Creak... creak... creak.

"Belmont, I could kill you and bury your body in my home wood, nobody the wiser."

"Better to bury your guilt and leave it to rot among the regrets we all collect on the road to adulthood. Theresa had no mother, not an aunt, not even a proper companion, and yet you say, somehow, she was a good girl."

She had been. Sweet, fierce, a little too bold sometimes, but *good*.

Thomas settled on the swing beside Belmont and brought the damned thing to a halt.

"I came home from university for the Christmas holidays, and my cousins were holding a house party at Sutcliffe that made the revels of Bacchus look like a tea dance. For some reason, they knew not to inveigle me into their debauchery, but Grandpapa was off at some shooting party. Theresa was not the sister I'd known."

She'd deserted all decency, all sense, and she'd been barely seventeen years old. Thomas and his sister had fought, loudly and often, with the cousins placing bets as if they'd been ringside at a bear baiting.

"I wanted to take her away," Thomas said. "I pleaded with Grandfather by letter to send her away from the influence of my cousins, but once my studies were done, the old man sent me away instead. I finished university without spending much more time at Sutcliffe, but I never thought—"

Belmont was a relaxed presence beside Thomas. Did parenting teach a man such impregnable calm? Apprehending felons? Sorting through differences in the parlor sessions? Or was it a gift bestowed by the Almighty?

"The feeling of betrayal stains a relationship, doesn't it?" Belmont mused. "My wife betrayed me, and yet, there was my son, an innocent baby, one deserving of the love and protection of two parents. I held him in my arms, an blameless, squalling, red-faced tiny fellow who weighed little more than a stout puppy. I realized I could do for love of the boy what I might never do for love of his mother."

Thomas was acquainted with the circumstances of Belmont's marriage, but what woman would have rewarded her young husband's gallantry with anything less than complete loyalty?

"What did you do?"

"I forgave her, Thomas. I forgave her for her weakness, and me for my arrogance."

Thomas was feeling murderous, not arrogant. "You saved her good name and provided for another man's child. How is that arrogance?"

"Don't be obtuse. I was seventeen, and in exchange for saving Matilda's good name, I expected to exercise my conjugal rights. I was owed those intimacies— she'd promised them to me in good faith, though she was in love with another. The poor woman was sorely confused, and I was a clueless ass."

"You were young."

"*Theresa was young*, you were young. We make mistakes, we learn from them. I have been puzzled about Theresa's situation, though."

Thomas gave the swing a push. With more weight on the chains, they didn't creak.

"Say on, Belmont. You're a clever fellow, and I doubt much puzzles you."

Then too, Belmont was inconveniently competent with his fists, *and he'd been right.*

Seventeen was miserably young, from any perspective, twenty not much older.

"Wait until your youngest child is fifteen years old," Belmont said, "alternately raging down the rafters and silently fuming. Your capacity for puzzlement will acquire new dimensions. In any case, I can understand why a young woman would go astray. Wild oats are not the exclusive province of young men."

"Theresa was bored at Sutcliffe," Thomas said. "I know that." Bored, lonely, too smart for her own good, with a grandfather too parsimonious to get her proper tutors or governesses.

Thomas could admit that much.

"She was dowered." Belmont stated this fact as if building a case before a jury.

"What do you mean, *was?*"

"She claims whatever funds were set aside, they were gone before your grandfather died. Perhaps your cousins appropriated them."

Well, of course. They'd been shameless, the pair of them. "Theresa should have applied to me, and I'd have held them accountable." Except even as he spoke, Thomas felt a sense of the ground under his righteous feet eroding further.

Theresa could not have applied to him, because once he'd finished university and been cast out of Sutcliffe Keep, he'd stopped opening her letters.

"She likely had a dowry at one time simply as a function of her mother's marital settlements and subsequent estate," Belmont went on, as if Thomas hadn't spoken. "From what Theresa says, she had no respect for these cousins of yours. Her best avenue forward would have been marriage to some proper fellow of good means, and she was well-born enough to pursue that avenue."

Belmont was closing in on some conclusion Thomas would not like at all. "Matthew, she ruined herself before she even came out. She had no come out, in fact, because she'd become such a disgrace."

Belmont halted the swing. "Do not tempt me to resume my pugilistic displays. A woman cannot ruin herself, particularly not a woman who has yet to reach her majority, who has no funds of her own, and no reasonable future outside of marriage. Under those circumstances, she must connive at her ruination with relentless determination."

Thomas rose, and a chilly wind shook the few leaves clinging to the trees beyond the garden.

"So Theresa connived. She got the bit between her teeth, threw in with our cousins, and wrecked her chances at a decent match. She's very bright, and stubborn."

The squire remained on the swing. "Hmm."

As a manager of a brothel, Thomas had been amused at men who lost their tempers. They shouted, they smashed handy breakables, they called each other out, all the while hoping somebody would stop them from blowing each other's brains out.

Thomas wanted somebody to shove him down the porch stairs, to get him out of this calm, patient conversation with Belmont.

"Say it, Belmont. Whatever damned conclusion you're coming to, just damned say it."

Belmont rose and draped his lean length along the porch post. "Not a conclusion, but a question of motive, Sutcliffe. Theresa Jennings was, as you say, bright, dowered, from a titled family, and comely."

"Quite comely, unfortunately." She was still pretty, though her attractiveness was contained in plain clothing, severe hairstyles, and a mother's constant vigilance regarding her child.

"So she had every reason to guard her virtue. A few more months of proper behavior and she would have been presented at court. She was less than a year from gaining the freedom of her own household. An intelligent, determined, attractive, decent, and pragmatic young woman threw away her chance for a happy future. Despite considerable thought devoted to this very puzzle, I cannot for the life of me fathom *why*."

Belmont sauntered down the steps, offered Thomas a parting salute, and disappeared around the corner of the empty cottage.

* * *

"Tea won't help," Theresa said, willing Matthew to come up the garden path. "I should be packing. If you would write to me—write to Priscilla, I mean—I'd be grateful."

The baroness looked so pretty, pouring out over a service that had to be antique Sevres. At least Theresa had got to meet her.

"So you kissed Matthew Belmont," Loris said, sitting back with her teacup cradled in her hands. She was not a conventionally pretty woman, being dark rather than fair, and inclined to marching rather than mincing. "Many women would envy you, and I daresay Matthew has not been celibate in widowerhood."

He had been lonely, a far worse affliction for a man of Matthew's disposition than sexual deprivation.

"I kissed him in a public place, and I kissed him shamelessly." The word was literally applicable—without shame, in the sunshine, for anybody to see. Theresa was proud of that much, at least.

Porcelain tinkled delicately, and Loris appeared at Theresa's side bringing the soothing scent of lilacs with her.

"So Thomas and Matthew will pound each other to flinders, you'll marry Matthew, and all will be a little awkward, but we'll muddle through."

Matthew would be dreadfully effective with his fists, but so would Thomas.

"I hate it when men brawl. When Thomas was young, my cousins would bait him until he lost his temper, and then they'd laugh as they blacked his eyes and split his lip."

"Two against one?"

"Thomas was younger by five years. One was enough, while the other taunted and derided. When Thomas learned to withstand their derision, they took up the sport of insulting me."

That recollection unsettled Theresa's insides yet further, for she had heard Matthew's fist connecting with Thomas's stubborn jaw.

"Thomas had it coming," Loris said, looping her arm through Theresa's. "He's so wonderfully pigheaded, else I should not have married him. I hope we have a lot of boys, who will teach their papa a little of diplomacy and patience."

Matthew was diplomatic and patient, and now Theresa would never get to meet his children. Emmanuel Capshaw would rejoice, as would half the spinsters in the shire.

"They won't kill each other," Theresa muttered. "I gather they are friends, and Thomas needs friends."

"As does Matthew. If you won't have a cup of tea, at least have a biscuit."

"No, thank you."

Where was Matthew? Thomas was younger, and he was furious, and if he hurt Matthew, Theresa would not answer for her reaction.

"You are more worried for Matthew than you are for yourself," Loris said, easing away. "You needn't be. Matthew can handle himself. We treat him as if he's a house cat, all soft fur and elegant movement. He purrs, he never brings mud in the house, he's comfortable and handsome. At the assemblies, he stands up with the wallflowers, he makes up the numbers at dinner parties, and nobody comes to grief in the hunt field if Matthew's casting the hounds."

Theresa had come to grief. She'd fallen in love, and for once, chosen a man whose regard mattered to her.

"Matthew is more than the male equivalent of a spinster," Theresa said. "I would trust him with my life."

More porcelain gently tinkled from the direction of the settee and still, Matthew did not come striding across the garden.

"You would trust him with Priscilla's life," Loris said. "And you'd be right to. There was a girl born to a local family—the sort of family every village has and wishes they didn't. Their chickens were scrawny, the husband drank too much, the wife was too quiet. They had gaunt, ragged children, and the youngest girl…she wasn't right."

Clouds were starting to gather to the east, above the Downs. Priscilla would be drawing snowflakes soon, though she'd be drawing them at Sutcliffe.

"I know you're listening," Loris said, sounding as though she talked around a bite of biscuit. "In any case, the parents treated the child awfully. She didn't learn to speak, she didn't mind them, she became like some sort of ill-favored human dog, tied more often than not, and allowed to grow even thinner than her siblings. Matthew came upon the father beating the child at the village well one day."

"How do you know this?"

"At the posting inn, this is one of the stories they tell about the king's man," Loris said, "but in this case, I happened to be present. I could not interfere, for a man may do with his children as he sees fit, and this man was both violent and inebriated."

Theresa had experience with violent, inebriated men. "Matthew interceded?"

"He confiscated the child," Loris said. "Confiscated the child as if she were livestock, and I will never forget the sight of him holding that filthy, mewling little girl in his arms and, with all the calm in the world, facing down the father. The child clung to Matthew, as if she knew by instinct he would never harm her."

"One can't confiscate a child," Theresa said. "A man's power over his wife and his legitimate progeny is without limit." Fortunately, illegitimate progeny remained in their mother's custody, but the wife part—oh, that had been a troublesome detail when Theresa had been younger.

Loris was beside Theresa again, holding out a piece of shortbread. "Take it. My guess is Thomas will appear here a chastened baron, and you will need your strength. I cannot stand against my husband, but neither will I sit meekly by while he does something he'll regret. I grew up without family, and I will not allow him to squander what little family he's brought to me by marriage."

Theresa took a nibble of shortbread flavored with lavender. Matthew would have enjoyed this, which was probably why Loris had asked for it to be included on the tray.

"Please tell me the tale of the confiscated child." For if Loris did not complete the story before the men returned, Theresa might never hear the whole of it.

"We have aldermen," Loris said, "the same as any village, and they pass ordinances, many of which we ignore. Matthew, as the magistrate, knows those ordinances like a duke knows his ancestry. One of our little laws says a man can be fined for neglecting any creature having a value of at least one pound. The mistreated animal may be put into the care of a responsible party until it once again thrives."

"What's the point of such a rule?"

Loris passed over another piece of shortbread. "Matthew says it's related to a very old custom, dating back to when villages held livestock in common. If a man can provide for his sheep or cows, and he yet neglects them out of spite or laziness, then valuable livestock goes to waste. Most villages don't have the luxury of wasting food, so the law provides a means for the animal to be put into hands that will care for it properly."

The Sutcliffe barony was so old, it likely dated back to when such laws were simply unwritten custom.

"So Matthew likened this child to a skinny bullock?"

Loris dusted her hands together. "He did more than that. He held his parlor session at the local tavern that Monday, and he'd rallied the wives and grannies in the days prior. By sheer coincidence, Vicar's sermon the previous day had been about the kingdom of heaven belonging to little children. The tavern was packed to the rafters."

Oh, Matthew. "What happened to the girl?"

"Not a soul would argue when Matthew declared the child to have a value far in excess of one pound and to meet the definition of the word *creature*. He fined the father, who would never have parted with the coin even if he'd had it. Matthew put the girl into the care of a pair of spinster sisters pending payment of the fine. He deduced that the child is deaf, and while she cannot speak clearly, she can communicate in her way. Matthew will not fail you, Theresa."

"Matthew cannot change my past, he cannot make Priscilla legitimate, he cannot change my brother's heart."

Footfalls sounded across the parlor, a ringing, confident stride Theresa already knew.

"Only you can change your brother's heart," Matthew said, marching into the parlor and kissing her cheek. "Ah, I see we are having shortbread. I adore a buttery sweet with my tea, assuming I'm welcome?"

CHAPTER FOURTEEN

"I saw Mr. Belmont hit you," Priscilla yelled down from the hayloft, ready to hit somebody herself. Why must grown-ups always ruin everything?

Uncle Thomas peered up at her from the barn aisle below, his hands on his hips. When he and Mr. Belmont had left the stable yard, Priscilla had been too upset to leave her tower. She was still too upset.

"Priscilla, you ought not to spy on your elders."

"Elders ought not to hit each other where I'm playing. I wasn't spying, I was waiting for Mama to come home from the hunt."

Priscilla was unwilling to come down the ladder until she had to. She liked being above Uncle Thomas, who was a tall fellow, like Mr. Belmont. Uncle did not ride a white horse, though.

"Mr. Belmont was trying to get my attention," Uncle Thomas said, coming up the ladder. "I was distracted."

The ladder shook with each step he took, and if Priscilla had had any Greek fire—whatever that was—she might have poured it on her uncle's head. The hayloft was *her* tower, and stupid grown-ups were not allowed up here.

"If somebody is distracted," Priscilla said, "you say excuse me, and you wait—without fidgeting or pulling on their arm—until they stop talking. That's only if you must interrupt, which is a *rare occasion*."

When Uncle Thomas stood up in the hayloft, his head almost touched the roof of the barn.

"Your braid's coming undone, child."

"I'll tidy up before Miss Alice or Mama catch sight of me. Beckman or Jamie can fix my braid because they braid manes and tails. I've helped them."

The hayloft was much smaller with Uncle Thomas in it, less of a tower, more of a dusty old hayloft. Priscilla couldn't very well ask her uncle to leave his own hayloft, which was a great pity.

"I'm sorry you saw that altercation," Uncle Thomas said, taking a seat cross-legged in the hay. "What were you doing up here all by yourself?"

"I'm always all by myself when I'm up here, unless Nick or Beckman see me. They know I'm here, though, and Mr. Belmont knows where I am from the tracks I leave. What's an altercation?"

Uncle Thomas fished through the hay and plucked out a long stem of grass. He smelled good and spoke in a lot of languages that sounded very pretty. Right now he looked sad, which suggested he was truly sorry, not simply grown-up sorry.

"An altercation is when I get more angry than I should, maybe a lot more angry than I should. You saw your mama kissing Mr. Belmont?"

They had kissed at Belmont House too, so Priscilla had gone around to the parlor door rather than tapping at the library window, and she'd been careful to make *a lot* of noise as she'd cantered up to the library.

"I saw them kissing each other," Priscilla said, taking the place beside her uncle. The hay was scratchy, but Uncle needed to understand a few things, and scolding him in private seemed the wiser course.

"They did, indeed, kiss each other. A fine distinction," Uncle Thomas said, turning so he could get his hands on Priscilla's loose braid. "The squire pointed out that very same fact to me. Do you like him, Priscilla?"

"He has ponies, he's teaching me to ride Tut, and Miss Alice likes him. Mr. Belmont makes Mama smile."

Uncle Thomas's touch was not like Mama's or Miss Alice's. He was slower, and the braid would be looser. Not a proper braid for going into the hunt field, in other words.

"Your mama doesn't smile much, does she?"

"She does sometimes, when I get my sums right. I like sums and languages."

"So did I," Uncle Thomas said, sounding more like a grandpapa than an uncle. "So did your mother. She was much like you."

"Was she im-per-ti-nent? That's my word for today. It means I speak up when I ought not."

Uncle Thomas hugged her. He had a good hug, quick but firm, like Miss Alice, only with more muscles.

"I do that—speak up when I ought to hold my peace," he said. "I did that, which is why Mr. Belmont had to get my attention."

From the corner of her eye, Priscilla could see Uncle was smiling, though not a happy smile. More of a thoughtful smile. He tied a snug, lopsided bow at the bottom of her plait than flipped the braid forward over her shoulder.

Priscilla scooted around and sat up as tall as she could while perched on a pile of hay.

"You yelled at my mama. A gentleman doesn't raise his voice to a lady. He doesn't argue with a lady."

This was important for him to know, though perhaps nobody had told Uncle Thomas this rule yet. He and Aunt Loris had not been married for very long.

"How do you know this, Priscilla? Last time I checked, no gentlemen lived at Sutcliffe Keep. I fear that's been the case for a very long time."

He had found some more grass stems about the same length and was braiding them together now in the same loose fashion.

"Mama told me you lived at the Keep. You grew up there."

Uncle pitched his little grass rope away. "I was a boy when I lived there, and not always a very nice boy."

"Did you yell and say bad words?"

"I did, though sometimes I was justified." He grabbed Priscilla and scrubbed his knuckles over her crown, which she sort of hated. "Sometimes I was horrid."

"You cannot yell at Mama again, Uncle. You will make her sad, and she's been sad too much. When she got your letter, she cried."

"I nearly cried when I wrote it, but your aunt said I must."

"I like Aunt. She makes scents and always has biscuits on the tea tray."

"I like your aunt too, and if you're lucky, she and I will provide you with a few cousins—" Uncle Thomas fell silent, and Priscilla let him think for a moment. A fellow who went around yelling at people and getting hit in the face might not be too quick to figure things out.

"Priscilla, do you have any playmates?"

Tut was much more than a playmate. "Real ones?"

"Real ones, real children."

"No, not at Sutcliffe. Here, I play at the vicarage."

Uncle Thomas studied her for a long time, as if trying to find the right words in English to say something he knew how to say in French. Miss Alice said he was a prodigy with languages, which was fortunate, because apparently he wasn't very bright otherwise.

He kissed Priscilla's forehead and rose, making him very tall compared to Priscilla's perch in the hay.

"I'm sorry, Priscilla."

She had the sense he wasn't speaking to her, but to himself. Priscilla knew what to say though, because the rule for this situation was simple.

"I accept your apology, but please don't do again whatever you did that you're sorry for." She popped to her feet and held out her hand, because Mama said words meant more when accompanied by deeds.

Uncle Thomas bowed over her hand—he was supposed to shake it—then went back down the ladder without another word. Perhaps he was off to apologize to Mama, because he ought.

Sometimes, Priscilla felt like the whole world ought to apologize to Mama.

* * *

All the anger Matthew hadn't expressed when sitting beside a befuddled baron on the cottage porch swing threatened to choke him along with his shortbread.

Sutcliffe, with a few words, had shaken his sister's confidence. Family could do that. A meal with the Capshaws could cast Matthew back into the role of weary, bewildered young husband, or equally weary, bewildered young father... of one, then two, then three lively boys.

Agatha and Emmanuel, despite having no offspring of their own, had been full of suggestions for how Matthew ought to have gone about raising his children. Emmanuel had frequently pulled Matthew aside and explained how to go on with a new wife, despite the fact that the Capshaws' own marriage appeared merely functional.

Emmanuel's guidance had invariably been stupid. Even as a young man, Matthew had realized as much.

"Would you care for a sandwich, Matthew?" the baroness asked, holding up the dish.

Every offering on the plate was slathered with yellow mustard, which Matthew could not abide.

"Thank you, no," Matthew said, the first time he could recall refusing food in ages. "I'd best return to Belmont House and see that the leftovers from the hunt breakfast have been sent round to Vicar Herndon. I need to look in on the hounds, and Spiker will want a report from me as well. Miss Jennings, might you accompany me to the stable?"

There were, of course, no leftovers from the hunt breakfast, and the hounds were doubtless napping. Spiker was likely still occupying the posting inn's snug, treating the near-loss of his entire arm with liberal doses of gossip and winter ale.

Theresa had changed out of her borrowed habit, back into one of her wren-brown dresses. She appeared composed, but she darted glances at the door, the clock, the window, Matthew's hands.

Those hands yearned to touch her, though she might remonstrate with him for his presumption, which show of spirit he'd welcome.

"I think Priscilla has hidden herself away in the stable," Theresa said, rising. "I'll spare Alice the effort of retrieving her, if you can wait for me to fetch a shawl."

The trip across the gardens was made in silence, while Matthew mentally rearranged a recounting of his interview the baron.

"Your brother loves you," Matthew said as they approached the stable.

In that breathless moment when Theresa had smiled at him over her half-eaten pear, and all Matthew had wanted was for her to see herself as he saw her, he'd admitted to the same emotion: He loved this woman. Desperately, endlessly, wonderfully.

She drew her shawl closer, another plain brown garment, but at least this one looked warm.

"Nine years of silence means Thomas loves me?"

Argument, rather than polite agreement, was surely a hopeful sign. "You love him, though you haven't spoken to him in nine years."

"I wrote to him, I prayed for him, I did what I could at Sutcliffe. He's my brother, and the only family I had worth claiming until Priscilla came along."

Mention of the child's name steadied Matthew's resolve. "You are privy to much of my situation with Matilda, and you have not judged the man you know now for the misguided steps I took in my youth." Theresa did not know the entire truth of Matthew's marriage. Not yet.

"You were trying to do the right thing," Theresa said, taking Matthew's arm. "You very likely *did* do the right thing, and you have not one but three boys to show for it. Your decision to marry a woman in difficulties could not have been entirely foolish."

Well, yes, it had been. Did Theresa think she was the only person to pay for one blundering season with year after year of her happiness?

"I love my sons without limit, and they are ample consolation for a marriage that bitterly disappointed both parties." Matthew ought not to air this linen now, with such turmoil brewing between Theresa and her brother, and yet, he wanted Theresa to know the truth. "Matilda never gave up her first love, Theresa. Not in any meaningful sense."

Matthew trusted Theresa Jennings. He hadn't made a decision to trust her, hadn't pondered evidence and hypotheses, the trust had simply taken up residence in his heart, like Maida had appropriated the library hearth the same day Matthew had accorded her house privileges.

Theresa fretted over a cranky mare, she mothered the hell out of her lone child, she still protected a brother who had wealth, worldly wisdom, and position in abundance.

"Matilda was not faithful to you even after the vows were spoken?"

Theresa also didn't mince about when the terrain became boggy.

"For at least the first several years of our marriage, Matilda pined for her lost love, and after that, I focused on the boys. She was the mother of our children, and in that sense, we had a functional marriage."

A lone hedge of honeysuckle had got hopelessly confused by the Martinmas summer apparently, and was sporting a few fragrant blossoms.

"You did not set her aside."

Matthew had had the means and the motive to do just that. He might have sent Matilda to visit fictional relatives in Wales or Cumbria, might have established her in London, so she could maintain a relationship with the boys. Agatha would have taken her in, though in Matilda's most histrionic moments, she'd never threatened to join her sister's household.

Matthew plucked a sprig of honeysuckle and presented it to Theresa. "I didn't hate Matilda, and the boys loved her. We muddled on, and for the most part, it wasn't awful."

"Which means at times, the whole situation was horrid." Theresa twirled the honeysuckle under her nose, then drew her fingers over the few, sad leaves still sheltering the blossoms. "You love your sons, so you protected them from the horrid parts."

Had Matthew had his hunting horn, he might have blown the view-halloo.

"Precisely. One is protective of loved ones; therefore, I conclude you must have had a very good reason for pushing your only sibling away, Theresa Jennings."

She turned into Matthew's embrace, as naturally as a leaf falls to the forest floor at winter's approach. The fragrance of honeysuckle rose between them, a poignant contrast to the chill breeze.

They would be visible from the house, and Theresa had suggested Priscilla was lurking in the stable, so Matthew led his lady to the bench across the lane. In summer, the oak tree provided magnificent shade, but today, the bench was cold and hard.

"You leap to conclusions, Matthew."

"I do not leap, my dear. I study the evidence, read the signs, and ponder the possible explanations. Thomas's stubborn silence suggests he cannot bear to know particulars of your ruin, and you've respected that, but he must also once again respect *you*."

Sutcliffe came striding out of the stable as if summoned, slapping at his breeches and coat sleeves until he spied Theresa and Matthew on the bench.

Priscilla charged forth next, and when she might have barreled straight across the lane to her mother, Sutcliffe prevented her with a hand on her shoulder.

Beside Matthew, Theresa silently bristled. He felt the war in her, between wanting Priscilla to have her uncle's protection and resenting that such protection might cost the girl her mother's company.

"You grew up without a mother," Matthew said. "Do not inflict the same misery on that innocent child." Further than that, Matthew dared not go. He could dower Priscilla, pay for her education, and otherwise usurp Sutcliffe's patriarchal role, but without marrying Priscilla's mother, such arrangements would support the very worst conclusions.

Theresa slipped her hand into Matthew's, a gesture not lost on the baron, and probably not on the child either. Matthew did not move closer or put an arm around the lady's shoulders, though he remained beside her, waiting.

And hoping.

* * *

How well Theresa knew the expression Thomas wore now. A wintry breeze tousled his dark hair and riffled the lace at his throat, but he stood unmoving, a monument to fraternal ire. Priscilla looked wary too, and for that, Theresa nearly hated her brother.

These feelings, of resentment and protectiveness, were as old as the first memory Theresa had of holding her baby brother, and they had grown more burdensome with time, not less.

Matthew rose and offered Theresa his hand, the courtesy both innate and deliberate. He kissed her knuckles, then tucked her fingers into the crook of his elbow as he escorted her to the stable yard.

"Sutcliffe, you will have acquainted yourself with Tut, I trust," Matthew said. "Priscilla does very well with him and has already cantered nearly halfway around the arena."

They'd cantered a few steps, mostly by accident. Matthew was making small talk—and a point, about civility, about a child being present.

"The Jennings family has an aptitude for all things equestrian," Thomas said, releasing his hold on Priscilla. "Thank you for the loan of the pony."

"I could mount a regiment of youngsters on my pensioners, and exercise does them good," Matthew said, patting Theresa's hand. "Priscilla, when I left the parlor, the baroness was urging shortbread upon me. Perhaps a piece or two remains."

"You may have one," Theresa said, "and one cup of tea if the baroness offers. Come here, Priscilla, one of your braids is coming unraveled."

Let Thomas think of the child's state of disrepair what he might. Priscilla turned her back to her mother and submitted to a quick tidying up, while Thomas's expression remained unreadable.

"Brush the hay from your stockings before you reach the house," Theresa went on, turning Priscilla toward the garden and sneaking in a quick hug. "One piece of shortbread and one cup of tea, and you will let Miss Alice know you've had both."

"Thank you, Mama!" Priscilla said, racing off. "Good-bye, Mr. Belmont!"

Silence descended, and still Matthew remained beside Theresa.

Thomas watched Priscilla's retreat, and abruptly, Theresa was exhausted. Tired of measuring every look and word, tired of apologizing, tired of worrying. Tired of hoping that her brother—not a stupid man, by any means—might someday understand.

"Thomas, when you have a moment, I'd like to speak with you."

Priscilla stopped by the honeysuckle hedge and bent a sprig to her nose, then scampered around a bend in the path.

"I am at your service," Thomas said. "I'll be in the parlor, trying to prevent my wife from stuffing the child with sweets. Belmont, if you'll consider selling the pony, I'll happily take him off your hands."

Was that Thomas's idea of an olive branch, or an opening salvo?

"I couldn't sell that little fellow if I wanted to," Matthew said. "The pony doesn't belong to me, but rather, to my son Richard. We can't sell what we don't own, can we?"

"If you change your mind, let me know," Thomas said, offering Matthew his hand.

Something passed between them, not exactly cordial. Prizefighters shook hands before pummeling each other. Thomas would be scandalized that Theresa even knew of such a bizarre ritual.

And that was tiresome too.

"I'll see you at the house," Thomas said, bowing to her then following in Priscilla's footsteps. He walked past the honeysuckle without pausing and was soon out of sight.

This time tomorrow, Theresa might be in a coach bound for Sutcliffe Keep, but she'd leave behind all the fretting, trying, and hoping where Thomas was concerned.

"He can take Priscilla from me," Theresa said. "He's rich, he's titled, he's married to a lovely woman, and I'm a disgrace."

"What you are, is mistaken," Matthew said, leading Theresa out of the cold and into the relative warmth of the stable. "For nine years Sutcliffe turned his back on you. We might excuse him for that rudeness while your cousins were extant, but we cannot excuse his indifference for the past two years, can we?"

In the middle of the day, no work went on in the stable. The stalls had been mucked, the water buckets filled. The only sounds were horses—and one fat, furry pony—munching hay and shifting about on thick beds of straw.

"You're saying Thomas is the disgrace?" A month ago, Theresa would not have grasped that possibility, but she'd since had the benefit of Matthew's perspective.

And she'd fallen in love.

"Thomas is wrestling with the suspicion that he's behaved more shamefully than he can admit," Matthew said, "and it's about damned time. I'm wrestling with other possibilities, for which you should probably slap me."

Matthew braced her against the wall of Tut's stall and brought her hips against his falls. His movements were measured and deliberate, an invitation rather than a demand.

"I am wanton," Theresa said, kissing Matthew on the mouth. "Don't mistake me for some martyred creature who longs for a nunnery. I behaved myself all morning, only smiling at you the once, and my self-control has been taxed past bearing."

"You are not wanton, you are passionate," Matthew said, kissing her back. "You are determined, you are lovely. All morning, all damned morning, I dealt with the hounds, the hunt staff, the small talk, with a vixen too concerned for her kits to seek her own damned covert, and all I could think about…"

"Was you," Theresa said, smiling against his mouth. "How easily you manage the hunt, how handsome you are on horseback, how people naturally follow your lead, and how the sunlight—"

"Finds all the highlights in your hair," Matthew said, pressing closer. "Madam, at this rate, I'll have to walk home, and a drenching cold rain will be necessary to restore me to a respectable state."

Theresa rested her forehead against Matthew's shoulder, loving the scent of him, the warmth and solidness. This kind of intimacy was new and wonderful, not simply of the body, but of the heart.

She did not want to let him go, did not want to face the cold drenching rain of her next discussion with Thomas.

Not quite yet.

CHAPTER FIFTEEN

"Come with me," Theresa said, taking Matthew by the hand. "This won't be dignified, but my dignity doesn't overly concern me when I'm around you." Finding privacy concerned her. One never knew when a judgmental brother might appear, breathing fire on all of her hopes and dreams.

"I treasure that about you," Matthew said. "You don't stand on ceremony, don't put on airs. You get on with—"

Theresa opened the door to the granary, the portion of the stable reserved for storing feed. To keep out the birds and rodents, this room had a solid plank floor, thick oak walls, and only one window, which could be latched tight against the elements.

The window was open now, the sole source of light. Wire mesh covered the opening, protecting the grain from the birds while letting in fresh air.

"We won't be disturbed," Theresa said, though the setting was hardly conducive to reckless desire. The scent of oats permeated the space, reminiscent of porridge and freshly baked bread. Dust drifted in the sunbeams slanting through the window, and a shovel was propped against the wall.

A sturdy table stood in one corner. Feed buckets, a wooden scoop, a few smooth red apples and a bunch of carrots occupied one side of the table. A pencil hung from a string suspended from a nail above the table, and sheets of foolscap weighted with a horseshoe sat on the other side.

"One of these days," Matthew said, wedging the shovel under the door latch, "you will allow me to share a bed with you, madam. You'll enjoy it. Beds have pillows, fluffy mattresses, and clean linen scented with sachets. Beds allow one to disrobe entirely. You will doubtless be shocked to know that the idea of you without clothing has filled more than a few of my waking hours."

A bird fluttered against the window screen, then bounced away.

"Matthew, if you'd rather not…" Theresa had initiated this, this… interlude. A first for her. In a dusty, chilly barn… when Matthew's house probably had two dozen rooms better suited to such folly.

"I see you, and I want you," Matthew said, stuffing the carrots and apples in one of the buckets and putting the lot on the floor. "Do you know how marvelous that is?"

"Marvelous? I thought most men regarded their base urges as inconvenient half the time and undeniable the other half."

The stack of paper and the horseshoe went next, so the table surface was free of clutter. Matthew stuffed his gloves into a pocket, then withdrew a handkerchief from inside his riding jacket.

"A man regards his base urges as a treasured inconvenience as long as they plague him," Matthew said, scrubbing at the table with the handkerchief. "Then comes a day when he realizes… they haven't plagued him for some time. Come here, my dear."

Theresa was across the room in two strides, then found herself hiked up onto the table.

"A perfect height," Matthew said, standing between her spread knees. "At first, I told myself my marital situation was to blame. Matilda tried to accommodate me intimately, but that's… that's hell for a man, particularly a young man. Utter, unrelenting hell. I think she even wanted to want me, if that makes any sense, but one can't conjure desire when not even a spark of attraction exists."

Theresa unbuttoned Matthew's hunt coat rather than look into his eyes. "Hell for you both, then."

"Precisely, and the road to that hell was paved with"—he let Theresa push the coat from his shoulders then took it from her and hung it on a peg—"animal spirits, so I learned to keep busy and to keep to my own bedroom."

Theresa started on his falls next. "And you had the children."

"The children, the magistrate's duties, the estate duties, and then I had an ailing wife."

"Right now, Matthew Belmont, you have me, and my animal spirits are much revived by the simple sight of you."

Theresa hauled him closer by his elbows, and he came unresisting, his falls half undone, his recounting both sad and precious.

"I had opportunities," Theresa said, after a long, hot kiss. "The curate of all people would come around every few months, soliciting for this charity or that subscription. He was unmarried, as curates tend to be, and lonely, and hopeful. Not bad looking, had all his teeth and a sweet smile. I was tempted."

"Do you think I'd blame you?" Matthew asked, arms looped around her. "The sheer hypocrisy of a churchman soliciting donations while pandering to a woman without protection… and you politely pretended not to grasp his invitation. Very nearly humorous, also a pathetic comment on the Church of England."

And yet, somehow, this coupling with Matthew, in a private little corner of a horse barn, was not pathetic. Theresa purely hugged him, wrapped him in her arms, and hooked a leg around his hips.

"You are so dear, Matthew Belmont. Please make love with me."

Thank goodness she was not in her habit, because Matthew's hands, warm and competent, could slide up her legs, past her gartered stockings to her thighs.

"The sheer feel of you…" he said, resting his forehead against hers. "You bring me to life, Theresa Jennings. I go along, a decent fellow who breaks up the fights on darts night, and then… then you happen, and I'm eighteen again."

Theresa scooted closer, shoving skirts aside and wishing she'd thought to pad the table with at least a horse blanket.

"Eighteen," she said. "Full of hope and determination, full of possibilities and desire, but we'll never be eighteen again. Never again so naïve, never that ignorant. Never that willing to squander our affections or our time or our—"

Matthew shifted close enough that Theresa could feel him probing at her sex, but in this position, the initiative had to be his.

"You understand," he said, finding her and easing forward. "You understand so much."

The sheer glory of Matthew's loving, relentless and yet utterly controlled, sent Theresa off into pleasure despite her determination to hold back. Despite the humble surroundings, despite the looming altercation with Thomas, this was how lovemaking was supposed to be.

An island of intimacy and joy amid all of life's vicissitudes. Why did no one explain this to naïve eighteen-year-olds?

"I love to give you satisfaction," Matthew said, pausing for some lazy kisses. "Love to hear the wanting in the way you say my name. Come again, Theresa."

She did, and again, until her back ached, her braid was tumbling down her back, and she would have melted into a puddle of bliss on the plank floor, but for Matthew's arms around her.

"You'll be sore," Matthew said, when for the third time, Theresa had gone boneless against him, the beat of his heart the only sound in her world. If they ever did find a bed, she might not survive the experience.

"I don't want to let you go," was what came out of her mouth. Not now, not when Thomas sent her back to Sutcliffe. Not ever.

Matthew started moving again, and at any moment, Theresa might have begun another climb to satisfaction. She mustered some self-restraint and instead memorized the feel of Matthew in her arms, the scent of him, the sensations of being joined with him.

"For now, let me go, you must." He hilted himself against her, an offer, in case Theresa's greed overcame her determination not to beg.

She kissed him thoroughly, then allowed him to ease from her body.

"Matthew, look at me." Theresa was not eighteen, thank God. Not seventeen. She was not innocent, and most of all, *she was not ashamed.*

He met her gaze, and she scooted back, sliding her skirts up and up yet more.

"Look at me," she said again, more softly. "If we were in a bed, we'd have not a stitch of clothing between us. I'd be looking at you, touching you, kissing you…"

He wrapped his hand around his cock as Theresa got her skirts above her waist. She rocked against the table, giving him as much of an eyeful as she could. She'd never done this before, never been so wonderfully wicked, never been as determined to please a lover.

"I want to close my eyes," Matthew said, "lest I spend immediately, and I never want this moment to end."

Theresa jiggled, she rocked, she spread her legs as Matthew's fingers traced her folds and secrets. He looked at her as he pleasured himself, caressing her, making her very, very glad she was a grown woman who'd taken a detour or two from the path of propriety.

Matthew was silent in his passion, the only clue to impending satisfaction a hitch in his breathing, a shift in the rhythm of his hand. Theresa passed him the dusty handkerchief and lay back against the table, as exhausted as if she'd come yet again.

The beams above were festooned with cobwebs, the poor bird made another attempt to fly through the window's wire mesh, and Matthew climbed onto the table to crouch over Theresa.

Peace settled inside her, the peace of having loved and been loved, intimately. For a moment, Theresa simply rested in that peace, and in Matthew's warmth all around her.

"I ask different questions now," Theresa said, stroking his hair. "Before Priscilla was born, I never understood why, if fornication was such a great sin, so many people were hell-bent on indulging in it. Some thrashing about, a momentary pleasure if the fellow had any consideration, nothing more. *That* was ruin? *That* was the great wicked pleasure young women are warned against? I have a harder time resisting tea cakes."

Matthew's sigh breezed past Theresa's ear. "And don't forget the moments afterward, when there's nothing to say, and you honestly hope she doesn't want you to linger for another go, even as you make plans to leave the house party before breakfast. You ask yourself what in the hell you could have been thinking—again."

"But lonely people don't think," Theresa said, kissing Matthew's eyelids. "Now, I ask myself how something this sublime, this… *precious* could ever be a sin. I have so many regrets, Matthew, but I assure you, this will never, ever be one of them."

"I have no words, Theresa Jennings, other than thank you, and please marry me."

Thank you, a respectful sentiment between adults who'd been lonely for too long. Theresa trailed her fingers through Matthew's hair as she searched for the right words to reciprocate that sentiment, because a mere thank you was also—

The sense of his words smacked into her mind, like the bird who'd flown into the window screen.

"You're proposing *now?*"

Matthew eased up to his elbows. "The setting isn't exactly romantic, I know, but we'll never forget this occasion. I want you in my bed, Theresa Jennings. I want to ride to hounds with you, I want to surprise you under the mistletoe two weeks from now. I want to dream and argue and while away afternoons with you, to grow old with you. If I'm stealing down to the stable before breakfast, I want you stealing with me. Please say—" He fell silent, gaze focused on Theresa's shoulder. "I hear—"

Theresa put her finger over his lips, because she heard it too.

"Spiker says he'd cleaned the gun just the week before." Jamie's voice was perilously near, a few yards beyond the window.

"Guns misfire," Beckman replied, as Matthew silently climbed off the table. "Pistols especially. We carry them about, stuff them into saddlebags. If the gun was stored in Belmont's stable, then dust was a factor."

Theresa sat up, praying Jamie's inherent contrariness would prolong the discussion.

"Belmont is the father of three boys," Jamie shot back. "He's not careless with his firearms and his stable is spotless. You ever see him shoot from the saddle?"

Matthew helped Theresa off the table, and as she smoothed down her skirts, he got to work on his falls.

"I haven't seen Belmont shoot from the saddle," Beckman replied, his tone impatient. "But I've shot from the saddle on occasion. What's your point?"

"Matthew Belmont's damned good with a gun," Jamie said, which inspired a small smile from Matthew. "But in the hunt field, you can come across a rabid animal, an injured horse, a dog that's got itself in bad trouble. You sometimes have to shoot to kill."

"You're not telling me anything new," Beckman retorted. "My father put us up on ponies from the time we could walk."

"A killing shot has to be steady, the first bullet has to count," Jamie went on.

Matthew had gone still, clearly listening to the conversation. Theresa took it upon herself to silently reposition the feed buckets, carrots, and apples on the table.

"Because the noise alone will cause an injured animal to panic," Beckman said.

"If you're shooting from the saddle, your own mount will dance around, or at least flinch when your gun goes off," Jamie said, as Theresa tried to recall the exact position of the horseshoe on top of the sheaf of papers.

"And because you're holding the gun," Beckman said, "you can't have both hands on the reins. Jamie, what are you getting at? Belmont is a first-rate huntsman, and his horses don't panic at the sound of gunfire."

Theresa moved the shovel away from the door.

"Beckman, *think*," Jamie said. "Picture this: Squire is in the hunt field and comes across a stray dog, a sickly cur that might be rabid. He won't dismount, he won't waste a moment. He'll get out his pistol, signal his mare to stand. The shot has to count. Belmont raises his left arm to eye level, and steadies the barrel of the gun on his forearm. I've seen him do this. He sights, lets a breath halfway out, the gun practically at the end of his nose, and bang."

Theresa nearly dropped the shovel as the import of Jamie's words struck her.

"That pistol could have blown up in Belmont's face," Beckman said. "The gun he routinely carried as master of fox hounds, the one unlikely to have ever been fired by another hand, could have blown up in his face. I don't think you're right, I don't think you're half right, but somebody needs to find Matthew Belmont and put this before him, immediately."

* * *

Agatha's hip was paining her. She, of course, did not say a word, but Emmanuel knew from the compressed line of her lips, from the quality of her silence, from the way she perched *on* the saddle rather than rode *in* the saddle, that she was uncomfortable.

"Did you enjoy the morning's outing?" Emmanuel asked, tipping up his second flask and finding it empty.

"I did, thank you, though the cold weather feels like it's about to pounce in earnest. I take it you had a good time?"

She was reliably civil, his Agatha. Also boring as hell. "Racketing about in the undergrowth while catching up on the latest gossip isn't exactly a riveting diversion. Matthew's idea of riding to hounds has little to do with ridding the countryside of vermin, and the rest is so much tedium and protocol."

"To take the fresh air is still a healthful pastime," Agatha said, which for her was close to outright disagreement. "You did not wish Matthew good night."

One always wished the master good night when leaving the hunt breakfast, even if sunset was hours and hours away.

"I dispensed with hunt protocol because our dear Matthew was too busy ogling the Jennings creature." Miss Jennings was worth an ogle too. Not only was she generously proportioned in the places that fired a man's imagination, she was bold.

Matthew had apparently developed a taste for a bold, curvaceous strumpet, which would not do at all if matrimony was under consideration.

"Her name is Theresa," Agatha said, sitting taller, "and she's a baron's granddaughter and a baron's sister. If Matthew has taken a fancy to her, she'll be treated with the same courtesy as was shown to my own sister. Don't publicly disrespect her, Manny. We mustn't have it said there's discord in the family."

Oh, the hilarity of marriage to a decent woman. The horses plodded along, while Emmanuel considered just how badly to shock his dear wife.

"Theresa Jennings was once known as the Sutcliffe Strumpet, madam. She wasn't exactly available on street corners, but neither was she... don't give me that look. Her daughter is nearly half grown, a pretty little thing by all accounts, brought along on this visit to Linden as bold as you please. I tell you these things that your judgments about Miss Jennings might be well informed."

Though Agatha, in her quiet way, seemed to come across all the gossip. Quilting parties, social calls, and even Bible study gatherings allowed the women to exchange information without benefit of male supervision. Fortunately, she passed anything relating to Matthew Belmont along to her devoted husband.

"Spare me your lectures, Manny Capshaw. The holidays approach, and Miss Jennings will doubtless be included in the Linden household's socializing. You will be on your best manners, or after all these years, the neighbors will think we are no longer cordial toward Matthew."

Manny. Emmanuel hated that nickname, but he hated more that connection to the Belmont family fortune was doubtless the gossamer thread from which Emmanuel's own meager credit dangled.

"We will always be cordial toward Matthew, my dear." They'd remain cordial toward Matthew's wealth, at least. "We owe our nephews that effort, and we owe it to dear Matilda's dear memory."

Agatha—good, silly woman that she was—probably held herself responsible for all the trouble Matilda had got up to. Invoking Matilda's memory usually resulted in Agatha falling into fuming silence.

This morning she merely shot Emmanuel a displeased look, touched her mare's quarters with the whip, and cantered off in the direction of home. Watching her ride away, Emmanuel realized that she needed a new saddle, one that fitted a matronly figure rather than a young woman's.

Finances did not permit that extravagance, alas for Agatha. Lately, finances hadn't permitted *any* extravagances, though Emmanuel had made some interesting investments and had reason to hope the situation would come right. And soon.

* * *

Thomas kept his horse to the trot on the way to Belmont House. Rupert was a good fellow, but he'd recently made the journey from Sutcliffe Keep to

London, and then from London to Sussex. A sedate pace was only considerate of the horse.

Thomas also needed the time to think, for Matthew Belmont would not want to hear what must be said.

And yet, Belmont was gracious as ever, welcoming Thomas into his estate office as if they'd last seen each other over a pint on darts night at the Cock and Bull.

"Baron, shall I ring for a tray, or may I offer you a brandy to ward off the chill?"

"Brandy wouldn't go amiss. Jamie says we're due for snow." Jamie had said a lot more than that, but a pair of English gentlemen embarking on a difficult discussion might as well start with the damned weather.

Belmont passed over a neat portion of spirits in a cut crystal glass. His own serving was more parsimonious.

"A health to your womenfolk," Belmont said, saluting with his brandy.

Thomas silently drank to Belmont's continued good health, which was apparently in jeopardy.

Where to begin? "My thanks for looking in on Penny."

Twenty years from now, Matthew Belmont's appearance would be much the same. He'd be lean and fit, his gaze genial to the casual observer. His hair would be wheat rather than gold, and he'd still fool most of the world into thinking he was merely a wealthy yeoman content to tend his acres.

If he was alive in twenty years.

"Sutcliffe, whatever has sent you haring from your baroness's side, you'd best just say on. The daylight is nearly gone, and the clouds will obscure the moon when it eventually rises. I should hate for harm to befall you because you sought to spare my sensibilities, particularly when I took no pains to spare yours earlier today."

"Harm," Thomas muttered, stalling with another sip of his drink. "I've come to discuss that very notion. Might we sit?"

Belmont propped a hip on his desk, while Thomas took a reading chair positioned before the blazing fire.

The room was both a business office and a county gentleman's retreat. Behind the desk hung a portrait of an eighteen-point red deer amid verdant summer foliage. Small portraits of the three Belmont children were arranged on top of a bookcase, and a painting of hound puppies tussling over a whip hung above the fireplace.

The air bore the scent of leather and old books, of contentment and ease, but also of loneliness. Not a bouquet of dried flowers, not a miniature of the late Mrs. Belmont, not an embroidered pillow suggested the man who ran his empire from this room was beloved of any woman.

"Jamie and Beckman have put a theory before me," Thomas said, easing back into an exquisitely comfortable chair. "I'd like you to hear me out before you dismiss what they have to say."

"A magistrate learns to listen, as does the father of three imaginative boys. Out with it, Sutcliffe."

Thomas had the sense Belmont knew exactly what was coming, and yet, the squire's gaze conveyed nothing so much as patient interest.

"A harrow was found on my property at the exact spot a bridle path crosses the boundary with your woods," Thomas said. "The placement of the implement was dangerous, for you often take that shortcut when calling upon Linden."

"Beckman moved the harrow, and I have since stored it at my home farm."

"Your hunting pistol misfired, and Spiker's hand is the worse for it."

Belmont shoved away from his desk and ambled to the bookcase, where he fiddled with the portraits of the children.

"Pistols misfire, Sutcliffe, though I can guess what you're thinking."

Belmont's offspring were handsome boys, all brown-haired and brown-eyed, and in their expressions, Thomas saw the same calm, settled outlook Belmont shared. Those children would want their father safe. Thomas wanted their father safe too.

"Jamie and Beckman are worried that somebody tampered with your pistol and left that harrow where you'd come to grief on one of your morning gallops." Loris was of a mind to agree, and Thomas hadn't asked Theresa her opinion.

Not that he was avoiding his sister.

"I appreciate their concern," Belmont said, taking out a handkerchief and dusting along the frame of one painting. "I asked our local blacksmith about that harrow, and he doesn't recognize it. He did recognize the welding that had been done on an old repair, and said a man whose forge is the other side of Trieshock does such work."

That Belmont had made inquiries was both unnerving and reassuring.

"Who would move a harrow nearly seven miles to leave it where it could cause severe injury or death?"

The next little portrait also got a careful dusting. "You're making the first mistake of a new magistrate, Sutcliffe. The harrow might have been mended years ago and then sold to my nearest neighbor shortly after that—my nearest neighbor besides you. It might have been sitting in my woods for the past two years, rusting away, and some disgruntled poachers moved it, the better to hide their activities."

And the bad fairies might have conjured that harrow from thin air. "Would a sane man poach from the magistrate's own home wood?"

"My woods are extensive and teeming with game. Any man's sanity can be imperiled if he's had sufficient drink, or has too many mouths to feed. One learns this, being a magistrate, and one learns to proceed by rational steps."

Thomas took another swallow of brandy rather than point out that when dealing with Theresa, Belmont's capacity for reason had apparently been mislaid.

"I'm leaping to conclusions?"

Belmont picked up the third portrait, this one of the youngest boy. "You are leaping to cause and effect. *If* the mending looks like it came from a forge seven miles distant, *then*, you conclude, some malefactor from that direction has recently moved the harrow, intent on causing me harm. You leap to cause and effect, rather than study the facts until a solution appears. Richard does not want to come home for Christmas."

"We are talking about a possible attempt on your life, Belmont. Two possible attempts on your life. What matter a boy's sulks?"

Belmont set the portrait down. "My children are due to join me here, along with my only brother, and remain for the holidays. If you have wisdom to dispense, then I'm all ears, Baron. Do I bring my children to the scene of possible murder attempts, or, because of nothing more than speculation, do I forgo a holiday with family, possibly the last time we'll all be together?"

Thomas shoved out of a chair that invited a man to grow old by a cozy fire. He should have brought Loris with him, and then this discussion would be taking place in a parlor or library, not this patriarchal confessional.

"I hate messes," Thomas said. "This is why I was such a competent factor for Lord Fairly. I cannot abide untidy situations. I put them to rights, or I unravel what makes them untidy. Instinct tells me you have a mess on your hands, Belmont. A magistrate makes enemies, and a wealthy, well-liked magistrate has too much power to be openly confronted."

Opposite the hearth, burgundy velvet curtains had been drawn back to let in the last of the afternoon's light. A single flake of snow drifted down outside, or perhaps it was stray ash from a chimney.

"Did you leave your ancestral home ten years ago because matters there were messy, Sutcliffe?"

Good God. No wonder the district had so little crime. A pack of hounds in full cry was lackadaisical compared to Matthew Belmont intent on making a point.

"That is none of your business, Squire."

Belmont nudged the curtain back from the window. "I've offered for your sister, you know. You and I might well end up as family, Sutcliffe. I care about my family, and my friends."

"Belmont, you are in love. Because I am familiar with that affliction myself, I will make allowances. Theresa was not the innocent you want to believe her to be. She embraced ruin, and when I tried to dissuade her, she made it plain my efforts were unwelcome. Grandfather offered me a sum upon graduation from university as a remittance for leaving the family seat. I took it with Theresa's blessing."

The window rattled in its casement, suggesting that the wind had picked up with the gathering darkness.

"She started it?" Belmont mused, wandering to the mantel behind his desk. "A juvenile corollary to the doctrine of self-defense. I do not dispute that Theresa started the rift, Sutcliffe, but please consider why a shrewd woman, one who professed to care for you, would cast from her side her only ally."

This much Thomas had worked out. As he'd inspected each room at Sutcliffe, the furniture draped with Holland covers, the porcelain, linen, and silver all carefully stored under lock and key, Thomas had admitted to himself at least part of Theresa's motivation.

"She was ashamed, Belmont, and didn't want me underfoot to see that. By then she was probably anticipating motherhood, and well she should have been ashamed."

Belmont took an inlaid wooden box down from the mantel, possibly a humidor.

And then he withdrew a pistol. "Motherhood is a cause for shame. Why has nobody explained this to me? Does fatherhood subject one to humiliation as well? I do hope you've acquainted your baroness with these facts, for she admires you exceedingly, and in the natural course of early marriage—"

"Shut your mouth, Belmont."

He sighted down the barrel of an elegant little piece, one of a matched pair. The mouth of the pistol was pointed at the hearth, but at close range, Belmont could have hit any object in the room he pleased.

And this entire digression had done nothing to disprove Thomas's theory that somebody was trying to seriously injure, or possibly even kill, Matthew Belmont.

CHAPTER SIXTEEN

"I will shut my mouth," Belmont said, "if you will open your mind, Sutcliffe. You don't even know if Priscilla's conception was a consensual undertaking, and yet, you—who left the scene, lucre clutched in your righteous fist—presume to judge. Priscilla must get her imagination from you. Marriage to your sister will not be dull, and that's before my sons have made any contribution to the festivities."

Marriage—to Theresa. Thomas set that topic aside as a man might a draught of poison.

"Is that firearm William Parker's work?" And did Belmont plan to use it on his intended's brother?

"I favor Parker over Manton, and I favor cordial relations over awkwardness. What do you propose should be done about a potential threat to my life?"

Thomas felt as if Belmont were delivering another series of unexpected blows to the chin. Each well placed, well timed, and all of them still somehow unexpected.

"I suggest you be careful," Thomas said, "though if somebody wishes you evil, they've had ample opportunity to do you in, and failed to accomplish that objective."

Belmont replaced the pistol with its twin in the velvet-lined box. "I offered to lend Priscilla a book about equitation, though the best teacher of equitation is the horse. Accompany me to the library, and I can send the book back to Linden with you. What are these opportunities for murder you allude to?"

Thomas was relieved to quit the estate office, relieved to be moving. He was not relieved to notice that a few flakes of snow had organized themselves into a steady, light downpour.

Belmont moved through the house at a good clip, though Thomas was aware as they traversed steps, the main hall, more steps, and a lengthy corridor, that this entire house was now the residence of one somewhat retiring man.

A decent fellow he was too. Theresa's tastes had improved considerably.

"You should gather your family for the holidays," Thomas said. "Safety in numbers being a consideration."

"Fewer chances to shoot me out of the saddle?" Belmont mused, leading the way into the library.

"Well, yes. If somebody truly wanted you dead, then this morning's hunt was a good opportunity. You're off with the hounds, well ahead of the first flight, and anybody who knows the local foxes would deduce where to lie in wait for you."

Belmont crossed the library—a chilly room, despite a fire blazing in the hearth—and disappeared between two rows of bookcases.

"Nobody knows the local foxes like I do, Sutcliffe, and the foxes and I have an understanding. They leave my chickens alone, and I leave the foxes alone. The fox who disrespects those rules repeatedly is the only one who must deal with the king's man. Where could the damned book have got off to? When you have children, you'll find that whatever item you seek will levitate—here we go."

Thomas liked Belmont's library. Liked the sense of quiet, the gently crackling fire, the balance of elegance and comfort. The old hound lay flat out on the hearth rug, and on Belmont's desk, a plate held half a sandwich, the crusts cut off to expose generous portions of ham, slices of cheese, and smears of mustard.

Belmont's library was not a museum for books. He spent time here, he lived here. Theresa had always loved books, and yet, the library at Sutcliffe hadn't held but a few hundred volumes.

"Is that your late wife?" Thomas asked, for on the wall between the bookcases hung a portrait of a blond, blue-eyed woman barely into her adult years. Her appearance was more girl than matron, though she bore a resemblance to Belmont's children.

"The late Matilda Belmont. I keep that portrait here for the boys. Richard once told me he could barely recall her appearance, so I've made sure Emmanuel and Agatha know I've bequeathed that portrait to my youngest."

"She was very pretty." Something in her smile suggested she'd also been vain.

"Matilda was very mendacious," Belmont said, emerging from the bookshelves, "and I don't think she knew much happiness, though she loved the boys and did the best she could with me. For many women, beauty is as much a burden as a blessing. This is the book I promised Priscilla, but I'm in no hurry to have it back. I particularly like the illustrations."

Theresa was beautiful, more beautiful than she'd been as a younger woman, even, though she'd never been vain.

Thomas accepted the book. "Do you ever stop sermonizing?"

Belmont regarded the dog, who remained unmoving before the fire. "I'm simply a country squire who misses his children, Sutcliffe. A humble, rather smitten, fellow facing possible attempts on his life, and—Maida?"

From the old hound, not so much as a tail thump indicated she'd heard her master call her name. Belmont crossed to the hearth, knelt, and stroked a hand over the dog's brindle shoulder.

"Maida, my dearest, have you finally left me?"

Surely a touch that gentle, a voice that loving would rouse the hound from her dreams?

"She's...?"

"Taken in her sleep," Belmont said, his hand smoothing over the grizzled head. "Carried off while napping before a cheery fire, exactly the way an old hound should go. The boys will miss her. She was a gift from them, though Matilda was of course complicit in that generosity, and if ever a man didn't need another canine—"

Thomas had to look away. For something to do, he took himself to the sideboard, intent on pouring the bereaved—or himself—a consolatory tot.

"You barely touched your brandy," Thomas said, pouring out two measures. "Doesn't look like you finished your luncheon either."

Belmont had risen, nothing in his features suggesting he'd lost a friend of long standing only moments before. He was instead studying the half sandwich on the desk.

"Sutcliffe, in point of fact, I have touched nothing on that plate. I didn't know any sustenance awaited me here when I returned from Linden."

Thomas set his glass aside as cold slithered up his spine. "You went straight to the estate office when you returned from Linden?"

"I came in through the kitchen. Because my cook has absented herself indefinitely, I foraged for bread, cheese, ham, a few pickles, some biscuits, two boiled eggs, a glass of milk, a slice of cinnamon cake—what?"

"So a single sandwich wouldn't even constitute a snack for you?"

Belmont peered at the desk. "The kitchen has orders not to waste the crusts unless a loaf has been burned. I also have a violent dislike for mustard. The young ladies on my kitchen staff know that. The mustard overpowers all else, though that could be useful if poison were... Sutcliffe, am I daft?"

Thomas's mind took a progression of moments to assemble the hypothesis Belmont had formulated with a glance, a hunch, and a suspicion.

Was it daft to wonder if mustard had been used to disguise the taste of poison?

"You wonder if Maida ate half a sandwich left for you," Thomas said, "and now she's dead. Your kitchen help knows better than to waste crusts or use mustard on your food, and yet, somebody left that food here, on the desk you probably occupy daily."

Belmont sniffed the sandwich, which Thomas would not have thought to do.

"Next you'll take a taste." Thomas snatched the uneaten portion from Belmont and pitched it into the fire.

"I might have fed that to the rats and determined if it was indeed poisoned."

"Shite."

"Or I might have concluded that the meat had gone bad," Belmont said. "In the alternative, the rats might not be susceptible to the specific poison involved, and I'd have erroneously concluded that Maida's time had simply come, when in fact, a killer was loose in my own library."

A peaceful library, not a place where murder should be done, not that murder should be done anywhere.

Amid the blaze in the hearth, the sandwich went from toast to ashes in moments.

"You are welcome to come back to Linden with me," Thomas said, though Belmont's intended dwelled at Linden, and Thomas did not want to watch his sister working her wiles ever again.

"And leave my staff here to contend with some homicidal miscreant in my absence? Not bloody likely, Sutcliffe. Half the shire was on my property today, and the house is always open when we have a hunt meet. The weather was nippy, and some people prefer to eat indoors. Mrs. Dale is prone to chills, and Mr. Dale's gout means he wants a comfortable chair when he's ridden in. Your own sister might have needed the retiring room, and all the while—"

"We might be jumping at shadows," Thomas said, because nobody else was on hand to say it. "Old dogs die. Somebody might have fixed that plate for themselves and left it here inadvertently. The situation is no different from when your gun misfired or your mysterious poachers left a rusty harrow in the worst possible location."

Thomas picked up his drink, intent on fortifying himself against a cold journey home, steadying his nerves, or toasting the departed hound. Something—

"Don't touch that brandy," Belmont said, moving toward the door. "Any food or drink that was not under lock and key at all times today must be regarded as suspect. My home must be treated as a potential crime scene."

"As must your stable and your home wood," Thomas said, setting the brandy down. "I can't like this, Belmont. How many people have you seen tried, transported, or hanged?"

Belmont paused at the door, sparing his departed hound a look. "I don't think I need fret over the three I've sent to the gallows. They were thorough-going scoundrels, caught red-handed committing robbery and rapine on the king's highway."

"You still need to consider their aggrieved families, their mates, their partners in crime."

Belmont preceded Thomas into a corridor grown both chilly and gloomy. "What a cheering companion you've turned out to be, Sutcliffe. While you're spouting such encouraging sentiments, perhaps you'll explain to me how I rescind the proposal of marriage I made to your sister? Anybody who wants me dead won't quibble at endangering my intended or her daughter to accomplish that goal."

Well, damn…. As if sibling relations in the Jennings family weren't already beyond delicate. At least Belmont hadn't referred to Theresa as his fiancée—yet.

"You need not rescind your offer. I'll simply send Theresa and Priscilla back to Sutcliffe Keep, at least until you've determined why your favorite dog died, your favorite pistol misfired, and your favorite bridle path became the potential scene of a fatal ambush."

* * *

Axel Belmont had gathered all the intelligence he could without asking brother to peach on brother, or cousin upon cousin. He'd written to Matthew, he'd consulted his journal for clues that might lie between its pages. He'd been as patient as the uncanonized father of two adolescent males could be.

The journey to Sussex began in the morning. Time to confront the rebel nephew directly.

"Hand me that thread," Axel muttered, the heat of the lantern overhead making the propagation house almost cozy.

Richard passed over a three-foot length of black silk thread. "How do you know how tightly to wrap the graft?"

The boy had a good mind, restless, but capable of focus. Considering he was not yet fifteen, this boded well.

"You wrap it quite snugly," Axel said, winding the thread about both graft and root stock. "You're not introducing two young people at a tea dance. You're creating a marriage, where one partner provides sustenance and the other brings all the good breeding, grace, and beauty. That takes more than a passing interest if it's not to fail."

Though to be honest, Axel knew precious damned little about what made a marriage work. He'd loved his wife, and she had loved him. More than that, the passage of time was mercifully obscuring.

"How did you learn to do this?" Richard asked, as Axel knotted the thread and knotted it again.

"Practice, my boy. So what do you think of your papa's interest in Miss Jennings?"

Richard became fascinated with a pair of freshly sharpened pruning shears. "She has a daughter, and yet she's *Miss* Jennings."

"Is that why you're determined not to return to Sussex for the holidays? You are going with us, you know. If I have to wrap you in heavy silk cords and tie your skinny arse to the saddle, you will not remain behind by yourself."

The trick with adolescent males was to know when to be an authority, when to be silent, and when to be a knowledgeable resource, ready to step in, but unwilling to interfere uninvited.

Dayton and Phillip were good fellows, and Axel had had their entire lives to learn their moods, while Matthew's boys were more subtle. As Matthew himself had put it, Christopher had appointed himself Assistant Papa upon Matilda's death, Remington was appallingly canny for a boy just up from the shires, and Richard…

Richard was growing secretive and difficult.

Richard snipped at the air with the shears. "I could run away. You might force me to go with you, but you can't keep your eyes on me every moment. We'll stay at inns between here and Sussex, and I could sneak out in the middle of the night."

Well, then. Axel would be sure to share a room with his youngest nephew en route, though a boy who announced a plan to run off was not a boy who truly *wanted* to run off.

"You don't want to face something or someone in Sussex," Axel said, turning the rose bush so the graft was closest to the lamps. His plants did not need sunshine to grow—he'd done experiments—any sort of light would suffice, though sunshine was best.

"I'm not a coward," Richard retorted, bending the bush's single bloom toward his nose. "Belmont House is my home. I'm not afraid to go home."

"That bloom hasn't much scent," Axel said, sweeping leaves, dirt, and twigs into a pile on the work table. "The prettiest ones often lack a beguiling fragrance."

"What do you think of this Miss Jennings?"

Richard's tone was carefully neutral, as boys of a certain age must be when discussing the reality of adult female sexuality. Axel was glad for the opening, however, because the conversation was far from over.

"What I think of the lady matters naught. If your father is taken with her, then in the first place, I'm relieved. Matthew has been a damned monk, and with you lot out from under foot, that appalling transgression against commonsense can be addressed."

Richard pulled a single yellow leaf from the rose bush and tossed it on the pile of detritus.

"In the second place?"

In the second place, Miss Jennings was not who or what was troubling the boy. His sulks and broods had been going on since he'd left Sussex.

"In the second place, if your papa is enamored of her, then she must be a good sort. He's no fool, and neither are you."

Richard wandered away and hiked himself up on the second work table, which was free of clutter and mostly clean.

"She might be after Papa's money."

Interesting theory, and not one most adolescent boys would come up with on their own.

"She might well be after his money," Axel said, brushing the leavings into a dust bin, "because a woman has so few avenues of acquiring wealth in her own name in these enlightened and chivalrous times."

"Uncle, not the lecture on France, please."

"Mark my words, Nephew: Most Englishmen are cowards posing as knights in shining armor, and one day soon, Englishwomen will call that bluff. I thank the Almighty I have no daughters, for that day will be lively indeed."

"About Christmas," Richard said, with the air of a young man schooling a fractious puppy. "I'd really rather not go home."

Axel fired his dust rag at Richard's chest, which was not as skinny a chest as it had been six months ago.

"I don't want to go either," Axel said, leaning back against the work table and crossing his arms. "Travel in December is invariably unpleasant. The coaching inns are full of influenza and worse. Riding horseback on frozen roads holds even less appeal, and if your father is in the middle of a courtship, pretending to ignore that farce will tax my nonexistent stores of tact. Then there's your dear Aunt and Uncle Capshaw."

Richard shook out the rag he'd been twisting. "You don't care for them?"

Was that hope in the boy's voice? Relief?

"Your aunt is a good woman, albeit tediously pious and incapable of setting a decent table on a constrained budget. Your uncle is an utter buffoon, and a trial to the nerves. Five minutes in Manny Capshaw's company explains why your aunt has turned to no less comfort than Almighty God, whose mercy she must augment with genteel tippling."

Richard fired the rag back at his uncle. "You don't like Uncle Emmanuel?"

"Don't like him, don't respect him, and don't trust him either. Matthew says the Capshaw tenant farms are not in good repair. Your brothers have noticed that Manny philanders, which euphemism is as much delicacy as I'm capable of."

"So Miss Jennings being thoroughly ruined and having a bastard daughter is just fine, but Uncle Manny philandering is beyond the pale?"

Axel studied the boy, who sat, hands braced on the table's edge, shoulders hunched. This question had been vexing Richard for some time—an interesting question, too.

"What your father has told me of Miss Jennings's situation suggests she was quite young at the time of her downfall, had no one to properly guide her decisions, and has since become a pattern card of probity. I'm inclined to give her the benefit of the doubt. Emmanuel, by contrast, took vows to your aunt and has been so lacking in discretion that his own nephews know of his rutting and strutting."

Richard pushed off the table and dusted his backside. "Uncle's fault is a lack of discretion?"

"You should be a barrister," Axel said, cuffing the boy on the shoulder. "Miss Jennings failed to show proper respect for herself, in succumbing to the charms of some bounder." Or several bounders. The stories Axel had unearthed hinted at a spree of determined dissipation, not a single romantic mis-step. "Capshaw shows a lack of respect for your aunt in allowing his foibles to become common knowledge."

Richard's brows rose in a gesture reminiscent of his father when that worthy had stitched together seemingly unrelated bits of evidence into a possible solution to a criminal mystery.

"Uncle disrespects Aunt Agatha, but Miss Jennings disrespected herself," Richard said. "I see the difference."

"Then you will also see that Miss Jennings has apparently regained her self-respect, or at least improved the company she keeps. Will you please not run off on the way to Sussex?"

Richard studied the grafted rose, for which Axel had high hopes. "I might be sick a lot once we get to Belmont House, have a deal of studying to do, that sort of thing. If Aunt threatens to have us over for supper, I will fall victim to a violent megrim."

"The first contagious megrim in medical history," Axel assured him. "For I will be prone to the same ailment."

Richard smacked him on the arm—a good, hard blow, the blow of a young man, not a mere boy—and dashed out the door.

CHAPTER SEVENTEEN

Supper at Linden had been a tense affair, reminiscent of the many difficult meals Theresa had endured growing up at Sutcliffe Keep.

Often, Grandpapa's complexion had grown more choleric with each course—and each bottle of wine—until one of the twins said or did something outrageous, and crystal was hurled the length of the table. Theresa had learned by the age of fourteen to excuse herself with an impending megrim after the soup course when Grandpapa was in particularly loud form.

"Theresa, will you join me in the family parlor after you've looked in on Priscilla?" Thomas asked as he assisted Loris from her chair.

A request, but like many requests from powerful men, also an order.

"Of course," Theresa said, rising and avoiding the baroness's worried gaze.

Loris was besotted with her handsome husband, but she was also the daughter of a steward, and caretaking was in her bones. If Thomas had shared with his wife what Beckman and Jamie had doubtless confided in him earlier in the day, then Loris would be worried for Matthew too.

By the time Theresa reached the nursery suite, Priscilla had fallen asleep, and even Alice was on the point of retiring.

"You were so happy when you rode off to the hunt meet," Alice said, closing the book in her lap. "You're not happy now."

Theresa latched the door that led from the playroom to Priscilla's bedroom, though that would mean less warmth in the bedroom.

"Matthew proposed to me today. I feel as if those words can't possibly mean what I know them to mean. He offered marriage—to me. Not mere courtship, holy matrimony. His affection for Priscilla is without doubt, he's well-fixed, handsome, and he's offered to marry me."

Alice pushed her spectacles up her nose. "Priscilla matters. Handsome does not matter, well-fixed only matters some. His regard for you matters a lot."

"But I never, ever, in my wildest fairy tales imagined that such a man—he's good, Alice. He's kind, he's honorable. He's... he's worth every year I spent at Sutcliffe, ignoring the curate and keeping the books to the penny."

"You trust him, in other words."

Oh, the situation was even worse than that. Theresa loved Matthew Belmont. "*He trusts me.* Alice, you cannot imagine what a gift that is. He's not scowling at me from the back of my mind, waiting for me to pounce on the gardener's boy beneath the hawthorns, or gamble away my pin money."

"Your brother doesn't know you very well. Give it time, Theresa, and don't stay up too late. Tomorrow is another day."

Alice rose stiffly, set her book on the mantel, opened Priscilla's door a crack, and retreated to her own bedroom.

Thomas was waiting in the corridor when Theresa left the nursery suite, the flickering sconces making him look like a demon haunting his own home.

"Did you think I wouldn't heed your summons, Thomas?"

He turned down the lamp's wick, which made the shadows denser. "I thought you would join me, but I neglected to have the fire lit in the family parlor earlier in the day. That room will be freezing."

Because at Linden, nobody used the family parlor. Theresa knew where it was, but hadn't spent so much as an hour there.

"Let's talk in the playroom," she said. "It's cozy, and we won't be disturbed." They wouldn't be disturbed, provided nobody got to shouting.

Theresa crossed the corridor first, but Thomas beat her to the door. He opened it and bowed her through, the idiot.

"You never smile at me," he said. "Or is it more accurate to say, we never smile at each other?"

His mood was hard to decipher, but then, they'd avoided anything approaching a real conversation for nearly a decade.

"You smile at your baroness," Theresa said, taking the seat Alice had vacated. "I like Loris very much, Thomas."

Thomas took the second rocker, the chair creaking as he set it in motion. "What I feel for my wife is so complicated, and so fine, I don't try to put words on it. I suspect you're to become an aunt, and that…. That…."

Doubtless, Thomas had intended to raise some other topic, and yet, impending parenthood was too enormous, too all-consuming to ignore.

"Are you afraid?" Theresa asked.

He looked at his hands, elegant, competent hands, but not yet a father's hands. "Terrified, now that you ask. Terrified I could lose Loris so soon after I've found her. Terrified for the child, terrified I'll bungle it all, terrified Napoleon will escape again fifteen years hence, and my darling firstborn will run off to join some damned regiment. I've gone quietly daft, and nobody warned me about any of it."

In the next room, Priscilla stirred. Her dreams had always been vivid, almost as if a single day wasn't enough to hold all the fancies and fears her imagination could conjure in twenty-four hours.

"That terror is normal, Thomas, for us at least. Priscilla was five years old before I realized that most of my fear was not for her, but was instead the fear I'd grown up with, no parents worth the name, in a rackety old castle full of dangerous staircases, crumbling parapets, and indifferent servants. The twins' waking joy was teasing me when they weren't taunting you into a round of fisticuffs. Your child will be safe, Thomas, far safer than you were."

Thomas had had a sister looking after him, but Theresa had had a brother who'd at least tried to look after her too. How she longed to have that brother back again.

"I don't like to think of you, alone at the Keep, becoming a mother, raising Priscilla on your own."

An admission and an understatement.

Becoming a mother was a careful euphemism for three days of agony and blood. Priscilla hadn't wanted to be born, or perhaps Theresa hadn't wanted any distance to come between her and her child.

"The Keep became peaceful once the twins removed to Town. Grandfather's passing was peaceful too."

Thomas nodded, suggesting no more need be mentioned on that topic. "Belmont says he's offered for you. He apparently did not feel inclined to ask my permission to court you."

Good for Matthew. "Are you angry at him?"

A log fell on the hearth, sending sparks up the flue. Loris had ordered wood burned in the nursery, an extravagance Theresa would never have dared at Sutcliffe Keep.

"I am angry at you," Thomas said, his tone rueful. "My wife says anger is a way to stay connected with the object of my ire without having to examine more tender sentiments. Brave woman, my baroness."

And one to whom Thomas listened.

"We needn't plough old ground, Thomas. You have acknowledged me and Priscilla. I'm grateful for that."

"Grateful. I suspect such gratitude applied to my backside would smart considerably. Belmont says we must talk. He has suggested, scolded, ordered, threatened, and dared me to talk with you. In the past few weeks, my neighbor has learned to know you better than your own brother ever knew you, and that is... that is not right."

Thomas was merely stating a problem rather than tendering an apology.

Though he was *trying*. Matthew had inspired Thomas to *try*, when all of

Theresa's letters and prayers had not.

"Matthew is ruthless," Theresa said, "all the more so for being good-hearted about his objectives. He cares little about how I conducted myself ten years ago, and has asked very few questions. What shall we talk about?"

Theresa knew exactly what they must *not* talk about, but other matters could be spoken of, and probably should be.

"How much of your descent into ruin was your own doing, and how much was the twins leading you astray?"

In other words, how much guilt should Theresa bear, and how much should she reserve for her younger sibling? For years, a part of her had longed for absolution from Thomas, for understanding, for anything. Now she wanted only for peace between them, and a way forward.

"Much of what befell me was my own doing," Theresa said, an admission she could not have made as an angry, hurt, bewildered young woman. "By the time I was seventeen, Bertrand and Rothchild had introduced me to strong spirits, wagering, and worse, though I was still making an effort in the direction of discretion, particularly when you were home from school breaks. Grandpapa realized what was afoot though."

"Go on."

So Thomas sensed there was more, and none of it good. He was finally listening, and he might never afford Theresa another opportunity to discuss the past.

Because Matthew expected it of her, she'd share with her brother what she could.

"Grandpapa never had any intention of seeing me presented at court, which came as a bitter surprise. For years, I'd told myself, 'When I have my Season...' 'When I make my bow....' 'When I'm old enough to be presented...' I'd have friends in London, lovely girls who'd laugh and tease and share secrets with me.

"I'd have new dresses, gentlemen might tell me I was pretty, not simply a bother and a brat. I would waltz away to a lovely new life, with my own husband and my own household far from the stink and noise of the sea."

Thomas rose and took up the fireplace poker, shifting the logs back and adding another to the blaze.

"If Loris and I cannot have children, then the barony can be preserved through your line. Neither the twins nor I had married when you turned eighteen, and Grandfather should have presented you at court for the sake of the succession."

"*I* can preserve the title?"

"Baronies tend to be old, their patents liberal in some regards." Thomas resumed his seat, the room a little brighter for his attentions to the fire. "I gather Grandfather's decision to keep you at the castle left you peevish."

"I was furious, heartbroken, disbelieving. I'd never been fond of Grandfather nor he of me, but after that… he hated me, Thomas. He must have simply and purely hated me. I felt like a prisoner, as if I'd preserved my virtue and the best part of my innocence—despite all temptation to the contrary—for nothing."

Thomas crossed an ankle over his knee and tugged off a boot. The second boot followed, and he set them away from the fire. A gentleman would be so informal before only family or close friends.

Regret rose up, like a wave from the sea, deluging Theresa's heart with nine years lost forever.

"You had a tantrum," Thomas said. "Apparently, the Jennings family excels at the protracted public tantrum. Grandfather certainly had his share, and the twins tantrumed themselves right into early graves."

An hour ago, Theresa might have asked Thomas if that was an apology for his own tantrum, but the need to be right, to be vindicated, had slipped from her grasp.

While the need to protect her younger brother was probably a life sentence.

"For years, I had a tantrum, to the delight of our cousins, and the dismay of our grandfather. When I learned I wasn't to have a London Season, then realized I wasn't to have any escape from that damned stinking pile of rocks, I considered running away, I considered throwing myself into the sea—except you had taught me to swim, and I could not allow Grandfather to win. Then he found somebody willing to take me off his hands, and my rebellion became instead a battle for my own survival."

Thomas sat forward, his elbows braced on his thighs, his head in his hands. "Why didn't you tell me? I had an allowance. I had made a friend or two at school. I might have done something…"

His protest warmed Theresa's heart, because a part of him still wished she had sought his aid. She remained silent, though. Thomas was a man of the world, and while stubborn, he'd never been stupid.

"You did not want to involve me," he said, sitting back, "because in the first place, my paltry funds would not have sustained you for long, and in the second, you were not of age. Grandfather would have hauled you back to Sutcliffe Keep at the figurative cart's tail and restricted your freedom even more. I'm told this is the same reason slaves seldom run away—because the prospects upon recapture are too horrid to contemplate."

Priscilla spoke clearly from the other room. "Top of the trees!"

Thomas was half out of his seat when Theresa put a hand on his arm. "She's dreaming, reliving a moment on horseback with Matthew. She's quoted Shakespeare in her dreams and done an amazing imitation of Sutcliffe's butler rhapsodizing on the subject of cooking sherry."

He sat back, wary gaze on the door to Priscilla's room. "I hardly know my only niece. I hardly know you, Theresa, and yet I want to know who you've become and why. Who was your fiancé?"

"I would not have told you unless you'd asked. Sir Peter Hockstetter."

"Shite."

Oh, exactly. "I believe much of the time he was mad. He was certainly violent, and childless, but he and Grandfather had made the Grand Tour together. Sir Peter was willing to take me on because Grandfather had been able to keep my initial forays into wild behavior from becoming common knowledge among his cronies."

"While I memorized Cicero and wallowed in the delights of Hindu."

"While you finished growing up," Theresa said, and that gave her a fierce satisfaction. Whatever else was true, Thomas had stomped, thrashed, and worked his way to a good life, free from Sutcliffe. She'd prayed for that too.

"Your letters from university were what sustained me, Thomas. I read them over and over, though I had to keep them hidden. Bertrand and Rothschild would have burned them if they'd found them." Or exacted some extortionate fee for giving them back to their rightful owner.

Thomas rose, taking his boots to the door. "When I went to London, after university, I tried my hand at gambling and was good at it. I'd watched our cousins win, lose, cheat, and win some more. Most games of chance involve mathematics. Somebody suggested I frequent a particular hell, because Randy and Rotten played there, and one could win handsome sums off of them on a good night. Those two always won the sums back, for some reason, unless a fellow knew when to be called away from table."

"You had no idea who Randy and Rotten were?"

"Not until they walked through the door, and I dodged out the back. They had aged, Theresa. Instead of high-spirited, idle young aristocrats, they were nothing more than their nicknames suggested—randy and rotten, and all I could think was that you had chosen them over me, over decency, over your own good name. I booked passage on a ship the next week."

He stood by the door, and Theresa hoped he'd quietly slip into the corridor. She'd told him more than she'd intended to, and he'd believed her.

But no, he resumed his seat. "Tell me about Priscilla, but before you do, please be aware that Loris and I went up to London and met with my solicitors on the way back here from Sutcliffe. A trust has been established for my niece, and she'll be handsomely dowered, if she ever chooses to marry."

If she found a man willing to take an illegitimate bride to wife? Theresa was too grateful to press that point.

"Thank you, Thomas. I would never have asked, but thank you. Priscilla deserves to have choices I did not."

Thomas's silence was diplomatic, for given the circumstances of Priscilla's birth, she might have very few choices indeed.

"Belmont raised the possibility that Priscilla's conception was not consensual."

Oh, Matthew. And yet, would Thomas be sitting in this darkened playroom had Matthew not forced such a consideration upon him?

"Tally ho!" Priscilla called, a heartwarming sound, even when the child was fast asleep.

"Grandfather's health was failing," Theresa said, choosing her words carefully. "I was still not yet of age, and Bertrand and Rothschild were coming around the Keep more and more often, whispering in corners, and casting glances my way that made my flesh crawl."

"While I was..." Thomas waved a hand in circles. "Learning how to hold my liquor and flirt with tavern maids."

While he was coming of age, far from the influence of two cousins who would have ruined him for sport.

"I needed to confirm my fall from grace for all time," Theresa said, "and for that a child was necessary. I am not proud of the strategy I devised—I realized too late how Priscilla would suffer for my actions—but only a child proves a woman has entirely surrendered her chastity. If I could choose again, I'm not sure what else I might have done. Grandfather kept the eligible bachelors away, while the twins ensured the ineligible variety were ever close at hand."

Not as close at hand as the loneliness, but examining that heartache took more courage than Theresa could summon in her brother's presence.

Thomas scrubbed a hand over his face. He'd been a beautiful boy, and he was a handsome man. Theresa hoped she could watch him age, could have the comfort of his cordial regard as her own hair grew gray.

"I am relieved to know you were the author of your own ruin," he said, "relieved being the closest I can come to naming a confusion of sentiments. You looked after Sutcliffe for me?"

"I knew you would inherit it eventually, and the twins left me alone as long as I became their free house steward." They'd left Priscilla alone too, more to the point.

And Thomas.

"I've pensioned off most of the staff," Thomas said, "and given the housekeeper leave to hire replacements. You did the best you could with a poorly disciplined, aging lot of slackers. In future, you'll find the household more attentive to your needs, and to Priscilla's."

His tone was mild, simply a man tidying up a loose end two years after acquiring a title, but Theresa was studying her brother, watching the way firelight found the fatigue and sadness in his eyes.

Thomas was sad, not as a boy might be sad—mostly disappointment, some resentment—but as a man regrets what he cannot change.

Perhaps Thomas thought Theresa would turn down Matthew's proposal, out of some excess of old shame, or desire to avoid her brother's company.

"I had hoped never to return to Sutcliffe for anything but a visit, Thomas."

"I do not relish sending you back there, but somebody is trying to kill the man who has offered you marriage. The attempts on Belmont's life began only when he took an interest in you, which signal fact he doesn't seem to have realized. I'm hoping you'll return from whence you came, and for once allow me to protect you as I should have all along."

* * *

Priscilla stared at the blank page, her sharpened pencil poised in her hand.

"Is that the story of your mama's great adventure?" Miss Alice asked.

"Yes, Miss." So far, the story was merely an empty page, a way to keep Miss Alice from fretting while Priscilla pondered a problem. "Are we to return to Sutcliffe Keep?"

Miss Alice was a prodigious knitter. Priscilla probably owned more scarves, caps, mufflers, stockings, and mittens than any other child in England, all courtesy of her governess's knitting needles.

Those needles went still at Priscilla's question, then resumed their steady clicking at a slower pace.

"Are you homesick, Priscilla?"

Priscilla wrote on the page: *Once Upon A Time in a faraway land by the sea...*

"Do *you* get homesick, Miss?"

... where seagulls pooped on everything, and nobody had any friends...

"I do miss my home, Priscilla, especially around the Yuletide holidays. Cumbria is far to the north, and the seasons are different. We have a forest, a true forest, and high hills, almost like Scotland, but kinder."

... and nobody ever rode a magical white horse, there lived three beautiful maidens. Their names were Alice, Theresa, and Pendragon, and they were kept prisoners in their castle by an awful monster named...

"Do you miss your family?" Priscilla asked.

The name of the monster was important, for he was very bad. He could have a simple name—Thomas the Terrible—or he could have a sermon-y name, like... MakeTrouble Meanface.

"I miss my siblings, Priscilla, but you mustn't tell your mama I said that. I see my brothers occasionally, and they are very dear. After the first of the year, I'll nip up to London and look in on them."

"Before we go back to Sutcliffe Keep?"

Nothing had been said at breakfast, but Mama and Uncle Thomas had avoided looking at each other, while Aunt Loris had offered everybody tea a million times. Grown-ups thought they were so clever, but they were like the trails Mr. Belmont followed in the woods.

Easy to follow once you took the time to study them.

"I'm not sure what your mother has planned in terms of a return to Sutcliffe Keep," Miss Alice said, starting a new row. She was working with solid black yarn made of lamb's-wool, soft, but not at all pretty.

The monster was very hungry, and snatched seagulls right out of the sky for his dinner, but he'd eaten every seagull in sight, and so the beautiful maidens were growing alarmed...

Priscilla was not alarmed, she was furious. They had only just got here to Linden, Uncle Thomas and Aunt Loris had only just come home from their wedding journey, and Mama and Mr. Belmont had only just kissed each other twice.

Now was not the time for the beautiful maidens to freeze and rattle their way back to the castle, and yet, at bedtime last night, Miss Alice had said that Mama and Uncle Thomas were having a discussion after dinner.

Discussions were not happy. Nobody laughed in the middle of a discussion, nobody made up a story with a happy ending.

"Miss Alice, would you tell me if you knew we were going back to the castle?"

Miss Alice rearranged her stitches along the needle so they were evenly spaced. "I would leave that discussion to your mother, Priscilla. I take it you do not want to leave Linden?"

"I hate Sutcliffe Keep. Here, I can play at the vicar's house, and I have Tut. Nothing is made of stupid stones, and the food comes hot from the kitchens. The servants smile, and they don't smell like mildew and fish. Sutcliffe is awful, and Linden is pretty. Mama doesn't want to go back to Sutcliffe."

Priscilla took little comfort from her mother's position, though, because Mama's *discussions* were peppered with unhelpful observations such as, *"We must all occasionally do things we'd rather not, Priscilla Undine Jennings..."*

"We are guests, Priscilla," Miss Alice said, needles clicking away. "Your uncle is our host, and when he says our visit is over, then the visit is over."

Uncle Thomas had said a great deal more than that. Priscilla hadn't eavesdropped on purpose last night. She'd even tried to warn her elders that she was awake without letting them know they'd been overheard.

They'd been too busy having their *discussion*, much of which Priscilla hadn't understood. That part about somebody trying to kill Mr. Belmont though, she'd heard that just fine. Mama had said Uncle was being fanciful and over-cautious, but then they'd gone off to *discuss* the whole business with Aunt Loris.

At breakfast today, nobody had discussed much of anything other than *"pass the butter"* and *"the snow makes everything so pretty."*

Priscilla was angry at the thought of returning to Sutcliffe, not simply because the castle stank and had the creeping damp, but also because Mr. Belmont was a capital fellow who made Mama smile even when he wasn't kissing her.

He rode white horses, he had golden hair, and his kiss had woken Mama from her enchanted sleep. A villain had entered the story, though, if Uncle Thomas was to be believed.

The monster's name ought to be Vexatious Villainous, except both of those words were hard to spell right time after time.

"Is Mr. Belmont coming over to work with you and Tut today?" Alice asked.

"I hope so. Tut hopes so too." Mama probably hoped so more than anybody. If somebody was trying to hurt Mr. Belmont, Mama would be upset.

Priscilla was upset, but she also knew that every handsome prince needed two things besides a princess: He needed a trusty steed, of which Mr. Belmont had an entire stable, and he needed a loyal page who guarded his back and kept a watch for wicked monsters.

If Mr. Belmont was in trouble, then Sutcliffe Keep was the worst place for his princess, and for his loyal page.

CHAPTER EIGHTEEN

Matthew's family had descended, Priscilla's riding lessons were casualties of holiday disruption, and Theresa was once again avoiding her brother.

"This is simply a Sunday meal between neighbors," Loris said, tucking the lap robe around Theresa. "The open house isn't until Tuesday. Matthew's brother and his sons are all on hand, and they will defend him stoutly."

Not as stoutly as Theresa would. "A bullet can cut down many defenses."

Thomas left off pretending to gaze out the coach window. "Belmont is the king's man. He knows the criminal mind, and he has the loyalty of every member of his household. They are alerted to report any odd goings-on, any muttered threats at the Cock and Bull. We don't even know for sure that he's the target of ill will."

Theresa wanted to smack Thomas for spouting reason, and she wanted to hug him. They weren't on hugging terms, though, and might never be again.

"Have you met Matthew's sons?" Theresa asked.

Thomas's eyebrow—when had he acquired such eloquent eyebrows?—said he knew the change of subject for the dodge that it was.

"I know them," Loris said. "Young gentlemen, of course. Christopher, Remington, and Richard. They have their father's lively curiosity, his affection for hounds and horses, and they're good-looking fellows."

"If they treat you with anything other than perfect courtesy," Thomas said, "you will apply to me, and I'll address the situation."

He could do it—now. Thomas could *address* situations involving his sister. The notion was heartwarming, also unsettling.

"Thank you, Thomas. I suspect Matthew's sons will be civil on the few occasions they must deal with me."

With Loris as referee, Theresa and Thomas had reached a compromise. Theresa would remain at Linden through the holidays, for that had been the original plan, but she would limit her dealings with Matthew to situations involving social groups, and if the risk to Matthew wasn't resolved by the New Year, she would return to Sutcliffe Keep.

Matthew was concerned that ill will toward him could endanger Theresa, so she and Priscilla were to be sent away to the Keep for their own safety.

The irony of the Keep as a refuge was painfully exquisite.

"The boys won't be civil to you if you're scowling like that," Alice said. "Priscilla will cast you as the monster in her latest story rather than the heroine, and that is a fate to be avoided. I wish we'd either get more snow, or the ground would dry out."

The coach slowed to make the turn at the bottom of the Belmont lane.

"Watch out what you wish for," Thomas said. "I don't like the look of those clouds, and yet it's too warm for December."

The mild day was why Priscilla was up on the box with Beckman, that and Theresa's unwillingness to tell her daughter of the planned return to Sutcliffe. Priscilla had made friends with two of the vicar's daughters, she was enthralled with Tut, and already attached to her aunt and uncle.

Thomas tapped Theresa on the knee. "Smile. We'll get Belmont sorted out. He's a canny fellow, and if his regard for you is genuine, it will survive a little distance."

"I'm sure you're right." Of course, Theresa had reassured herself with the same platitudes nine years ago: Thomas would sort himself out, make his way, and come back to Sutcliffe. He'd forgive, he'd see reason, he'd apologize for being so passionately offended.

He'd give Theresa a chance to explain and apologize as well.

Instead, he'd gone to the ends of the earth rather than make peace with his sister. Whoever wished Matthew ill might wait two years to strike again, and by then, some casserole-wielding sweet young thing with great, big—

The coach rocked to a halt, and Spiker opened the door. "Welcome to Belmont House. I see you've hired a new groom, my lord. A most fetching addition to your staff."

Loris preceded Theresa and Alice from the coach. When Theresa emerged, Priscilla was still beaming down from the box, her cheeks rosy, her braids already coming undone.

"Mama, Mr. Beckman let me drive almost the whole way! The horses were ever so gentlemanlike and didn't put a foot wrong."

Thomas pried Priscilla loose from the coach and affixed her to his hip.

"Next you'll be demanding wages from me," he said, poking Priscilla gently in the ribs. "And your own livery and a place to sleep above the coach house."

Beckman climbed down, the coach rocking with his descent. "Cease fretting," he muttered to Theresa. "I kept my hands on the leaders' reins the whole time. She's a natural whip. Few children are."

He sauntered off in the direction of the stable, and Thomas led the way to the manor house, Priscilla chattering madly the entire time.

"Priscilla is nervous," Theresa murmured. "She knows she's to meet Matthew's sons."

"You're nervous," Loris countered.

"Uneasy, certainly. An ambush on a bridle path, poison in the library, tampering with a firearm, all on a man's own property... Anybody would be uneasy."

And furious. Theresa hadn't endured this same blend of outrage and dread since she'd realized that conceiving a child was the only certain means of extinguishing her cousins' interest in marrying her to the highest bidder—or worse.

And yet, Theresa calmed amid the normal hubbub of introductions and holiday wishes. The Belmont family had decorated their home, wrapping holly about the bannisters, hanging mistletoe from the rafters, and draping greenery outside the front door. The party repaired to the library, with Matthew's sons taking Priscilla up the spiral stairs to the reading loft, while the adults sipped punch and gathered before the fire.

Matthew looked tired, but put on a show of genial good manners, doubtless for the sake of the children. He kissed Theresa's cheek in greeting, and kissed Alice and Loris in the same fashion.

"Mama, there are more books up here!" Priscilla shouted, leaning over the railing. "Books about art and sculpture; books in French and German. I have never seen so many books!"

"We have a book about castles too," Richard said. "But if you fall over the balcony and break your head, you'll never get a chance to read it."

"Mama would catch me," Priscilla retorted, disappearing from view. "I live in a castle, I'll have you know, but we haven't this many books."

The young people fell to quiet murmuring, and Matthew excused himself to let the kitchen know his guests had arrived.

"Cease worrying," Thomas said. "He's hale and whole, and as focused as ever on his victuals. His sons are on their best behavior, and Priscilla has them well in hand."

"If nobody objects, I'd like to have a look at Mr. Belmont's collection," Alice said. "Priscilla isn't the only one in raptures at the sight of so many books."

While Theresa didn't even like the idea of Matthew strolling the corridors of his own home alone. She excused herself after asking Loris for directions to the ladies' retiring room, and found her quarry at the first turning of the corridor.

He had his back to her, and her first thought was that he really was overdue for a trim about the collar. Mistletoe hung from above, though Theresa hardly needed that excuse.

She wrapped her arms around him from the back. "I have missed you so, Matthew Belmont, and worried for you awfully."

He turned, but even as strong arms settled gently around Theresa, her mind was registering facts at variance with her assumption.

He was a shade too lean.

His scent was lavender rather than cinnamon and spice.

His embrace was *off*.

"To envy one's brother is exceedingly bad form, and yet, honesty compels me to admit that I do."

The voice was too… gruff.

Theresa stepped back. "You're not Matthew."

"Axel Belmont, at your service." He executed a deferential bow. "If you're not Miss Theresa Jennings, then my brother has much to explain."

Axel Belmont bore a disconcerting resemblance to Matthew. He was the same height, his hair nearly same shade of gold at the back, but darker around his face. His smile, though, was ironic rather than warm.

"Mr. Belmont, my apologies. I assure you I'm not in the habit—"

"Brother, I will thrash you silly if you attempt to flirt with Miss Jennings." Matthew's arm slid around Theresa's waist. "She's shy, and unused to you university types. Now that you've torn yourself free of my glass house, please join the gathering in the library. We've matters to discuss."

Axel Belmont's gaze cooled to downright chilly, then he kissed Theresa's cheek, plucked a berry from the mistletoe above, and dropped it into his pocket.

"Welcome to the family, Miss Jennings," he said. "You'll have your hands full with the southern branch of the clan, but if ever you need a thrashing administered to your handsome swain, I'm your man."

He marched off, but not before Matthew had tossed the entire sheaf of mistletoe at his brother's retreating backside.

"He likes you," Matthew said. "That's mostly a good thing."

"But he looked so fierce." Surely Theresa hadn't imagined the chill in those blue eyes?

"Axel regularly lectures on botanical topics at Oxford, where he must deal with half-drunken, unruly, randy young fellows in quantity. His glower is the envy of the other professors, though his own children taught it to him. Come along, or your brother will be on patrol next."

Theresa didn't *come along*. She stood right where she was, wrapped her arms around Matthew, and held on.

"Thomas is sending me back to Sutcliffe Keep after the holidays. He says you've asked this of him."

Matthew obliged her with a snug embrace. "I ask it of you, too, and ask that you take Priscilla and Miss Portman with you. These difficulties I'm having are serious, and once my family has returned to Oxford, I expect more trouble."

For all that Matthew's arms were around her, he'd already ridden away to battle in a sense.

"You *want* me to leave?"

"I care for you very much and want you and Priscilla to be safe. My own selfish wishes don't signify."

"I'm being banished while you remain here to fight dragons." *As she'd had Thomas banished.*

"Not merely fight the dragons, slay them. I have many reasons to prevail, my dear, not merely to survive."

Theresa slid from his embrace. "And the less favor you show me, the safer I'll be?" This was how the king's man would organize his pursuit of justice, with innocent bystanders well away when he drew his weapon.

"I will write to you, I will do my utmost to apprehend my malefactor, and I will carry you in my heart until the end of time, if need be."

Or the end of his interest in her, or hers in him. The young girl who'd developed a naughty smile and tolerance for liquor knew how dreams could die, slowly, silently. Sutcliffe Keep might never crumble into the sea, but dreams certainly could.

"Matthew, I don't want to leave you."

"I don't want to send you away. Please trust me on that much, at least."

Theresa blinked back the tears and took the handkerchief Matthew offered.

"I hate this, Matthew, when all my choices lead to either danger or heartbreak for somebody I love. I'd choose the danger for myself, because I'm convinced if I remain here, I can keep you whole."

The urge to argue, to rant and reason and insist until she got her way, came from an old, unhappy place. Nobody listened to "the girl," nobody paid attention to her. When Theresa might have tossed Matthew's handkerchief back at him, she noticed Thomas standing outside the closed library door, his expression grave.

"Priscilla is agitating to visit the ponies," he said, extending a hand to Theresa. "For what it's worth, I don't want to send you away either."

Theresa took her brother's hand, and he pulled her closer, into a tight, fierce hug.

"I didn't want to force you away from Sutcliffe, Thomas," she whispered.

As rotten as the situation was, as badly as Theresa longed to stand in front of Matthew with a gun aimed toward any who'd try to harm him, in Thomas's arms, she took comfort from a moment of grace.

Absolution without further penance, forgiveness even in the absence of a complete understanding.

"I'll go back to Sutcliffe," Theresa said, "but don't expect me to bide there month after month like some hermit. Priscilla is old enough to enjoy the sights in London, my wardrobe is a disgrace, and the Keep is long overdue for some new furniture."

Matthew's expression was thoughtful, though he did not offer to jaunt up to London to meet her. When the king's man undertook to keep a woman at a safe distance, then at a safe distance, she would remain.

The sheaf of mistletoe lay on the carpet, a forlorn little sprig of pale greenery with a half-dozen white berries yet clinging beneath the leaves. Theresa picked it up, held it over Matthew's head, and kissed the hell out of him.

* * *

Theresa's kiss gut-punched Matthew's resolve, and the only sympathy he got was a stout blow on the shoulder from the baron as the lady flounced off to the library.

"If you break my sister's heart, I will kill you, Belmont."

"If I break her heart, and somebody else doesn't dispatch me first, then you are welcome to end my days as you see fit." Though Matthew would expire of heartache in any case.

Sending Theresa back to Sutcliffe was necessary, but it was not... not *right*.

"I should have killed my cousins," Thomas said, slinging an arm around Matthew's shoulders. "I see that now. A pair of thoroughgoing scoundrels, and I left my sister to deal with them. I've been an idiot. She sent me away to keep me away from harm, and now life is serving me the same dish."

"Most brothers are idiots from time to time. Ask Axel for his opinion on the matter, or Richard. My youngest has a fine sense of martyrdom as a result of being outnumbered by his idiot older brothers."

Which sense of martyrdom, the boy had not left at Oxford. If anything, Richard was more taciturn and withdrawn than ever. Matthew joined his guests in the library and ignored the empty space on the sofa next to Theresa.

"Priscilla, gentlemen," Matthew called up to the reading loft. "If you would come down for a moment?"

The sound of the boys' boots on the spiral staircase had changed since summer, becoming heavier and slower. They were no longer pirate lads quitting their crow's nest for a portion of grog. They were the Belmont heirs, budding scholars, and young men to be proud of.

How Matthew had missed them, and how he would miss them.

"Richard, I understand Miss Priscilla longs to see the ponies," Matthew said. "If you would oblige her and take the old guard some carrots?"

Get the boy outside, was all Matthew could think. Get some color into his cheeks.

"Yes, Papa," Richard said. "Come along, Miss Priscilla, and if you refuse to wear your gloves and scarf, I will tattle to your mama and *you will never be allowed to visit the ponies again.*"

Priscilla stuck her tongue out at Richard, which provoked the first smile Matthew had seen from him for months. She then took Richard by the hand and dragged him from the library.

"His voice is changing," Matthew said, shoving back to sit on the desk. "Christopher and Rem, you will not tease your brother about this. Tease him about growing too tall, eating too much at one sitting, or bankrupting me with his tailor's bills, but not about his voice."

"Yes, Papa," they chorused.

Matthew ought to have convened this gathering in his public parlor, the place where he held the magistrate's sessions on Monday mornings when criminal wrongdoing had been alleged, or an arrest made. The library lacked sufficient chairs, and Matthew was keenly aware of Maida's absence.

"Rem and Christopher, if you'd fetch yourselves chairs?"

Remington folded to the hearth rug in one lithe movement, Christopher doing likewise.

"Uncle Axel said there's trouble afoot," Remington said, sitting cross-legged. "Perhaps you'd best come back to Oxford with us."

"From the mouths of babes..." Axel muttered.

Matthew ignored the attempted mutiny—a remove to Oxford might well bring the danger to Axel's doorstep—and summarized for the assemblage the facts as he knew them.

"So you don't have solid evidence of attempted murder," Christopher said. "But you have too much coincidence to ignore. You're beastly careful with your firearms, and any fool could have seen that the harrow was left in the worst possible location. As for the poison..."

The poison Matthew might have casually ingested, but for Maida's bad manners.

"It strikes me," Theresa said, "that this person knows you, but not as well as they think they do. They know you eat prodigious quantities, but not that you abhor mustard. They know that you use a certain pistol in the hunt field, but not that Spiker routinely fires that weapon in the vicinity of your hounds and hunters through the week."

"You are suggesting I can eliminate my staff from suspicion." Theresa's insight yielded Matthew significant relief. His children and his only brother were dwelling at Belmont House, after all.

"And yet," Loris said, "it has to be somebody the staff would expect to see about the area and on the premises. A neighbor who typically attends the hunt meets, though not a groom or a servant, for they would not presume on your library."

"They might have helped themselves to the hunt breakfast and come in through the French doors," Theresa said, chewing a nail.

"Damn," Axel muttered at the same time Thomas said, "Shite."

"Stealth has been part of this campaign," she went on. "Nobody saw the harrow being dragged about the countryside, suggesting it was moved at night. Nobody saw anybody tampering with the pistol, suggesting that happened when the stable was quiet, which again, occurs every night and often throughout the day. Any Sunday morning or afternoon, the stable would be deserted. The poison was left out when a crowd made it easy for anybody to gain access to the house."

"What are you saying?" Matthew asked.

"This person is a likely suspect," Theresa replied. "They cannot afford to provoke you even to speculating about their involvement."

"I think I know what she's saying," Rem interjected. "When we realize who it is, we'll wonder how we could have missed him. You locked up somebody who was innocent, you settled a dispute and left somebody with a grudge, you got the magistrate's job when somebody else wanted the prestige or power of it."

"Nobody in their right mind wants the magistrate's job," Thomas said.

"I certainly didn't," Matthew said.

"I damned hate it," Axel added, "begging the ladies' pardon for my language. I think we're dealing with a simple case of cowardice. Some criminals like a bit of risk about their undertakings, a sense of sporting fair play. Whoever we're dealing with here..."

"Is not a professional," Theresa murmured. "There are professionals, bully boys, thieves, forgers. Evil for hire abounds in London."

"Criminal expertise certainly does," Thomas said. "One can hire murder done, for a price, but our murderer has been unsuccessful, suggesting he's an amateur. Poison is often considered a woman's weapon because only stealth is needed to wield it, and anybody can shove an obstruction into the barrel of a pistol."

"What motive would a woman have?" Loris asked. "Matthew is unfailingly polite, a reliable guest for making up the numbers, a gentleman..."

"Greed, passion, and revenge are the typical motives for murder," Axel added, oh so helpfully.

Though thank God others were capable of seeing the situation rationally, because all Matthew could think was that in less than two weeks' time, if this damnable business weren't resolved, he might never see Theresa Jennings again.

His mind went to work on that problem—for it was a problem—the way he'd often start to worry an unsolved crime. Loose ends tumbled around in his imagination sometimes resulting in insights when he least expected them.

"Papa isn't the type to inspire passion," Christopher said. "Well, you aren't. You're the Harmless Old Squire, who takes little old ladies to church and to market. The widows adore you, but you never dance with the same one twice."

Was Christopher being delicate?

"You are popular with the ladies," Loris said. "Though I believe I'm the last woman you offered for, and that was more than two years ago."

Remington looked intrigued, while Christopher twitched at dog hair caught on the fringe of the hearth rug.

"We can safely assume her ladyship has not conceived a violent dislike of you," Axel observed. "Besides which, the baroness has been off on her wedding journey. If we rule out passion as a motive, that leaves greed and revenge."

"Papa's wealthy," Remington said, "but we're his heirs, and our uncles are the estate's trustees. As much as Richard is being a pest lately, I don't think he's had the means or the motivation to plot murder."

"Not unless he's planning on conjugating and declining Papa to death," Christopher said.

"So we're down to revenge," Thomas said. "Belmont, make a list of all the people you've arrested, all the cases you've heard in the past year, all the parties who've muttered into their beer about the magistrate being a blight on the king's justice."

"I made such a list last night, and it's quite short."

Theresa was watching Matthew from halfway across the room, and he could nearly hear her thoughts. They had made no progress with all this discussion, and they likely wouldn't make any progress unless or until the killer made another attempt on Matthew's life.

By which time, Matthew had insisted that Theresa and Priscilla would be safely returned to their castle by the sea.

Their lonely, drafty, crumbling castle by the sea.

CHAPTER NINETEEN

"If you would send Beckman back with the coach in an hour or so," Theresa said, "I will remain here and make a final inspection of the kitchens. Matthew has no hostess, and somebody needs to see that all is in order before the open house."

Thomas paused with half his coat buttons undone, but before he could make some brotherly protest, Loris passed him her cloak.

"Sending the coach back will be no bother at all," she said. "Shall we take Priscilla home with us?"

"Please do. She's bound to be tired from her adventures today. I won't be long, assuming all is in readiness."

Richard Belmont, may the young man be eternally blessed, had taken Priscilla on an inspection of the retired ponies, then given her a stall-by-stall tour of the Belmont stable. She'd returned to the library tired, elated, full of story ideas, and none too tidy.

"Priscilla will need a soaking bath," Alice said. "Mr. Belmont, thank you for your hospitality."

The good-byes were cheerful and interminable, and Thomas's farewell was accompanied by a glower or two in Matthew's direction. Then the front hallway to Belmont House was empty, save for Theresa, the man she loved, and an ache larger than the sea.

"Come here," Matthew said, holding his arms wide. "I was wondering how I might scale the walls of Linden Hall to appear by moonlight in your bedroom tonight."

"Your family—"

"Axel has dragged the boys out to the glass house and will use the time to acquaint Richard with the topics discussed in the library. We'll cover the same ground over brandy, but right now..."

He kissed her, and unlike Theresa's earlier overture, Matthew's approach was tender, savoring, and delicate.

"I want a bed, Matthew. I want a bed right now, with you in it. I want your clothes off, my clothes off, and a stout lock on the door."

"My dearest love—"

"Don't you dare be reasonable and noble now," Theresa said, taking him by the hand and leading him to the steps. "Save your gentlemanly balderdash for the assemblies. If we have one hour of privacy, I want to spend it in your arms. We deserve one experience of sheer glory before I go back to worrying about you, and dreading my next journey."

At the top of the stairs, Theresa had to pause, because she simply did not know in which direction Matthew's rooms lay.

"I know what you're thinking," he said, leading her down a carpeted corridor. "You think if we make love, then I won't be able to send you away."

"You dratted, stubborn, idiot man, I'm not thinking at all, but if I were thinking, then perhaps I might conclude that I won't be able to leave you unless we have at least one memory to sustain us, one occasion of passion in a proper—"

The next instant, Theresa was pinned against the wall, fifteen stone of Matthew Belmont stealing her words in a kiss so ravenous, she had to cling to him to remain on her feet.

"I already have more than one memorable occasion with you, Theresa Jennings, and I intend to have many more of them. Do you believe me?"

Looking into his eyes, Theresa saw not the country gentleman, not the perceptive widower, and not even the handsome, passionate man with whom she'd been intimate on too few occasions.

She saw a warrior who would stop at nothing to protect those he cared for.

"Be careful, Matthew. I believe you, but three times, your continued survival has been a matter of chance. Leave nothing to chance, I beg you, and be careful."

An overcast day in December was a gloomy affair, and no footman had come around yet to light sconces or start fires. Matthew's private parlor was thus mostly shadows, and his bedroom darker still.

"I wasn't expecting company in here," he said. "The sheets will be chilly."

"No, they won't." The room was cold, but Matthew's embrace was all the warmth Theresa needed.

"You are sure, my dear? You never did accept my offer of marriage."

Theresa left off nuzzling Matthew's shoulder. "That matters to you? Your life is in danger, and you're preoccupied with vows you may not live long enough to speak?"

He turned Theresa by the shoulders and started on the hooks at the back of her dress.

"I offered in good faith, and I'd like an answer." He knew what he was doing with a lady's apparel, for cool air trickled down the middle of Theresa's back.

"I'll marry you, Matthew. The very first chance I get, I'll marry you gladly."

His arms came around her. "I'll hold you to that. Though no one outside of family may know of it, we are engaged from this moment forward. Finish undressing, and I'll light the fire."

Then he was away, probably in search of a taper or carrying candle, while Theresa stood in a cold, shadowed room trying to locate her wits.

Matthew Belmont, in the midst of attempts on his life, had recalled his offer of marriage, renewed it, and wrung an acceptance from her.

Though he hadn't had to wring very hard. Was he tidying up his affairs in the event he soon lost his life, or was he offering Theresa assurances of his love in the most time-honored way?

He wasn't about to cry the banns or announce their engagement, of course. That would rather defeat the purpose of slinking off to Sutcliffe Keep.

And yet, they were *engaged*.

"You're standing right where I left you," Matthew said, using a spill a moment later to light a candle on the bedside table. "I also notice you have yet to shed a single article of clothing. Shall I assist you to undress?"

Theresa marched off toward the privacy screen rather than let the sheer seduction in his question buckle her knees.

"You warm up the bed, Matthew Belmont. Once I get my hands on you, there will be no stopping to deal with tapes, bows, or buttons. This is your only warning."

"Feel free to use my toothpowder, and you'd best take the pins from your hair too."

Now *he* was dispensing warnings. A smile bloomed, as incongruous as roses in December, despite Theresa's worry.

"Are the sheets warm yet, Mr. Belmont?"

His waistcoat came sailing over the privacy screen. "Patience is a virtue, Miss Jennings."

By the time Theresa emerged from the privacy screen, the fire in the hearth was giving out a cheery heat, and Matthew Belmont's coat, cravat, breeches, and shirt were draped over a chest at the foot of his bed.

"You see before you the king's man, dutifully warming the sheets," he said from the depths of the bed. "While I see you have purloined my favorite dressing gown."

Theresa loved the scent of the blue velvet, pure Matthew Belmont. "You look cozy in that bed." That enormous bed.

"I look lonesome. Quit stalling, Theresa. I'll close my eyes if you're feeling bashful."

Theresa let the dressing gown cascade to the floor. "I'm feeling many things, Matthew. Bashful is not among them."

Darkness was falling beyond the window, and Matthew had lit only the hearth and the one candle. The light was adequate for Theresa's purposes, though. She wanted Matthew to see exactly who was joining him in that bed, exactly who had accepted his proposal.

He held up the quilt. "If you do not get your luscious, brave, naked self over here this instant, these sheets will spontaneously ignite."

Theresa dashed for the bed and hopped in, only to be enveloped in a warm embrace.

"What was that glorious display about?" Matthew asked, kissing her ear.

"I've never been entirely naked in the presence of a man before. I wanted you to see me. I want to see you too."

"So you've never flaunted your wares before an entire regiment? Never been the toast of the Cyprian's ball?"

What was he asking? "I drank strong spirits to excess, Matthew. I gambled, I used foul language, I flirted shamelessly, I... smoked cigars, or tried to."

He arranged himself on his side, the firelight glinting off his smile. "You didn't fall so very far, did you?"

"Far enough, but I simply hadn't a taste for true wickedness. My cousins were too strong a cautionary tale."

Matthew kissed her brow. "Syphilis?"

"I suspect so, and stupid wagers, and vile associates one could never consider friends. The occasional basically decent fellow stumbled through their house parties too, Priscilla's father among them. I don't want to talk about that, though. All too soon, I'll hear the coach rattling up the drive, and then I must find a way to leave you."

"You might part from me for a time, but you will never leave my heart."

His lovemaking was infernally patient. When Theresa wanted to pillage and plunder, Matthew teased. She pulled his hair, wrestled, squirmed, swore, and finally surrendered to the mood he set.

Lazy kisses, soft caresses, a slow transition from lying beside her to bracing his weight above her. The result of all Matthew's languorous passion was an urgency that for Theresa bordered on desperation.

"You drive me to madness, Matthew Belmont."

"Only fair," he murmured against her throat. "I've dwelled there since our first kiss."

He dawdled about, his mouth on Theresa's breasts, his hands in all manner of locations, and even as desire beat through her veins in a joyous, unashamed tattoo, sorrow as relentless as the sea beat with it. This might be all they knew of loving, all they had of pleasure.

"Matthew, I can't wait."

"You've waited far too long."

Bliss, sweet and hot, accompanied their joining. Matthew knew just the right tempo, just the right *everything*, to send pleasure cascading through Theresa's soul, subduing the worry, the loss, and even the fear that gripped her heart.

"This…" she whispered, moving with him. "I can't lose you now, Matthew."

"You'll not lose me. I promise you, you will not lose me."

He sealed the promise with his body, with slow, relentless loving, with kisses and pleasure, until Theresa was replete with sated desire.

"Again," he whispered.

For nine years, Theresa had told herself that her life had meaning because Sutcliffe prospered, because Thomas was well and whole, because Priscilla was a happy, well-loved child. All the schemes and sacrifices had paid off, her goals had been accomplished.

And her heart had been broken.

Matthew had mended that heart, and if she lost him, nothing would ever come right again.

"Again," he whispered, more softly.

Theresa locked her ankles at the small of his back, denying her own satisfaction until she felt Matthew's control unraveling.

"Theresa, we must not…"

"We are betrothed. We deserve this. You deserve this. Come with me, Matthew."

A battle ensued, between good sense and hope, between respect and reverence. Between a man's need to protect, and a woman's determination to consummate promises made with the heart. The victory went to Theresa, to hope and to love, as Matthew surrendered to passion, and the coach came clattering up the drive.

* * *

The damned Belmont open house was a tradition that went back at least to Matthew's great-grandfather's day, and invitations had been sent out weeks ago. The invitations were mostly reminders of the date chosen from year to year, for everybody in the shire, along with their guests, relations, and the occasional well-behaved dog, attended.

And part of the tradition was that the Belmont menfolk gathered in Matthew's rooms to prepare for the day. The routine would vary today— providing Theresa didn't change her mind—and Matthew would sleep better that night as a result.

"Why do we do this?" Axel groused, fluffing the folds of Matthew's cravat. "Why do we bankrupt the larders, aggravate our offspring, and waste an entire day spreading good cheer and better drink on the same people you see in the churchyard every Sunday?"

"Uncle Axel is shy," Remington said, wiping at the toe of his boot with the handkerchief Matthew had left folded on his vanity. "I get my own retiring charm from him."

Christopher had appropriated Matthew's hairbrush and was giving his curls a final smoothing. His hand paused, a minute disruption of focus Matthew saw any time heredity and his sons were mentioned in the same breath.

"Papa, Rem knows," Christopher said, setting the brush aside and tucking Matthew's second-best flask into his coat pocket. "I think Rem knew before I did."

Richard, thank a gracious Deity, was off with Phillip and Dayton hanging the last of the greenery in the conservatory.

"What does Rem know?" Matthew asked, avoiding Axel's watchful gaze.

"I know you're not my papa either," Rem said, bouncing onto Matthew's bed. "Not that it matters."

"Now is not the time—" Axel began in his best lecture-hall tones.

"If the boys have brought it up, now is the time," Matthew countered, though Theresa and her family would be arriving any moment, and Nicholas and Beckman were already making a tour of the decanters in the library with no less personage than Vicar Herndon. "How did this disclosure come about?"

And how did Remington, the sweetest of Matthew's children, feel about it?

"I was eight or so," Rem said, flopping to his back, long legs dangling over the side of the bed. "You'd been called away to the Longacre's, where domestic discord was once again the order of the day. When you came home I asked you why two people with children to love and a tidy cottage of their own had so much trouble getting along."

"They've squabbled as long as I've known them."

Rem sat up. "You said when two blue-eyed people have a brown-eyed child, squabbling can result. That made no sense to me, because you and Mama both had blue eyes and seemed to get along well enough, and yet, all three of your sons are brown-eyed."

A casual aside, intended to deflect a boy's curiosity, and even as a child, Remington had caught every possible significance of the words.

"That's hardly proof," Axel said. "All manner of babies result from all manner of unions."

"Not proof," Matthew said, chagrin warring with pride in his son, "but Remington is the thoughtful type. My comment was inspiration for further speculation, I'm sure."

"I know Christopher isn't a Belmont by birth," Rem said, rising from the bed, "and he and I look quite alike. I know Mama wrote letters to some fellow she didn't want anybody to know about, because I caught her at it, twice. I saw one of those epistles, and the salutation was, 'My Very Dear Man...'. After that, I knew not to surprise her at her correspondence."

And all those years, when a small boy ought to have been growing up secure in the knowledge of his patrimony...

Axel became fascinated searching through the cravat pins, watch fobs, cufflinks, and other adornments Matthew kept in a dish on the clothes press.

In the fleeting silence, no brilliant insights came to Matthew, no subtle, philosophical comforts. His only concern was for his son—for they were his sons, all three of them.

"Remington, I'm sorry," Matthew said, dropping onto the hard stones of the hearth. "I'm so very, very sorry, that you've been burdened with this knowledge for years. I hope you know—"

Rem was scowling at him, and Christopher had taken to studying the view out the window—the drive, which would soon be thronged with damned coaches.

"I know you love me," Remington said. "I couldn't ask for a better papa, and that's all that need be said. One feels sorry for Mama, but only a little, because a gentleman ought."

Christopher took out his flask and tipped it up, the gesture striking a chord of memory Matthew couldn't place.

"I don't know what to say, Remington, other than that you're entirely correct. I would lay down my life for any of my boys, and consider you my beloved sons, and nobody else's."

"Now see here," Axel said, appropriating Christopher's flask. "There will be none of this talk of laying down anybody's life. Bad enough we must endure the open house without protestations of martyrdom on every hand. If you lot are determined to air the linen now, then I'll take it upon my humble self to ensure the punch has been mixed in accordance with the appropriate recipe."

"I love you too, Uncle Axel," Remington said, neatly swiping the flask before Axel could sample its contents. Rem gestured in Matthew's direction. "Happy Christmas, *Papa*."

He took a sip, and again that flash of something tapped Matthew's memory on the shoulder. He ought to have purchased flasks for them all as Christmas tokens, the Belmont crest engraved on both sides.

"You will please refill that," Christopher said, "and before I'm overcome with sentiment too."

Remington passed his uncle the flask, bent to kiss Matthew's cheek, and hauled Axel from the room.

"My brother is too good for the church," Christopher said. "I didn't know how to tell you that all your discretion, all your attempts to spare him, were for naught."

As Matthew's concept of his family went tumbling in all directions, he yet knew three things. First, he wanted to share these developments with Theresa, for she could sort emotion from reaction, and help him make sense of a situation he'd failed to accurately grasp.

Second, Christopher had also borne the burden of secrecy.

"Sit with me for a moment, Christopher, and if you need to cry, then for God's sake cry. I'm so proud of my sons I'm nearly in tears myself."

Christopher knuckled his eyes with his cuff, then took the place beside Matthew.

"You're proud of us for keeping something like this from you? I argued with Rem at first, but that's like arguing with the sea. He's so... so like you. Determined, polite, canny, all private and honorable. One doesn't know how to—"

Matthew locked his arm around Christopher's neck, pulled him close, kissed the top of his head—and then let him go.

"You protected his confidences, and you tried to protect me, and we have to be the most protective lot of fools ever to tiptoe about with the same last name. We've traumatized the professor, who is similarly afflicted with noble sentiments, so please keep an eye on him for me."

"Uncle Ax always samples the punch. That's simply tradition, but I think the spirits give him the courage he needs to get out his violin."

Axel played only at Christmas, that Matthew knew of, and he always played magnificently.

"So are you and Remington at peace with your paternity?"

"He is," Christopher said. "He's at peace with every bloody thing. Schoolwork, the other fellows, the ladies... only Richard defies Remington's ability to pour oil on troubled waters."

Richard. God yes, Richard.

"What about you, Christopher? Does it bother you, not knowing with whom your mother was in love?" For whoever that bungler was, he didn't deserve the name father.

Matthew rummaged around in his own emotions, which were about as organized as a pile of autumn leaves on a windy day: concern for his children, longing for Theresa's company, resentment toward whoever had made three clumsy attempts on his life—and during the damned holidays, no less.

And—the third verity he knew for certain—love.

Love for his family and for his intended filled every corner of Matthew's heart, along with determination that next Christmas, the Belmont family would be here together again, with no secrets and no shadows to haunt them.

Christopher rose and made free with Matthew's hairbrush again. "When I was small, I wanted to know who my father was. I never asked Mama, though, because I was afraid she might tell me. What if she'd fallen in love with old Mr. Dale? Or the late Squire Pettigrew?"

"She fell in love with somebody," Matthew said, though he could understand Christopher's ambivalence. Would knowing be preferable to ignorance? Would Matilda's choice make better sense of the past, or throw it into greater confusion?

"People do fall in love," Christopher said, setting the brush on the vanity and passing Matthew the handkerchief Rem had used. One corner was wrinkled, which mattered not at all.

"I have fallen in love," Matthew said, "in case that escaped the notice of my ever vigilant offspring."

Christopher extended a hand and drew Matthew to his feet. "We like her, Papa. Even Richard likes her. He says Priscilla will be good for us, and Richard lately doesn't like anything but his books."

"So you truly don't care to know to whom your mother gave her heart?"

"Mama gave her heart," Christopher said, inspecting himself in Matthew's cheval mirror. "Maybe one can't help giving that sometimes, but did Mama have to give her body too? When she'd married you, had the protection of your name, a child to love in the person of my humble self, and all the wealth and comfort of the Belmont family fortune, did she have to repeatedly give more than her heart to this fellow?"

Christopher fiddled with a cuff-link, having borrowed the sapphire set. "What sort of man," he went on, "accepts a woman's advances—or continues to make advances—when his attentions have already left that woman's honor dangling over the Pit?"

What truth could a devoted father offer in the face of such an unresolvable heartache?

"She loved you awfully, Christopher. Loved the three of you, and maybe that's all that need be said. I have a question for you, though, which you are of course free not to answer."

"Don't be an idiot, Papa. Ask me anything."

"Did you and Rem ever argue about your birthright where Richard might have overheard you?"

Christopher left off fiddling with his cuff. "Ballocks. You think—"

"I damned near know he overheard you, or read your diary, or eavesdropped on a conversation. The evening of the final hunt meet last year, I noticed that my darling baby boy had abruptly become disagreeable company. I attributed it to adolescent humors, the impending remove to Oxford, fatigue, or the thought of leaving home."

"Rem and I had a bloody great row in the stable that morning," Christopher said. "Papa, I'm sorry."

"You needn't be. I should have known what bothered Richard, should have paid as much attention to my sons as I do to my foxes and hounds."

"I hear a coach," Christopher said, peering out the window. "The Linden crowd is here, which means your presence is required in the library, and I'm for a stop at the punch bowl."

Matthew would not stop by the punchbowl, but he would find a moment to have a quiet word with his youngest son, no matter what else filled the day's agenda.

CHAPTER TWENTY

The wounded pride of a young boy fueled Thomas's reaction to the gathering in Belmont's library: He resented, utterly, that Belmont had come up with this solution. A quiet, private wedding was so… so, Matthew Belmont, and so right, and so gentlemanly, Thomas wanted to hit the man who'd soon be his brother by marriage.

"How did you get Theresa to agree to this?" he asked Matthew.

Axel Belmont was at the punch bowl, carefully ladling holiday mayhem into flasks, while Nicholas, Beckman, and the vicar supervised. The children were up in the reading loft, arguing as children did on special occasions.

"I proposed, and being a woman of great good sense, she accepted," Belmont said.

This acceptance had come after Theresa and Matthew had spent an hour unchaperoned following the Sunday meal.

"You compromised her," Thomas said, not at all sure he wouldn't be on the receiving end of violence for that observation. More violence—his chin was still a trifle sore from Belmont's last pugilistic display.

Belmont's gaze was on the door, but he spared Thomas an amused—pitying?—glance.

"We had plighted our troth, Sutcliffe, and one looks damned silly maundering on about gentlemanly honor under certain circumstances. You're married. I needn't draw you a sketch, and yet gentlemanly honor matters exceedingly. A private ceremony will allow Theresa the protection of my name, while deterring disrespect from opportunistic curates or other fools. Then too, the lady will become my wife, which result seems to please her endlessly."

Axel Belmont was an expert on roses, and thus Matthew's lapel bore an elegant bloom, despite the season. He looked every inch the bridegroom, and yet his gaze was riveted on the door.

"You're nervous," Thomas said, somewhat comforted. "You're worried about these attempts on your life, but you're more nervous of your ability to make Theresa happy. *You* want to please her endlessly."

Good. Theresa deserved a man who took her happiness seriously.

"You're jealous," Belmont countered, mildly. "You've finally had the good sense to reconcile with your sister, and I'm snatching her away. We'll be right down the lane, Sutcliffe, and our children will be friends as well as cousins. You will be sick of seeing me, ere long, and I of seeing you."

The enormity of that gift, of having family on the next property over, seeing them every Sunday, celebrating the seasons and years together, had Thomas taking a sip of his drink.

"What the hell is in this punch? It's wickedly delicious."

"Axel won't say, but hard cider plays a discreet and dangerous role. I will take the best care of her, you know. Her and Priscilla. I was denied the right to dote on my first wife, and by God, I intend to make up for lost time."

Thomas declined to point out that prior to any doting, Belmont would have to find a certain would-be murderer. The plan was that none outside the immediate family would know of this marriage for the present, Theresa would retire to the safety of Sutcliffe Keep, and Matthew Belmont would solve the crime posthaste.

A fine plan, for Thomas hadn't come up with anything else that would keep Theresa safe. His contribution had been to send Beckman pelting up to London to procure the special license.

"I discussed the settlements with Theresa," Thomas said, taking another sip of very tasty punch. "She fought me, until I pointed that they mostly benefit Priscilla."

"They benefit your conscience. Priscilla, as the oldest daughter of my house, will be handsomely dowered."

Already, Belmont spoke of the girl with a father's smug protectiveness, which a doting uncle was honor-bound to trifle with.

"Loris would like you and Theresa to be godparents to our first-born. You'd best get this other business tidied up, Belmont. I'd hate to disappoint my baroness with the news of your untimely death."

Belmont's smile probably had a lot to do with why Theresa had agreed to marry him: Shy, proud, pleased, handsome… and already, plotting how he'd corrupt Thomas's children in the manner of godfathers from time immemorial.

Loris came through the library door, Belmont stood straighter, and Thomas downed the rest of his courage—his punch.

"Don't muck this up," Thomas said, as Theresa followed Loris into the library. "Don't make her a widow before she's had a chance to enjoy being a wife."

Belmont clearly didn't hear him. His smile had become radiant, the children up in the reading loft were clapping, and Theresa was a woman transfigured. She did not look young, or innocent, or blushing, or any of those other wedding-day platitudes.

She looked happy, and determined. Very, very determined.

"Children, come down," Axel Belmont called. "We have a wedding to supervise."

The vicar leafed through his prayer book, Loris stood with Theresa, and Axel Belmont took the place beside his brother.

Thomas was assailed by an anxiety, a sense that his role as brother was about to end. Priscilla edged in front of him, a notebook and pencil clutched in her hand.

"Reese," Thomas called.

Everybody turned to look at him, though his sister only smiled.

"That was my pen name—Reese Belmont," she said, "so nobody would know I was a girl. Thomas gave it to me, and I've always preferred it to Theresa."

Priscilla wrinkled her nose. "What's wrong with being a girl?"

"Nothing," Richard Belmont said, "provided you're a quiet girl, who never gets dirty or spooks ponies."

Vicar cleared his throat, but Thomas wasn't quite finished. "Reese Jennings, you look lovely, and I'm proud to be your brother."

Axel Belmont cast a longing glance toward the punch bowl, though Theresa, if anything, became more beautiful. Her smile was benevolent, full of forgiveness and pride in her younger brother.

"I'm proud to have you for my brother, Thomas Jennings."

Vicar looked up. "Now that we've established that deal of a family pride bears on the nuptials, shall we begin? Who gives this woman in marriage to this man?"

"We do," Priscilla said, over her uncle's more conventional reply. "But we get to keep Mr. Belmont and his ponies, and we're not really giving Mama away. We're just letting her live happily ever after with Mr. Belmont."

Matthew took Theresa's hand. "A fine introduction. Vicar, if you'd proceed?"

The rest went quickly, with Loris tucking her hand into Thomas's, then accepting his handkerchief as Matthew and Theresa spoke their vows, and kissed beneath a bough affixed beneath the reading loft.

"Will you write us a story about this, Priscilla?" Thomas asked, when the shaking of hands, and kissing of the bride had concluded. The girl had already been warned repeatedly not to mention her mother's marriage to any of the day's guests. Vicar Herndon, fortunately, agreed with the need for extreme discretion.

"I won't write a story," Priscilla said, sniffing at Thomas's refilled drinking glass. "Stories are make believe, and this is better than a story, because Mama and Mr. Belmont are really, truly in love. I have brothers now, like Mama has you."

The child had a papa, too, and a good one. Loris passed Thomas back his handkerchief.

"To have brothers is wonderful," Thomas said. "Though I wouldn't know about that first hand."

Priscilla tossed him a patient glance that made her look very much like her mother.

"Yes, you would. Uncle Axel told me how it works. Mr. Belmont married Mama, so he's your brother now, and you are his brother too. Maybe Aunt Loris can explain this to you."

"I'll do that," Loris said. "Priscilla, why don't you come with us to inspect the buffet?"

"No, thank you. I'd rather stay here with the books."

With her new brothers. *Ah, well.* "Be patient with Christopher, Remington, and Richard," Thomas said. "Having a sister is a new privilege for them, but they soon won't know how they managed without you."

Before Priscilla was halfway up to the reading loft, Loris kissed him, even though they weren't anywhere near the kissing bough.

* * *

The day was unseasonably mild, a sunny reprise of late autumn, perfect for a country gathering. Theresa allowed the joy of the moment its due—her joy at Matthew's greeting, and at the ceremony in the library was considerable—but worry would not be set entirely aside.

"Stop fretting," Matthew said, as Axel herded the children from the room.

Matthew's brother had promised slow, painful, death-by-memorization to any young man who brought shame to the family name that day, even as he'd scooped Priscilla onto his back and threatened to imprison her beneath a sheaf of ever-blooming mistletoe.

"Axel let her have a taste from his flask, Matthew," Theresa muttered as the library grew quiet. Theresa did not know what to make of her brother-in-law, but Priscilla had taken to Axel Belmont easily.

"Today is a day for nipping from one's flask, but I assure you, all Axel offered Priscilla was lemonade, perhaps fresh cider, nothing more. Would you like a celebratory tot?"

"No, thank you. I'd like some of that ever-blooming mistletoe."

A murmur of voices drifted up the corridor, as Theresa stole one more embrace from her beloved.

"Thank you," she whispered. "I started the day among family, celebrating, being celebrated. I never thought to have that, Matthew."

His arms tightened in a hold that felt like home. "We belong to each other.

I wish—"

"I do too," Theresa said, kissing him. "But we have today, and until the New Year at least, and you've promised me forever after. For now, I will focus on that much and on keeping you safe."

He'd promised her *until death did them part*, which thought was like somebody walking over Theresa's figurative grave.

"As long as I stay away from Axel's devil's brew," Matthew said, "the king's peace is secure for another day."

Mr. and Mrs. Dale arrived, followed by more neighbors, the rest of the vicar's family, the Capshaws, and more jolly souls than the library could hold. The conservatory was pressed into service, and before noon, people were sitting on the terrace in groups, children were chasing each other about the corridors, and the occasional scrap broke out between dogs.

"This is what you've been missing for years, isn't it?" Thomas asked, passing Theresa a plate with a buttered scone on it and a dollop of jam on the side.

She'd always liked her scones this way, jam on the side.

"This is wealth, Thomas," she said, biting off a corner. Linden's kitchens had provided much for the buffet, and neighbors had brought contributions as well. "This is the difference between people showing up to rebuild your stable, and struggling alone for years, hoping next year's harvest is better than this year's. You should start a comparable celebration at Sutcliffe."

He wrinkled his nose, looking very much like an overgrown eight-year-old. "Loris said the same thing, only she says I must establish such traditions at both Linden and Sutcliffe. I'll be fat as a market hog before my firstborn is sitting a pony."

Theresa held up her scone, Thomas took a bite, and all was right with the world... almost.

"Whose turn is it to keep an eye on Matthew?" she asked. Today, Matthew would eat nothing that hadn't come from Linden's kitchens, and he would never be out of sight of a family member.

"Mr. Axel Belmont has that privilege. I take over at one of the clock, when the professor serenades us with his fiddle. As far as that goes, the time has come to assemble in the conservatory."

An informal concert would ensue, opened by Axel Belmont's violin, followed by a choral offering from the five cousins, and further entertainment from whatever neighbors were inspired to perform.

Theresa was free to enjoy the music, because Agatha Capshaw and the vicar's wife had taken on the job of monitoring the buffet.

"Have you seen Priscilla?" Theresa asked. "She won't want to miss the cousins singing."

"She might be down in the stable," Thomas said. "Or up some tree, or reading in the library. My niece is a young lady of infinite parts."

Theresa had once been that busy. "I'll start with the stable, and don't you let Matthew out of your sight."

Thomas bowed, twirling his wrist. "Ever at your service, dearest sister." He snitched another bite of her scone and sauntered off, while Theresa blinked madly at her plate.

She was his dearest sister, and he was her dearest brother. This visit had restored them to each other despite all the trouble and worry swirling about, and for that, Theresa was more grateful than words could convey.

Theresa gathered her skirts—her composure eluded capture—and hoped the walk to the stable would give her time to regain her dignity. She hadn't been this prone to sentiment since she'd been—

Her hand went to her middle. "Gracious, everlasting powers."

She meandered through the dormant garden, wonder crowding out all else. Priscilla might have a sibling, Matthew would have more children to love, Thomas would be an uncle again…

The stable was an oasis of quiet after the crowding and noise at the house. The contented sound of horses munching hay blended with the scents of equine and leather. The aisle was tidily raked, though small boot prints led from stall to stall.

"Priscilla?"

No answer. Matthew's gray mare looked up, pausing with a mouthful of hay half-chewed.

"Priscilla Jennings!"

"I haven't seen her," Emmanuel Capshaw said as he emerged from the saddle room. "Though on a day like today, losing a child would be easy enough. The little dears tend to be underfoot until you need to gather them up, then they're nowhere to be found. May I say, you look very fetching, Miss Jennings?"

He'd said that several times on the day of the hunt meet. Then as now, he had a silver flask in his hand.

"Thank you, Mr. Capshaw. I believe the concert will soon begin, and I'm sure the boys will want to see you among the audience."

A violin pierced the quiet of the early afternoon with a rapid ascending minor scale that put Theresa in mind of gypsy campfires.

"The annual musicale," Emmanuel said, pocketing his flask. "Don't suppose you'd care to miss the entertainment with me?"

His question was far from innocent, and beyond tiresome.

"I'm looking for my daughter, sir, and I would dearly love for her to join me in the conservatory."

The violin began running through phrases, intricate flourishes in the higher register. Axel Belmont was talented, and his performance would hold everybody's attention.

Unease crept down Theresa's spine as Emmanuel Capshaw took a step

204 | Grace Burrowes

closer. He was not a young man, but he was taller than Theresa, and from the scent of his breath, he wasn't entirely sober.

"Your daughter apparently doesn't want to be found," he said. "Nobody will notice your absence, and isn't that just the most convenient gift a man could ask for at the holidays?"

* * *

"Richard, a moment," Matthew said. "You've been avoiding me all morning, and you needn't." Had been avoiding his devoted papa for months, in fact.

Richard closed the book he'd been reading, for Matthew had tracked his youngest to the reading loft in the library.

"Uncle's concert is about to begin," Richard said, shoving the book back onto a shelf. "We're the hosts, and he'll expect us to be there."

"Your brothers and cousins are likely wondering where you are, but as for Axel, he'll dazzle everybody. The ladies will declare him dashing and talented, and then he'll put his violin away for another year."

Richard made no move to leave. "He is dashing and talented, also grouchy."

"And I am your father."

Ambushing the boy was unfair, but left to his own devices, Richard would likely disappear back to Oxford in a cloud of sullenness, and that, Matthew could not allow.

"Whose turn is it to watch you, *Papa?*"

"Sutcliffe's, but the simple expedient of leading him to the mistletoe beneath which his baroness stood has gained me a moment of privacy with my youngest son. Somebody is trying to kill me, Richard, and in the event they succeed, I want you to know that I love you, I consider you my son and mine alone, and I'm sorry if the circumstances of your birth were conveyed to you without my knowledge."

"You're *sorry?*"

Richard's expression gave away nothing. Matthew had seen men with the same bleakness in their eyes marched to the dock to face a certain verdict of guilt.

"I'm very sorry you overheard your brothers arguing—and they are your brothers—but I am not sorry at all, I have *never* been sorry, to be your father."

Axel's violin had fallen silent, which suggested the neighbors were assembling in the conservatory and the concert about to begin. Axel could play for hours, though he'd limit himself to perhaps fifteen minutes of public brilliance.

Richard braced two hands on the railing overlooking the library, much like a captain on the deck of a ship might brace himself against an approaching storm.

"Priscilla claims Sutcliffe's family sent him away when he came of age," Richard said. "Stuffed a packet of money in his pocket and told him to be gone."

Bloody hell. Matthew had never considered that Richard might be frightened by the facts of his parentage, tossed adrift amid fears and uncertainties too terrible to name. Matthew joined his son at the balcony, pleased that the boy had a few inches to grow before surpassing his father's height.

"Richard, I cried like an infant the day you left for Oxford. Got sloppy drunk, shut myself in this library and fell asleep before the fire next to Maida on the rug."

Richard alone deserved to know this. Matthew would probably describe his grieving to Theresa one day—one day soon.

The boy bowed his head as if warding off blows. "Why would you cry to finally get rid of us? We cost a perishing lot of money, we make endless noise, you have no privacy with us around. We eat like a bloody p-plague of l-locusts, and we—"

Matthew wrapped Richard in a hug as secure as the love wrapping around his own heart.

"I miss you every day, Richard. I'm proud of you every day. You are my son, and since the day I first held Christopher in my arms, all I've wanted in this life was to be worthy of the honor of raising your brothers and you. Some man, some pathetic fool, took advantage of your mother's tender heart, and his penance is that he hasn't seen you become the magnificent young men you are. I pity him, and I thank God every night for my boys."

A great sigh went out of Richard, while Matthew simply held his son, reveling in a sea of sentiment too complicated and vast for mere words. The house became quiet, and one wayward child was welcomed home.

Richard sniffed, then turned away and fumbled at his pockets. Matthew passed him the handkerchief Rem had wrinkled earlier.

A friendly round of applause came from the direction of the conservatory.

"You don't know who he could be?" Richard asked, blotting his eyes with the handkerchief. "You've no idea? I suspect Rem has figured it out, but the bloody bugger will never say."

Tears had deepened Richard's voice. He dashed his hair from his eyes and reached for his flask, for apparently Matthew was the only Belmont on the premises unarmed with holiday spirits.

And in that gesture, that reaching, uncapping, and tipping up of a silver flask, Matthew's memory and instincts collided with an awful insight, followed by a worse premonition.

"I have my suspicions, Richard, about which we can talk at greater length when the house isn't full of tipsy neighbors and overfed dogs. Would you happen to know where your Uncle Emmanuel has got off to?"

Richard tucked his flask away. "Doubtless, he's getting drunk, groping somebody's cousin, and disgracing his vows, the usual."

Axel's violin began a sweet, soaring melody, while cold settled in Matthew's bones.

"Belmont, are you up there?" Sutcliffe called from beneath the balcony. "I've been looking all over for you, and Loris will have my hide—Theresa will have my hide too, and Priscilla will serve me up in little pieces to the nearest dragon—if I can't report your whereabouts."

Footsteps clomped up the spiral stairs as Sutcliffe's head, shoulders, and then the rest of him came into view.

"I am sorry to interrupt," Sutcliffe said, "but the professor has started his performance, and you, Belmont, are the last person permitted to play least-in-sight today."

"Thomas, where is Theresa?"

The baron's demeanor shifted without a change in his posture. "She went looking for Priscilla, whom I also haven't seen, now that you mention it."

"And did you happen to note Emmanuel Capshaw among the audience in the conservatory?" For Richard's benefit, Matthew tried to keep the question casual—and mostly failed.

"He was half in his cups and lurking near the mistletoe before noon," Sutcliffe said, "but no, I didn't see him in the conservatory just now."

Perishing hell. "Gentlemen, my every instinct tells me we have trouble. We have serious trouble and I fear Theresa is in the middle of it."

* * *

The only gift Theresa needed to make her holidays complete—Matthew's love, for the rest of her days—had already been given to her, and to Matthew's side, she would return.

"Mr. Capshaw, I think you'd better leave."

Capshaw stood between Theresa and the open barn doors. Instinct warned her to keep her distance from him, and that same instinct urged her to flee.

"Leave, well yes. Bit difficult, when a fellow has no means. The tenant farms barely make their rent, which my dear wife assures me is because they're poorly managed—by me, one supposes. I would love to decamp for a life of gay abandon on the Continent, but I'm held fast to Sussex by necessity. For now. Investments in train and all that, but none of the ready at present. Don't suppose you'd care for a nip?"

He took a step closer, close enough that Theresa could see a slight tremor in the hand grasping his flask.

"No, thank you." She moved left, and he dodged the same direction, a parody of a dance partner.

"You're no one to judge me," Capshaw said. "No one to judge anybody, in fact. Time somebody relieved you of your high-and-mighty airs."

Theresa shifted her right foot back, ready to relieve him of his very breath, when movement behind Capshaw caught her eye.

"Emmanuel Capshaw, you will miss your nephews' performance."

Never had Theresa been so glad to hear a man scolded. Agatha Capshaw, wearing a cloak but no bonnet, stood in the sunlight at the end of the barn aisle. Her expression was calm, suggesting she hadn't overhead her husband's philandering, or perhaps the poor woman was accustomed to Emmanuel's unmannerliness.

He turned, hands wide. "My dear, I simply wanted a bit of air and to exchange my flask for a fresh one. The younger Miss Jennings has apparently absented herself from the gathering. If I see her, I'll send her to the conservatory, shall I?"

"Thank you, Mr. Capshaw," Theresa said, though Priscilla had better sense than to come within ten yards of him.

"Miss Jennings and I will follow shortly," Agatha said. "Run along, Manny."

Capshaw tottered off, and Theresa recalled Axel Belmont's admonition that today, nobody was to disgrace the family name. Emmanuel Capshaw was an embarrassment, at least, if not a disgrace.

"You probably wonder why I don't leave him," Agatha said, advancing into the stable. "But you of all women should understand my circumstances."

"We depend on our menfolk for necessities, at least until we're widowed," Theresa said. "I'm not fond of this system, myself."

How odd, to think that Theresa had something in common with Agatha Capshaw.

"My portion wouldn't suffice to keep a mouse in summer stockings," Agatha said. "Emmanuel 'invested it,' in his pocket flask and his fancy ladies, I presume. He visits his soiled doves almost nightly, when he thinks I've gone to my solitary slumbers. I've made shift as best I can. You know all about making shift, I'm sure."

The observation bordered on pitying, which was worse than if it had been snide.

"You are Matthew's family, Mrs. Capshaw. I'm sorry for your circumstances, but I'm sure Matthew will not let you become destitute."

Agatha peered at Matthew's mare, who'd gone back to munching hay.

"Haven't you found, Miss Jennings, that relying on the good offices of some man is a poor substitute for managing matters oneself? Women are pragmatic, determined, and much smarter than men give us credit for. You have emerged from a scandalous past to capture the attention of a handsome, wealthy man, for example. I commend you for that, I truly do."

Theresa was formulating an innocuous reply to that odd compliment when Mrs. Capshaw pulled a sleek, heavy pistol from beneath her cloak.

She pointed the gun at Theresa. "I most sincerely regret, Miss Jennings, that for all your cleverness—because of your cleverness, in fact—you must die. And at the holidays too—such a pity."

* * *

Nicholas and Beckman had been subtly beckoned from the audience in the conservatory, Sutcliffe was sniffing at the decanters, and Richard had gone to assemble the cousins and brothers, intent on keeping them singing until sunset, if need be.

"All those years of shared Sunday dinners," Matthew fumed, "and I was sitting down with the author of my marital failures. I cannot fathom—well, I can, but I don't want to. Emmanuel is not even very bright, and yet Matilda was woefully besotted."

"And now he's going after Theresa?" Sutcliffe asked. "But why?"

"Because she caught the squire's eye," Nick Haddonfield said, "and when a man's eye is caught, his purse is likely caught as well."

"Particularly if the lady becomes the mother of his children," Beckman added, studying the portrait on the back wall. "You were generous with your first wife. What provisions might you make for the second, and her child, and any subsequent children?"

"So the motive is greed," Matthew said, as Axel stomped into the library. "Emmanuel is one of the trustees of the estate, and of all the obvious connections to overlook, I chose that one."

"The baroness would provide me no details," Axel said, pacing the carpet before the fire, his violin in one hand, his bow in the other. "Trouble's afoot, that's all she said. Get to the library, she said, so I tear myself away from more simpering beauties than—Matthew, what the hell is wrong?"

"Emmanuel Capshaw cannot be accounted for, and Theresa and Priscilla are missing as well."

"Emman—?" Axel came to a halt. "He's passed out under some bush, or swiving somebody's widow. Don't be daft."

My very dear man, Rem had quoted. Not man, but rather, Man. Short for Manny.

"Emmanuel is the father of Matilda's children," Matthew said, taking the violin and bow from his brother and setting them on the sideboard. "I hear Emmanuel's voice in Richard's words. I see Emmanuel in the way my sons raise a flask. I know it, when I look back on all the times the family was together, and Matilda offered Emmanuel her cheek for a kiss."

Axel braced a hand on the mantel. "That's—that's... Bloody hell. Shall I kill him for you?"

"Let's find him first," Sutcliffe said. "We can take turns killing him after we find him."

"That means tracking him in a crowd," Matthew retorted, crossing to the window nearest the corner, "which is damned near impossible without an excellent scent hound. Agatha might know where he's got off to, but she's been flitting from the buffet to the guests to the kitchens all morning. We could organize a searching party and obliterate any sign of where Capshaw has—"

Emmanuel came sauntering across the gardens, a flask glinting in his hand. His complexion was ruddy, his gait somewhat unsteady.

Matthew was out the French doors in the next instant. "Where the hell is my wife?"

Emmanuel blinked. "In the churchyard, best as I recall. Pity about that too."

"Not Matilda, you idiot, Theresa—the wife I married not three hours ago, before witnesses that included your sons."

Emmanuel pitched the flask off into the bushes. "Tilly said you'd never know. I told her you knew all along. Wish I'd been wrong. I wish a lot of things, come to that."

At that moment, Matthew wished this pathetic fool were dead, but for one question. "Have you seen Theresa?"

"Miss Jennings is immune to my charms, much like my dear wife. Left them in the stable. Agatha chased me off. Agatha's not usually the jealous sort, but she likes your Miss Jennings, or feels sorry for her. Agatha's a fine one for feeling sorry for her inferiors."

Agatha? For an instant, Matthew was suffused with relief. Agatha Capshaw might sniff and mutter and thank-the-Lord Theresa into a stupor, but Theresa had nothing to fear—

Be happy while you can.

With the next beat of his heart, Matthew knew Theresa had *everything* to fear. Agatha had managed through years of penury, watched her own sister repeatedly fall prey to Emmanuel's dubious charms, and could well have authored attempts on Matthew's life. If Matthew were dead, the Belmont wealth would be that much closer to Agatha's control.

"Beckman," Matthew snapped, moving off toward the stable, "take Mr. Capshaw to the estate office and don't let him out of your sight."

"Well, that's a relief," Nick said, falling in on Matthew's left. "A pity, but a relief. Not a word of this—"

"Nicholas, you will please shut your mouth. Theresa Jennings is alone in the stable with a woman who was for years scorned by her own spouse. If Emmanuel is concerned I'll squander my wealth on a second wife, Agatha is likely rabid to prevent the possibility. If anything happens to me, Axel becomes guardian of my sons, but the Belmont estate lands will come under Emmanuel's immediate supervision."

"Nobody would suspect Agatha Capshaw of anything save an over-fondness for elderberry wine," Sutcliffe said from Matthew's right. "Though perhaps we ought to find a gun or two, or three."

"The guns are all under lock and key in the armory above my office," Matthew said, "and Spiker has the key. By the time we locate Spiker, discreetly draw him aside, and procure and load weapons, Agatha could have done her worst."

"I'm guessing she was here the day Maida died," Axel said, bringing up the rear. "She could easily have hired one of the tenant farmers to move that damned harrow. She knows you eat like a regiment on forced march, and she might have slipped into your stable on some family visit and tampered with your gun. Good God, hell hath no fury—"

"Hell hath a much greater fury," Matthew said, "and Agatha Capshaw is about to come face-to-face with him."

CHAPTER TWENTY-ONE

Theresa had realized in earliest adulthood that death could be the ultimate temptress, and death's handmaiden was despair. Alone at Sutcliffe Keep but for a contemptuous grandfather and leering cousins, faced with a worse fate even than that, death had whispered to Theresa of peace, of a final righteous indictment of an unfair world, of lasting woe for those who'd wronged her.

Common sense had retorted that Grandpapa and the twins would have congratulated themselves on having accurately ascribed a weak mental constitution to Theresa. They'd have made free with her settlements, while Thomas....

Thomas would have been devastated to lose the only person who loved him as he deserved to be loved.

So love had preserved Theresa from death once before, and then love for Priscilla had preserved her from folly many times since. More love was hers to claim now—love for Matthew, for his family, for life itself, and for a future full of hope and promise.

"Mrs. Capshaw, you will please put that gun away. You apparently fear that Mr. Belmont and I have conceived an interest in each other, though how that affects you, I neither know nor care."

Indecision flickered in Agatha's eyes, while the gun remained unwaveringly pointed at Theresa.

"Matthew is besotted—he intends to offer for you, of all the outlandish notions—and you are no debutante to refuse him your favors. I cannot risk him becoming entangled with you."

Thank God that Matthew had insisted the wedding be kept secret. Theresa mustered the glower that had subdued even her cousins.

"I am also no stupid girl to permit a man intimacies before he's earned the right to enjoy them."

A cat or some other creature shifted in the hayloft and Matthew's mare hung her head over the half door.

"You confirm my worst fear, Miss Jennings. You have given Matthew an incentive to marry you. If I allow that to happen, then I've no doubt Sutcliffe will replace Emmanuel as trustee for the Belmont estate until Christopher turns five-and-twenty. Needs must, Miss Jennings, and now we must take a short walk into the home wood."

Fear choked Theresa, but rage and determination gave her courage. "So you're the one who's been trying to kill Matthew?"

"And nearly succeeding," Agatha said. "It was too much to hope Matthew would consider himself the victim of that much bad luck, but more bad luck will head his way, I can assure you. He rides about the shire without so much as a groom, he eats like a starving apprentice. I'll think of something once the boys are out from underfoot."

The rest of the puzzle wasn't hard to solve: Matthew would die, his children's inheritance would be liberally raided at the behest of their embittered aunt, and years hence, when Christopher was old enough to manage the estate on his own, Agatha would be comfortable for life. Emmanuel would become expendable shortly thereafter, and nobody would be the wiser.

"What has Matthew ever done to earn your enmity?"

"We can discuss that as we walk," Agatha said. "March, madam, and do not think of screaming, or my dear husband's gun will accidentally discharge, to my everlasting, eternal horror—not that anybody would hear your scream or the gun go off over all that holiday music."

* * *

Matthew would have run to the stable, except that his one advantage was the element of surprise. Agatha's attempts on his life had nearly succeeded because she'd moved under a cloak of long-suffering decency. If she was threatening Theresa in the midst of a holiday gathering, then she'd grown cocksure.

"Perhaps we shouldn't be hasty," Sutcliffe said. "Agatha Capshaw has never by the least indication shown any animosity toward you, Belmont."

"Agatha Capshaw threw her younger sister at Emmanuel, would be my guess," Axel replied. "In the alternative, Agatha knew exactly what was afoot and did nothing to discourage Emmanuel's philandering."

Memory intruded, of Matilda beneath the mistletoe with her brother-in-law, and Agatha smiling benignly from the foot of the family dinner table.

"Agatha _knew_," Matthew said. "She can't be held responsible for the initial liaison, but if Emmanuel's attentions had grown tiresome, she probably turned matters to her advantage as best she could. I made out my will practically before Christopher was baptized—with Agatha and Emmanuel as his godparents—

and I didn't change it when Rem and Richard came along. Why I missed the evidence staring me right in my very—"

Priscilla came pelting around the corner of the grape arbor, running smack into Matthew and lashing her arms around his waist.

"Mr. Belmont! She has a gun, and she has Mama, and I'm scared."

Matthew was afraid, furious and very determined. He hoisted a panting Priscilla to his hip.

"We know, child, and we're off to rescue your mama. Catch your breath, and all will be well."

"Mr. Belmont, that lady hates you. She wants your money, and she hates everybody. You have to save M-Mama."

"You were with us in the parlor this morning, Priscilla. Do you recall what I promised your mama?"

"For better or for worse? This is worse, Mr. Belmont. This is awful."

And Matthew hadn't time to properly comfort the child. "I'm your papa now too, and that gives me the right to protect your mama from every harm, and you as well. Nicholas, take the child to the library and read her a story."

"I want to rescue Mama too."

Nick plucked the girl from Matthew's hold, set her on the ground, and kept her hand in his.

"You have already rescued your mama by warning us about the gun," he said. "The rest will be easy for a man as brave as our squire."

Nick winked at Priscilla, though the child ignored that nonsense.

"Bring Mama to the library when you've rescued her, please. And rescue her very soon."

"We will," Sutcliffe assured her. "Very, very soon."

"Priscilla," Matthew said, "did you see which why they went?"

"Into the woods on the path behind the stable."

Into hundreds of acres of woods, where the paths would all be carpeted with leaves—and that was to Matthew's advantage too.

* * *

"I suppose you're curious," Agatha said as Theresa shuffled along one of the myriad trails in Matthew's home wood. "How did I abide all that nonsense between Manny and Matilda?"

What nonsense—?

The truth landed on Theresa's fear with a nauseating weight.

Matthew had done nothing to earn Agatha's enmity, but Agatha had reason aplenty for bitterness toward life in general. Agatha's pretty sister had poached on her older sibling's marital preserves, the Capshaw finances were in disarray, and Emmanuel had bumbled and tippled even a tiny jointure into oblivion....

"You must be very angry," Theresa said, leaving as clear a trail through the bracken as she could without attracting Agatha's notice. "Very hurt."

"Saints in heaven, of course, I was upset at first, then I was relieved. Matilda's first season in Town didn't go at all according to her dreams. She expected from Polite Society the cosseting our parents had always showered upon her, but there was only Emmanuel, ever willing to flatter and flirt. Matilda flirted right back. Take the trail to the left."

Agatha had had years to learn these trails and apparently had a destination in mind.

While Theresa had only a glimmer of a plan. She pretended to stumble over a root and snatched at a hanging vine.

"Watch where you're going," Agatha snapped, the pistol muzzle digging into Theresa's back.

"I'm not wearing boots," Theresa retorted. "Marching off to my own execution through the wilds of Sussex wasn't on my agenda today."

"Of course it wasn't. You were too enthralled with the prospect of becoming Matthew's hostess. Belmont House is beautiful, isn't it? I've loved that property since I was a girl."

Agatha spoke about the house with more longing and respect than she did her husband.

Theresa paused for a moment to fuss her skirts free from some brambles, straining her ears for the faintest sound of pursuit.

"That estate is Christopher, Remington, and Richard's birthright. Do you think to take it from them?"

The only sound was the lapping of water against rocks in a wide stream running alongside the path. The woods would be beautiful in summer, but now, they were chilly and deserted. Not a bird or a squirrel moved overhead, not a breeze stirred the bare tree limbs.

"I'm very fond of my nephews," Agatha said, "and they are not to blame for their parents' venery. My husband took a fancy to Matilda, and I saw an opportunity to turn that betrayal into a connection with the only wealth attached to the family tree. Matilda probably tried to be a good wife to Matthew, but Manny was her first love, and she was never able to deny herself anything. Why Matthew put up with such a wife is beyond me, but he's helplessly dutiful."

Matthew had put up with Matilda in part out of duty, in part out of pity, and very much for the sake of the children. He'd said that his first marriage was concocted by the women of the family.

One woman, apparently. One very determined woman.

Theresa stumbled again, falling to her hands and knees on the soft earth of the path.

"Get up slowly, Miss Jennings, and quit delaying the inevitable. The fatal wound will be to the head, and you'll barely know an instant's suffering."

Matthew would know endless suffering, though, if the woman he'd taken to wife that very morning died before the sun set. Priscilla would suffer, Thomas,

Loris, Alice…

This is different. The woman being marched at gunpoint through Matthew's woods was not a lonely young lady, consigned to isolation or worse in a castle by the sea. Her brother's love had been restored to her, and so much more besides. She had allies, she had family, she had many, many reasons to live.

Though little reason for hope.

"Do you think to make it appear that I've killed myself?" Theresa asked.

"Precisely. Matthew has failed to offer for you, and your disappointment has deranged you. Matthew will go back to being a boring widower who occasionally risks a flirtation at a house party—until tragedy befalls him, of course. Not much farther to go, thank goodness. I shall return to the festivities before I'm missed, and I do so enjoy hearing the boys sing."

* * *

"There are more trails in this damned wood than Oxford has books," Axel muttered as he tramped along at Matthew's heels. "Where in the hell can Agatha be going?"

They faced another fork in the trail, but unlike the previous turnings, Matthew could not easily see the signs. The ground wasn't as soft, no carpet of leaves was conveniently disturbed by the passing of two—

A vine had been torn free of the branches overhead. A thorny raspberry cane was broken two inches from the end.

"This way," he said, marching off to the left, "and this trail leads to one destination."

"To the river," Axel said. "I dislike this, Matthew. The water level is high because of the snow melt, and few women swim well in winter clothing."

"I bloody hate it," Sutcliffe muttered. "I cannot see danger when it lurks at my sister's very elbow. Why you had to lock up all the guns up in your armory today of all days, I do not know. Why I had to leave my knife at home—"

"Voices down," Matthew whispered, breaking into a trot. "We always lock up the guns when children are loose on the property, particularly if strong spirits will be served in abundance as well. Now listen to me, for we'll have only one chance. They're heading for the vixen's covert, and Theresa has been leaving us as clear a trail as she can. "

* * *

"I've chosen a pretty place for you to die," Agatha said, as Theresa emerged onto the banks of the river. The water was at least fifty feet across, running fast and high.

"You've chosen a remote place for me to die," Theresa replied. "Do you hope my body won't be found until spring?"

"There's no good time to find a suicide's body." Agatha shaded her eyes against the afternoon sun. "If Matthew is lucky, he won't live long enough to come upon your remains. A good heavy snow would help, but some things even

I can't control. At the river's edge, please."

That damnable pistol muzzle dug into Theresa's side for the third time.

Theresa spun and grabbed Agatha's wrist, but the older woman was surprisingly nimble, twisting free and wrenching the gun straight up. She hopped back, smiling at Theresa.

"I wondered when you'd show some spirit, and I don't blame you for trying, but your time to die has come."

"Or maybe yours has," Theresa said, dashing left to put a sizeable willow between them. "Attempted murder is a hanging felony, and your little plan has yet to succeed."

"My little plan has yet to fail, you mean. I might still be biding my time, except Emmanuel has bungled our finances to the very brink of ruin, and Matthew's regard for you was obvious to the whole shire at the hunt meet. If you run, I'll have a clear shot, and if you remain cowering back there, I'll simply wait you out. I've been waiting for years, and for the Belmont fortune, I can be patient a little while longer."

Agatha was not mad, not in the sense of having lost her sanity, but she was furious, at the end of her tether with the fate she'd been dealt. Theresa entertained one instant of pity for the woman, and silently tore off a twig from hanging willow branch.

"I can be patient until my husband comes to find me," Theresa said. "Today is my wedding day, you know, and brides and grooms don't like to be parted from one another on their wedding day."

Theresa tossed the willow sprig to the right and took off at a dead run in the other direction.

Only to find herself face-to-face with Agatha's pistol.

"Turn around," Agatha said. "And say your prayers."

* * *

Matthew crept closer to the clearing by the river, until he could see Agatha Capshaw holding a gun on Theresa, a stout, double-barreled horse pistol that would be accurate at close range.

Matthew counted to twenty in keeping with the only plan he could devise on no notice whatsoever, for tackling Agatha where she stood might mean injury or death for Theresa.

"Turn around," Agatha said. "And say your prayers."

Matthew stepped forward, making certain to slide his boot through the carpet of leaves as noisily as he could.

"Perhaps Agatha, you had better be the one importuning heaven," Matthew called, "because the king's man has arrived, and in the name of our sovereign, and in the name of justice itself, *you are under arrest.*"

Agatha stood between Matthew and Theresa, and unless she was an excellent shot, she was unlikely to wound them both.

"Theresa, my dearest, simply step back," Matthew went on. "You will eventually be beyond the range of Agatha's pistol, and it's me she wants to kill, isn't it?"

Theresa took one step in retreat, and Agatha's pistol swung in her direction. "I will shoot your dearest lady love, if you take even one step closer to me, Matthew. Shoot her right through her heart."

Thomas Jennings moved out from behind a holly bush and took the place before Theresa.

"You'll have to shoot me first," he said, "and there's rather a lot of me for that one silly little gun. Theresa, you will please honor that vow to obey Mr. Belmont, and step back."

To Matthew's endless relief, Theresa retreated, keeping her brother between her and Agatha's gun.

"You truly *married* her?" Agatha said.

"We married each other," Matthew replied. "For richer, for poorer; for better, or for worse. I'm looking very much forward to the part about having and holding each other. Give me the gun, Agatha."

"I haven't done anything wrong," Agatha said, training her pistol on Matthew. "You can't prove anything."

He took a step toward her. "The harrow left where I was likely to send my horse leaping into its teeth? I'm nearly certain one of your tenant farmers will be able to identify it."

"Stay back," Agatha said, her finger closing on the trigger.

"You were at my house the day my dog ingested poison—for it was poison. I had a post-mortem done on dear Maida, and the evidence was clear."

He was close enough to Agatha that a single bullet could be lethal. Not yet close enough to disarm her.

"I should have killed you years ago," Agatha said, raising the gun to the level of Matthew's heart.

Theresa called from the edge of the clearing. "Or you should simply have asked him for help."

That unexpected—and quite sensible suggestion—gave Matthew the instant he needed to leap forward and snatch the gun from Agatha. Axel had his arms around her from behind the very next moment, and though she struggled, she was no match for his strength.

"Attempted murder," Axel growled, as Theresa ran into Matthew's embrace. "Not one but multiple counts, against three different unarmed individuals, including a magistrate. Malice aforethought goes without saying. We heard you, madam. Heard you admit your greed, your bloody *patience*. Matthew, please give me permission to throw this blight upon the species into the river."

"If she should survive the first immersion," Sutcliffe added, taking the gun from Matthew's hand, "I'll push her under again—and again, and again."

Matthew eased his grip on his wife, lest Theresa be unable to breathe. Death awaited Agatha, if the king's justice was brought to bear, and she deserved that at least.

"I cannot serve as magistrate in this case," Matthew said. "I'm a witness, and so, Axel, are you. Agatha's fate must rest in the hands of—"

Theresa stirred in his arms. "Matthew? Might we discuss this?"

"No," Matthew said. "Not here, not now. The boys will be frantic with worry, Belmont House is bursting with guests, some of whom have already over-imbibed, and my temper is strained beyond bearing. *She tried to kill you.*"

All the terror and rage Matthew had carried inside for the past hour, all the nightmares he'd have for the rest of his life, were boiling up inside him. His hands ached to choke Agatha where she stood—except that would mean turning loose of Theresa, which he could not do.

Possibly not ever.

Theresa eased from Matthew's embrace, keeping her fingers linked with his. "She tried to kill you too, but she is family. Emmanuel is family."

Oh, worse than that. Emmanuel was *close* family to Matthew's sons. "We will discuss this later, but justice must be done, Theresa. Agatha will pay for her crimes."

Five yards away, Agatha looked small, homely, and old. Axel could easily have pitched her in the river and clearly still wanted to.

"Sutcliffe, please fetch a rope to the stable," Matthew said.

Agatha sagged against Axel on a moan.

"He doesn't intend to hang you, more's the pity," Axel said, as Sutcliffe passed him the gun. "Back to the stable now, madam. My nerves are not as steady as Matthew's, and I've been drinking the holiday punch since early morning. Make your choices accordingly."

Agatha walked off, head held high, Axel holding the gun trained on her back.

Theresa leaned against Matthew, and all over again, he saw his wife facing a bullet, because he'd been blind to evidence that had been staring him in the face for years.

"She's gone," Matthew said. "You need never lay eyes on her again."

"Matthew, if you send her to the gallows, it will haunt you for the rest of your life. I know what it is to feel desperate, at the mercy of selfish men, without options other than those I can create myself. I hate her for trying to hurt you, for planning to steal from her own family, but I know what it is to make wrong choices."

Matthew turned her in his arms and for long moments tried to find some peace in the sound of the river rolling past.

"She is dangerous," he said at last. "She nearly killed me, nearly killed you. She exploited a foolish younger sibling who'd looked up to her. She had a hand in destroying any hope my first marriage had of success. She lied to and manipulated her idiot of a husband. I'm enraged simply listing her transgressions."

Theresa kissed him, a wifely, comforting sort of kiss. "I'm furious, and my luncheon is threatening to reappear. Let's get back to the house. Our absence will have been noticed, and our children are doubtless worried."

Two words—*our children*—pierced Matthew's awareness like a beacon of light across a foggy midnight sea. Truly, he'd married well this time.

"Come," Matthew said. "Time enough later to argue over the fate of the prisoner, if my brother doesn't accidentally shoot her and toss her remains into the river."

Theresa kept his hand in a snug grip, and even when the trail narrowed and they had to walk nearly single-file, she didn't turn loose of him.

Nor he of her.

CHAPTER TWENTY-TWO

"Agatha is being held under armed guard in the dower cottage," Matthew said, leaning an elbow on the library mantel when all the guests had been cordially sent on their way. "Mind you, I'm not asking you three to make a decision regarding her fate, but your opinions are welcome. As far as I'm concerned, Agatha has broken the law, and is guilty of multiple felonies. Nonetheless, she is family, as is her spouse."

Theresa had never admired her husband more, for Matthew was trying so hard to be fair and rational, despite his continuing ire toward Agatha. Thomas too, was maintaining his peace, sitting beside Theresa on the library sofa, when he'd made it clear he'd rather be building a gallows at the foot of the drive.

Christopher settled into the reading chair by the fire, a brandy in his hand. "Rem, Richard, and I have talked, Papa, and you needn't be so careful. He's Uncle Emmanuel to us, and that's all he'll ever be."

"I doubt I'll be writing to him any time soon," Richard said from his end of the sofa. "Agatha's sentence ought to be hard labor while subsisting on a diet of her own pear compote for the rest of her life."

Remington was sitting behind the library's desk, looking much like... Matthew. *Like his papa.*

"Do they have pears in the Antipodes?" Rem asked.

At the sideboard, Axel ceased fiddling with his violin's tuning pegs. "Excellent question."

Matthew exchanged a look with his brother. In twenty years, Theresa might still not entirely understand such looks, but she wouldn't need to. She understood her husband.

And she understood that his sons—her sons, too, now—were brilliant. "Are you suggesting transportation?" she asked.

"That would get Uncle Emmanuel out from underfoot if he emigrated," Rem said, "and he's much in need of a fresh start. Aunt was a model of Christian charity and decorum, as far as anybody knows, and her bad behavior seems to have limited itself to family. Maybe transportation is what she deserves."

"And pear compotes," Richard said. "For his stupidity, Uncle deserves *her*."

Thomas laid an arm across the back of the sofa. "You won't miss your uncle?"

Thomas knew what it was to be sent far from home, but how perceptive of him, to realize those left behind might miss the one banished—terribly.

"Uncle can come home to visit in ten years if he's of a mind to," Christopher said. "Or not. I don't fancy a long sea journey, myself."

"Nor I," Richard said.

"I'm prone to a bilious stomach on the high seas," Remington observed. "Though a jaunt over to Paris this summer to work on my French might be in order."

Axel sighted down the length of his violin bow. "If I see Capshaw again, I'll kill him. I'll enjoy killing him. If he'd been a half-decent husband, a half-decent man, we would not be in this contretemps. He took advantage of Matilda, neglected Agatha, neglected his very acres, and disrespected Theresa. My nephews are more compassionate than I can be, so I'm off to practice in the conservatory."

The library door closed softly behind him.

"He'll play the Kreutzer Sonata," Remington said, getting out from behind the desk. "Second movement."

"First," Christopher countered, rising. "Five quid on it."

"You're on," Richard said, standing and stretching. "But he'll play the last movement. It's the most fiendish."

"Also the jolliest," Remington said.

Each one of them paused to kiss Theresa's cheek before heading out the door. Thomas rose and looked about the library. "I seem to have misplaced my baroness."

"She's in the kitchen with Priscilla," Matthew said. "Defending the remains of the buffet from Nicholas and Beckman."

Theresa had burst into tears at the sight of Priscilla, who'd been reading a story to a rapt Nicholas in the loft. Alice had eventually peeled mother and daughter apart, but not until Theresa had promised to relay every moment of her adventure to her daughter.

"I should be in the kitchen," Theresa said. "I'm your wife."

Matthew prowled over to the sofa and took the place Thomas had vacated. "Sutcliffe, go cadge a meat pie from your baroness."

"I'll cadge something from her. Theresa, I take it you'll bide here tonight?"

"Of course, she will," Matthew said, gesturing toward the door with his chin. "As will Priscilla and Miss Portman. We can sort out the rest *later*, your lordship."

Thomas stayed where he was, standing before the sofa. "I realize you sent me off to keep me safe from the twins, Theresa. That's the only explanation that makes sense of all the facts. Those two would have cozened me into drinking, gambling, and worse dissipations, had I not been packed off to university, and then sent away from Sutcliffe."

Well, of course. The day needed only this.

"You're not to bring that old business up now," Matthew said, tucking an arm around Theresa's shoulders. "Go find your baroness and tell her to take you home, Sutcliffe."

"Matthew, it's all right," Theresa said, letting Thomas draw her to her feet. "Thomas has guessed the whole of it. I made an agreement with my cousins. My pin money in exchange for them leaving Thomas alone. Then I hadn't any pin money, because Grandfather concocted a scheme to marry me off."

"So you got me banished, ruined yourself, and they divided up your settlement," Thomas said, taking her in his arms. "Or did I get some of your settlement?"

Theresa could not find the words to lie to him.

"Thomas got every last groat, didn't he?" Matthew muttered. "Your settlement for his freedom. Sutcliffe, you really must leave. Not the house, of course, but the room. My wife and I need to have a succinct discussion about her overly protective nature."

Thomas's arms remained around her. "Today, you reminded Agatha that she might have sought Matthew's help. I know what you were thinking: You should have sought my help. Don't be daft. We've had that discussion. I was all but penniless, eager to see the world, legally powerless where you were concerned. No matter how you might have cautioned me, no matter my own common sense, if the twins had been set on wrecking my life, my life would have been wrecked."

Once again, Theresa burst into tears, and these too were tears of relief. "I should have told you, Thomas. I should have confided in you, trusted you. But you wouldn't have taken the money, you wouldn't have left me. You were no match for them. I should have—"

Matthew's handkerchief dangled in Theresa's line of sight. "He was a university boy, ignorant of life, and full of himself. For God's sake, if I could be talked into marriage prior to my majority, and me a sober, upright, sensible fellow, just imagine what quagmires of debt and vice Sutcliffe could have landed in."

"Entire swamps," Thomas said, dabbing at Theresa's cheeks. "Oceans in fact, I'm sure of it. I would probably be transported by now myself, or worse, if I'd fallen in with those two."

"I was afraid you'd call them out," Theresa said. "They were such bad apples, Thomas. When they called each other out, all I could think was, they didn't get you."

Thomas kissed her forehead. "Listen to me, because this needs to be said: Thank you, but—"

"If you ever do anything like that again," Matthew interjected, "we will both be quite wroth with you. Sutcliffe, you've made your point. Turn loose of my wife."

Thomas kissed Theresa's cheek this time. "You've married a jealous man, Sister. If he's ever difficult, you have only to apply to me."

Matthew took him by the arm and marched him to the door. "I made the same offer to your baroness, on your wedding day, and I have both sons and a brother to back me up."

Thomas's smile would have put the sun to shame. "Sons, brothers—plural—and now even a daughter, thanks to the Jennings family. What matters all that, when Theresa is *my sister?*"

He sauntered out, and Matthew—wisest and most loving of husbands—let him have the last word. Then Matthew advanced on Theresa, hands on his hips.

"Madam, if that buffoon ever makes you cry again, I shall thrash him, family or not. Neighbor or not. If *anybody* makes you cry, I shall thrash them."

Theresa sank back onto the sofa, and Matthew came down beside her. "I thought you were the king's man, Matthew. A model of good sense and rational thinking." She loved his good sense and his ability to patiently create order from chaos.

He kissed her knuckles and kept hold of her hand. "Bother good sense and rational thinking. I am *your* man, and it's high time some other damned fool spent all of his waking hours searching for laundry thieves and prodigal hogs. Perhaps I shall take up the violin."

Theresa snuggled closer and looped Matthew's arm around her shoulders.

"Will you learn to play lullabies?"

"For you, my beloved, I will learn to play—lullabies? One hasn't a need for a lullaby outside the nursery. Priscilla is too old for a lullaby and much too imaginative."

Theresa searched for the right words, cheerful, but casual. Thrilled, actually, but ready to be mistaken.

"Earlier today," Matthew said, "you mentioned that your luncheon threatened to make a reappearance."

Of all the dire threats, he would recall that one. "I did say that."

"Now you're prosing on about lullabies." He treated Theresa to a fierce perusal. "Mrs. Belmont, my nerves are delicate right now. You mustn't tell my brother or my sons I ever said such a thing, though I suspect Priscilla would be very understanding. Have we conceived a child already?"

Tears trickled down Theresa's cheek. "I become lachrymose when I'm carrying. You mustn't think anything of it."

Matthew's embrace was all the tenderness any princess might have wished for from her prince. He kissed Theresa's closed eyes, her cheeks, and each finger.

"I've barely made proper love to you," he whispered. "Oh, this is marvelous. You are marvelous."

"The improper approach will sometimes do the trick. You aren't upset?"

"I'm... in awe. Awash with wonder, enraptured, delighted, and my brother will be so jealous. We must be considerate of his sensibilities."

What they must do was find Axel a wife. "You can't say anything, Matthew, not yet. It's very early days, and one can't be certain about these things."

Except Theresa was certain, and all four times she bore Matthew a daughter, she knew early, and she turned into a watering-pot. The former king's man was patient, doting, and prone to lecturing with each confinement, but he bore up under the ordeals with good grace, and when the time was right, found the perfect pony for each daughter.

And granddaughter.

And even for the great-granddaughters.

-THE END-

To my dear readers,

I hope you enjoyed Matthew and Theresa's story, but Theresa is absolutely right—we MUST find a true love for Axel Belmont! Which brings us to…
Axel: The Jaded Gentlemen, Book III

In the Belmont family tradition, Axel occasionally takes a turn serving as magistrate in his little corner of Oxfordshire. When the owner of a neighboring estate is the victim of a homicide, Axel initially suspects the man's much younger wife, Abigail Stoneleigh.

But then Abby appears to be in harm's way, and Axel's investigation uncovers longstanding deceptions aimed at cheating her out of wealth and happiness. The solution to this deadly puzzle remains elusive, even as Axel captures Abby's heart and surrenders his own. Axel is a fine investigator, a devoted father, a brilliant botanist, (and an excellent kisser), but will he solve the mystery before villain strikes again?

I've included a sneak peek in the pages that follow, and you can already order the ebook version from my website at graceburrowes.com.

In case you missed the first tale in The Jaded Gentlemen trilogy, *Thomas: The Jaded Gentlemen--Book I* is also available in both ebook and print versions.

And if that's not enough happily ever after to add to your To Be Read pile… in November, the second book in my True Gentlemen trilogy comes out, *Daniel's True Desire.* If you recall Daniel Banks from the Lonely Lords series, you'll know the good vicar is very much in need of a lady to set him to rights, but instead he gets a pack of rotten little boys, a few rambunctious toads, some shaggy ponies…and true love.

Find all of my books on my website at
graceburrowes.com/books/main.php

Happy reading!
Grace Burrowes

PS: Stay up-to-date on all my book releases and other news by signing up for my newsletter at graceburrowes.com/contact.php. I will never sell, give away or share your information, and I only publish a newsletter 4-6 times a year.

"Mrs. Stoneleigh." Axel took her cold hand, bowed over it, and examined her as closely as manners and candlelight would allow. She was tallish for a woman, though still a half foot shorter than Axel's own six foot and several inches. Abigail Stoneleigh was also, he admitted begrudgingly, pretty in a quiet, green-eyed, dark-haired way.

Because she was—had been—another man's wife, Axel's assessment of her beauty had never gone further, though if she weren't so perpetually aloof, if she ever once smiled, she might even be beautiful, not that he'd care one way or the other.

She had to be chilled to the bone from the temperature of the room. Axel led her over to the hearth, where a dying fire was losing the battle with the January night air.

"I should warn you, Mrs. Stoneleigh, I am here in the capacity of magistrate as well as neighbor."

"To come at this hour was still considerate of you."

The woman's spouse was crumpled over the desk, not fifteen feet away, and she was offering pleasantries? Everybody coped with death differently. Caroline's passing had taught Axel that.

He took off his jacket and draped it around Mrs. Stoneleigh's shoulders. "Why don't we repair to the family parlor? I've asked Shreve to bring the tea tray there."

Mrs. Stoneleigh's gaze swung away. She peered through the French doors into the darkness beyond.

"My—the colonel would not want to be alone."

Wherever Stoneleigh's immortal soul had gone, the life had departed from his body. Axel knew better than to argue reason at such a time.

"The deceased cannot be moved until I've looked the situation over more closely, and I would prefer privacy to do that."

"You may have your privacy, Mr. Belmont, but I'll send Ambers to stay with him thereafter. I'll await you in the parlor."

As imperious as a bloody queen—a pale, bloody queen. "You don't want Shreve with him, or perhaps his valet?"

"Ambers. Shreve is overwrought."

While the lady was glacially calm. She also bore the faint fragrance of attar of roses, which realization had Axel longing for his glass house all over again.

He escorted her to the door, then turned his attention to the question of how a man reasonably well liked, in good health, with wealth aplenty, and no apparent vices had managed get himself shot through the heart at close range in his very own home.

* * *

"Let me tell you what I've observed so far," Axel suggested, when he joined Mrs. Stoneleigh in the family parlor. "Shall I pour?" A widower would expire of dehydration if he didn't learn to navigate a tea service.

"I've had a cup, thank you," Mrs. Stoneleigh replied. "Shreve brought the brandy if you'd prefer."

Well done, Shreve. Tea at nearly midnight, at the scene of the crime, was insufficient fortification given what Axel had to tell her.

"Brandy would be appreciated."

Mrs. Stoneleigh poured him a generous portion, the glow from the hearth creating fiery highlights in her dark hair. Her movements were elegant and graceful, and that was somehow wrong.

Was she surprised by her husband's death? Relieved?

"First," Axel said after taking a bracing sip of fine spirits, "my condolences on your loss."

"My thanks." Two words, and grudgingly offered. She took one side of a brocade loveseat pulled close to the hearth. "Won't you sit, Mr. Belmont? The hour is late, you have to be tired, and you are about to discuss difficult matters. I'd rather be able to see your face."

Blunt, Axel thought, running a hand through his hair. Mrs. Stoneleigh had a way of expressing herself that made him feel as if he were trying her patience and insulting her intelligence.

All thorns and no blossom. Axel could be blunt too. He lowered himself not into a wing chair, but to the place right beside her.

"I have reason to believe your husband was the victim of foul play. To quiet misgivings from our vicar, I will preliminarily rule death by accident."

Mrs. Stoneleigh was silent for a moment, not reacting at all, and then she sat taller.

"Please explain yourself, Mr. Belmont."

"The cause of death was likely that gunshot to the chest—to the heart—as you no doubt suspected." Contrary to what the gothic novels propounded, once the heart stopped, little bleeding occurred—and Stoneleigh's heart had stopped instantly.

"I did not move the body," she said, her hand going to her middle. "I knew he was dead, because I put my fingers to the side of his neck, and I saw blood spattered on the desk and blotter. I also saw the gun in his hand, but I did not... I did not *look*."

"You were wise not to disturb the scene." Was she reacting now? Was there a slight tension around her eyes and mouth? She was mortally pale, though many English women went to pains to protect their complexions.

"You needn't flatter me, Mr. Belmont. I simply did not know what to do, other than to send for my nearest neighbor."

Who had the bad luck to be serving as the temporary magistrate—something she apparently hadn't known.

"Given the gun in your husband's hand, a casual observer might think he had, indeed, taken his own life, or perhaps had an accident while cleaning his equipment."

Axel took another swallow of brandy, resisting the urge to down it all at once.

Mrs. Stoneleigh reached toward the tea service as if to pour herself a second cup, but her hand drifted to her lap instead.

"God help my late husband if, after twenty-five years in the cavalry, he was attempting to clean a loaded gun."

"True." Axel hadn't considered that aspect of the situation. "The difficulty with the theory of suicide, though, is that the gun in your husband's hand has not been fired and was, in fact, still loaded. Your husband was shot, though the fatal bullet was not fired at point blank range."

Axel braced himself for a swoon, some ladylike weeping, even a fit of hysterics. People took their own lives. This was tragic, of course, but in Axel's estimation, suicide was preferable to murder most foul two doors down the corridor.

"Is there more?" she asked, still calm, still gazing thoughtfully into the fire.

"Not much." Would a second brandy be rude—or stupid? "The absence of an exit wound suggests a small gun was used. Such weapons—pea shooters—are notoriously inaccurate. They lack the length of barrel to steady the projectile toward its target, and such a small weapon seldom fires with much force."

"I've carried such guns and you are correct. Their greatest value is in the noise they create, but somebody apparently had good aim."

Would a woman guilty of murder make such an admission?

"Who heard the shot, Mrs. Stoneleigh?"

"I did. I was in my apartments, directly above, and the colonel was in his study, where he usually finished his evenings. Shreve would have heard the shot, because he was in the corridor, having just brought the colonel his customary ten o'clock night cap. Those servants still awake belowstairs heard it, as did Ambers, who was outside the groom's quarters smoking. Ambers was the first to arrive at the colonel's side."

The murderer had also heard the shot, then taken off across the snowy grounds, footprints conveniently obliterated by the brisk wind.

"The colonel never finished that nightcap," Axel said. "I'll want to talk to Shreve, sooner rather than later, and to the rest of your staff."

What Axel truly wanted was to return to the quiet and warmth of his glass house, there to work on grafts until his back ached and his vision blurred.

"Shreve is busy now," Mrs. Stoneleigh said. "He should be available to speak with you mid-morning tomorrow."

Axel was the magistrate, for pity's sake, investigating the murder of her husband in her own home. She ought to want answers more than she wanted her next breath.

"What can Shreve possibly have to keep him busy?"

Mrs. Stoneleigh turned faintly pitying gaze on him. Her expression was as close to warm as he'd seen it, ever, then Axel realized the direction of her thoughts.

"When a spouse dies," she said, gently, "there is much to be done. The windows must be hung with crepe, and the portraits and mirrors in the public rooms, as well. The liveried servants must acquire black armbands, the deceased must be laid out, the coffin built, the surviving family's wardrobe must be dyed black, the hearse hired, and so forth. You know this."

Axel did know this, and he resented her bitterly for making him recall that he knew it. Maybe resentment fueled by fatigue prompted his next observation.

"You seem to be coping with this tragedy well, Mrs. Stoneleigh."

"Am I a suspect?" The pity, at least, was gone from her eyes.

"No." *Not yet.* "But if murder was done in this house, while others were about, then we have both a crime and mystery on our hands."

"And a tragedy," she replied. "Have you more questions, Mr. Belmont, or shall I see you out?"

"I can see myself out," he replied, unhappy with himself for his little pique. "And again, my condolences." He rose, surprised when she did as well, albeit slowly, and walked him to the door.

"You are fatigued," she said. "Unusually so, not merely like a man at the end of a long day."

Her observation wasn't rude, but neither was it... useful. "I've just arrived this afternoon from my brother's home in Sussex, hailed back to Oxfordshire by Rutland's decision to nip off to Bath in the dead of winter. Phillip and Dayton chose to remain with their uncle until spring."

"You are orphaned, then. I am sorry to have disturbed you when you are much in need of rest. Shall I tell Shreve to expect you tomorrow morning?"

Axel spared a thought for his grafts and for his crosses.

"By eleven," he replied, taking her hand—still cold—and bowing over it. "Will you be all right?" he asked, not knowing where the question had come from, and not releasing her fingers, either.

"I don't know." She seemed unaware of their joined hands, or at least unconcerned. "I've heard of people being in shock, and I suspect that term fits. My husband is dead, and though we were not... entangled, as some spouses are, I did not expect such an end to the day, to any of my days. The colonel was not ill, he was not reckless, he did not drink to excess...." A minute shudder passed through her, one Axel detected only because he was holding her hand.

"I expect," she went on, "I will realize more fully what has befallen this house when Mrs. Pritchard and I lay out my... the body."

"Mrs. Pritchard will charge you good coin for tending to that office, and she needs the money, too. You are not to return to the study until the morning." Axel made it an order, which was bad of him. The father of two adolescent boys learned that giving orders all but guaranteed his wishes would be disrespected.

Mrs. Stoneleigh withdrew her hand. "I want to argue with you, but only to argue for argument's sake, not because I want to see my husband's naked corpse, particularly, not with a bullet..."

Another little shiver, two...

"Mrs. Stoneleigh?" Axel took her by the hand and drew her back over to the hearth, grabbing an afghan from the back of the loveseat and draping it over her shoulders. "Have you somebody who can sit with you, get you up to bed?"

"I do not use a lady's maid," she said, much the same as she might have eschewed sugar in her tea. "The colonel regards it.... *regarded it*.... Well, no. I do not have a lady's maid."

Axel endured an inconvenient stab of compassion—one that temporarily obliterated the question of her role in her husband's death. She was alone, more alone than a woman expected to be at the age of... eight-and-twenty? Her husband had died violently, and even if she'd killed him, who knew what her motivations might have been.

Time enough later to locate some outrage if she'd done away with the old boy for pestering her once too often in the marriage bed.

Axel took a moment to study her, the way he'd studied each and every specimen in his glass houses when he'd returned to Candlewick after weeks of absence. Mrs. Stoneleigh looked overwatered and undernourished, ready to drop leaves and wilt.

"I don't want to leave you alone."

"I'll manage." She didn't exactly smile. "I've been managing alone for quite some time, Mr. Belmont. My thanks for your concern. Until tomorrow."

Axel had no authority to gainsay her, so he bowed and took his leave. He was back on his horse—why on God's good green earth had nobody devised a means of warming a saddle before a man settled his innocent, unsuspecting arse on cold leather?—when he put a name on what he'd seen in Mrs. Stoneleigh's luminous green eyes the last time he'd bowed over her hand.

Fear. Mrs. Stoneleigh was afraid, but was she afraid of the murderer, or of having her part in the murder revealed?

Order your copy of *Axel: The Jaded Gentlemen—Book III*
at graceburrowes.com/books/axel.php